continued . . .

BOOKS BY STEVEN HARPER

THE BOOKS OF BLOOD AND IRON
Iron Axe
Blood Storm

THE CLOCKWORK EMPIRE
The Doomsday Vault
The Impossible Cube
The Dragon Men
The Havoc Machine

BLOOD STORM

The Books of Blood and Iron

STEVEN HARPER

A ROC BOOK

ROC
Published by New American Library,
an imprint of Penguin Random House LLC
375 Hudson Street, New York, New York 10014

This book is an original publication of New American Library.

First Printing, December 2015

For more information about Penguin Random House, visit penguin.com.

ISBN 978-0-451-46847-5

Printed in the United States of America
10   9   8   7   6   5   4   3   2   1

PUBLISHER'S NOTE
This is a work of fiction. Names, characters, places, and incidents either are the product of the author's imagination or are used fictitiously, and any resemblance to actual persons, living or dead, business establishments, events, or locales is entirely coincidental.

Penguin
Random
House

*To Michelle Singer, who unwittingly dragged me
into a new phase of my life. Thank you.*

NOTE ON PRONUNCIATION

The people of Erda tend to sound out all the letters in their names. Aisa's name therefore has three syllables and rhymes with "Theresa." Most vowels have a European flavor, so the *A* in "Danr" is more like the one in "wander" than in "Daniel."

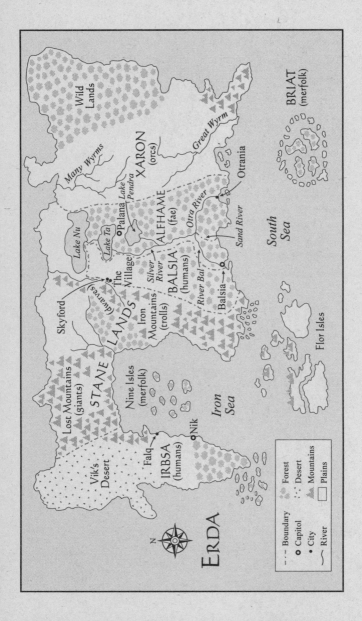

The Story So Far

Well, really! A standing ovation, and I haven't even said anything yet!

Yes, I'll get to the story. But you have to expect at least a *little* lead-in. Do you have any idea what I went through to get it? How many hours I spent translating manuscripts in stuffy studies and moldy book rooms?

So. The story we have tonight—and the next several nights—details more history for Danr of Balsia, the Second Great Hero of Erda, and of Aisa the Slave, who became . . . Well, we know what happened to *her*, don't we? And yes, folks, the rumors are true. Aisa *did* confront Harbormaster Willem near Bosha's Bay, and Aisa *did* take up Kalessa's magic sword, and—

Er, sorry. I don't mean to give things away.

Let me assure you all that this story, called *Blood Storm*, stands alone all by itself, and you can follow it fine, just fine, without hearing *Iron Axe*. But does anyone want a quick refresher? Raise your hand if you do. Ah. Right, then.

If you haven't heard *Iron Axe* and do not like a good story being spoiled, how about you trot over to that inn over there and get something to drink? Tell the barkeep I sent you and he might even give you a discount. I'll wave this little red flag here when I'm ready to start the next bit, so you'll know when to come back, yeah? And I wouldn't say no if someone brought back a nice mug of something foamy.

All right—*Iron Axe*, the short version. Hard to decide where to begin, you know? Does the story start when the downtrodden Fae went to war against the oppressive Stane? Maybe. The king of the Stane ordered the dwarfs, craftsmen extraordinaire, to create a weapon so powerful it would destroy the Fae—elves, sprites, and fairies—forever. But when the dwarfs created an axe of iron, the Fae stole it and used the weapon's power against its own creators. In desperation, the Stane worked out a way to destroy the Axe, though it would require cooperation between the trolls and the Kin—humans, orcs, and merfolk. The trollwives provided the magic, and the Kin provided a blood sacrifice. Together, they slaughtered a young human on a stone table and gathered enough power to crack the Axe into pieces. Unfortunately, something went wrong. The spell not only broke the Axe; it sundered part of the continent itself. The land dropped straight down, creating the Iron Ocean, with the Nine Isles poking up like dead fingers.

The Sundering drove the Stane under the mountains, which allowed the Fae to do as they liked. At first, the Fae worked diligently to restore the world, but over time, a taste of power drove them to want more of it. They enslaved humans and used glamour to force their slaves to love them. They kept the Stane in their underground caverns, never to see the light of the moon or taste the good fruit of the mountainside. They grew in their power and their arrogance, and they were draining the world dry.

A thousand years after the Sundering, one troll managed to push open the Great Door that led out from under the mountain. He slipped out to explore and encountered a human woman in the forest. After she got over her fright, she found him more attractive than horrific, and they fell in love. But when she became heavy with child, it became clear that neither Kin nor Stane would accept them, and the troll abandoned her. The woman bore a baby she called Danr but whom everyone else called Trollboy.

As a half troll, Danr grew up an outcast (this was long before the enlightened era in which we find ourselves, folks), and when his mother died, he had one friend—a young slave named Aisa, who came from the land of Irbsa across the Iron Sea. Aisa was once owned by elves, and she became addicted to their glamour, but she angered her master and he sold her away. The sudden separation from her beloved (and be-hated) elven master nearly tore her apart.

Aisa was eventually charged with witchcraft, and Danr was exiled from his village for defending her. They both fled and spent some time with the trolls, where they learned that the Stane were slowly starving under the mountain and planned to free themselves. Through a complicated series of events involving a trio of dreadful giants, Danr was blessed, or perhaps cursed, with the power to see truth through his left eye.

At this point, Death herself intervened. The Stane had bound her with a mystical chain nothing could break, and it meant no one could die. The trollwives were harvesting the power of the ghosts stranded in the world of the living to force all the mountain doors wide-open and make war against the elves again. Death asked Danr to reforge the Iron Axe, the only object that could break the chain and set her free.

More complicated and fascinating events followed. Danr and Aisa were joined by Talfi, a young man who turned out to be not so young after all. Indeed, every time he died, he came rather shockingly back to life. Unfortunately, every resurrection wiped away Talfi's memory, and he had to content himself with what he could remember of his life since his most recent revival.

The little group traveled to Xaron, the land of the orcs, in search of the pieces of the Iron Axe. There, an orc princess joined them and became close friends with Aisa. They found one piece, the haft, and discovered the head was in Palana City, where Aisa had been held as a slave. Reluctantly, they traveled to that town and learned that more than two hundred years ago, Talfi had been involved with an elven prince named Ranadar, who still harbored deep feelings for Talfi. Ranadar's love for Talfi forced him to betray his own people and help the growing group recover the head of the Iron Axe. In a dreadful twist of fate, they also learned that Talfi, who was the original sacrifice that had broken the Axe in the first place, was the third piece. Only his final death would fully reforge the Axe.

Meanwhile, it turned out Ranadar's parents, the elven king and queen, were themselves harvesting the power of the dead in order to Twist—that is, teleport—the entire Stane army cross-country the moment they emerged from under the mountain. In their weakened state, the Stane would be easy to slaughter.

Danr and Aisa somehow found the strength to slay Talfi and reforge the Axe just in time to stop the war, though they destroyed most of Palana City in the process. Aisa also killed her former elven master and discovered that his death released her from the terrible addiction.

Armed with the Axe, Danr and the others visited Death and cut her free. As a reward, Death allowed Ranadar to give half his remaining days to Talfi so he could come back to life one more time.

Danr returned to his village something of a hero, but he realized he couldn't stay. Ranadar, as an elf, wasn't well liked in a human habitation, and Talfi's love for him only made matters more complicated.

Besides, Aisa wanted to see mermaids.

All right, let me wave the flag here so the folks who are drinking can—ah! Here they come. And there was a discount after all? Well, the night can't get better than this.

Unless we add a giant squid.

Chapter One

The orc woman flew backward and landed in the cave pool with a great splash. Danr didn't even have time to shout before a great tentacle slammed into him and swept him aside like a toy. He crashed hard into the tunnel wall. Air burst from his lungs and stars danced before his eyes. Vik! It was always monsters, always fighting.

"To the left!" Talfi shouted. "Aisa! It's going to the left!"

The great squid at the back of the cave pulled in its tentacles and struck again, this time to the left. Aisa ducked, and for a heart-stopping moment Danr thought the creature had hit her, too, but the tentacle went over her head and smacked the stones with a nasty, rubbery sound. The tunnel rumbled. Bones and skulls from the squid's previous victims tumbled about the cave floor. Maybe this was the reason Death had sent them after the creature—she was tired of collecting its prey.

Ribs aching, Danr yanked himself upright. The body of the squid was enormous, at least fifteen feet long and twice as high as Danr, who himself topped nearly seven feet. It filled the rear of the tunnel with writhing tentacles and a fishy, salty reek that turned Danr's stomach. The creature made no sound when it attacked—tentacles whipped through the air like gristly lightning and no noise at all emerged from a wicked beak that was easily big enough to crush a human skull. The creature took up the entire rear wall of the tidal cave, which was damp because the tunnel rose a little here. Opposite the squid, hard daylight filtered in from the distant—much lower— mouth of the tunnel, which was filling with seawater as the tide came in. Damn it, they had to *move*.

Danr caught the sound of Kalessa, the orc woman, splashing about, probably looking for her sword. If she was disarmed, they were in trouble. Although Danr's troll half made him feel perfectly at home in caves, the confined space gave the squid a definite advantage.

"Ranadar!" Talfi shouted from the edge of the water. He had brown hair and sky-blue eyes and didn't look more than seventeen, though Danr knew he was much older. "Twist in there with your knife and—"

The squid snatched up a large rock and flung it at Talfi. Shit, shit, shit, Talfi didn't see it coming. Danr shouted a warning, but the rock caromed across the cave straight for Talfi's head at lightning speed.

There was a flash of light. Next to Talfi, an elven man with longish red hair flicked into existence. He tackled Talfi, shoved him to the ground, but the rock clipped the side of the elf's head. He staggered and rolled, gasping, into knee-deep water.

"Ran!" Talfi shook the elf's shoulder.

The squid threw another rock, this one at Danr. He ducked. It exploded against the stone wall where his head had been. His heart pounded, and he could barely think. The squid's beak snapped between its enormous eyes, eyes that looked strangely human, but also cold and hungry.

Water continued to rise higher in the tunnel and lap Danr's toes. In a few minutes, the squid would win by default. He cast about in desperation. His club was gone, knocked from his hand in the first moment they had found the squid, and he hadn't gotten around to learning sword work. He felt slow and out of his element.

Kalessa emerged from the tunnel, water streaming from the weave of her armor. She held a small knife in her hand. Her orcish yellow eyes and faintly greenish skin created a striking contrast with her long auburn braid. Kalessa charged the squid, and her battle cry echoed off the walls. The squid flung a tentacle at her. Kalessa dodged neatly to one side and swung at it with her little knife. In midswing, the tiny blade flickered into a full-length broadsword. It sliced neatly through the tentacle, spewing purplish ichor across the tunnel floor. The severed tentacle, easily as thick as Danr's leg, writhed like a dying serpent. Kalessa gave another high-pitched shout. A second tentacle flanked her and caught her hard in the solar plexus. Kalessa's shout died in a burst of air. Her sword clattered to the ground and changed back into a knife as she dropped beside it.

"Sister!" Aisa ran to her. The squid pulled back its tentacles again, ready to strike at both of them. Oh no, it didn't. Danr snatched up a rock of his own and threw it as hard as he could. It bounced off the squid's rubbery head near the beak.

"Hey!" he shouted. "Over here!"

Both eyes focused on Danr, and he saw his own reflection in hungry pupils the size of dinner plates. He looked both big and tiny at the same time, and he swallowed. Maybe that hadn't been such a good—

The two tentacles snapped at him. Danr waited until the last second, then jumped. His leap carried him above both tentacles, and he pointed his toes to land straight on one. Danr's weight was considerable. His mother might have been human, but his father was a troll, and even as a child, he had been heavy. As an adult, he used that weight to his advantage and crushed both squirming tentacles to the cave floor.

"Do something!" he barked. "Ranadar! Twist closer and get it in the eyes!"

"He's hurt," Talfi yelled back. "No Twisting!"

Talfi's shout got the squid's attention. It flung out another tentacle, and this one wrapped around Talfi's neck. He gasped and clawed at the thing, but the squid jerked hard. Bone snapped. Talfi went limp, neck broken. Vik! But no time to deal with that now. The tentacles squirmed beneath his bare feet like angry worms, and he danced on them, trying to keep them under control.

Aisa produced a vial from her pocket and was fumbling with the stopper. It was probably something to wake Kalessa. He felt a swell of pride at her skill as a healer, and a simultaneous stab of fear that she might get hurt. Before he could consider the situation further, both tentacles freed themselves from Danr's weight and wrapped around him. It was like being engulfed by a pair of muscular, smelly snakes. The cold suckers pulled at his neck and bare arms. He struggled, but could barely move.

The squid snatched up another rock. Where in all Vik's realm had it learned to do that? It didn't seem fair. It threw one at Aisa, who was just rolling Kalessa over.

"No!" Danr shouted in horror.

Aisa ducked, but the squid threw a second rock in quick succession. Time slowed. The rock spun lazily through the air. Even though he was too far away, Danr reached for it. It cracked the side of Aisa's head and she went down.

Danr's world went red. Rage swept him into a bloody storm, and a roar burst from his chest. The muscles on his arms bulged with new strength. He tore the tentacles away from his body. One of them he ripped in two, and cold ichor gushed over him. With another roar, he grabbed the other tentacle and heaved. The surprised squid slid forward several yards from its lair at the back of the tunnel. It focused all its attention on Danr now, trying to brace itself with some of its tentacles and whipping at Danr with the others. Danr barely noticed. This thing had injured Aisa. This thing would pay. He pulled and pulled. The squid, wriggling and writhing all the way, skidded across the rocky tunnel toward Danr with dreadful inevitability. Its beak snapped and its cold eyes stared. Danr wrapped a squirmy tentacle around his free arm and reached for the squid's head. How many people had this thing eaten? How many fishermen had it devoured? And it had *hurt Aisa*.

The beak snapped and caught Danr's fist, but it couldn't close entirely. Danr's fist was too large. Terrible pressure crushed his hand. The pain broke through the bloody rage, but only for a moment. Grimly, Danr shoved forward. He thrust his hand, his arm, his shoulder straight down the squid's throat. It made a gurgling sound. With his other hand, Danr let the tentacle go and punched straight through one of the cold eyes. It burst in an explosion of jelly.

Danr braced himself and yanked. Both his arms came free, tearing a large part of the squid's head with it. A huge chunk of smelly flesh came free with an awful ripping noise. The squid went into convulsions. Its remaining tentacles lashed in random directions, slamming against the walls and ceiling. The tunnel trembled. Rocks fell from above.

"Hamzu!" A hand touched his arm. Danr whirled, expecting another attack, but it was Aisa. Blood ran down the side of her face, but she looked otherwise fine. Relief drained his rage, and the strength left him. The cave trembled beneath his bare feet. "We do not want to be here!"

"Are you all right?" He reached out to touch her face.

Aisa closed her eyes for a small moment beneath his hand, then took his wrist. "Sweet as you are, we should save this for when there is less danger. As one example: squid!"

Danr spun. The squid was still convulsing, and it was bringing the tunnel down. A stalactite smashed to the floor near them like a giant's leg. Kalessa was getting to her feet, knife in hand, and hauling Ranadar up. But they couldn't leave. Not yet.

"Kalessa!" Danr shouted. "Your blade! Ranadar, get Talfi!"

Kalessa tossed her knife across the cave. Danr snatched it out of the air and used it to slice through flesh and gristle until he found the black bladder that made up the ink sac. In seconds, he slashed it free, and with another stroke cut the squid's beak away. The squid convulsed once more and died.

"Now!" Aisa said. "We have to leave now."

The tunnel was trembling, and almost entirely dark. The rising tide had nearly filled the exit. Cool seawater was knee deep in the cave. More rocks tumbled from above and splashed into the tide. Kalessa and Ranadar had Talfi's dead arms around their shoulders and were dragging him toward deeper water.

"For you." Danr thrust the sac and beak into Aisa's hands.

"Hmm. Most men give flowers," Aisa remarked.

"You're glad I'm not most men, admit it." He waded over to Ranadar and easily hauled Talfi over his own shoulder. The young man hung there like a warm rag doll. The water was waist high now. Danr flinched away from another falling boulder that exploded into the water only a pace away. At least the sea was washing off the smelly ichor, though Danr hoped the stuff wouldn't attract sharks. He waded fast for the tunnel mouth with the others in his wake.

"Ranadar, can you Twist us out yet?" Kalessa demanded.

"Not enough power," Ranadar muttered. "Will Talfi be all right?"

"He is dead," Aisa said. "What do you think? I will have some choice words for Death after this."

The others were swimming now. Danr was up to his neck, grimly trying to keep Talfi's head above water, more out of habit than necessity. The tunnel mouth and dim daylight were only a few yards away, but the exit was now submerged, and a current pushed against Danr's body. It wasn't going to be easy, especially carrying Talfi. Danr wasn't a skilled swimmer, and already Talfi was starting to drag him down.

"We'll have to swim underneath," he said. "It's only about ten feet, but the current's stiff."

"Do not think," Kalessa advised. She had the beak now, along with her knife. "Just do." And she dove.

The tunnel rumbled again. Ranadar breathed deeply and dove. Aisa clasped Danr's hand in the darkening cave, though his trollish eyes saw her lovely face perfectly well. It was a face he had only recently come to know. When they first met, she had hidden herself behind rags and scarves. Over time, she had come out of hiding, but the novelty of her beauty, like a new-risen star, hadn't worn off. Her deep brown eyes and tan skin and arched eyebrows and lovely mouth made his heart swell, and he wanted to touch her face, even here, with the cave coming down around them.

"I know what you're thinking," he said quietly.

"There are no mermaids this close to the city," she replied. "And not at this time of year. I will see none."

"But you're still hoping."

"You worry about the wrong thing, my strong one," she said, still clutching the ink sac. "Bring Talfi home." And she dove as well.

The sea rose farther and Danr's feet left the floor. Above him, the ceiling splintered with earsplitting cracks. Danr shifted Talfi across his shoulder, took several deep breaths, and dove. Rocks thundered into the water behind him, but he swam and swam through the soft light. Hard stone hemmed him in overhead. The current tried to push him back, but he used all his troll's strength against it. Ahead was brightness. His lungs were bursting within his chest and Talfi's body grew heavier. Blood pounded in his ears. Oh, he wanted air. Just one breath. The water was a great hand, shoving and pressing, trying to hold him down. He could let Talfi go and make it easily. Then he felt ashamed that the thought crossed his mind. He cleared the tunnel, and the light grew brighter. Danr kicked upward hard, and suddenly he broke the surface. Sweet air filled his lungs. He hung there, just breathing, while his dark hair plastered his skull.

The golden sun burned bright overhead, drilling his eyes and giving him an instant headache, the downside of being part troll. He treaded water with Talfi over his shoulder. He was at the base of a low cliff. Away to his right, the rocks went off into the ocean, but to his left the cliff came abruptly down to a sandy beach. The water swirled and vibrated— the last of the tunnel collapsing. Vik's balls, he'd gotten out just in time. Talfi had damn well better appreciate this.

Danr swam alongside the cliff toward the beach. The ocean was shallow here, and it didn't take him long. Aisa, Kalessa, and Ranadar were waiting for him, and they helped drag Talfi across the damp sand until he was above the tide line. Talfi's tongue protruded, and his head lolled at an angle that turned Danr's stomach. They all flopped down on the beach.

"My *Talashka*," Ranadar said sadly, stroking Talfi's slack face. Ranadar was handsome, even for an elf. His cheekbones were sharp enough to strike flint on, and his emerald eyes gave quick contrast to his sunset hair. He avoided the usual overly embroidered robes and vestments other elves wore in favor of rough silk in forest brown and green. Talfi was no slouch, either. Even soaking wet and . . . well, dead, his brown hair and fair skin and molded face created a handsome picture. Kalessa was striking, in her own way, with her lithe build and alien skin and hair. Danr felt the odd one out—tall and blocky, with shovel hands and coarse black hair and a jaw that jutted pugnaciously forward. Aisa said his eyes—brown—were deep and rich and that she could fall into them, but Danr always felt a pang of jealousy at Aisa's beauty, Kalessa's exoticism, Ranadar's sharp features, and Talfi's fine ones. It came of being a half-blood, caught between races, and there were times he hated it.

"He still looks dead. This is disappointing." Aisa dropped the ink sac on the damp sand with a flopping noise. She wore a loose-fitting red tunic and trousers instead of a dress, done in the style of her homeland across the Iron Sea to the west. Although she bared her face these days, she usually wore a hood or scarf over her hair. Right now everything was sticking to her, and Danr forced himself not to stare at the outlines of her body, though he still peeked. She caught him, and shook a mock finger at him.

"Never mind Talfi," Danr said, flushing a little. "How's your head?"

"Achy." Aisa touched the spot where the stone had hit her. The sea had washed the blood away. "I will have a bruise beneath my hair, and it would be best if someone woke me at least twice tonight, but I will be fine."

"I am fine as well, in case anyone wants to know," Ranadar complained. "Only my *Talashka* is dead."

"You are a prince among elves," Kalessa said. "Surely your head is harder than any rock. Talfi's is another matter."

"You know, sister, Slynd would have been an enormous help back there," Aisa said. "A wyrm would have destroyed that squid without trouble."

Kalessa shrugged. "It is mating season back home in

Xaron. As the saying goes, 'You can't keep salmon from the spawning grounds, and you can't keep wyrms from the mating nests.' Slynd will find me when he is finished."

"My *Talashka*," Ranadar repeated, and kissed Talfi on the lips. Danr shifted uncomfortably and glanced away. Learning that his best friend was *regi*—not a nice word, but Danr had never learned a polite one—had caught Danr off guard, but he had finally forced himself to realize it was foolish for anyone, especially a half-blood, to judge someone based on who he fell in love with. Still, it looked odd to see two men together like that, especially a human and an elf. Danr supposed eventually he would take it in stride, but for now he had to remind himself not to flinch. And he would remind himself. Talfi was his best friend, and Danr wasn't going to give that up over a few strange kisses.

"What is taking him so long?" Kalessa drummed her fingers on the squid beak. "Usually, he's—"

Talfi gasped hard in Ranadar's arms. He jerked once and sat up, blinking in the sunlight and the surf. "What—? Where—?"

"You're with me, my *Talashka*," Ranadar said, touching his hair. "Everything is fine."

"Vik!" Talfi massaged his neck. "And, ow!"

Everyone breathed a relieved sigh. Danr felt a little weak. Last year, Death had awarded Talfi half of Ranadar's remaining days to keep Talfi out of the underworld, which apparently meant that Talfi couldn't die, but no matter how many times Talfi came back to life, a small part of Danr always wondered if this death would be the last, and it was always a rush of relief when he came back.

"What do you remember?" Aisa asked.

Danr leaned closer to hear the answer. Aisa's question was more than academic. At one time, each of Talfi's deaths also wiped his memory clean. That had changed, but only last year.

"I remember you." Talfi pointed to Ranadar, then to Danr and Aisa and Kalessa. "And you, and you, and you."

It was an old joke, but they laughed anyway.

Talfi continued to rub his neck. "That was not a fun way to die."

"Are any of them fun?" Kalessa inquired. "I only ask because one day, I am sure it will happen to me, and I want something to look forward to."

"None of them are fun," Talfi said, then looked at Ranadar and smiled. "Well, maybe the little death isn't bad."

"The little death?" Danr said.

"It's an elvish phrase," Ranadar said, "for that moment when a mama and a papa—or just two papas—become very close to each other, and they—"

"Let's get back to town," Danr interrupted, standing up. "Before another squid comes looking for a meal."

"Hello, little one," Aisa said.

For a moment, Danr thought she was talking to him, and that was strange. Not even his mother had called him little. Then he realized she was looking past him to a small boy. He looked to be five years old. His fair hair was bleached by the sun, and his skin tanned by it. He had inquisitive blue eyes and a pug nose.

"Hello," the boy said. "What are you people doing so far away from the city?"

"We might ask you the same question," Talfi said. He was still sitting on the sand with Ranadar's arm around him. "Are your parents nearby?"

"They're back home." The boy carried a stick, and he poked at the damp sand with it. "I come down here sometimes to see if Lady Bosha has washed anything up onshore.

Sometimes I find bottles or even a barrel from a shipwreck, and we can sell it. We don't have much money."

The boy didn't seem the least bothered by finding a group with a half-blood troll in it, or two men with their arms around each other. Danr said, "I'm Danr. What's your name?"

"Joshuah."

"Well, Joshuah, we just killed a monster squid in the tidal cave down there, so if you're in the habit of wandering around this beach, you'd better keep an eye out."

The boy's eyes widened. "Really?"

Kalessa obligingly held out the squid beak, and Joshuah touched it with the awe only a little boy could muster. "And you're an orc, aren't you?"

"A tribal princess," Kalessa said. "And he's an elven prince. And he"—she pointed to Danr—"is a prince among trolls, though he likes that as a secret, so don't tell."

"And what are you?" the boy asked Aisa.

"The commoner who worships at their feet," she said.

Now recognition rushed over Joshuah's face. "Wait! You're the heroes of the Twist! Danr, the half troll! I heard all about you from my dad! Are you real?"

Here we go, Danr thought. "Real as you," he said gruffly.

"You killed a giant squid all by yourself?" Joshuah asked.

"They helped a little," Danr said.

Talfi shot him a mischievous look. "He tore the beak and the ink sac out of the squid with his bare hands. You're the first one to see it."

"Wow!" Joshuah said breathlessly. "Wait'll I tell my brother! He'll never believe it."

"Here." Talfi took the ink sac and squeezed a dot onto the back of Joshuah's arm. "Now they will. Go tell them."

Joshuah ran off, trailing laughter.

"What did you do that for?" Danr groused. "We were

trying to avoid more stories. By the end of the day, the whole city will be saying I tore the squid in half with my bare hands."

"You *did* tear the squid in half with your bare hands," Aisa pointed out. "I was impressed."

"Really?" Danr said, a little surprised. Aisa was rarely impressed by anything.

"Really."

"Thanks," Danr said with a laugh of his own. The last of his tension was evaporating and his mood lifted despite the sun headache. He tried to put an arm around Aisa to hug her close, but she abruptly drew away. Vik. She did that a lot. Just when things were getting good between them, she pulled away, and he didn't know why. Danr dropped his arm as if it had turned into a dead fish, and his face grew hot. The others studiously failed to notice. After a moment, Kalessa cleared her throat.

"We must get back to the city and clean up," she said. "Seawater will eat my armor faster than that creature."

"Can you walk, *Talashka*?" Ranadar asked.

"Always." Talfi scrambled to his feet, sending sand in all directions. "Coming back from the dead always fills me with energy. It's like drinking sunlight."

"How is it to die and come back?" Kalessa asked curiously.

Talfi spun in a glorious circle. The rising surf washed at his feet, and a flock of seagulls cried overhead with a high, free sound. He dashed back to Ranadar and caught him in a breathless embrace. Danr gave Aisa a sidelong look and tried not to get jealous. Talfi and Ranadar had gone through more than one hell, including separation for more than two hundred years and Talfi losing his memory, before they'd been united, so it wasn't as if they didn't deserve what they had. But Danr had gone through a number of hells himself, and why didn't he have this with Aisa? He glanced at her again. She gave him a small smile, then sighed and looked away. He wasn't sure what to do. Always caught in between—troll and human, love and neglect, half of one and not quite the other, that seemed to be his lot in life.

"Happy," Talfi said. "It makes me happy. I don't remember everything that happens, though. I remember the squid grabbing my neck, and then I was here with all of you. With Ran. Now I want to run to the moon and back."

"Let's run back to the city to clean up," Aisa said. "We have dinner with the prince tonight, remember."

"Blargh," Talfi said. "I should have stayed dead."

"The city," Danr sighed. "What am I going to look like this time, Ranadar?"

Chapter Two

Aisa threaded her way through the crowded streets, trying to look in all directions at once without trying to
appear that she was doing so. She had pulled her wet scarf
over her sodden hair, and she kept her face down as best she
could. Normally, she favored a hooded cloak, but she had
not brought one to the squid's cave. Kalessa came a little behind her, proud and upright and refusing to hide her face.
Farther behind were Ranadar and Talfi. Ranadar's face was
schooled in concentration because he kept the glamour on
Danr, who walked in the center of them.

At the moment, Danr looked like a pudgy, balding human
in a brown robe, utterly nondescript, which was the way they
wanted it. If anyone waved their hand in the air above the
"man's" head, they would have encountered a half troll's
chest. Elven glamours could change only appearance, not
shape. No one, not even the Fae, could change shape. A
powerful trollwife had once told Aisa a story about the Kin
having the power to change shape, long ago and before the
Sundering, but Aisa had never seen any evidence of such a
power and now she found herself deciding that the story was

nothing more than a legend. A pity, too—such power would come in handy.

She hurried forward, eager to get home and change clothes. Danr called for Kalessa, and the orc woman dropped back so the two of them could converse in low voices.

The city of Balsia dozed in the sun like a warrior gone to seed. Streets sprawled lazily in all directions, without plan or purpose, sprouting buildings of wood and stone as they went. Here and there, the bones of an ancient stone palisade rose several stories, providing a back wall for some buildings. A mass of people, mostly human, shouted and laughed and rang little bells and begged and cried and created a cacophony that continually assaulted Aisa's ears and mixed with a continual pungent miasma the place belched up— garlic and oil and body odor and waste. Always the waste. Didn't people know how to dispose of personal sewage other than to throw it into the streets?

Despite the noise and smells, Aisa still found this place exciting and interesting. Balsia slurped everyone in—young, old, wealthy, beggar, pious, vulgar—and mixed them into a glorious tangle she had never understood until now. Even here she watched a woman in a blue dress drop a coin into a beggar's bowl below. Years and years ago, she mused, the woman in blue had been a child and made many choices, all of which had brought her to this spot at this moment, where that beggar, who had also once been a child and who had made an equal number of choices, was sitting. And all those years ago, neither of them had any idea that one day their lives would intersect in even this small way.

The woman in blue turned away from the beggar, and her face dripped with blood. The beggar fished the coin from his bowl, and blood ran down his hand. The standing water in the street turned scarlet. The cacophony turned to screams of fear. Aisa froze.

And then it all snapped back to normal. The woman in blue ambled on her way, the beggar pocketed a perfectly normal coin, the water was only scummy water, the noise was only street noise. A scream, however, echoed inside her mind. Aisa tried not to listen.

Kalessa broke away from Danr and hurried forward. "Are you all right, sister?"

Aisa coughed and forced herself forward. "Fine. Just lost in thought."

"Troll," Talfi said, oblivious. He jerked his head at a hulking figure who stumped down the street like an angry cartload of stone. Every inch of skin was bundled beneath rags and bandages. Heavy gloves and boots covered hands and feet, and a heavy cloak with a deep hood was pulled across its head, pushing the features into shadow. It—he?—kept well to the shady side of the street.

It was unusual to see an actual troll out in full daylight. Even the tiniest ray of sunlight caused the Stane great pain. Danr's human side allowed him more free passage through the day. He was also better-looking, with that strong chin and that husky voice and that smooth, dark skin she wanted to run her hands over. And those eyes. Those brown, soulful eyes that turned her insides to sweet butter whenever she looked into them. It was probably a good thing that Ranadar's glamour changed them, or she would melt right here on the street. She almost smiled at the thought.

A pair of nut-brown figures pushed a cart piled high with bread over the cobbles. They chattered and snorted behind knotty fingers while their saillike ears quivered in the dank air. "And there, two fairies," Danr said in that wonderful voice.

"Don't say it," Ranadar warned.

"Would we dream of it?" Aisa shot back, feeling better with the banter.

"And here, an orc." Kalessa tapped her own chest as they walked.

Aisa smiled. "Did anyone ever think Kin and Stane and Fae would live together in the same city?"

"Not even the Nine foresaw such a thing," Kalessa admitted.

Danr twisted around to watch the troll disappear around a corner. "Huh. Out in daylight," he said, echoing Aisa's earlier thought. "I wonder why."

"Everyone has emergencies," Ranadar said. "Perhaps he—"

What happened next came so fast, it was not until later that Aisa was able to fully sort it all out. A man carrying a small keg slipped—probably on excrement—and dropped his burden just as he passed Ranadar. The keg burst open on the stones, flinging hundreds of nails everywhere. Iron nails. One of them flew up and landed in Ranadar's collar. He cried out. Talfi, acting on instinct, snatched the nail away and yanked the white-faced elf free of the debris. But the damage was done. Danr's glamour burst like a fragile bubble, and he stood in full view of the street. The man with the nails yelped and scuttled away.

"What the—?" Danr looked down at himself.

"Oh no," Kalessa moaned.

"Quickly!" Aisa said. "We have to get him out of here." It was too late. A man pointed. "Hey! Half troll!"

"It's Danr the Hero!"

"Danr! He's on our street!"

"The Iron Axe."

A crowd swirled toward them like a gathering storm as word rippled up and down the street. People boiled out of shops and leaned out of windows. Traffic came to a halt. Kalessa drew her knife and it sprang into the shape of a broadsword nearly as tall as she was.

"Stay back!" she barked.

The crowd faltered, then someone said, "It's Kalessa! And Talfi—the boy who can't die!"

"The Nine," Talfi swore. Twice in the past year, people had unexpectedly killed him just to see if he would come back to life. It was alarming, but Aisa did not find it in the least surprising. People could show wonderful acts of compassion and wonder, but more often they were selfish and thoughtless. Talfi continued to prop Ranadar upright. Now that the elf wasn't so close to the cold iron, he was recovering, but slowly.

Aisa flicked a glance up and down the street. They were trapped smack in the middle of a block, with a wall directly behind them, street in front of them, and no handy alleys or intersections to make good an escape.

"It's all right, Kalessa." Danr faced the crowd, forced a smile to his face, and waved a meaty hand. "Good day, everyone! We're just out for a walk! Nothing special."

"Tell us about the Battle of the Twist!" someone shouted.

"As if a half-blood could be that brave!"

"How did you face down the Queen of the Elves?"

A pregnant woman thrust her belly toward him. "Will you bless my baby?"

"Don't let a half-blood touch her!"

"I don't think—" Danr began.

A girl, not yet twenty, dodged around Kalessa and snatched the hat from Danr's head. Aisa saw how the pain sunlight struck his face, and she grabbed angrily for the girl, but she was already gone.

"Half-blood, all monster!" shouted someone else.

"He's so ugly."

"Is it true you talk to Death?"

The crowd pressed forward, half in admiration, half in hostility. Kalessa swung her sword in a short arc, causing the people in the front to flinch back, but those behind pressed forward. Aisa desperately looked about. It was always like this. Half the crowd adored him, half the crowd hated him. She and Danr had never met another half-blood, and for all either of them knew, Danr was the only one. But the Stane—and the Fae—were mistrusted at best, despised at worst, and just the idea of mixing one of them with the Kin set off waves of revulsion among otherwise peaceful people.

"Ranadar!" she hissed at him. "Can you—?"

"I can try," Ranadar gasped. "But not all of us, and not far. That iron hurt."

"Half-blood filth!"

"He's a hero, you Vik-sucking pig!"

"Don't call my wife a pig."

A glob of mud flew at Danr. He ducked, and it struck the wall behind him. The street before them was a mass of people, pushing and shoving. Aisa's heart pounded.

"Back away!" Danr roared.

Suddenly, Aisa was back at the Battle of the Twist. The Iron Axe sizzled in Danr's hand. The crowd was an army of Fae, and they fell in clouds of blood beneath the Axe's blade. Flames devoured entire trees and fairies dove screaming into the lake. A cloaked figure watched from the flames. Then Aisa was back beside Danr, her heart pounding so fast her head ached. She forced herself to keep control. Danr's face was tense, and Aisa understood that he was balanced between fear and anger, just as he had been during the Battle of the Twist. Vik. The crowd was provoking someone who could tear a squid in half with his bare hands. A roar rose, half cheer, half growl. Danr made fists.

"Ranadar, now!" Aisa snapped.

Ranadar made a small sound. There was a flicker, and Danr was gone. So were Ranadar and Talfi. The crowd fell silent again, then set up a confused babble. Aisa took advantage of the moment to wrap her head scarf around her lower face and melt into the crowd. Kalessa, she knew, was well able to handle herself. Aisa eeled through the crowd toward home, trying not to shake.

Sometime later, both she and Kalessa crept through the side door of a tall, blocky house whose back wall was one of the original city palisades. The moment they entered the main room inside, Danr caught Aisa in a relieved embrace.

"Thank the Nine!" He held her tight. "I was so worried. Again."

"*You* were worried?" She disentangled herself lightly. "I had to run all the way here and wonder if the Twist had killed you."

"We just got here ourselves," Danr said. The main room of Mrs. Farley's rooming house had a fireplace, a long table with benches, and a few other pieces of furniture. Danr liked it, Aisa knew, because the windows were small and the room was usually dimly lit. He dropped to one of the benches. "Ranadar only managed to Twist us to the other side of the wall the crowd had pushed us against. It wrecked him. We had to carry him home without being seen, and that was a trick. Talfi's upstairs with him now."

"That boy has it bad," Kalessa said.

"So do I," Danr added, reaching out for Aisa's hand. "Let's not do this again."

"Gladly." Aisa squeezed. "Though it will make for good conversation at the prince's celebration tomorrow."

Danr groaned and put his face in both his hands. "Could we just send him a note saying I'm sick?"

"We could," Aisa said, "but we would still have to attend. The event is in your honor."

"You avoided the prince's invitation for nearly a month," Kalessa added. "No small feat."

"I'd rather avoid it forever," Danr sighed. "I'm a farmer, not a . . . whatever it is the prince thinks I am."

Aisa nodded. This was not something they had foreseen. Word of the half man, half troll who had wielded the Iron Axe, killed countless Fae, razed the elven city of Palana, and faced down the Queen of the Elves herself had spread with incredible speed. The stories were embellished with every telling, until Danr became twenty feet tall, the son of Olar the bird king and a trollwife, able to tear mountains from their roots. Talfi figured in a number of stories as the boy who could not die, as did Kalessa, the warrior orc whose sword could cleave an oak tree. Somehow Aisa was largely missed, and for this she was glad, though a few stories mentioned a slave girl who stopped the angry troll from sundering the continent a second time. Ranadar had escaped notice entirely.

However, vanishingly few people had ever seen a half troll, which made it easy to pick Danr out of a crowd. Talfi and even Kalessa could hide their identities, but Danr attracted attention no matter where they went. Whenever they passed through a village, town, or city, the local lord or mayor or other person in charge insisted on showing hospitality, which sounded nice at first—free food and shelter were never a bad thing—but such events often evolved into problematic celebrations that lasted days or even a week. Danr was asked to judge jousting events, attend special religious ceremonies, bless marriages, and even battle local champions. Danr did his best to be graceful, but he had the manners of the farmer's thrall he had been until just last year, and he was never comfortable in the center of attention. After a particularly embarrassing incident involving a wedding and a pair of kittens, Aisa had appointed herself his social assistant, and she had learned to steer him through difficult waters.

She had definitely learned the value of the polite *no*, but the receptions and parties and parades had delayed them over and over, which was why it had taken them more than a year to get to the city of Balsia. They had hoped that in a city as large and cosmopolitan as this one, they could blend in, but they had quickly learned that more people in a city just meant more people to recognize them, and the local ruler—a prince—was that much harder to refuse.

"You'll do fine, my Hamzu." Aisa stroked his hair. "I'll be right there to ensure it."

He grabbed her hand. "Don't leave me alone for a moment. You remember the kittens."

"We *all* remember the kittens," Kalessa said.

"I will not dare leave you," Aisa promised with a laugh. "Except to change out of these wet clothes."

Upstairs, Aisa poked her head into the room Talfi shared with Ranadar to ensure that they were indeed all right. Ranadar was resting, and Talfi assured her he would be perfectly fine in a few minutes. Twisting was draining enough, let alone under duress and with so much iron about.

In her own room with Kalessa, Aisa quickly changed out of her chilly clothes while Kalessa worked her way out of her woven armor. She sponged away the stench of squid, donned dry clothes, and settled her nerves by fussing with the potted plants on the room's little balcony. The plants didn't need tending, but touching and pruning and plucking calmed her, made her feel at home in ways she hadn't realized were possible. Back when she was a slave in Farek's house in northern Balsia, gardening had been a terrible chore done to benefit someone else. Now that she was a free woman, living in the world's largest city and able to grow what she liked, she found she enjoyed it.

When she planted seeds or started a cutting, she could almost see the plant that would emerge. When it finally did, it often produced a surprise or two—a diverging stem or flowers of a different color or faster growth—but still the plant remained true to its nature. Marigold still cured thrush and helped when a woman's cycle became irregular. Vervain relieved fierce, light-sensitive headaches. Ginger eased morning sickness. It didn't matter if the plant had one stem or two, green flowers or red—it always followed its inner self. How admirable.

One of the echinacea plants was nearing its bloom. The head, however, had two nascent flowers instead of the usual one. Both tiny buds were beautiful, but already Aisa could see that the plant had barely enough resources to bring out one flower. With two buds, neither could bloom. Aisa held out her scissors, then hesitated. Perhaps the echinacea could manage with both.

But no. The greater plan would be served by sacrificing the errant bloom. Without further thought, she snipped it off.

As it fell, the other plants stirred in a passing breeze. For a moment, Aisa thought the leaves formed a tired face. The breeze even made the face nod. Then it was gone. Aisa shook her head. A trick of light and shadow.

"Excuse me, sister." Kalessa edged around Aisa with her armor, which was woven together from strips of wyrm-skin leather fashioned into a supple but strong creation that both protected her from blades and granted mobility. She hung it over the balcony rail.

"Don't let that drip into the pots," Aisa cautioned. "Tannin is bad for the plants."

"It is damp, not dripping." Kalessa checked to make sure nothing would tumble over the edge to the street three stories below. Finding this rooming house had been a small miracle. The rent was affordable, the landlady had accepted two humans, an elf, an orc, and a half troll without blinking, and the rooms had decent-sized balconies that opened out onto the street. Mrs. Farley was also willing to keep their presence a secret, something that seemed to come out of both

a sense of awe and a sense of self-preservation. If word got
out that Danr was living here, regular crowds would no doubt
gather outside on a regular basis, and if their previous experi-
ences were any indication, more than a few people would
barge right in.

Kalessa leaned on the balcony rail. A busy, smelly street
clambered down the gentle slope below. "Now I must tell
you something, my sister," she said. "Before our walk home
provided us with other concerns, Danr asked me for a favor."

"He did? What favor?"

"He asked me to intercede on his behalf." Kalessa flicked
her auburn braid over one shoulder. "I am to ask you, as a
sister, to go and talk to him."

"I talk to him all the time," Aisa replied too casually.

"He wants to discuss the two of you because something
is wrong, but he says every time he tries to bring it up, you
avoid him. Is that true, sister?"

The pointed question—the only kind Kalessa asked—
caught Aisa off guard. "Somewhat, I suppose."

"Why?" Another pointed question.

"Because I . . . have not wished to discuss it."

"Huh. That seems foolish. How will he know what you
want if you will not say?"

Aisa wanted to say that he should already know, that he
should be perfectly aware of what she wanted after all this
time. But her practical side would not allow such foolish-
ness. "He cannot."

"Then it is settled." Kalessa strode for the door. "I will
tell him."

"What?" Aisa turned for her. "I never said—"

But Kalessa already had the door open. Danr was standing in it, filling the doorway with his bulk. He must have
been standing outside it. And for how long?

"She is ready to talk now," Kalessa reported. "I will ask Mrs. Farley to fetch strong drink."

"I really don't want anything," Danr said.

"For me," Kalessa clarified, and left.

Danr blinked at the closed door, then turned to Aisa. "Hello."

"She is blunt as a boulder," Aisa complained, dropping to the bed.

"It's why we love her," Danr agreed. "Uh . . . should I leave anyway?"

Aisa sighed. "No, my love. Stay. Kalessa has pointed out that I have been unfair to you and she is right."

Looking both relieved and apprehensive, Danr sat tailor-fashion on the floor next to the bed. This brought his head on a level with hers. His feet were bare, as was his habit. He would probably never grow accustomed to shoes. She liked that about him.

"What is it, Aisa?" he asked in his husky voice. "You say you love me, but sometimes I think Ranadar and Talfi are closer than we are. What are we doing?"

"I do love you," she said quickly. "Forever. It is just . . . complicated."

"I'm not as stupid as everyone thinks, you know. I can follow what you talk about."

"Only a fool would think you are stupid." Aisa smoothed his coarse hair. "I am not sure you want to hear this, but I will say it." She paused for a long moment, gathering herself as if to jump off a cliff. "Our relationship has been difficult. The fame you bring to it has created an obstacle."

"You're backing away because of everyone else?" Danr said incredulously. "That's not—"

"If you want me to speak, you may not interrupt," she admonished. "And you may not jump to conclusions or get angry until I have finished."

"I'll try." A dubious note entered his voice.

She sighed. "It is unnerving the way everyone treats you, yes. It will make many things difficult. People want . . . pieces of you. Of your story, of your time, even of your clothes. You refuse to let Kalessa and Ranadar guard you—"

"It feels wrong," he interrupted, ignoring her earlier admonition. "I'm a farmer. Guards and servants are wrong for someone like me."

"And that is one reason why they love you so much," she said. "You are one of them. But you are also not. They look at you and see a half-blood."

"Yeah, Danr the Stane." He spread his hands and looked down at them. "Half the crowd today wanted to hear a story. The other half was ready to throw shit. *Did* throw shit. I'm always caught between." Something seemed to occur to him. "You're not unhappy because I'm part Stane, are you?"

"Certainly not!" she said. "That is who you are. Everyone *else* has the problem with half-bloods."

"Everyone else," he repeated softly. "Yeah."

"At any rate, I am trying to say that you attract attention wherever you go, and it has caused us problems. Delays, mostly, and for that I am . . ." She took a breath. "I am angry. I love you, but I am angry."

This caught him by surprise. "Angry? What for?"

"Why have we come to Balsia?" she countered. "The city, not the country."

"Lots of reasons," he replied, puzzled. "We wanted to see if we could blend in here, and wanted to see if it was a good place to live, and . . ." He trailed off as he caught sight of the temper rising in her face. "Oh."

"Yes." The word was clipped. "Oh."

"The merfolk," he was forced to finish. "Like we said in the cave. Maybe I am stupid."

Despite his admission, her temper was getting away from

her like a galloping horse, and she fought to keep it under control. "Ever since the merfolk boarded my ship when I was first sold as a slave, I have wanted—yearned—to swim with them, or just *touch* one. I cannot explain why or what it is. They call to me, so free and so fine. The desire was muted when I became addicted to the Fae. But after I killed the elven king, the merfolk came back to me. In thoughts. In dreams."

"Is it another addiction?" Danr asked, looking more than a little alarmed.

"Nothing like!" she almost snapped. "I . . . long for them the way a sky yearns for a rainbow, or the way a willow tree leans toward a river. But when I ran away from my owner in Balsia, I did not go to the ocean. I followed you under the mountain, and outwitted giants with you, and helped you find the Iron Axe, and more. Afterward, you said we would look for merfolk. Those words thrilled me like a new butterfly realizing it has wings! Except it has been more than a year, and we have only just now arrived in a place on the ocean. Not only that, we arrived just when the threat of storms prevents us from venturing out. For this, I am . . . angry."

"It's not my fault," Danr protested. "How was I supposed to know word would spread about us? Everywhere we went, people stopped us."

"They stopped *you*," Aisa corrected pointedly. "They do not know who I am."

"Do you want them to?"

"That is not what we are discussing."

"And then Death had those other quests for us," Danr said. "Were we supposed to say no?"

"I am angry, Danr," Aisa said evenly. "Ever since we went under the mountain, I have lived my life for you. I have done what you wished, gone where you needed, fulfilled your quests."

"They were your quests, too." Danr was growing heated now. "You killed the elven king and cured your hunger for him. Now *everyone* knows how to cure elven hunger, and the elves don't take humans for slaves anymore. Should we have turned back? Do you want to be hungry again?"

"So I did not spend a year following you around," Aisa snapped. "I did not find the haft for the Iron Axe for you, or save Talfi's life when he lost his leg."

"He didn't need saving, it turned out," Danr shot back.

"This is why I did not wish to talk to you." Aisa folded her arms hard. "I knew it would hurt your feelings and you would become angry."

The scream echoed in her head again. *Liar*, whispered a small inner voice. Aisa tried to ignore it.

Danr made a visible effort to calm down, though his hands were still tense. "So that's why you've been pulling away from me. I'm famous, and we haven't been able to look for the merfolk fast enough."

"It is how I feel," she said.

Liar. Tell him the rest. But Aisa folded her lips. There were times when she *wanted* to talk about it, when the words swirled around inside her in a bloody storm of emotion that demanded release. But years of slavery had locked up Aisa's ability to share. Danr couldn't help but tell the truth. Aisa couldn't help but hide it. They made the perfect pair.

"And me being half troll isn't part of the problem?" he asked.

The exasperation started again. "I have already said—I love you whether you are half troll, half dwarf, or half tree. But I would be a liar if I said your birth never made things difficult. A lot of people think you a monster, no matter what you have done. When we marry, they will think me a monster, too, I suppose."

"A monster," he repeated sadly, and Aisa was instantly sorry for her choice of words. Danr had been called a monster all his life, and Aisa had only barely managed to convince him that he was not one in time to stop him from cracking the world in two during the Battle of the Twist.

"You are not a monster," she said. "I have never thought so."

"I know." He touched her small, callused hand with his large, hairy one. "But you're right—other people will think differently, and that will make life hard for . . . well, for both of us. When we're married."

She seized on the change of subject. "Married. Hmm. Is that a proposal, then?"

"I don't know," he said, and coming from him, that had to be the truth. "I didn't think of it as one."

Her face grew warm. "It is the first time you have used the word *marriage* with me."

"Is it?" His own face had the most peculiar look. "I . . . I guess I didn't think. I mean . . . I always just assumed you and I would . . ."

"A woman needs to be asked, you know," she said tartly. "In the right way."

"Oh. Sure. Er . . ." He shifted again and started to get to one knee. "Aisa, will you—"

"Not now!" she interrupted. "We are fighting!"

He sat back down, confused. "I thought the fight was over. You told me why you were angry, and I agreed with you. Are you still angry?"

She looked away. "I don't know. It's all so complicated."

The scream returned. *Liar,* said her inner voice again.

It is not a lie. It is true.

You are not telling the whole truth. That makes it a lie.

"All right." Danr got to his feet. "Aisa, I'm really sorry we delayed after everything you did for me—for us. We couldn't have done any of it without you. All I can do is promise you that the day storm season ends, we'll go look for merfolk, and when I promise, you know it's the truth." He tapped his left eye. "I love you forever, yeah?"

A great deal of the tension went out of the room. "And I love you," she said. "But now I should gather my things and head down to the Docks."

"The Docks?" Danr cocked his head. "What for?"

"The slaves."

"Oh. Right." He was still standing at the door. "Can you put it off? We were supposed to visit Death after we killed the squid. This is sort of important."

"How can you think *this* is unimportant?" Aisa's temper flared all of a sudden. "Death is not going anywhere. Those people are in *pain*!"

"All right, sure." He held up his hands. "I don't want to fight again."

She closed her eyes. What was wrong with her? But the screams in her head answered that question. "I don't, either. I'm just tired."

"Then don't go. Let's do something together. Just you and me. It's been . . . I don't know how long."

"I would love to, but after I get back." She rose, caught up a pack, and rummaged through it. "Tell Mrs. Farley not to wait supper on me. And . . . I await your proposal."

"Just need the right moment," he said at the door, then paused. "Just to be clear, you're going to say yes, right?"

"What woman can refuse a man who brings her a handful of squid ink?"

He grinned and left, but Aisa noted the expression had an air of sadness to it.

After a considerable walk from Mrs. Farley's rooming house, Aisa arrived with her pack at the Docks. Because Balsia was a port city—perhaps *the* port city—the Docks had a life of their own. Countless quays, dock, slips, berths, and piers jutted like the warrior's toes into the green water of Bosha's Bay, and hundreds of vessels of all sizes, from tiny rowboats to massive ships that moved under sails as big as clouds moored themselves here. The bay was protected from the South Sea by a spit of land that lay across the mouth, keeping the bay calm in even the strongest autumn storms. The spit was called the Sword of Bal, and legend said the great hero had fought a great fire-breathing wyrm on this spot countless centuries ago. They had killed each other. The wyrm's blood created the bay, and Bal's dropped weapon created the spit of land that sheltered it. At one time in her life, Aisa wouldn't have given the story a shred of credence, but after watching Danr wield the Iron Axe, she half wondered.

Sailors, merchants, dockworkers, rope weavers, prostitutes, innkeepers, coopers, sail makers, and others created a city all its own down at the Docks. Like the city of Balsia itself, the Docks were split in half by the river Bal—Aisa noted the lack of originality in names for this place—which emptied into Bosha's Bay. As she always did when she arrived at the Docks, Aisa paused to shade her eyes and look out over the water in case one of the merfolk might be swimming there. There never was, but she always looked.

At least the sky was clear for the moment. When they had first arrived in the city of Balsia, Aisa was hoping to board a ship right away and go looking for merfolk, but they had arrived in early autumn, the beginning of storm season. Dreadful typhoons blew up out of nothing in the Iron Sea and rushed across the coast. Only the most desperate or foolhardy captains put to sea at this time of year. Instead they cozied up to Balsia's forgiving port for a month, made repairs, and let their sailors get into fights on land, where it was the busy season for innkeepers and whorehouses. Aisa tried to tell herself it was only one more month, but the time dragged, and the ever-present ocean tempted her daily.

Some days, the ocean called to her, almost sang to her, like a mother humming a lullaby, and she wanted to . . . what? It was hard to say. She had no real desire to sail, could barely swim, but the ocean was mysterious and powerful and gentle all at once. It held secrets, and she wanted to know every one. She had no real idea why she felt this way. It was simply a fact that she did. Most likely it had something to do with the conversation she had had with the mermaid all those years ago when she was first sold into slavery. She would have liked to ask the merfolk in person about it. But merfolk never swam the filthy waters of Bosha's Bay, and the ocean hid its secrets beneath the greasy little waves of the harbor.

On the west bank where the river met the bay stood the gleaming azure jewel that was Bosha's temple. Since Bosha was the goddess of the ocean, her priests were in charge of the Docks, and her temple showed their wealth. A high wall studded with shards of blue glass surrounded the temple complex, and within rose a number of intricate buildings designed to appear that they flowed and crested like waves. More glass, and even real jewels, were inlaid on the pale stone so the place sparkled and shone like a bit of ocean dragged up on land.

It made a stark contrast to the cages and pens of the slave market directly across the river. Most of the pens were long, low buildings with cages or shackling areas inside. If the city was a seedy warrior, this place was a festering sore on his buttocks. Here, the smell of fear and feces made the wind heavy with hopelessness. Today, every pen was filled to capacity, and more slaves of all ages, including babies, were chained outside them. Slave dealers in black moved among the pens, mingling with customers—wealthy estates intending to buy in bulk, whorehouses looking to fill beds, homeowners seeking a cheap maid or houseboy.

Aisa's teeth ground until her jaw ached. She hated this place, but she couldn't stay away. The pens were packed because of what she and the others had done to the Fae. Before the Battle of the Twist, the main market for human slaves had been the elves in Alfhame, just up the coast to the east. The Fae used slaves the way a pampered lady devoured sweetmeats, and many humans had been sent to Alfhame as tribute, but just as many were exchanged for elven silver.

Almost no humans ran away from slavery among the Fae. A lingering touch by an elf put on a glamour that made the human love the elf, worship him, yearn for him. Aisa remembered very well how badly she wanted her elven master, the king, to touch her, or simply say her name aloud. And then Aisa had displeased her master and he leveled on her the worst possible sentence: exile. For two years she had lived in Farek's cold house, hungering for the elven king's touch, until the Nine had given her the chance to lay the elf king low. The moment he died at her feet, her hunger had ended. It was a revelation—killing the elf ended the hunger among the human slaves. Once that knowledge got out, the Fae no longer wanted human slaves. With the main buyer no longer interested, a glut appeared on the market. Prices fell sharply. And with lowered value came an increase in abuse of the merchandise. The combination of guilt and outrage brought Aisa here.

Aisa filled two buckets of water at the common pump and made herself stride toward the first pen. The guard stationed there recognized her and let her pass inside with a simple nod. The smell of the pen hit her with a ghostly fist. The streets had nothing on the pens, where sanitation was a bucket or bowl, where few people were able to wash, and where people often vomited or soiled themselves from fear.

The stench of misery, pain, and waste lay thick and pungent on Aisa's skin. Slaves were chained or tied to a series of low walls that ran the length of the pen. Voices bounced off the walls and ceiling in a mix of conversation, moans, cries, and soft sobs. There was no laughter in this place.

"Here you are." A plump human woman in a red robe bustled up to Aisa. She had a wrinkled face, twisted hands, and thinning white hair. Her name was Kuri, and she was a priestess for Grick. The temple of Grick officially disliked slavery, but did not have the political clout to make its displeasure known. It did send its priests and acolytes to the slave pens to practice their healing. Aisa was no acolyte, but the temple never turned away volunteers, partly in the hope that they might become converts. Aisa wondered what the priests would think if they knew Aisa and Kalessa had once kept house for Grick for several months while the Old Aunt herself called up Aisa's personal demons in single combat. As a reward for defeating her inner monsters, Grick had given to Kalessa a sword that changed into any blade Kalessa desired and to Aisa an old fireplace poker that unexpectedly turned out to be the handle of the Iron Axe.

"A new lot came in early this morning, and they need seeing to," Kuri said to her. "Over in the corner. Do you have what you need?"

"I do, and good morning to you."

Kuri waved a hand and hurried off to a knot of children who were chained together. Aisa watched her go, a little glad Kuri had not requested that she deal with them. The adults were heartbreaking enough.

Aisa was carrying her buckets to the corner when a hand lifted one of them from her. Surprised, she turned. The helper was a dark-haired woman in her fourth decade, old enough to be Aisa's mother. She wore a patched blue cloak with the hood cast back, and she carried a broom in her other hand. Her name was Sharlee, and Aisa had come across her and her broom in the slave pens a number of times.

"Let me carry this one, honey," Sharlee said. "Do you need a hand today?"

Out of habit, Aisa almost refused, then changed her mind. It was silly to turn down help. "Thank you," she said instead.

In the corner, three women were chained to the wall by ankle shackles that gave them spare movement. The first had a festering cut, and the second was coughing uncontrollably. The third seemed healthy, but Aisa would have to examine her anyway. The first two women flinched when Aisa set the buckets down.

"My name is Aisa," she recited in a quiet voice. "I'm not a buyer, and I do not work for the slavers. My friend Sharlee and I wish to help with your sickness and injuries."

She wet a cloth in the first bucket and handed it to the first woman so she could clean herself. Aisa had learned from experience that people were more likely to trust her if she let them do something for themselves, like wash or eat a bit of food. Some slaves became violent if she offered too much too fast.

"Thank you, lady," the first woman said.

"Now you, dear." Sharlee wrung the cloth and gave it to the second woman, and then the third.

"May I see the cut on your hand?" Aisa asked. The first woman's cut was indeed infected, and Aisa cleaned it with supplies from her pack and bandaged it while the woman sucked in her breath. "Do your best to keep it clean. I'll check on you later."

"If no one buys me, you mean," the woman said sadly.

The second woman coughed hard and spat out a throat full of phlegm. "Why are you here, if you don't work for the slavers?"

This question Aisa had heard often. She poured some water from the bucket into a cup and crushed a handful of different medicines into it. "I used to be a slave. Now I help where I can."

"Can you help me escape?" the woman asked boldly. She had greasy brown hair and hard lines around her mouth. "I have a son back home."

Sharlee shot Aisa a glance. The request pulled at Aisa's heart. She wanted to say yes, she could help. The unfairness of this place fanned an outrage that swelled her chest with tears—and made her want to explode. She wanted to beat the guard over the head, take his keys, and let every slave free. But she also knew what would happen if she did. Perhaps two or three slaves might actually escape. The rest would be recaptured and beaten for their trouble. Aisa would be arrested, imprisoned, and probably executed.

It was the suffering that drew her here. She couldn't look at these people without stopping to help. It was too little, but it was something.

"I know of no way to escape," she said. "But if you try, I will not stop you. This will help your cough."

Aisa started to hand the second woman the cup, but she caught Aisa's wrist. "You say you used to be a slave," she hissed. "But now that you have your freedom, you won't help me? Traitor!"

She dashed the cold cup down Aisa's front with a snarl and turned her back with a clanking of chains. Aisa stood there for a long moment, dress dripping, face flaming. The other slaves either stared or looked carefully away. Sharlee bit her lips. Aisa trembled as tears warred with anger. Perhaps she was a traitor. But how dared this woman?

After a few deep breaths, Aisa sighed and took up her packs and the buckets, intending to move on to the next group of slaves. For a moment, she remembered the little blossom falling beneath her scissors. Sometimes a small sacrifice must be made in order to help the whole, and sometimes that sacrifice was her own self.

Sharlee touched her shoulder. "I'm sorry, honey. You're only trying to help."

"We'll check her again later," Aisa decided. "Come on."

They worked together, along with a too-tiny group of priests from the temple of Grick. Some slaves accepted aid gratefully, some barely noticed her presence, others raged and snarled at her. The unfairness of the place continued to press at her, but Aisa knew if she didn't do it, these people would suffer, so she kept at it. Sharlee stayed with her the entire time, and for that, Aisa was grateful. It was good to have more female friends. Kalessa was a wonderful sister, but sometimes it was like befriending a pile of swords and needles, and it felt nice to be with someone a little less . . . prickly. And while her hands were filled with work, her head remained empty of screams.

"So. How are things with your friends, if you don't mind some motherly prying?" Sharlee asked while they refilled the buckets at the well outside.

Why was everyone asking this today? Aisa's thoughts rushed back to the rooming house and the argument with Danr. A guilty flush came over her. "Er . . . fine." Aisa pretended to check her pack for burdock. "We are well."

Sharlee's lined face softened. "I'm so sorry."

"What?"

"This is me you're talking to." Sharlee hoisted a dripping bucket from the well. "You don't need to lie, honey. Not between us women. What happened? Was it something to do with Danr and the Battle of the Twist?"

"Ssss!" Aisa glanced around while Sharlee poured water over their hands to clean them. "Not here!"

"Honestly! You're heroes, all of you! I don't know why you want to keep so quiet about it. *I* figured out who you really were. Do you think no one else will?"

Aisa scrubbed her skin in the cold water. "Some may see us as heroes, yes, and an equal number wish us dead. Best just to keep quiet. Besides, I do not—Danr does not—wish for the attention."

"Of course, honey." Sharlee sent the bucket back down the windlass. "But what *happened* today? I can see you're upset. Tell Auntie Sharlee, and you'll feel better. Is it your young man?"

Aisa could not keep another guilty look from crossing her face. Wearing a scarf for so many years had gotten her out of the habit of disguising her expression. Sharlee noticed.

"Maybe I can help," she said. "What happened?"

The screams came back. Aisa looked down at her hands. For a moment, they were covered with blood. Then the blood vanished. She shook her head at Sharlee. If she wasn't going to talk about it to Kalessa or Danr himself, she certainly wasn't going to talk to Sharlee, a woman she barely knew. "It is nothing. I am fine."

Liar.

"Well, that's good, then." Sharlee patted Aisa's shoulder and let the subject drop, to Aisa's relief. "Are you hungry, honey? I'm absolutely starved."

As if in answer, Aisa's stomach growled. She had been so busy she had not noticed the passing time. "I could eat a wyrm's tongue."

"In this town, you could probably find a cook that serves it," Sharlee laughed, "but I was thinking about a place I know two streets over. My treat."

"Oh." Aisa hadn't meant to hint. "There are more slaves who need—"

"Aisa." Sharlee took both her hands, and Aisa was glad the blood had vanished. "You are a kind and giving person, but you can't clean up all the misery in the world. There will always be slaves who need treatment, and meanwhile you need to eat. Now come along! Auntie's orders."

Still a little reluctant, Aisa let herself be led away. Sharlee took her to a tavern north of the Docks, a place that was quieter and did not cater much to loud, vulgar sailors. This place seemed to specialize in food and drink more than rooms, and the great room smelled pleasantly of bread and mead and spices. Sharlee talked quietly with the proprietor, a balding thin man who reminded Aisa of a vulture, and they took up a table to themselves.

"You needn't feel guilty, you know," Sharlee said as a serving girl brought them fried apples, glazed carrots, beef ribs heavy with herb gravy, and mugs of mead. "The Gardeners have been kind to you. Enjoy the fruits of your fate."

Aisa thought of her own time as a slave. "I do not know that I can say the Gardeners were ever kind to me," she said, sipping from her mug. The mead was sweet and had a new taste Aisa could not identify. Quite good, and she wanted to share it with Danr. Then she remembered she was angry at him, and then she remembered she was not truly angry at him, and then she was confused. Perhaps bringing him here, just the two of them, could make things up. "The elven hunger . . . I lived with it for so long."

"And now you don't," Sharlee finished. "The entire world knows how to end that hunger, thanks to you."

"Sss!" Aisa glanced around, hoping no one heard. "I do not wish—"

Sharlee clucked her tongue. "You're too nice, Aisa. Do you know how many people—rich people—would love to have you at their homes to tell your story? Or who would pay to have you grace their gardens at a party? You could make a tidy living, dear."

"I do know," Aisa said. "And I do not wish it. *We* do not wish it."

"Have some more mead," Sharlee sighed.

It was good mead, especially with the fried apples, and Aisa was a little surprised at how fast the first mug went. Sharlee called for seconds.

"It must be so sad," Sharlee said after a while.

"What is?" Aisa reached for more bread and missed. The table seemed to be wobbling. Or maybe it was her chair. Was this funny? A bubble of laughter rose, and she swallowed hard to keep it down.

"The fight you had with your young man," Sharlee said. "You never did say what it was about."

"It was not a fight," Aisa said, and her words were a little slurred. "Not really."

"No?" Sharlee rested her chin on her hand. "Tell me."

Suddenly, it seemed unreasonably difficult and silly to keep everything back, especially with Sharlee. Sharlee was kind, so gentle, so like her mother. A well of emotion for the other woman burbled up inside her, bringing tears to Aisa's eyes and spilling words from her like wine from a jar. "I have lied to him all this time. I just today told him that I was angry at him because his fame delayed us in our travels."

"So that's a lie?" Sharlee prompted.

"Maybe a little lie." Aisa held up a shaky thumb and forefinger to show how little. "It's part of the lie. And I told him that if we get married, other people will see me as some kind of abnomin—ablomin—aboomin—"

"Abomination?" Sharlee supplied.

"Monster," Aisa agreed. "So he thought I was calling him a monster, and I was not. I said *other* people will think *I* am a monster. If Danr and I get married. 'Cause he is half troll and lots of people hate half-bloods, even if they have never seen one."

"I see."

"Oh, good. Because I do not." Aisa hiccupped and waved her mug, which was not quite empty and probably made her at least one enemy at the next table. "But that is not what truly bothers me."

"And what's truly bothering you, honey?"

She did not truly wish to say, but the words kept coming. "It is the Battle of the Twist."

"What happened at the Battle of the Twist?"

The truth popped out of its own accord. Aisa did not fight it. "Sometimes . . . sometimes I see blood. On me. On my food. On other people." She looked into her horn. It was almost empty, and then a barmaid handed her a full one. Aisa took it gratefully. "I hear screams in my head, too. Screams of elves and sprites and fairies. They scream because . . . because . . ."

"Because why?" Sharlee asked softly.

"Because Danr is killing them," Aisa whispered.

"With the Iron Axe."

"Yes." The room was spinning a little now. "I watched him kill them. He cut them in half by the dozens with the Iron Axe. He set fire to the trees and they burned to death. He made earthquakes that crushed them. I hear their screams. I see their blood."

"I thought you hated the Fae. You killed the king yourself."

"Yesh. It makes no sense. I despised the Fae. The king raped me and he was going to kill us all, so I killed him. But then I watched Danr slaughter so many Fae. All at once.

Like candles drowning in blood. All that blood. And *he* was doing it."

"Your love had become a killer of the masses," Sharlee observed.

Aisa nodded, which made the room swim. Her cheeks were wet. When had she wept? "I had to stop him. And I did. Barely. But sometimes . . . sometimes I have dreams when I fail to stop him, and he stands on a pile of bloody corpses and cracks the world in half with the Iron Axe. I wake up and my sweat is cold. I know Danr had no choice. The Fae had already killed dozens and dozens of Stane, and they planned to kill the rest of them. Danr stopped them in the only way possible. He did nothing wrong. But those thoughts do not keep the blood and the screams out of my head."

"You poor dear," Sharlee said. "You're afraid to tell him because it'll hurt him, but not telling him is hurting your love for each other."

"Yes." Aisa wiped at her face with her sleeve, and Sharlee gave her a handkerchief. "But that is not all of it. We are supposed to find merfolk, and we cannot because of the stormy season, and it's been more than a year, and it makes me even more short-tempered. I blame him, and I should not, and it is all mixed together."

"Mermaids?" Sharlee came upright. "You want to find mermaids? Really?"

"Yes." She blew her nose and reached for her horn again, but Sharlee pulled it away. "It is foolish, I know, but I have wanted to swim with the merfolk for a long time. We always seem to do what Danr needs or what Talfi or Ranadar or Kalessa needs, but not what I need." She sniffed again. "Heroes in stories never have such problems."

"That's because those are stories and this is real life." The warmth had left Sharlee's voice. She got to her feet and dropped a coin on the table. "I have to get home, honey. Use this to hire a carriage for yourself, all right?"

And she was gone, leaving Aisa with a tableful of empty mugs and dishes and the strangest feeling something significant had just happened.

Chapter Three

The gold-liveried footman helped Sharlee Obsidia down from the carriage, but she hardly noticed. Wrapped in urgency, she hustled across the great stone portico, barely giving the golems enough time to snatch open the massive front doors of the big house. Once inside, she dropped her patched cloak. A golem caught it before it hit the floor.

"Where is my husband?" she demanded.

"In the library, lady." The golem's voice was dead and dry, like stones rubbing together. It looked like a pile of clay flowerpots with arms and legs, and two glassy sapphires made up its eyes. Runes crawled across its head and body in blocky, artless script, and the runes at the top of the golem's forehead were smeared red-brown with blood. The golem had no mouth—the dead voice came from somewhere inside.

Only the dwarfs could make golems, and more of them were coming on the market now that the doors underhill had opened and more Stane were showing up. Dwarfs could make nearly anything, given enough time and the right materials, and golems were better than slaves. They didn't have to be fed, they never slept, and they never disobeyed. The only disadvantage was that they were blood-all expensive. Sharlee had, in fact, balked at buying golems at all, but Hector had pointed out that in the long run, golems paid for themselves in food alone, and she had given in. Then the Battle of the Twist had caught up to the slave market, and Hector's foresight in hiring dwarfs to make golems had turned out to be the most prescient move in all history.

Or it would be, once the final pieces were put into play.

For a tiny moment, Sharlee considered heading upstairs to bathe and change out of the nasty, itchy peasant's disguise she wore whenever she was spying on the fool girl Aisa, then just as quickly decided against. This was too important, too much *fun*, to wait. Instead she all but scampered across marble floors and thick rugs toward the library. Slaves, servants, and golems all jumped to get out of her way. It was always a treat to bring good news to Hector.

Light and bright air filled the library. Its floor-to-ceiling windows, which they had spared no expense to have built, let in every bit of Rolk's golden fire to make reading easy, and Sharlee drank in the warmth and heat like wine after the filth of the slave pens. Why people allowed such things to happen to them, she didn't understand. Three entire bookshelves, each six feet high, were crammed with books. Two bookshelves were fitted with pigeonholes for scrolls. It was the largest library in Balsia, outside anything the priests might have, and no guest was ever allowed to see it.

Hector was standing at a table, looking dapper in his sun-red silk shirt and dark, perfectly cut trousers. A proud smile crossed Sharlee's face and mingled with the anticipation. Even now that he was over forty, he hadn't lost his fine figure, and his hair was still thick and black, with only a hint of silver that called for her fingertip to brush across it. Her heart fluttered a little to see him, even after twenty years, and she liked that he could do that.

Across the table from Hector huddled a pale, pudgy man in brown whose name was Irwin. Sharlee knew his name because she knew the name of all the people in their employ. She also knew that Irwin was a damp sponge of a man who had a drab wife and two daughters just entering marriageable age. Lately, he had made a number of mistakes, and judging from the look on Hector's face, Irwin was in for it. That would be fun, too. Hector did know how to put on a show. Partly interested to see what Hector was up to and partly annoyed that Irwin's presence was spoiling her grand news, Sharlee approached the table.

"The dwarfs you hired have all left me," Hector was saying to Irwin. "All but one. They're defecting to the temple of Bosha just when I need them most."

"All but one?" Sharlee interjected, her previous pleasant thoughts thrust aside. "When did this happen?"

"Moments ago, darling." Hector didn't take his eyes off Irwin. "I wasn't able to alert you, and now I have to deal with the aftermath."

Sharlee's hands chilled, and she glared at Irwin with barely concealed ire. Losing the dwarfs was a complete disaster! And just when she was bringing good news, too. "How could this happen?" she demanded.

Arranged on the table between Hector and Irwin were nine small goblets with wine in the bottom. A golem stood to one side, arms at its sides. Whatever Hector planned, it wouldn't be enormously entertaining for Irwin, the little sop. Good. If he was responsible for letting the dwarfs go, he would deserve it, whatever it was. Interested despite her pique, Sharlee came around to Hector's side of the table. He raised his eyebrows at her.

"Please, my lord," Irwin quavered. "The temple offered more than you authorized me to pay. I'll find more dwarfs. We'll build all the golems you need. I won't fail you again."

"I know you won't," Hector replied in a mild tone Sharlee recognized with a little thrill. She almost felt sorry for Irwin, but he had been well paid for his work, and if he couldn't live up to Obsidia expectations, he shouldn't have entered employment with them. Honestly.

"Hello, darling," Sharlee said, and gave Hector a quick kiss on the cheek. He always smelled good. She couldn't put her finger on what it was—a bit of smoke, a bit of sweet wine, a bit of . . . him—but it made her happy, and that was all that mattered.

"I'm glad you're home, love." He pressed her hand with the wide smile that still gave her a kick of happiness after years of seeing it. "You look ravishing, even in that awful disguise. I hate it when you wander around that filthy slave market."

"You're sweet, darling." She brushed imaginary lint off his soft shirt and let her touch linger. If Irwin hadn't been there, she would have whirled him around with excitement over what she had learned. But instead they had to deal with the dwarf problem. Good news and bad news at the same time. It wasn't fair. She suppressed an urge to smack Irwin on the head with a hammer and lowered her voice instead. "We need to talk, Hector. Very important stuff."

"Every word you say is important to me, my sweet." He kissed her hand. "But I do have to deal with this first, if you don't mind."

"I wouldn't dream of interrupting," she said, shifting from one foot to the other. "Perhaps we can do both at once."

Hector saw her agitation—he knew her perfectly well. "Why not? It'll be like pears and cheese together."

"My favorite, darling!"

He turned back to Irwin. Sweat ran down the drab man's face. Sharlee's gaze swept the goblets, and instantly she worked out what was coming next. It surprised her that Irwin hadn't. Poor man. Well, he deserved it.

"One of the nine goblets is poisoned, friend," Hector said. "If you can get through four of them, everything will be forgiven. The odds are in your favor. Just."

Irwin licked his lips. Sharlee automatically noticed the bad stitching on his clothing, the scuff marks on his worn shoes, the placement of the calluses on his right hand. This was a man who was spending a lot of time losing money at the dice tables. No wonder the dwarfs had left. If there was one thing dwarfs couldn't stomach, it was someone who couldn't handle money.

"If I don't drink?" Irwin asked.

Hector snapped his fingers. The golem reached for Irwin, who backed away. "No! No, I'll . . . I'm in. Thank you, my lord."

He reached for one of the goblets with a trembling hand, changed his mind, and picked up the one next to it.

"I really should discuss this with you, my dear," Sharlee said, letting some impatience show.

"Of course, of course." Hector folded his hands in front of him. "Tell! I'm dying to hear."

"I've had a breakthrough with Aisa and Danr." She couldn't keep the smile from her face. "I finally persuaded her to have a drink with me. A little of Tikk's tincture in her cup at the right moment, and everything came spilling out."

Hector's face lit up, reminding her of the young man she had met so many years ago, and her impatience abated. "Darling—genius!" He kissed her again. "You were absolutely right, as usual—volunteering in the slave pens was the perfect idea. Tell me everything, and then tell me again."

Irwin drained his goblet, waited a moment, then gulped

hard and reached for a second. The golem watched through impassive azure eyes.

With relish, Sharlee related the essence of her conversation with Aisa. Hector listened with an intensity that told her she was the only person in the universe, so she told it again, and still he listened. He had a way of doing that which made her feel special, completely unlike her father, who had treated her with . . . well, less than specialness. People who said girls married their fathers were idiots. When she finished speaking, Hector drummed his fingers on the table with the abstract look on his face Sharlee associated with deep thought.

"So," he said, "you believe the key to controlling Aisa is her fear of that troll boy. I like the way you think."

"I believe we need to hurry," Sharlee countered. "Three problems are bothering Aisa, you see. The first is that her life will be difficult if she marries a half-blood. A *famous* half-blood. This fear is utterly groundless, and she knows it. She's using it to cover up the second problem."

"The battle nightmares," Hector said.

"Absolutely. I've seen it before, usually in men who return from war. They bring the battles home with them, and it tears at them. Sometimes they recover, sometimes they don't. Aisa saw Danr as a battle monster. She knows he had no choice and she hated the people he killed, but she nonetheless saw him mow down a *lot* of people, and this tears her in two directions. We need to act quickly. She is on the edge of telling him about this."

"What makes you say that, darling?"

"Now that she had said these things aloud to me, she will be willing to tell Danr. The moment she does, she will become useless to us."

Irwin picked up a third goblet. His hands were shaking now, and the sweat shone on his face. What little sympathy

Sharlee felt for him was rapidly vanishing. He was putting it off for too long. Best to do what was necessary and get it over with. Only a fool drew it out.

"What are your thoughts?" Hector asked. "Sharp as knives, I'm sure they are."

"We need to ensure that Danr thinks the first problem, the famous half-blood problem, is the real one," Sharlee said. "Because the solution to *that* problem is—"

"The power of the shape!" Hector put out a hand, and a slave hurried up with a separate goblet of wine. Sharlee held out her own hand and received one as well.

"The power of the shape?" said Irwin timorously. "That's just a legend. Only a few people have even heard of it."

Sharlee pursed her lips. So close. Irwin was sporting some spine by daring to insert himself into their conversation and showing he might know something useful. For a tiny, tiny moment, Sharlee could have seen him spinning his meager knowledge into a second chance. Then he had thrown it away by contradicting what she and Hector clearly already knew—that the power of the shape was more than legend. Involuntarily, she glanced at the shelves. Every book, every scroll, contained at least a scrap of information about the power of the shape. It was the most extensive library on the topic in the world. And every book they kept *here* meant the knowledge stayed a secret from someone out *there*. Sharlee didn't worry about the slaves or golems— they couldn't read—and in a few minutes, Irwin wouldn't be able to, either.

"You have wine to finish," Hector said shortly, as Sharlee knew he would. "In silence."

Irwin raised his third cup with lowered eyes and a shaky hand. No doubt it was mostly vinegar—no point in wasting the good stuff on someone in his position. Sharlee tried her own. Sweet and light.

"I see it now," Hector said, sipping again. "Danr will want to find the power of the shape to solve Aisa's problem."

"And his own," Sharlee said. "He's still uncomfortable being a half-blood."

"You know all this from just spying on him?" Hector asked.

Sharlee drew herself up, wounded. "Darling!"

"Apologies." Hector brandished the cup. "This wine is stronger than I thought. No one manipulates like you, my love."

Mollified, Sharlee raised her own cup while Irwin shakily contemplated his next choice. "And no one makes the long plan like you, my dear."

"Then how do we manipulate him into going after the power of the shape?" Hector asked.

"For that we'll use Aisa's third problem." Sharlee revealed her nugget of information like a magician pulling a dove from his sleeve. "She seeks the merfolk."

Hector's reaction did not disappoint. "I *knew* it!" he crowed. He took Sharlee by both hands and danced about with her for a moment. "I saw it from the beginning! This is wonderful news! That last venture into the Iron Sea was worth every lost sailor."

"Especially since we didn't pay them," Sharlee put in. "You're a genius, darling."

"So are you, my love. The merfolk know the location of the Key, and that means we'll get everything we want. Our families . . ." Hector rubbed his hands. Sharlee waited with a wife's patience.

"Do you know how much this means to us?" he said.

"Of course, darling."

Hector went on, as if she hadn't spoken. He was heading into a tirade, and Sharlee, recognizing the signs after years of marriage, held out her goblet for more wine. The slave obliged.

"We were *powerful*, Sharlee," he said. "Your family and mine. Kings begged to lay their broken crowns at our ancestors' feet. Now all we have is money. Money! As if money meant real power to anyone!"

"Any child can earn money on a street corner," Sharlee said, giving the reply she knew he wanted. "But only the right people can wield the power of the shape."

"And we will become the right people. All we need to do is get everyone in the right place at the right time." Hector looked thoughtfully at Irwin's selection of goblets. "Danr is attending the prince's reception tomorrow evening, and that will allow me to set everything into motion. Can you get our heroes of the Iron Axe into proper position?"

"No." Sharlee set her wine down as Irwin snatched up a fourth goblet

Hector raised his eyebrows. "No?"

"It'll have to be you."

"Oh." Hector thought again. "A little man-to-man talk. Can I handle that?"

Irwin downed the fourth goblet in one desperate gulp. Sharlee laughed and put a hand on Hector's arm. "You absolutely can't, darling, but don't worry—I'll tell you what to say."

Hector heaved a sigh of relief. "That's why I keep you around, my dear."

"Only that?" she asked archly.

He put his arms around her and kissed her. She tasted wine on his lips, and her body molded warm against his. "Some other reasons leap to mind," he whispered in her ear.

"M-my lord?" quavered Irwin.

Hector looked over Sharlee's shoulder in annoyance.

"Oh. Four goblets. Yes, you may go, Irwin. I should run, if I were you. We still need to figure out what to do about the lost dwarfs."

"And we need a mermaid," added Sharlee. "No small detail."

"Thank you, my lord." Irwin rushed for the door. After four steps, his knees buckled and he went down. He choked and gasped and convulsed. His face turned reddish purple, and his tongue protruded from between his teeth. Then he gave one final breath and died.

Sharlee laughingly boxed Irwin on the shoulder. "I knew it! You poisoned all of them, didn't you?"

"Never leave your opponent a choice." Hector kissed her again.

"A fine philosophy," said a nonvoice.

Sharlee jerked away from Hector as a tall man in blue and white stepped over Irwin's body, but she relaxed when she saw who it was. "Really, Will! Can't you knock?"

"I let myself in," the man said, "and I see poor Irwin has paid for the traffic I encountered on my way here. I'm afraid he wasn't truly responsible for the loss of the dwarfs. That was me."

"Well, obviously." Sharlee put her hands on her hips. "No one else would have the money to pay them. What in Vik's name do you mean by leaving us with a single dwarf?"

"You need to think bigger, my dear," said the man. "I have a deal for you."

"A deal?" echoed Hector. "One that will give us something better than an army of dwarfs that can make golems? We want them back, Will. Now."

"I couldn't help overhearing what you said about the girl Aisa," the man said, ignoring Hector's demand. "I've noticed her as well, you know. Eyes and ears all over the slave market. And speaking of slaves, I have the final thing you need to make her get the power of the shape. Let me keep the dwarfs, and I'll give it to you."

"What's the final thing I need?" Hector asked.

"Stop by the slave market on your way to see Danr," the man said, "and I'll show you."

"You ready to talk?" Talfi asked for the third time since Aisa had left.

"No." Danr thumped his horn down. He'd never been fully drunk in his life—as a thrall he hadn't been able to afford it, and as a truth-teller he'd always avoided it—but maybe now was the time to try it. This was the proper place: a dark tavern next door to Mrs. Farley's rooming house. It had fresh rushes on the floor and women who brought drinks and a smoky fire in the fireplace. Danr wore a voluminous cloak and kept the hood pulled so no one would recognize him—he hoped. He gulped from the horn again. The ale was new in the barrel, and cheap—more than a little sour and tasting too strongly of yeast. Perfect if you wanted to get drunk with little money.

"Why is being in love so hard?" he asked the table morosely.

"You're asking *us* for advice about women?" Talfi said wryly. Ranadar was sitting next to him, holding his hand under the table. Balsia was live-and-let-live in a lot of ways—Vik, there was an actual troll sitting in the corner of this very tavern—but *regi* men attracted mixed attention. The priests of Olar, who held sway farther north where Danr had grown up, taught that such men were an abomination, but Grick, his lady wife, was a little more accepting. The ocean goddess Bosha, powerful in Balsia, was happy to accept men and women who loved their own sex into her temple. The war gods Fell and Belinna did as well, but they required celibacy of such people. It was all very confusing.

Sometimes, though, Danr was sure the Nine meant all relationships, *regi* and not, to be confusing.

"It does seem fitting that Fell and Belinna are gods of both love and war," Ranadar said, unconsciously echoing his thoughts.

"I'm wondering if it would be all right to ask what she told you," Talfi put in. Danr understood what he was doing. It was a trick Talfi had worked out over the past few months to make both his and Danr's lives easier. Last year, Danr had visited three powerful giants, and they had told him that everyone, Stane, Fae, and Kin, had small splinters of wood or stone in their eyes that clouded their vision just enough to keep them from seeing the truth. Then they had knocked the splinters out of Danr's left eye. It let him see the truth about people and places, but it had also removed Danr's ability to tell even a small lie, and he had to answer any question put to him with utter, complete truth, even if the listener didn't want to hear it. Talfi was asking a question without actually asking a question, which left Danr the freedom to refuse an answer. This put him in a better mood.

"Yeah," he said. "We can talk about it."

"So you talked about . . . stuff," Talfi said.

"Why do women have to be Vik-all difficult?" Danr burst out. "It's been a year. I didn't mean for it to take so long to get here, and now she's mad at me."

"Woman trouble, eh?" said a new voice, and a man in an expensive-looking red tunic sat at the table, uninvited. Danr tensed. The man looked to be something over forty, still fit and relatively handsome, despite silver in his black hair and lines webbing his face. "I can recognize it a league away."

"This is a private conversation," Ranadar said in his prince voice. "You may leave now."

In answer, the man waved the barmaid over and tossed a gold coin on her tray. "A *real* round for my friends here. None of that thin piss. And some of that roast, with the apples, and the bread."

"Who—?" Talfi said.

"My name is Hector," he said with a wide grin. "And I'm something of an admirer of yours, if you're all who I think you are."

"And that would be?" Ranadar said.

The man Hector lowered his voice. "You're the ones from the Battle of the Twist. You stopped an entire war. Vik, you're Danr the Hero, and you wielded the Iron Axe itself. Isn't that right?"

Danr didn't want to answer, but Hector had asked him a direct question, and a reply pushed at the back of his throat. The words piled up like water behind a dam and finally spilled out of him. "I did, and a lot of people died for it, so keep it to yourself. We don't want a lot of—"

"Attention, I know. Don't blame you. I just want to buy you a round or two and say thank you."

That surprised him. "Thank you?"

"For stopping the slaughter. I have family in northern Balsia, and if that war had begun . . . well, in my book you're the biggest heroes since Bal himself." Here, Hector looked a little sheepish. "I just wanted to give you something back."

Huh. Usually, people wanted something from Danr. The gratitude made him feel . . . warm. Appreciated. It was nice. Maybe an unexpected stranger wasn't so bad. The barmaid arrived with her heavy tray. She laid out bread, meat, and two pitchers of ale. The food was plentiful—Danr was almost always hungry—and the new ale flowed like liquid gold. The food and the man's kind words made Danr feel a little better, though he was still a bit put off by the man's forwardness.

"How did you recognize us?" Talfi asked. "We're kind of hiding right now."

"I told you—I have family in northern Balsia." Hector

sipped from his horn. "And everyone's heard of the half troll, the elven sorcerer, and the boy who can't die. But isn't there an orc swordswoman?"

The much stronger ale warmed Danr's stomach and he didn't bother trying to fight the question. "Kalessa's at a leather worker's, seeing to her armor," he said.

"So it's just us men, and you're having some woman trouble, eh?" Hector tore into the bread with strong white teeth.

This was more a statement than a question, but Danr responded anyway. "How did you know that?"

"Danr," Talfi said, "maybe—"

"Not hard to spot." Hector raised his horn to Danr, who obligingly toasted with him and drained most of it. Drinking the smooth ale was like drinking sunlight. "Your lady isn't here and you look sad. And I overheard the last part of your conversation."

This last struck Danr as funny, and he laughed. "Well, you're right, and these two"—he waved his horn at Ranadar and Talfi, who ducked—"aren't much help."

"Understandable." He poured more ale into Danr's horn. "But I can understand your lady's problem, at least a little."

"Yeah?" Danr leaned toward him, curious. "How?"

"Just look at you!" Hector raised his horn yet again, and Danr obliged him with another drink. "You're half troll. Not a lot of people like half-bloods. They're an abomination. *I* don't feel that way, of course, but I'm sure you've seen it."

"Sure," Danr said dryly.

"There you are, then." Hector scratched his chest. "Once she marries a half-blood, all those people will see her as a traitor to humans. And since you're famous, they'll all know about it. No way to escape it. Must be hard for her."

Half-blood. Traitor. The words stabbed Danr with an icy dagger and he sat still as a winter boulder. That was it. Hector's words made cold, terrible sense. Really, it made a number of thoughts rush together, like streams trickling into a gushing river. Aisa was angry about the merfolk, yes, she was, and she was nervous about marrying a half-troll because of the shit it would bring into their lives. Would their marriage last with people always judging them, attacking them, making both of them outsiders the way he was now? Still, she had indeed said she would marry him, if he asked. That was hope. A tiny fleck of warm hope. If only he could figure out what to do with it. He sat up straighter.

"Too bad you can't be, I don't know, fully human or something," Hector continued with a pull on his ale. "No one would recognize you, and the half-blood problems would just . . . vanish. Poof." He drummed his fingers on the table. "Well, we're what the Nine made us, and no changing it."

"You're awfully forward for someone we just met." Talfi hadn't touched the food. "You say you spotted us across the room? This dark room? With Danr wearing his cloak?"

"You have keen vision," Ranadar agreed.

Danr ignored them. *Fully human.* How had he not thought of it before? Being half human and half troll was really the source of everything that had gone wrong in his life. He wasn't entirely welcome among either race, only half welcome—ha!—which was as much to say he wasn't welcome at all. He only had half a relationship with Aisa. Really, he only had half a life. What he really needed was to be fully one thing or the other. Then he could live his life, a full life, in peace. But that wasn't possible.

Or was it?

Hector reached up to clap him on the shoulder. "I can see you're deep in thought, my friend. Maybe my advice was the right thing, eh? Glad an ordinary man could help a true hero."

Danr blinked at him. The man had been helpful indeed. And extremely coincidental. With only a moment's hesitation, he closed his right eye and looked at Hector only through his left.

Through his left eye, he saw Hector. The first thing he saw was . . . the truth. The man wasn't lying or misrepresenting. He was telling the truth as he knew it. Danr also saw things he had missed before—the exacting cut of Hector's clothes, the ease with which he carried himself, the hidden pouch of money in his tunic. This was a man of great wealth, and he had acquired it himself, not through inheritance. And Danr saw more.

The light dimmed and the air chilled despite the fire. Gooseflesh crawled over Danr's skin. Darkness oozed through Hector like a rotten worm. The darkness coiled around a strange power, a presence, a *thing* Danr couldn't put a name to. The thing had no shape. It was possible Hector didn't even know it existed, wrapped in darkness as it was. It wasn't alive. It wasn't magic. It was a part of Hector himself, a terrible part of the man. It was hunger. This man was never satisfied with anything. He had devoured people, families, and businesses, and still he was hungry. He could devour a town, a city, a country, and never be satisfied. What was more, this man knew it, knew himself, and didn't care in the slightest. Nausea clawed at Danr's gut. He tensed and his guard went up. Hector might have been telling the truth about Aisa's fear, but there was more here than Danr wanted to become involved with.

"What's the matter?" Hector asked.

And from under his hood, Danr had to answer, "You're a rich man, Hector, but you don't appreciate your wealth because you always want more, and more, and more. The darkness and the hunger you carry inside will turn on you like a pair of starving dogs. I don't want to be near you, and you should leave this table before I hurt you to make you go away." He met Hector's eyes and crushed the drinking horn in his fist. It popped like a dead bone.

"Danr!" Ranadar said, more than a little shocked. Talfi's eyes likewise widened.

Hector seemed unruffled. He took a sip of ale from his own horn. Only Danr's left eye noticed the slight tremor in his hand. "So. You may be right."

"I'm right. Leave now."

"Does any of this make my advice about your young lady wrong?"

The true word popped out. "No."

"Think on that, then. Consider it my gratitude for saving the world, even if you're cruel to me in taking it." He drained the last of his horn and left the table. Danr watched pointedly until he left the tavern. Only then did he let out the breath he was holding. The air warmed again.

"That *was* cruel," Talfi said once the front door had shut. "Even if he was suspicious."

"If a terrible man asks me a terrible question and gets a terrible answer, he deserves what he gets," Danr said bluntly.

"What did you—" Ranadar began, but Talfi clapped a hand over the elf's mouth.

"Don't ask. He'll tell you."

Danr shuddered. "He was a bad, bad man. I don't know why he wanted to talk to me. He was grateful, and that was the truth, but more than that I can't say."

"Will you eat the meal he bought?" Ranadar gestured at the table.

"Sure." Danr shoved some bread into his mouth. "The food is good, even if the man is bad."

"And will you take his advice as well?" Ranadar added archly.

Danr thought. The question didn't require a true answer—there wasn't one yet—so the words didn't push themselves from Danr's throat. "Maybe. If he's right."

"You're the truth-teller," Talfi said, still watching the door. "Can't you tell if he's right?"

"Usually not until it's too late," Danr said mournfully. "The truth doesn't always tell you everything you want to know."

"Who does know, then?" Ranadar seemed unwilling to let the point go. The damn elf always had to be right. It came of being Fae. Or a prince.

But Danr had to answer Ranadar's question. "Death knows." He rose from the table, his meal only half-eaten. When you were unsure what to do, move forward, and no sense putting it off. "Let's go see her. Now."

"Now?" Talfi stuffed more meat in his mouth and followed it with a gulp of ale. "Shouldn't we wait for Aisa?"

"She doesn't like going," replied Danr.

"Does anyone?" Ranadar muttered.

"Of course not," Danr was forced to say. "Don't be an idiot."

"I only meant—"

Talfi put a hand over his mouth again. "Haven't you learned anything in the last year, Ran? Never argue with a truth-teller."

"I have a question of my own, Ranadar." Danr leaned over the elf, using his height and bulk and the elf's lifetime of mistrust for the Stane. Danr liked Talfi. Ranadar, on the other hand, he tolerated only because Talfi was in love with him, so he felt no guilt about pushing Ranadar around. Well, maybe a little guilt. But well within tolerances. "Can you Twist now?"

"I dislike doing it in the city," Ranadar answered. "You humans"—his lip curled—"use so much iron, and it drains the ambient power away. Some days, it is painful to be here.

With all this iron about, I can only Twist short distances, and my glamours are weak."

"But you can Twist," Danr pressed.

"Yes."

"Then let's go."

"What, here and now?" Ranadar's tone was halfway between jovial and serious.

"Only a fool would Twist in a roomful of people." Danr spat the words like hornets. "You aren't a fool. Except when it comes to your family."

Ranadar sucked at his teeth and actually reached for the bronze dagger at his belt. Talfi put a hand on his arm.

"Danr," Talfi said warningly. "You're going too far."

Danr sighed. It was always like this. He was surprised he had any friends left after this past year. It was probably another reason why Aisa didn't talk to him about what was bothering her—whenever she asked a question, he *had* to answer, and it always seemed he had to answer with the harshest truth he could. He backed up a step. "I'm sorry. I can't always help how the words come out. Talfi was right, earlier—don't ask me a question if you don't want a faceful of truth."

Ranadar's face relaxed, but with effort. "Right."

"Anyway," Danr said quickly with a glance about the tavern. It wasn't particularly crowded at this time of day. "Let's go back to Mrs. Farley's and see what Death has to say."

CHAPTER FOUR

U p on the slate roof of Mrs. Farley's boardinghouse, the
air was a little cleaner and the street noises were
fainter. Heavy clouds had moved across the sun, and Danr
was glad about that—he didn't need a hat or cloak to shield
himself against the damn headaches. A flock of pigeons
flapped overhead, and Danr peered dubiously over the edge
of the roof. Unsympathetic cobblestones lay a leg-breaking
distance below, while the rough wall of Old City rose high
and hard behind them.

"Explain to me again why we have to jump," he said
slowly.

"Up here, we are farther away from the iron." A breeze
teased Ranadar's red hair. "What with all the pots and pans
on Cook Street, I can barely work up a glamour, let alone
Twist. Some days I wake up with a headache that won't
go away."

"You do?" Talfi looked concerned. "I didn't know that."

"I did not want you to know," Ranadar replied. "You like
the city, and I like that you like the city. Iron and all."

Talfi was looking agitated now. "But if you're in pain—"

"I am an elven prince, even in exile," Ranadar interrupted. "I do not burden others with small troubles. In any case, there is enough energy up here that I can Twist the four of us, but the gate will have to open there." He gestured to a spot just below the lead gutter.

"This is wrong." Kalessa spat over the edge. "Aisa should be here."

"Aisa's busy," Danr said. "You yourself said. And I want to take care of this. Now."

"You mean you want to take care of it without her around," Kalessa contradicted.

Danr clutched his sack, a patched, ragged affair that had accompanied him across Balsia, under the mountain to Glumenhame, across the orcish lands of Xaron, and even to the elven land of Alfhame, and back. It had carried clothes, food, a golden torch, and a magic box. Currently, it carried the squid's beak and the ink sac. Danr hoped the latter wouldn't leak. Yuck.

"I don't need to do *everything* with her," he said. "And I want to handle this by myself. A betrothal present, yeah?"

Kalessa looked torn, as though she might dash away in search of Aisa. She had nearly done so when Danr came up to her and Aisa's room to fetch the beak and ink, but Danr had stomped up to the roof before she could object much. After a moment's hesitation, she set her mouth and stayed where she was.

"Do it, Ranadar," Danr said.

"The Twist will only stay open a moment, so jump when I say." Ranadar inhaled and made a series of gestures Danr couldn't follow. No glowing lines trailed the air, no bell-like sounds chimed, no air rushed. There was nothing at all that Danr could see. His heart beat faster. If Ranadar made a mistake—

"Jump!" Ranadar barked.

Kalessa leaped off the roof without hesitation, trailing her auburn braid. Talfi dove after her. Both of them fell, then vanished as if the air had swallowed them. Danr gulped and clutched his sack tighter. Shit. Stane were heavy, not well built for swimming or climbing—or falling. The street below him rocked dizzily. Even though he had seen Kalessa and Talfi disappear, his every instinct begged him, screamed at him not to jump. He would plunge to the stones, and they would crush his bones to—

"Jump!" Ranadar shouted again.

Danr forced himself to the edge. He hesitated half a second longer, one foot over three stories of empty air, then jumped.

He fell for a long, sickening moment. The ground rushed up at him, hungry and hard. Terror clawed at his chest. He had jumped too late. He had missed the Twist. He was going to hit. Then the world *wrenched.* Light exploded around him, and he felt as if he were being pulled in a hundred, a thousand, a million directions. He was every point in the universe, or every point in the universe was him. He was a great tree, branching in an infinite number of directions. He was near to losing himself in the diverse paths. Then a seed sprouted, one tiny bit of time and space that was stronger than the others. Gratefully, Danr grabbed it, used it to will himself forward. With another *wrench*, the world turned inside out, and Danr landed with a thud on a hard stone floor. A moment later, someone else thudded next to him.

Nausea squeezed his stomach, and his gorge rose. He swallowed hard, willing himself not to throw up. Not here, not now. Slowly, he pushed himself upright. He was in a cave, one with a rough floor and earthen walls. Tree roots twined thick through the ceiling, some as small as a finger, others thicker than the squid's tentacles. Soft light pushed through the roots, illuminating the cave, but not painfully so. The cave smelled faintly of fresh mushrooms, which Danr liked.

An unornamented door made of wood with stone lintels and a dark window of precious glass was set into one wall. Beside the door on a plain table stood two lit candles, one silver and one gold, and between them lay a scarred, rusty battle-axe. The Iron Axe. It looked as though it had lain there for centuries, but Danr happened to know the Axe had been there for little more than a year.

Between the table and door in a rocking chair sat a plump, motherly looking woman in a red dress with an ivory shawl thrown over her shoulders. Danr rocked uneasily, trying to control his nausea and show respect at the same time. Gray braids, pinned up, framed the woman's face, though her features were somehow thrown into shadow by the candles. A soft clicking sound filled the cave. The woman was knitting. Her bone needles moved in and out, up and down, never slowing or ceasing.

The others, including Ranadar, were also getting to their feet. The woman watched in polite silence until they had managed it.

"I feel like I should offer you something. Hot tea or little cookies or the skulls of your enemies," she said, and her voice was as low and rich as the liquid stones at the center of the world.

"No, thank you," Danr managed. "It was quite a trip."

"It amazes me that I got us here," Ranadar said. His face was even paler than usual. "Usually, only the most powerful of trollwives can Twist someone to Death."

The woman gave a gentle smile that didn't chill Danr at all, no, it didn't. "I'm hurt that you don't trust me. I told you last time that I would bring you here the next time you Twisted through the branches of Ashkame. Did you doubt the word of Death?"

"Not for a moment, great lady," Ranadar said with a courtly bow, and Danr felt a twinge of envy. What a fine thing it would be to show good manners and lie like that again.

"This one's a keeper, Talfi," Death said, still knitting. "Don't let him go."

Talfi was leaning against a wall, working his jaw as he tried to keep his own gorge from coming up. "Wouldn't dream of it, ma'am."

"Can we get on?" Kalessa asked. Her arms were crossed, and if the Twist had bothered her, Danr couldn't see it.

"Impatient," Death observed. "But I understand. Even my time is limited. Did you bring them?"

"Yes, lady." Danr fished the squashy sac and the sharp beak from his bag and approached the rocking chair. The stony floor felt rough under his bare toes, and the roots on the ceiling brushed the top of his head. It was both homey and surreal, comforting and awe-inspiring at the same time. He was walking toward Death herself, the end of all that lived, the final darkness, the guardian who watched the portal to Vik's realm. But she looked like someone who might at any moment leap up to check the stew kettle or bustle off to milk the goats. Danr wondered if she really did milk goats somewhere, and what those goats might look like. He decided he was better off not knowing.

Danr had first visited Death last year, after the Stane had chained her up and she had asked Danr to find the Iron Axe, the only object that could cut her bonds. After he had helped her, she had given him and the others a fine reward and then said she would call on them again, if they were willing. In the last year, she had called on them two other times, as it happened, and her requests had been instrumental in delaying their arrival in Balsia. This, the third time, was perhaps the oddest. Why had Death wanted parts of a giant squid?

"Set them on the table, dear," Death said. "I don't mind the squishy."

A moment's fishing in the sack brought out the smelly objects in question, and Danr set them on the table between the candles next to the Iron Axe. He shuddered at the sight of old blood on the Axe's blade, remembering where it had come from.

"Why did you want these, ma'am?" Danr asked. "It seems like you could get this kind of thing on your own."

"They aren't for me, sweetie." Death's face was still in shadow, but Danr got the impression she was smiling at him. "The ink is actually a present for someone else."

"I don't understand." Danr shook his head.

"That's all right, I don't mind." She finished a row on her knitting and started another. "Where's Aisa? I was looking forward to trading insults."

"She was occupied, lady," Kalessa said. "I could try insulting you, if you like."

"Thank you, but it won't be the same," Death sighed. "That girl's tongue can snap monkeys out of the trees. It's no wonder you fell for her, dear."

Danr nearly staggered at this unexpected hit. "Me? What?"

"Your mother had a sharp tongue, didn't she?"

And Danr had to answer. "Because she was a truth-teller, like me. That's a stupid observation. Sorry!" he added quickly.

"Haven't you ever heard that boys fall in love with girls just like their mothers?"

"I have, and it's a foolishly idiotic saying pushed around by idiotic fools—sorry!" Danr dropped the sack and clapped both fishy-smelling hands over his mouth in horror, though he knew the words would still come out if Death asked him a direct question. At least he truly was sorry—that much wasn't a lie.

But Death seemed unbothered. "Hmm. Perhaps not as foolish as you think. At any rate, I thank you for your service, dear boy."

It seemed a dismissal, and Danr didn't think that quite fair. Talfi had *died* to get those objects, for Vik's sake. Well, not really died, and Death of all people knew Talfi was in no danger. Rather than let him walk through her door, Death had offered to give Talfi half of Ranadar's remaining days, and Ranadar had accepted. But Aisa had been hit during the squid attack, and—well, it wasn't right of Death to brush him off.

"I want to ask a favor," Danr said quickly.

"Hmm," Death said again.

It hadn't been an invitation to talk, but neither had it been a refusal. Danr decided to hurry on. "I want a . . . solution to my problem with Aisa. You know what I'm talking about."

"And I think you need to say exactly what you want, love."

The others remained absolutely still behind him, whether paralyzed by unease or something stronger, Danr couldn't say. He forced himself to keep his eyes on Death. "Please don't. Don't ask me."

"You brought it up. What exactly," Death asked relentlessly, "do you think will solve your problem with Aisa?"

Shit. Danr didn't want to say. Even though Talfi and Ranadar already knew, and Kalessa had probably worked it out, he didn't want to say. The words seemed small in the presence of this large being. But they pushed themselves out of his mouth.

"I want to be fully human," he said hoarsely, "so that Aisa won't be unhappy when she marries me. It sounds small and stupid, I know that, but it's what I want."

Death continued to knit. "Very good, though I wish you

had said it without being compelled by the truth-teller's blessing."

"Curse," Danr muttered, looking away. His face burned.

"It all depends on your point of view," Death said amiably. "But the world turns on petty desires. It always has done so."

"What does that mean?"

"People think history is made when powerful princes and clever kings make long, careful decisions. Should I start my war this year or wait? Should I marry my daughter to my neighbor to the east or to the west? Should I try the duke for murder so justice can prevail, or let the matter drop because I need his army to defend our border? And so on. But really, it almost never works that way." She leaned forward, though her face stayed in shadow. "Did you know there was a king named Alessander who conquered large swaths of Balsia and Xaron, but when he reached Irbsa, he turned around and went home because the chief general, who was also Alessander's lover, died unexpectedly? One man couldn't overcome his grief, and an entire empire faltered."

Danr shot Talfi a glance. "No, I—"

"In another part of Balsia," Death continued, "a little-known king and queen were seeking a wife for their son. They paraded three women in front of him and told him to choose one. One of the women wore a yellow dress, and for the simple reason that he liked the color yellow, the prince pointed to her. They later had a son of their own and named him Bal."

"Bal," Danr repeated. "You mean Bal, the hero who—"

"Imagine how history would have gone if that woman had worn a green dress or if the prince had preferred blue. Meanwhile, you yourself are here because of small, petty decisions."

Danr stepped back. "Me?"

"Of course. Aisa begged you to stay out of it when they were beating her for witchcraft, but you mixed yourself up in it anyway and got yourself exiled. Later, your aunt Queen Vesha—such a lovely woman—asked you to be the Stane emissary to the humans, and you were all set to refuse. You only agreed because you felt guilty over what you'd done to that White Halli boy. Such a petty thing. And then, when you found out your friend Talfi loved men instead of women, you very nearly wrote him off. But at the last moment you decided you wanted to stay friends with him, and thank the Nine you did. Without his friendship, you would never have found the Iron Axe. Petty, petty decisions decide how the world will go. It's always been so, dear."

"All right," Danr replied slowly, unable to say that he understood—it would have been a lie. "But can you make me fully human? For Aisa?"

"I can't make you fully human for Aisa, or for you," Death replied, and Danr's heart sank. "Only you can do it."

Danr's heart jerked. "I—what?"

"In the end, only you can decide to change," Death said. "You know, Aisa herself said that if you give her enough time, she'll probably overcome her little problem."

"How long do I need to wait?" Danr cried out. "It's been more than a year. And you said *probably*."

Death shrugged. "So goes the world. Let me show you what we can do. Talfi, honey, you might want to cover your eyes."

"Really?" Talfi looked startled. "Why?"

"Because you won't like this very much." Death slid one of her needles free of the work in her lap and drew a perfect triangle in the air three feet across. It glowed with golden light. Ranadar gasped. Death struck the triangle with the needle, and it shattered into a thousand shards that gleamed like a shower of jewels. She jerked the needle, and the water-fall of shards froze in midair.

"You know that power runs through the Nine People of Erda," Death said. "The Fae—elves, sprites, and fairies—have power of mind, which lets them make glamours and illusions and such. The Stane—dwarfs, giants, and trolls—have power of the hand, which lets them tunnel and build and use shadows. And the Kin—orcs, merfolk, and human—have a power of their own."

"We do?" Talfi was ignoring Death's admonishment to hide his eyes.

"The power of the shape," Danr breathed. "I remember. Grandmother Bund mentioned it when I first visited her under the mountain, but I forgot all about it. So much has happened."

"After the Sundering," Death said, "there weren't many humans alive to remember the power existed. Even the legends became scarce."

"When did we have it?" Talfi demanded.

"I just said—in the days before the Sundering." Death waved her needle, and the multicolored shards rushed about the cave in a rainbow river. "You were there, dear. You just don't remember. Not yet."

"I don't know if I want to remember," Talfi muttered, and Ranadar touched his shoulder.

"A thousand years ago, when the Stane went to war against the Fae, they created the Iron Axe, a weapon so powerful it could sunder the earth itself." The shards formed into a great glowing axe that matched the one on the table, though this one crackled with power. "But the Fae allied with a group of Kin to steal the Axe away, and the Stane were left with one recourse—to destroy it before the Fae could use it against them."

Death waved her needle, and the Axe shimmered into a

shower of brightly colored dust that sculpted itself like sand into a small stone altar. A group of tiny people dressed in clothing so outdated Danr couldn't even think of it as old-fashioned were gathered around it. The people were a mix of dwarfs, trolls, giants, humans, and orcs. Danr did recognize that some of the trolls were actually trollwives, the most powerful magicians among the Stane.

"The Stane had their own allies among the Kin—humans and orcs and even a few merfolk," Death said. "The trollwives summoned magic to destroy the Axe. But magic requires a sacrifice, and rather than ask for one among themselves, the trollwives demanded one from the Kin, who gave them one."

Two robed men dragged a teenage boy to the altar and a blond woman in plate armor clasped a small medallion around his neck. Even though the image was small and the boy wore strange clothing, Danr recognized Talfi. Talfi, the real Talfi, went pale as milk, and Danr wanted to stop the whole thing, even though it wasn't real. Ranadar put an arm around Talfi and tried to turn his face away from the sight, but Talfi watched with steadfast determination.

"The trollwives fashioned a dagger," Death continued. "They used it as a conduit, you see, and they thrust it into the sacrifice's heart."

Her words were duplicated by the silent glowing figures of dust. Danr, who had watched Talfi die a number of times, still felt the terrible pang when the dagger went in, and he almost reached out to stop the trollwife who wielded the dagger, even though none of this was real and it had happened a thousand years ago anyway. The real Talfi made a small sound. The dagger stood upright in image Talfi's chest, beating with his heart, while dusty, glowing blood gushed from the wound. The medallion glowed white-hot. To Danr's surprise, battle-hardened Kalessa set her mouth and turned away for a moment.

"But the Stane back then were even more selfish than the Kin knew," Death said. "They didn't tell the Kin that the sacrifice's blood was a mere catalyst, a way to start the spell running. In order to destroy the Axe, the trollwives needed to draw on some power, a great deal of power. Rather than drain their own, they took it from the Kin."

The gathered trollwives raised their hands. From all the assembled Kin and from sources Danr couldn't see came streams of power. The power rushed through the dagger sticking out of Talfi's chest, focused through the medallion around Talfi's neck, and poured into a single trollwife. The Kin dropped to their knees, squirming and convulsing as the power left them. The trollwife exulted while Talfi writhed sickeningly on the altar. Now the real Talfi buried his face in Ranadar's shoulder. Danr's mouth went dry. These were his people torturing a young boy and hurting the Kin. Did Talfi blame Danr for any of it?

The trollwife gathered the power—all of it—and released it in a great geyser. The dust exploded into a shower of light again that reformed into the Iron Axe.

"The power destroyed the Iron Axe," Death said as the handle broke away from the Axe's head. The pieces bled light. "And the blow sundered the continent. Have you ever wondered why the spell would do such a thing?"

"No," Danr replied.

"Think on it, then. Why would the trollwives fashion a spell that would destroy the continent on which they were standing?"

"I don't know. I can't know, and you're trying to hold back information so you can look powerful and mysterious— sorry," Danr said.

"You do have a way to know," Death countered. "And I'm giving it to you, if you pay attention."

"It has to do with me," Talfi put in slowly. "Doesn't it?"

Death ignored him. "As I was saying, the Stane paid for the destruction spell in blood, and so did the Kin who colluded with them. Unfortunately, so did all other Kin everywhere. The power of the shape, the power that had destroyed the Axe, didn't return to the Kin after the trollwives used it. There was no way for it to do so, you see. Not with the catalyst dead and gone."

"But it—I—didn't die," Talfi said in a hoarse voice. "I lived."

"You did not live, child," Death contradicted. She tapped the dust with her knitting needle, and it all vanished. "The Axe split into three pieces—it haft, its head, and its magic. The magic entered you and kept you alive in the way a *draugr* is alive. A few days after the continent sundered and the sea flooded the place the Nine Races now call the Iron Sea, you washed up onshore, took a new breath, and wandered away with the trollwives' medallion around your throat."

Talfi's hand automatically went to the silver medallion around his neck, the one he had worn as long as Danr had known him. The edges were worn. It had an Axe on one side and the symbol of the Nine on the other.

"That was a busy time for me." Death went back to knitting. "The point of all this, though, is that the Kin lost the power of the shape."

"What does the power of the shape do?" Danr asked, relieved that the scene was over.

"Many things, depending," Death said. "The orcs once used it to change into the wyrms they can now only ride, for example."

Kalessa gasped. "We did?"

"Indeed. And you could bond more tightly with your wyrms—read their thoughts and command them from a distance. The merfolk changed into humans and walked on land, or they changed into other sea creatures, like seals and dolphins. But humans were the most versatile. They changed shape into any number of creatures—wolves and bears and eagles. Some could do it on their own, others needed a skin of the creature first. Some Kin learned to change the shapes of other people or animals. Witches turned their enemies into toads, and wizards created chimaeras and sphinxes by smashing three or four animals together. Some learned to grow to the size of giants, and others learned to shrink smaller than fairies. It was a heady time." Death rocked faster, caught in the memories.

"All the Kin could do this?" Danr said, amazed.

"Goodness, no." Death checked her knitting, discovered she had dropped several stitches, and unraveled a row with a click of her tongue. Danr thought he heard faint screams. "Talent for the shape runs in families, you see, though the occasional wild gift shows up. The more talent you have, the more you can do. Some talents let you only change your own shape, and some only let you change the shape of others. The truly gifted could do both. And it all takes power. Lots of power." She leaned forward, eyes sparkling. "That's where the fun began, dear."

"Fun?" Ranadar said.

"When you change your shape, it becomes easier to share your inner power with someone else. Change yourself into a cat, and another Kin can draw off your power more easily for his own magic."

"Familiars," Danr whispered.

"Draw too much, and the familiar dies," Death said. "As I said, fun."

"That doesn't sound like—" Talfi began.

"I didn't say it was fun for you," Death interrupted. "And now you're going to ask where the power of the shape can be found, yes?"

"That was the point of coming here, great lady," Rana-dar said.

"Hmm." Death tapped the tips of her needles against her chin. "I'm afraid I can't tell you."

Danr's heart plunged into his feet and his hands turned cold. "What? After all that I—"

"Really, dear," Death interrupted. "You need to listen more. I said *I* can't tell you."

"Oh. Uh . . . someone else can tell me?"

In answer, Death raised her head, though her features remained in shadow. "I think it's time, sisters."

The darkness behind her stirred. Vik! Danr backed up a step with a twinge of fear, and he clutched his old bag, feeling small and defenseless. When Death called something up, you didn't want to be close to it, no, you didn't. The others tensed as well. Talfi touched the amulet at his throat.

From the cool shadows slipped three women. They wore cloaks in different shades. The first wore the green of pale spring leaves and carried a bag of seeds. The second wore the rich green-brown of summer grass and carried a hoe. The third wore the riotous rainbow of an autumn forest and carried a sickle. The blade had a smear of blood on it. All three women had strange faces that were neither beautiful nor ugly, old nor young, though they looked tired. The third, the one with the autumn cloak and sickle, looked particularly pinched and weary.

Danr's legs went weak when he recognized them, though he'd only heard of them in stories. These were the Three Gardeners, the Fates Nu, Tan, and Pendra, and they planted a seed for every life in the shade of Ashkame, the Great Tree. Each seed grew in rows pushed and perfected by the Gardeners. Some plants they coaxed into full bloom and let them twine around those close to them. Other plants they ripped out and threw away. Even the Nine bowed to the

Gardeners. Most people lived their lives hoping never to gain their attention, and now they were looking straight at Danr. His blood stopped flowing.

"Great ones," Danr murmured, and managed a shaky bow. The others followed suit. Ranadar put his hand over his heart.

"You brought us a present," Nu said in a flutelike voice.

"A gift," said Tan.

"A sacrifice," said Pendra.

"I did?" Danr cast about, suddenly desperate. He hadn't brought anything, and in any case, what did you give the Gardeners?

"It's on the table, sister," said Death.

Pendra, with slow, tired hands, picked up the squid's beak in one hand. In her other, the sickle gleamed, and the air curled around it. For a moment Danr considered looking at it—at her—with his true eye, then recoiled at the idea. For all he knew, gazing at the Three with his one true eye might strike him blind.

"Delightful," said Tan. Her voice was ancient as a star and just as steady.

"You're too kind," said Nu.

"I thank you," said Pendra, and a droplet of scarlet blood dripped from her hand. It tapped the cave floor. Danr watched it fall, more than a little startled. Had she pricked herself on the beak? It had never occurred to him that the Gardeners could bleed.

"Are you all right?" he asked.

Pendra glanced down at her hand and shook another droplet of blood away. "When I think big, I am fine. But where is Aisa? Why did she not come?"

"Aisa?" Danr repeated. "She . . . I didn't ask her to come. I didn't want her here." His face flamed as the embarrassing answer forced itself from his chest. Why did they have to ask? Didn't they know the answer already?

"A pity," said Nu.

"A shame," said Tan.

"A loss," sighed Pendra. "A petty decision that will complicate future rows." She crushed the squid's beak in her hand and it crumbled to a dust that she wiped on the front of her autumn cloak. Some of her blood mingled with the dust. Danr stared, his embarrassment forgotten.

Also taken aback, Kalessa said, "Lady, may I ask why . . ."

"The beak itself was unimportant," Pendra sighed. "It was what it symbolized."

"What it stood for," murmured Tan.

"What it meant," finished Nu.

"I do not under—" Kalessa began again.

"You believe that the three of us direct your lives," Nu interrupted.

"You believe wrong," continued Tan.

"Observe," finished Pendra.

Nu opened her sack of seeds and put one in the palm of Tan's hand. Pendra spat on it. In less than a moment, the seed sprouted into a small yellow marigold.

"This plant, sweet and small, can be nothing but itself," Nu said.

"Its scent can chase away insects, and it is pleasing to the eye of the Kin and Fae alike," said Tan.

"Yet no amount of coaxing can make it live underwater or climb a trellis," finished Pendra.

"You are saying that you fail to control our lives at all?" Ranadar said.

"So young and so simple," Nu sighed again. "Everything is one or the other to you."

"Black or white," said Tan.

"In or out," said Pendra. Was that a leer?

"No, young one, that is not what I am saying," said Nu. "We plant the rows."

"We choose the seeds."

"We pluck the weeds."

"But the plants still do as they must," said Nu. "No amount of fertilizing could make you fall in love with a woman, Lord Ranadar, but we can plant young Talfi here in your row to encourage certain things to happen."

Talfi blinked. "You must have . . . planted me a long time ago."

"One does not become one of the Three without at least a little forethought," Pendra agreed.

"A pinch of planning," said Tan.

"A touch of caution," said Nu.

"And speaking of which, young Danr here wants to know about the squid beak," continued Pendra. "You did meet a small boy named Joshuah on your way back from the cave."

As Talfi had done in the tavern, Pendra was making a statement, not a question, which meant no words pushed at the back of Danr's throat and he could answer as he liked. That small thing made him feel enormously better toward her and more at ease. If only more people would talk to him this way.

"I met Joshuah," he said. "He seemed a nice kid."

"Joshuah will grow up to have a child," Pendra told him, "and that child will have a child who will change the course of history on Erda just as you are doing now. If you had not killed the squid at our sister's request, it would have devoured Joshuah when he went swimming in the ocean, and the future would have gone in a much more unsatisfactory direction. We asked our sister Death to have you intervene, and now the future will go where it should. We thank you."

"We give you gratitude," said Tan.

"We wish you well," said Nu.

"Oh." Danr thought about that. He was beginning to understand now. Every action, every decision, every act, no matter how small, caused ripples throughout the world, twisting the future down a different path. Something as minor as swatting a fly or choosing which chicken to kill for supper could echo across centuries, but there was no way to predict what would happen or how things might come out differently if you let the fly live or decided on potato soup for supper instead. It made Danr himself feel small, like a minnow suddenly understanding the size of the ocean.

"But we are not here to discuss Joshuah or even Talfi." Pendra dropped the marigold, which vanished, and Danr wondered if that meant that somewhere, someone had died. He glanced at Death and her door, but Death merely continued rocking and knitting. "We are here because you have done us a service, and this service is worth a reward."

"A payment," said Tan.

"A balance," corrected Nu.

Pendra said, "So listen carefully. Only one being still understands the power of the shape."

"He was alive before the Sundering, and managed to keep his power," said Ta.

"Away from the trollwives and their dreadful spell," finished Nu.

Danr snapped to attention. "Who is that?"

The Three said together, "His name is Grandfather Wyrm."

Chapter Five

A drinking horn landed in front of Aisa. It wobbled as if it were soft. "Drink this," said a distant voice.

Aisa fumbled for the horn. She was dimly aware that a pair of hands were helping her. The contents of the horn were thick and warm and both bitter and sticky-sweet. Her stomach recoiled and she tried to spit it out, but the hands were firm and most of it went down her throat. It left behind a nasty aftertaste, and she tried to grab for some of the leftover bread to rid herself of it, but her hands wouldn't obey her.

"What—?" she began. And then the world snapped back into focus with a nearly audible *ping*. Her senses leaped into crisp hyperalertness. Light speared her eyes with diamond-tipped arrows. She felt every splinter in the chair beneath her and on the table that pressed her forearms. She smelled the pungent sweat and thick smoke and dying meat and rancid butter and tiny bread crumbs and spilled ale and old wine. The cacophony of voices in the tavern crashed against her ears in an ocean wave. But most of all, her mind was clear, absolutely clear. She wouldn't need sleep for a month, and every thought she'd ever had rushed through her mind in even, orderly patterns for her simple perusal. Yes, she loved

Danr. Yes, it was foolish of her to keep things back from him. Yes, she'd been an idiot not to tell him about her fears and visions, since that stopped them both from *finding a solution*.

And Sharlee was an enemy who had drugged her drink and persuaded her to spill these secrets as easily as they had spilled drink down their throats. Fury tried to grip her, but it withered away beneath the harsh light of such clarity. Why hadn't Aisa seen it before? Too much self-pity, she supposed. Rolk and Vik! She glared at the drinking horn, then up at the woman who had helped her drink it.

"What is this?" she demanded.

"Kafre," the woman said. "It's frightful expensive, and if you drink enough, you'll see clear to the end of time. Your friend gave it to me and said you'd need it."

Aisa had never heard of it, which meant the stuff was rare. It also meant Sharlee had the money to pay for it. She had not presented herself as wealthy, which further meant she had deliberately hidden her wealth from Aisa. Why? Aisa doubted any answer would make her happy. "What was in the first drink she gave me?"

"No idea. Ain't never seen anyone get drunk that fast on so little, though."

"How long have I been here?"

"Three hours, give or take. Your friend paid extra, said to give you the *kafre* if you weren't awake in four hours, but we need the table. This ain't no inn."

The betrayal stabbed Aisa like a stone dagger. All this time, Aisa had thought Sharlee was a good friend. She got to rock-steady feet and strode for the door. This would not stand. She would find Sharlee and confront her, with a knife, if necessary.

Her crystal-clear mind told her she should first get Kalessa. When seeking revenge, far better to have a sympathetic orc

with a magic sword behind you. Still, she had to pass by
the slave market on her way back to the rooming house, and
there was no harm in checking the place on the way to see if
Sharlee was there, or if anyone there knew where she was
likely to be.

It was perhaps an hour before sunset when Aisa reached
the slave market, and the *kafre* was wearing off, leaving her
shaky and a little light-headed. The market was still open—it
never truly closed—and she scanned the stalls and sheds for
a familiar face, either Sharlee's or someone else who knew
her. As the *kafre* receded, the anger returned, simmering in a
slow boil. Aisa turned the conversation over in her head,
searching for a clue to what Sharlee had been looking for, but
all Aisa had talked about was her misgivings about Danr's
fame and the visions of the past that haunted her, and they
were not particularly valuable, not even as blackmail. Was
Sharlee planning to make public her identity as one of the
Heroes of the Twist? No. Sharlee had known about that before the drugs and the *kafre*. So what did—

Aisa turned a corner and almost ran into the tank. It was
made of wood with a glass front, and perhaps eight feet tall. A
ladder was bolted to the side. Murky water swirled around a
form within. For a moment, Aisa's heart stopped and climbed
into her throat. Her entire body thrummed like a harp string.
Within the filthy water swam a mermaid.

Her form was barely visible through the pebbled glass
and cloudy water, but her tail managed to gleam a little. Her
long hair tumbled about her head as she swam helplessly in
a series of figure eights about the tank. Aisa couldn't make
out her features—everything was too blurry—but it was
definitely one of the merfolk.

Aisa put both hands to her mouth. What was a mermaid
doing in the slave market? The answer came on the heels of

the question—obviously she had been somehow enslaved and was coming up for sale. Aisa's stomach tightened. Merfolk couldn't serve as slaves in the normal sense. They couldn't labor in a field or serve in a house. The only role they could play was ornamental. Or as the owner's concubine.

The thought of one of the free, powerful mermaids stranded in some wealthy man's fishpond or, worse, dragged into his bed made Aisa physically ill, and the awful lunch she had eaten with Sharlee threatened to come up. She forced herself to keep control and instead approached one of the workmen attending the tank. It was a man she knew slightly, and he nodded when she greeted him, her face carefully blank.

"When did this one come in?" she asked.

"Just now," he said. "It's going up for sale at a special auction at the Gold Keep."

"The Gold Keep?"

"Yeah. The prince is having a party, and the auction is going to be the entertainment. Just announced. Very hoity-toity."

"A party." Aisa couldn't seem to stop echoing the man. The party he meant was being thrown in Danr's honor. Aisa's thoughts and heart raced in tandem.

"I . . . should see to her." Aisa put a hand on one of the ladder rungs.

The workman stopped her. "Sorry. No one's allowed to touch it. Extra valuable."

The words made Aisa's blood boil. "Then why is *she* kept in filthy water?"

"It's hard to dip all that water out and replace it. They foul their water fast, you know?" The workman hawked and spat. "Nasty things."

"They're Kin," Aisa said. "Related to us humans, just like the fairies and sprites are related to the elves."

"Sure, sure." The man shrugged. "I have to feed it. You want to watch?"

Before Aisa could respond, the workman climbed up the ladder with a bucket. From it he took a fish, which he held over the water. The mermaid leaped out of the water and snatched it from his hand. She also tried to grab his arm, clearly intent on dragging him into the tank, but the workman yanked himself away in time.

Aisa gasped. Even caught in midair above filthy water, the mermaid was a breathtaking sight. She was strong and sleek, with long brown hair. A mask of blue-and-black tattoos covered her face. Her breasts were bare, and the man goggled at them before the mermaid splashed back into the water. That, Aisa realized, was the reason he had forced the mermaid to jump for the fish rather than just dropping it into the tank.

As the filthy water closed over the mermaid's head, the world . . . shifted. Aisa could not explain how, but everything became slightly different. It was as if she had spent her life seeing the entire world as a tangled garden and then suddenly seen it as a collection of individual seeds and plants. The mermaid was an important and powerful piece of that garden, and if she was moved to a new place, the entire garden would change. And if she did not move, the garden would wilt and die. But, oddly, the mermaid's new position in the garden was more dangerous to her. If she moved, she would probably die. If she did not move, the world would careen into chaos.

The sensation vanished. For a moment, Aisa thought she saw a face, a woman's face, in the swirling filth of the water. Then it was gone.

Aisa blinked. What was wrong with her? She saw visions of battle and now visions of . . . gardens. Her mind was falling apart. She set her mouth and hurried away. Regardless of her many fears, she had to save the mermaid, and for that, she would need Danr's help. His and Ranadar's.

"Grandfather Wyrm," Danr repeated softly. "He's a bad one."

"The biggest and most powerful of wyrms," Kalessa added. Her greenish complexion had gone pale. "His breath poisons armies. He knocks down mountains. He swallows ships."

"And he is nothing but a myth," Ranadar scoffed. "My nursemaid told me stories of him."

"What stories will nursemaids one day tell about Danr the troll boy?" asked Nu.

"Or of Aisa the escaped slave?" asked Tan.

"Or of Talfi the undying boy and Kalessa the warrior orc and Ranadar the traitor elf?" Pendra finished tiredly. "Myths all begin somewhere. As we have good reason to know."

Danr considered this for a long moment. "Grandfather Wyrm can tell us about Shape magic?"

"He was a great magician who was already ancient by the time of the Sundering," Nu said.

"He knows everything about shapes," Tan said.

"He will tell you what you want to know," Pendra sighed. "If . . ."

"Why is there always an if?" Kalessa sighed.

"Nothing worth having comes easily," Nu said.

"Or quickly," Tan said.

"Or without a struggle," Pendra murmured. "Grandfather Wyrm. He lives at the Key, which is in the center of the Nine Isles. The Key, in fact, lies directly over the spot where young Talfi gave up his life to destroy the Iron Axe and was created during the Sundering."

"It has become a place of transition," said Nu.

"Neither earth nor air," said Tan.

"Neither fire nor water," finished Pendra. "Only people

who walk between worlds, such as half-bloods, can survive there."

"So *I* can go there," Danr said breathlessly. Maybe being
a half-blood wasn't entirely a curse.

"It's almost as if you were fated," Pendra agreed blandly.

"Predetermined," Nu added.

"Set up," Ta said.

Pendra passed a hand over her face. "When you arrive,
you must persuade Grandfather Wyrm to give you his
secrets, or he will devour you alive. He likes to start with
the toes."

"I heard it's the fingers," said Nu in a casual voice that
chilled Danr's blood.

"It's the head," said Tan waspishly.

"You're not helping," Death pointed out from her rocking chair.

"How do we—I—persuade a thousand-year-old wyrm
to give us anything," Danr said, straightening his backbone,
"let alone the secret to shape magic?"

"Fortunately," Death said, "Grandfather Wyrm has a
penchant for squid ink."

"Squid ink?" Danr said stupidly.

Death held out the smelly pouch. "I did say it was a gift
for someone else."

With a number of horrified expressions, Talfi carefully
squeezed the squid ink from the sac through a funnel and
into a bottle supplied by the long-suffering Mrs. Farley
while Danr looked on anxiously. They were upstairs, in the
room Talfi shared with Ranadar. Danr often envied the fact
that Talfi had someone to share a room with. It was very
difficult and lonely to sleep by himself when Aisa was only
one door down the hall.

"Don't spill any," he warned.

"Do it yourself if you're worried," Talfi said. "This is disgusting. Like wringing out cold fish guts."

"My hands are too big." Danr splayed them. "Maybe when I'm human, things will be different."

Kalessa put her elbows on the table and arched auburn eyebrows. "Exactly how are we going to go find Grandfather Wyrm? We are in storm season, and Grandfather Wyrm lives in the center of the Iron Sea. That is where storms *come* from."

Danr looked down at the stream of ink funneling into the bottle. "Storm season will pass," he said. "And when it does—"

The door to the common room burst open and Aisa rushed in. Danr jerked around, already worried and tense. What was wrong? Was she hurt? Was she—

"We have to help," she blurted out. "And we have to hurry!"

"Who?" Danr said. "How? What's the matter?"

Aisa took Danr's arm and tried to tow him toward the door. He couldn't remember when he had seen her so agitated. "What is it?" he demanded again.

"Aren't you listening? They—"

"I'm listening," Danr was forced to interrupt. "You aren't being very clear."

"They have a mermaid for sale!" Aisa was all but jumping up and down, her usually calm face filled with an urgency and need that unsettled Danr and made him want to break whatever was causing her pain.

"Who has a mermaid?" Ranadar asked. "You must start at the beginning."

"We'll help, Aisa," Danr said. "Just tell us."

Aisa looked up and into his eyes. For a moment the entire world stopped. He felt the love within her like a flock of butterflies waiting to burst forth like a thousand tiny rainbows. Then she looked away and the moment was gone. He knew why. Hector, however evil a man he might have been, was right. And Danr was so tired of being neither human nor troll, yes, he was. But he had a solution. He only needed to find Grandfather Wyrm and learn how—if—he could become human. For her. For both of them.

"The slave market," Aisa said tersely. "They've captured a mermaid, and they're selling her at the prince's party tonight. We have to free her. We *have* to."

"Why?" Ranadar said, puzzled. "How is she different from any other slave? We don't need to—" He fell silent when he realized that Aisa, Danr, and Talfi were all glaring at him.

"Still one of the Fae," Aisa said. "Even now."

"We met while I was a slave," Talfi said softly.

Ranadar held up his hands. "That's not what I meant."

"What *did* you mean?" Danr said evenly.

Ranadar retreated a little. "I do not condone slavery any longer. What I meant was, why does this single slave matter so much when there are hundreds of others at the slave market?"

Aisa closed her eyes and seemed to be fighting an inner battle. She opened them and quietly sat on the bed. "I saw . . . I *felt* sensations I cannot describe when I discovered the mermaid in that filthy tank. Strange things are happening in the world, and the mermaid is part of it. She must go free for just that reason. But there is more. Humans enslave humans. The Fae enslave humans. Even the orcs enslave humans." Here, Kalessa looked away. "That is horror enough. We do not need to drag the merfolk into it."

"I still fail to see why not," Ranadar said.

"The nine races," Aisa said. "You know what we are. Each race is divided three ways—Kin, Fae, and Stane. But we're also divided another way—into the low, the middle, and the high. The low are the fairies, the orcs, and dwarfs, and they concern themselves with the physical ideas—building and fighting and working with the hands. The high are the giants, the sprites, and merfolk. They concern themselves with the mind and the spirit and other, stranger concepts the lower folk cannot understand. The middle are the humans, the elves, and the trolls. They walk between the two and serve as a balance."

"You sound like a priest," Ranadar said. "What does this have to do with the mermaid?"

Aisa closed her eyes again. "Humans are both slavers and slaves. It is terrible enough when we do these things to ourselves. When we enslave the merfolk, the higher selves of the Kin, we do more harm to all Kin. The merfolk are freedom, they are spirit, they are power. By enslaving even one, we reduce all Kin, and when other Kin see her enslaved, it encourages more destruction of spirit, and it allows us to ignore pain even more than we do. Rescuing the mermaid will help all Kin, not just the single mermaid."

Chills ran down Danr's back at her quiet, powerful words, but Danr found he himself couldn't speak, though his mouth was hanging open. He closed it. There was a long pause. Then Talfi breathed, "Wow."

Kalessa drove the tip of her knife, the magic one, into the tabletop. "We will free this mermaid, my sister!"

"We will," said Talfi.

"Yes," said Danr.

Aisa opened her eyes and breathed a sigh that seemed to come from her toes, and Danr wanted to wrap his arms around her. "Thank you, my friends. You cannot understand how much this means to me."

"You are attending the party tomorrow, Danr," Ranadar said, ignoring Danr's quiet groan. "The easiest way would be to buy her at the auction and then set her free."

"And where would we come up with that kind of money?" Talfi said. "Would your mother give us a loan?"

Everyone snorted at that, even Aisa.

"I was thinking Ranadar could Twist us to Death," Aisa said slowly. "She does like us. And we still need to give her the squid parts."

"Oh," Danr said uncomfortably. "Yes. About that."

Aisa turned narrow eyes on him. "What about that?"

"We already went to see Death," Danr said.

"Without me?"

Her tone was cold, but now Danr got a little angry again. He didn't try to resist answering her question. "Yeah. You left, and we had to deliver the squid parts."

Talfi gave him a hard look, which Danr avoided. The look reminded him that they had deliberately gone to see Death without Aisa, and Danr prayed Aisa wouldn't ask him a direct question about that.

Aisa sucked in her cheeks and remained silent for a moment, then said, "Granted, then. Did anything—"

Danr interrupted before she could complete her question and force him to go on at length about the entire visit. "She accepted the parts. She also told us something interesting about shape magic." He went on to explain, though he left out the catalyst of the conversation—his desire to become human for her.

"So Death and the Gardeners want us to risk our lives to restore shape magic to the Kin," Aisa said slowly. "Why would we do this when she didn't even reward us for kill-ing the squid?"

No words came to Danr. It meant he knew no single, truthful answer. For once, this caught him off guard and he was flummoxed.

"Did you not, my sister, just say that enslaving the merfolk hurt all Kin everywhere?" Kalessa said. "And have you not made it clear how much you hate slavery? Imagine what would happen to slaves everywhere if they learned to change their shapes. How long could a slaver hold someone in bondage if she need only fly away as a falcon or slip her chains as a cat or poison her owner as a snake?"

"Leave it to an orc to be practical," Talfi murmured.

"Oh my," Aisa said. "I had not thought."

"The Kin, especially the humans, have been pawns of the Fae for a thousand years because they have no magic to defend themselves," Ranadar pointed out. "Death is asking us to even the score. The Tree tips—"

"But we could stop it from tipping," Danr interrupted. "Once the Kin have their magic back, the Tree might stop tipping back and forth between the Fae and the Stane. The Kin could hold it."

"Very well," Aisa said. "I am willing."

And Danr let out a breath he hadn't known he was holding.

"If," Aisa continued, "we help the mermaid first. She will be sold at the prince's auction, and we have to free her. I wanted to ask Death for enough money to buy her and set her free, but you already saw her."

Danr shook his head. "She never gives us money."

"Just a vague promise of great rewards to come," Aisa groused.

"Uh, she did bring me back to life," Talfi said. "I'll take that."

"But what has she done lately?" Aisa asked peevishly. "We have completed a number of tasks for her, yet here we live, with little money and no way to get more, and now a mermaid to rescue."

"This is Death we are discussing," Ranadar said, "and the Gardeners. I rather think that if they ask us to do something, it is in our best interest to do it."

"Hmm." Aisa folded her lips in a way that said she had other best interests in mind. "I care more about the mermaid than the shape magic. She must be freed."

"All right," Danr said. "What's to stop me from going down to the slave market after dark, smashing a hole in the tank, and dropping her in the ocean?"

"Perhaps fifty guards," Aisa said. "Even your strength and Kalessa's sword would have difficulty with so many armed men. And they will be moving her to the Gold Keep soon in any case."

"You said we don't have enough money to buy her outright," Talfi said. "But what if we did?"

"I fail to understand," Aisa said.

"One way to get something cheap is to convince the owner it isn't worth anything," Talfi explained. "Then you swoop in and buy it for nothing."

"Where did you learn this?" Kalessa asked with narrowed yellow eyes.

"My face"—Talfi tapped his own chin—"is handsome but ancient."

"All right," Danr said slowly, "how do you make a mermaid worthless?"

Aisa gave a rare smile and got to her feet. "It'll take just a little work. We should dress for the prince's party."

Chapter Six

Danr peered anxiously out of the hired coach. Thick clouds washed across the sky, viscous and clingy, blotting out the moon and drawing a cloak across the stars. A long line of other coaches snaked around a tinkling fountain and bunched up at the marble steps to the Gold Keep, so named because of the faint yellow tint to the stones and because of the wealth required to build it. Every prince of Balsia, determined to leave his mark, had added something to it, and over the centuries, the Keep had come to resemble six castles crushed together.

Slaves held torches to light the courtyard. From the first coach in line, a footman helped a lady in a wide dress and richly braided hair alight. A man in a wine-red velvet tunic embroidered with gold phoenixes belted under a sword followed. Wealth dripped like blood across the carpet as they stepped smartly up the steps to the great doors, which stood open for them. Danr sighed and pulled at his own tunic. It was also velvet, blue and black, with artfully slashed sleeves and matching trousers that were drawn embarrassingly tight. He didn't wear a sword—even the Hero of the Twist was still a commoner—but he did wear boots, terrible, uncomfortable things that pinched. The clothing had been a present from an admiring duke or baron or some such four districts back, and he only wore it on these occasions.

"Are you sure we can do this?" Danr asked.

"For someone who faced down two armies at once, you have an awful lack of confidence," said Talfi. He wore dove gray and scarlet red, and his boots probably didn't pinch.

"How does my hair look?" fussed Ranadar. He wore a long robe of stiff mauve with a high collar and embroidered in heavy silver designs. Underneath, his shirt was sky blue, and his boots turned up at the toes. An impressively heavy pouch clinked at his belt.

"Did you truly just ask about your hair?" Kalessa smirked. *She* got to wear her armor, freshly cleaned at the armorer's. "How sweet! Did Talfi brush—"

"Finish that sentence, orc, and you will do it from the end of a spit," Ranadar interrupted. "This is serious. I need to know if I look the part."

"You look fine. Don't bicker." Aisa, who so far had escaped mention in the stories, was pale and drawn, though she looked stunning in a pale yellow dress that contrasted sharply with her dark hair and eyes.

"Pray to Tikk this works." Talfi flashed a grin.

Danr stamped twice and spat out the window. "Don't mention the trickster's name! He might notice."

"I hope he does," Talfi replied impishly. "We'll need his help."

The coach jerked forward. It was hot and crowded inside, and there were enough of them to justify two coaches, but Danr hated hiring even one driver for these events. It seemed a waste of money, even though Ranadar assured him that it would not do for the guest of honor to arrive on foot or in a farmer's cart, and these outings were how they made a living. Inevitably, the host or some other wealthy person wanted to give Danr gifts, such as the clothing they all wore, or jewelry, or even simple money, and they had to accept such gifts or starve. This made Danr deeply uncomfortable. Prince gifts were for warriors and knights and other nobles, not for half-troll thralls. The givers also had no idea that Danr had come within half a hair of sundering the world a second time, and it seemed hypocritical to accept presents for that. Aisa and Ranadar, however, had no such reservations, and readily took whatever came their way. It was the only income they had, and it went surprisingly fast. It always seemed that the more they had, they more they needed.

The coach at the front of the line halted, and a dwarf dressed all in red hopped down to open the door before the footman could reach it. The dwarf pulled down a ladder, and a woman in a belled dress so black it seemed to draw light into it emerged. Aisa, who was also watching out the window, shot to her feet with a gasp.

"That cannot be!" she cried.

"Shh!" Ranadar said. "What are you talking about?"

"That woman! It is Sharlee—the woman who drugged me."

Danr's head came around. "Drugged you?"

"I have had no time to tell of it," Aisa said. "So much has happened."

"And that's Hector!" Talfi pointed out the window. Hector, the man from the tavern, had clambered down beside the woman. He wore the same impossible shade of black, but no sword. She took his arm, and they marched up the steps.

"They must be married," Ranadar observed.

"What's going on here?" Danr said. "What do you mean that woman drugged you?"

And as the coach inched forward, Aisa told a story that raised Danr's hair and boiled his blood.

"I'll kill them both," he said, clenching hard fists.

"The line starts behind me," Aisa said

"No, no, no," Ranadar said. "Not here. They are obviously

friends of the prince. Besides, we need to learn what they are planning."

"It must have something to do with the mermaid," Aisa said.

Ranadar jingled the pouch at his belt. "Concentrate on the plan. Aisa, you should avoid Sharlee. She and Hector obviously know you are coming, but if they have a plan for you, there is no reason to give them a better chance to accomplish it."

Aisa folded her arms like a petulant child. "Fine. We will find a way to kill them later."

"Are you sure you want to marry someone that bloodthirsty?" Talfi remarked.

"It's one of her finer qualities," Danr replied.

The coach finally creaked up to the front of the line. If the footman recognized Danr, he gave no sign. Once everyone had disembarked and the coachmen were dispatched to the stables to await the evening's end, Aisa reached up for Danr's arm and they mounted the stairs. Danr felt as if he were on his way to either war or an execution, he wasn't sure which. The Gold Keep loomed ahead and above him.

"Remember," Ranadar murmured as they reached the top. "Prince Karsten is young, just twenty-one, and he took the throne only a year ago."

"His father nicked himself on a practice blade and died of blood poisoning," Danr recited. "He's still unhappy, so don't bring it up. I know."

"His mother, Lady Hafren, still makes some decisions on his behalf," Ranadar continued, undaunted. "Many people see him as weak, and they wonder if a change is coming. Some of them may be trying to create that change. The prince tends to make rash decisions, and he spends money a little too freely, so they may get their wish if he does not mature quickly."

They passed through the great double doors into an arched tunnel. Murder holes glared down from the ceiling. More slaves with torches lit the way across a courtyard to the building where the prince was receiving Danr. It was long and blocky, with high, thin windows that spilled light across the courtyard. Another big set of doors stood open, and music drifted on the muggy night air. The song was a popular dance tune. Danr gave Aisa a panicked look.

"We will keep the dancing simple, my strong and fearful one," she said.

"Is there a nickname for that, too?" Talfi said. "It's got to be better than *Hamzu*."

"When you become engaged to him," Aisa sniffed, "you may call him anything you like."

"Are you engaged to him?" Kalessa asked archly.

"It will happen soon, I am confident."

"So if we all know it's going to happen," Talfi said, "that means you're as good as engaged. And if you're engaged, you're practically married. And if you're practically married—"

"Door," Danr interrupted. "Big door. We can stop talking now."

They had indeed reached the great doors where the castle's aging seneschal, identified by the silver chain around his neck and the keys at his belt, was just shouting, ". . . Lord Whetherwark and his lady." The crowd of well-dressed people beyond the door paused what they were doing, briefly bowed toward the door where Lord and Lady Whetherwark were standing, then went back to their business. Lord and Lady Whetherwark entered the room.

The seneschal turned to ask their names, then caught sight of Danr and inhaled sharply.

"My lord," he said.

It had begun. "I'm not a—" Danr began, but Aisa elbowed

him in the side. He sighed. Did she expect him to lie? He clenched his toes inside tight boots.

"Who were the gentleman and gentlewoman dressed all in black?" Ranadar asked, slipping a coin into the seneschal's hand. "They arrived just ahead of us."

"Ah yes," the seneschal said, still a little flustered. "Hector Obsidia and his wife, Sharlee. Wealthy. Slave traders, mostly. Everyone calls them *the* Obsidia. The prince didn't want to invite them—they have something of a reputation—but they have more money than slaves have lice, and Prince Karsten's lady mother reminded him that inviting the harbormaster and the mayor but not the Obsidia would cause a rift in certain sectors, and so here they are. And may I say it's an honor to meet you, Master Danr?"

"Yes, and thank you," Danr said, answering the question as a truth-teller must and adding the thanks as Aisa had taught him. He couldn't say the pleasure was all his—being here wasn't a pleasure.

"May I have your names for the announcing?"

"Danr of northern Balsia, Aisa of Irbsa, Kalessa of the Sixth Nest, Ranadar of Palana, and Talfi," Aisa said. She was scanning the room for Hector and Sharlee.

"Talfi," the seneschal repeated. "Of . . . ?"

"Just Talfi," Talfi said.

The seneschal turned to the great room beyond. It was filled with glittering people who coasted across the marble floor like great ships or silver swans. A small group was dancing, but most people talked or strolled about. Servants and slaves sailed across the floor with trays of food and drink. Warm, stuffy air clotted with cologne wafted out the door. Danr, who had grown up in a stable and felt more comfortable among a herd of cows, tried not to grimace. Against one wall on a raised dais stood a tall chair, and beside that stood a young, dark-haired man with a long nose and too much chin. Next to him was a richly dressed older woman. She had the same dark hair and was trying not to run to plump.

The seneschal turned to the throng and announced the names in a booming voice that belied his skinny body, saving Danr for last. When he started speaking, everyone paused their conversation to bow again, but when the seneschal said, "And Master Danr, Hero of the Twist," in direct defiance of Aisa's instructions, the entire room burst into applause and cheers.

Danr forced a wooden smile onto his face and stood in the great doorway with Aisa next to him like a strange animal suddenly on display. The bright torches and candles hurt his eyes, and the explosion of applause shoved his ears an inch into his skull. Every eye in the room stared at him with curiosity, admiration, calculation, or hunger, and he felt his soul shrivel a little.

You can get through this, he thought. *Just like you have done a dozen times before.*

When the noise died down, the crowd surged toward him. Kalessa and Ranadar automatically stepped in front of him, hands resting lightly on their swords in a way that wasn't meant to be threatening, but *was* supposed to remind everyone both of their manners and of the fact that Kalessa and Ranadar were titled nobility, able to bear arms.

A short blast on a horn froze everyone and stopped the music. A herald near the dais shouted, "The prince will receive the Hero of the Twist!"

Like magic, a path opened up between Danr and the dais. Prince Karsten, his mother beside him, stood at the other end. Danr swallowed. A prince.

A map of Balsia looked like a stained glass window that had been hit with a hammer. The country was a crazy quilt of city-states, baronetcies, duchies, and districts that allied, squabbled, warred, and made up until no one really knew where any boundaries lay. The local ruler called himself by whatever title he felt strong enough to use, and over the last year, Danr had been received by knights, mayors, *Bürger-meisters*, barons, earls, dukes, and even a duchess, but never a prince. Still, he figured you did the same thing. Bow, make nice conversation, eat with your best damn manners, and pray they didn't ask stupid questions of a truth-teller.

Danr and the others made a little parade of it, as they had a dozen times before. Everyone watched in silence, and Danr felt very small despite his height. Irrationally, he wished he were shorter, less noticeable. What a fine thing it would be to simply be part of a crowd instead of the center of one.

They had walked perhaps five steps when the prince bounded down the dais and dashed up to them. Startled, Kalessa and Ranadar gave way.

"So you're the half-blood Hero of the Twist!" Prince Karsten said with a grin.

Aisa poked Danr, and he quickly bowed, as did the others. "Your Highness," Danr said.

"It must have been damn amazing to hold the Iron Axe. You were the most powerful man on Erda! And you gave it up?"

"Yes, Your Highness," Danr said.

"You'll have to tell us about it. What do you think of Balsia so far?"

Words crowded in his throat, and Danr managed a minimal reply. "It's very big and crowded, and a lot of people know me, even though I don't know them."

A titter ran through the crowd. "I'm sure they do," said Karsten. "We're all glad you could come tonight, and some friends have brought in some special entertainment."

Danr exchanged a quick glance with Aisa. The mermaid auction. Ranadar touched the pouch at his belt, and Talfi touched his elbow, reminding him not to call attention to it.

"I'm sure it'll be fascinating, Your Highness," Danr said, with utter truth.

Karsten clapped him on the shoulder, and Lady Hafren, his mother, winced from the dais. The entire room was still watching in silence, but Karsten spoke as if no one else were there. "We should introduce you around. Let's see, over here we have Harbormaster Willem, High Priest of Bosha, Our Lady of the Oceans."

A man in watery blue velvet robes trimmed with spotless white stepped quickly forward from a small knot of men wearing similar, less resplendent, robes. Servants or lesser priests, Danr assumed. One of the lesser men, a mousy, bald man with a worried expression, twitched the train of the harbormaster's robe back into place after he stepped forward. The harbormaster's carefully combed silver-white hair fell across his forehead in a style usually found on a much younger man, and his sharp gray eyes swept Danr with a hard gaze that lost nothing. When he spoke, his voice rolled like long waves. "Good to meet you, Master Danr."

He held out his fist. A gold and azure ring gleamed on the middle finger. Danr stared down at it, uncomprehending. The people in the room shifted uncomfortably. The harbormaster waited with a stone face, fist still extended.

"Kiss the ring," murmured the worried-looking man without moving his lips.

Oh. Danr, who could have swallowed the harbormaster's entire fist, didn't trust himself to merely kiss a target that tiny. Instead he leaned down and made a faint kissing noise in the general spot where the ring was. The lack wasn't lost on the harbormaster, who looked as if he'd swallowed a sea urchin. Danr forced himself not to flinch, and after a tiny moment, a patently false quicksilver smile flashed across the harbormaster's face.

"May the blessings of our lady Bosha wash over you, my son," he said. "You destroyed Palana, didn't you?"

"Nearly," Danr said.

"Then we will have to talk later." The harbormaster rubbed his ring. "Indeed we must."

Meanwhile, Lady Hafren was trying to get her son's attention from the throne dais, but he either didn't see her or was ignoring her.

The prince led Danr over to a short, dumpling of a man all in brown velvet. "And this is the mayor, Lord Bilking."

"So glad to meet you, so glad," Lord Bilking said. "The Iron Axe, the Axe! Just imagine you visiting Balsia! You must pose for a portrait, you must!"

"Oh," said Danr. "I—I—" He cast about for something to say.

"It sounds delightful," Aisa jumped in, lying for him.

"Wonderful! Wonderful!" Lord Bilking said. "Maybe once storm season is—"

"And this," the prince interrupted, towing the group along, "is Lord Whetherwark."

"Perhaps," Lady Hafren finally called from the throne dais, "Master Danr could be called on to address everyone now, and more introductions could follow later?"

The prince looked around and seemed to realize for the first time that the entire room had remained silent and was prepared to stay that way until the prince finished his business. The prince shot the room a look and ran his tongue around the inside of his mouth.

"Would you like to tell us your story, Master Danr?" the mayor said quickly.

And of course, Danr had to say, "No. I can't stand tell-ing it, and I hate it when people ask me to."

The mayor turned white. A gasp rippled through the crowd and Danr wanted to sink into the floor. This exact same thing had happened in the court of an earl several months back, and Danr's unwilling rudeness had started a riot. The group had barely escaped without hurting anyone—or themselves. Stormy tension built in the room, and Danr frantically searched for exits. The closest was over there, and the crowd was thin-ner in front of it. He could probably bowl some people over to clear a path for Aisa and the others—

But the prince laughed and clapped him on the back. "Well said, Master Danr! I've never liked giving speeches, either. But we'd take it as a great favor if you'd at least tell the short version."

The tension broke like ice in spring sunshine, and several people laughed along with the prince. Even the mayor re-laxed. The prince caught Danr's eye and nodded. In that moment, Danr liked Karsten a great deal. He nodded back. Right, then. Danr mounted the steps to the dais. More than one noble, he noticed, shied away when he passed, and twice he heard a whispered, "Half-blood."

"Enough of that!" Harbormaster Willem boomed unex-pectedly. "Kin, Fae, and Stane are all children of the Nine. Thanks to Danr himself, the Stane were freed from their prison under the mountain, and they freely enter our city, at the command of our new prince."

"And the harbormaster," murmured the mayor, though not loud enough to carry far.

"We need to think big," the harbormaster said. "Bigger than our own homes, bigger than our neighborhoods, bigger than our city. The Stane are our brothers and sisters. Bosha bless them all."

That was unexpected. Maybe there was more to the harbormaster than Danr had thought. The murmurings stopped, though a number of people exchanged looks. Danr glanced between the mayor and the harbormaster. This was an old fight, and the opposing bishops had decided Danr was a new pawn.

"Thank you, your holiness," said the prince. "Now maybe we could hear from Danr himself?"

Danr finished mounting the dais. Aisa remained at the foot, while Ranadar and the others mingled as they wished. On impulse, Danr shut his right eye and swept the crowd with his left. Instantly, he could see their attitudes toward him— and toward Aisa. Half the sparkling people were ready to worship him like the Bird King himself if only Danr gave the word. Two women looked at Aisa, their naked envy playing over their faces for only Danr to see. The other half of the crowd was repulsed by a half troll and by any woman who wanted to be with one. Hatred dripped in black pus from their faces. Danr opened his right eye again so he wouldn't have to see it anymore, though a cold feeling clenched his stomach.

This was going to be his life, wasn't it? Crowds following him everywhere, ready to adore him or attack him. Worries that his truth-telling tongue would trip him up in front of someone important. Wondering what people thought of him. Telling stories on cue for his supper like a trained animal. The life of a half-blood freak. And he had the gall to ask Aisa, the best of women, to share it with him.

His resolve hardened. It wouldn't happen. The power of the shape would change it all. No more crowds, no more politics. He wouldn't have to straddle two worlds anymore, and Aisa wouldn't have to live with the prejudice he had faced his entire life. He faced his audience, firm in the decision that this time would be his last.

"The first person to tell me to find the Iron Axe was Death

herself," he began. It was a familiar narrative. Talfi had worked it out, and Danr had memorized it. This audience listened with rapt attention during the hour it took to tell. Danr knew the story so well that he didn't have to concentrate very much, and let his gaze wander over the crowd. No sign of Hector or his wife, Sharlee. Strange, and more than a little unnerving. Better to keep enemies in the open, where you could see them, yes, it was.

He finished the story and accepted the applause. Karsten ordered the feast tables brought in, and servants brought in trestle tables, followed by benches, platters of food, and goblets of drink. During the setting up, a crowd of people surrounded Danr, all wanting to shake his hand or have a word with him or touch his arm. One person stole his handkerchief. Danr fell into the familiar rhythm of such events—shake hands or bow, say something both truthful and noncommittal, keep conversations short, and tell people Aisa handled invitations, which was the truth. Wrestling with the truth-teller in him made for exhausting work, and Danr would rather face down a platoon of orcs on wyrm-back.

Meanwhile, Ranadar, Kalessa, and Talfi scattered themselves about the room, all of them far more at ease than Danr felt. Kalessa, the warrior orc, found soul mates among a number of knights, and Talfi, the boy who couldn't die, made friends everywhere he went. Even Ranadar got on well. Humans were usually wary of elves for taking slaves and because their touch was addictive, but elven magic and wealth garnered respect, so Ranadar was able to create a small court of his own in short order among the young and daring. No one knew who Aisa was, and they simply assumed she was a woman Danr had picked up somewhere. Neither of them went out of their way to explain the truth.

Danr still didn't see Hector or Sharlee.

When the feast was ready, Danr and Aisa were led to the

table of honor to sit near Karsten and his mother, along with the harbormaster and the mayor. The prince raised his goblet and toasted Danr (who had learned not to drink during a toast to himself), and then called, "Where is the entertainment?"

Danr saw Aisa tense beside Lady Hafren. The giant double doors were still open to keep the stuffy air moving. Through them came Hector and Sharlee Obsidia in their deep black clothing. Behind came the dwarf leading two horses that towed the water tank Aisa had described from the slave market. The water in the tank had been cleaned. At the bottom crouched the mermaid. A startled rumble rushed through the party. The mermaid's hair moved in waves about her head and her gleaming, muscular tail was curled beneath her. Still, even from this distance, she exuded a kind of magnetism and power. Chaining such a wondrous and powerful creature was a travesty, like staking an eagle to the ground or pulling stars from the sky. Danr understood why Aisa wanted her to be free.

The harbormaster and the mayor both got to their feet. The dwarf halted the creaking, slopping tank in the middle of the floor near the feast tables while Sharlee and Hector Obsidia bowed before the head table. Danr's stare turned into a glower. He should have known. Somehow he should have realized that the mermaid auction would be connected to these two people.

"Your Highness," Hector said. "Lords and ladies! The Obsidia, purveyors of the best in slaves, bring this great rarity for your entertainment tonight."

"Examine the mermaid to your heart's content," Sharlee added, "and then we will conduct an auction. The winner will take her home."

A wave of excited discussion followed. The prince leaned

forward in his chair. Hector caught Danr's eye and winked. Unable to contain himself, Danr heaved himself upright.

"Filth!" he shouted.

The room went instantly silent. Talfi stared at him from his own table. Kalessa mouthed, *What are you doing?* This wasn't part of the plan. But Danr didn't care. Every eye was on him.

"Slave auctions with humans are ugly enough," he boomed over his pounding heart, "without dragging the merfolk into it. We should set her free immediately!"

A new hope entered Aisa's eyes, and Danr would have moved worlds to see more of it. He firmed his jaw. If he was saddled with fame, he might as well use it, and they wouldn't have to resort to an elaborate scheme to free the mermaid.

"My lord!" said Sharlee smoothly. "I'm sure our half-blood guest knows the wider world, but here in the great city of Balsia, we know the laws and traditions."

The mermaid knelt at the bottom of the tank. Danr wondered if she could hear them.

The prince seemed ready to say something, but his mother leaned over and spoke quickly into his ear. His face remained neutral.

Danr said clearly. "As Hero of the Twist, and the man—"

"Half-blood," murmured someone.

"—who wielded the Iron Axe for Death herself," he continued as if no one had spoken, "I ask the prince for a favor. Give the mermaid to me."

Another ripple went through the crowd. Sharlee looked stricken. Danr, Hero of the Twist, stared her down.

"My lord!" she said. "That would break the laws of ownership! Your Highness certainly has the right to do as he pleases, but if you set this precedent, you endanger the entire slave market, and it's damaged badly already. Thanks to our . . . noble trollish guest, the elves no longer buy slaves, and our city is running a debt. Do we want more of that?"

The crowd watched in hypnotized astonishment. This was turning into the greatest bit of entertainment in a decade, and the auction hadn't even begun. Like the audience at a jousting match, they turned their gazes from Danr to Prince Karsten.

"You're not arguing that giving one slave as a gift will damage the entire market, the entire market," the mayor said dryly.

"This slave is worth more than a thousand others," Hector pointed out. Then he turned to Karsten and fixed him with a hard look. "And I'm sure the prince will remember where the slaves came from last year when the army needed them. The crown still hasn't paid for them all, though we know it's been difficult times and so far we've been willing to wait."

The last was a clear threat. Karsten worked his jaw back and forth and looked uncomfortably at his mother, then at the harbormaster.

"Debts must always be honored, Your Highness," Willem said blandly. "Order and law. We were a great city once, and can only become one again if order is—"

"Yes, fine," Karsten said shortly, and sat back in his chair with poor grace. "The mermaid belongs to the Obsidia. Let the auction continue."

Damn it. Danr forced himself to sit as well. Aisa's hand tightened visibly on her wine goblet.

"My lords and ladies," Hector called quickly, before anything more could be said, "please feel free to examine this lovely specimen. The auction will begin shortly."

Benches scraped the floor and a glittering stampede started for the tank. Danr refused to take part. Aisa pointedly turned away. Karsten and the other guests of honor stayed at the high table as well. At least they still had the original plan. Danr caught Talfi's eye across the room and nodded. Talfi nodded back.

Karsten was chewing the inside of his cheek. Feeling bad for him, Danr leaned over to the prince.

"I'm sorry if I put you in a bad spot, Your Highness," he said over the noise.

"Nothing to apologize for," Karsten replied evenly. "I would have given her to you, but Hector is right—my father incurred debts to the Obsidia that we haven't repaid yet."

"Why did you look to the harbormaster?" Danr asked without thinking if it might be rude.

Karsten, however, didn't seem to take it that way. "The harbormaster is the most powerful man in the city, after me, though the mayor wouldn't like to admit it. Willem thinks the entire city belongs to him because his temple runs the harbor, and Mother is—*I* am—worried his influence is growing too fast. He pushed hard for a declaration to allow Stane into the city, though there I agreed with him."

"Why?" Danr asked.

"New ideas. I visited Otrania, the elven port, when I was a boy. Did you know the Fae have this thing called a sewer? It runs under the city and drains sewage and other waste away to keep the city clean."

Danr remembered his time in Alfhame. He had indeed noticed the lack of waste aboveground in the elven cities, though to him and his true eye, it had felt more as if the Fae had drawn a pretty blanket over waste and disease than drained it away.

"Sewers could clean Balsia, too," Karsten was saying. "They can even do the opposite and bring in fresh water from the mountains so people don't have to drink from wells and fountains. Aqueducts, the Fae call them."

The harbormaster was passing behind Karsten's seat with

the worried-looking man in tow, and he caught this last remark.

"You're telling him about our new sewers and aqueducts, Your Highness!" he said with obvious delight. "Yes! We must think big, dig deep! You like to dig like all trolls, don't you?"

Was that snootiness in the harbormaster's tone? Danr couldn't quite tell. The words rubbed his hair in the wrong direction, however, and he was almost glad when the truth-teller in him forced him to answer the question.

"No," he said. "You like to cheat on your wife like all humans, don't you?"

Another dreadful silence crashed across the table. Aisa raised a goblet and Danr saw she was hiding her laughter behind it. The worried-looking man looked even more worried. The harbormaster grew bloodred beneath his white hair. He opened his mouth to speak.

"Well," Karsten interjected, "I suppose you had that coming, Willem. As you yourself like to say, we can't make assumptions about the Nine Gods or the Nine People. Think big, and all that, right?"

"Right." The word came out like a half-bitten bit of apple. "If you'll excuse me. Come, Punsle." And he swirled away with the worried-looking Punsle behind him.

"I could have lived without that," Karsten observed. "The harbormaster is . . . aloof, but I need his support for the sewer project. Water is part of his purview, you know."

"I would say I'm sorry if I could," Danr said blandly.

Karsten sighed. "He has his fingers everywhere. He's even used emissaries to strike up a friendship with Queen Vesha."

"Queen Vesha?" Danr said in surprise. "She's my aunt."

Now Karsten looked surprised. "I didn't know that. I've invited her to visit, but she never comes. Do you know why?"

And Danr was forced to answer. "Death cursed her. Aunt Vesha will live forever unless she comes out from under the ground. Then Death will take her. It's a curse because Aunt Vesha has dreamed of coming into the open sky all her life."

"Oh." Karsten thought about that. "That's awful. But you don't want to talk about all this. Maybe I can give you a different favor."

"Could you bid for the mermaid yourself?"

Karsten shook his head. "I owe the Obsidia too much money and can't piss them off."

"Step aside, please!" Talfi barked from the throng below. "The elf lord wishes to inspect the merchandise."

Danr glanced at Hector, and a rush of anxiety swept him as he remembered that Hector had seen Talfi and Ranadar in the tavern earlier. They hadn't known during the planning stage that Hector himself would be auctioning off the mermaid. If he recognized Ranadar, the entire thing would fall apart. Fortunately, Hector hadn't been in the room when the seneschal announced Ranadar's name. But what about his face?

The sea of people parted for Ranadar—no one wanted to touch an elf for fear that his glamour might infect them. An elf glided forward, and it took Danr a moment to realize it was Ranadar. He had altered his appearance with a glamour. His hair was the rich ash blond of an oak tree, and his eyes were blue instead of green. Small shifts in his facial features had changed his face as well, making him all but unrecognizable. Relief made Danr limp.

Ranadar, as if by accident, adjusted the heavy pouch at his belt. It clinked impressively, though Danr happened to know it was filled with nothing but scraps of bronze. He chewed his lip and took a drink from his goblet to disguise the nerves that rose again.

A ladder was bolted to the side of the tank. Ranadar

climbed it, graceful and sure even in his robe. In the water, the mermaid stirred and looked up at him. Ranadar looked down at her, splashed the surface, and seemed to lose his balance a little. He caught himself and, because Danr was watching for it, saw him squeeze the little leather pouch of liquid into the tank as he did so.

"Fascinating creature," Ranadar said as he climbed down. "Very fascinating. Auctioneer, what is the starting bid?"

"Two gold hands, my lord," pronounced Hector. If he recognized Ranadar from the tavern, he gave no sign of the fact.

Others climbed the ladder as well, and the crowd resurged around the tank. Aisa got up and quietly slipped into the main group.

"Lords and ladies," Hector boomed at last, "we have before you a fine specimen of the merfolk, ready for an ornamental pond or fountain or other services. You will be the talk of Balsia with this unique item! The price includes this fine tank so you can easily transport your new prize home. Let the bidding begin! Do I hear two gold hands for—"

A filmy cloud burst from the mermaid's mouth and nose and the gills on the side of her neck. Her face went pale as milk, throwing her tattoos into sharp relief, and her eyelids drooped. She slid to the bottom of the tank. The crowd burst into mutters and low cries.

"What is wrong with it?" asked Aisa, who had stationed herself toward the rear. "Is it sick?"

"Is it dying?" Danr heard another voice—Kalessa. "I think it must be dying. That is disgusting—I do not wish to buy a slave that will die."

"It's dying!" Aisa repeated. "Who wants to buy a dying mermaid?"

The word *dying* washed through the bidders with astounding speed. Sharlee held up her hands. "Please, my lords and ladies! The mermaid is fully healthy and completely—"

The mermaid threw up again. The smell of rotting fish drifted from the tank, and the nobility closest to it shrank away. Ranadar drew himself upright. He nodded once at the Obsidia and strode stiffly toward his table. He sat with his back to the mermaid and took a deep draft from his goblet as if she didn't exist. After a brief pause, several other bidders did the same, scattering in a dozen different directions, some disappointed, some in a huff, but all of them taking their money.

"Wait!" Hector begged. "My lords! My ladies! Nothing is wrong here!"

"I bid two silver fingers," Aisa called from her new position near the tank.

Hector blinked at her. "Two—?"

"Indeed." Aisa held up the coins.

"That's below the starting bid, honey," Sharlee pointed out. She recognized Aisa, of course, but that didn't matter now.

"I have watched many slave auctions," Aisa replied calmly, "and I have learned the opening bid is nothing but a guide. I have also learned that when the bidding begins, you must, by law, accept any bid made in good faith. I have plenty of faith." Her face was bland, but Danr heard the quiet contempt in her voice. Danr slapped the table in front of him, and everyone looked at him.

"My lady placed a bid," he rumbled. "Two fingers."

"You have to accept the bid, you do," the mayor said from his own seat. Danr had all but forgotten about him. "We all heard you open the bidding and that's the law, the law."

"We must follow the law," Karsten said, not bothering to hide a smile.

Hector looked desperately around the room and swallowed hard. "My lord?" he said to Karsten.

"I'd like to help," Karsten said, "but the law is the law."

"The young lady has bid . . . two fingers. Do I hear . . ." Hector had to force himself to speak, and Danr kept a tight smile off his face. ". . . three?"

Every eye was riveted on the goings-on. The mermaid lay listlessly at the bottom of her tank. Someone dropped a spoon, and it rattled loudly on the stone floor.

"No other bids?" Hector said desperately. "Are we sure, lords and ladies? Going once, then." He paused in hope. "Twice? Three times." He sighed. "Very well. S—"

"Four fingers!"

Everyone turned to look. The bidder was the dwarf, the one dressed all in red. Danr stared, doubly startled. What game were the Obsidia playing at? The dwarf worked for them.

"He is a servant," Ranadar called in a haughty voice. "He doesn't belong here."

"Among the Stane, I'm just as noble as you, elf," the dwarf growled back. "I bid four fingers."

"Four fingers," repeated Hector quickly. "I have four fingers. Do I hear—"

"Five," Aisa jumped in.

"Twenty," said the dwarf. His voice was hoarse and deep. "The mermaid belongs with a proper owner, one who can appreciate her. Definitely not a woman who doesn't know to keep quiet in public or a half-blood whose mother took a troll to her bed because she couldn't find a pig."

"You dare," Kalessa hissed, reaching for her enchanted sword.

The words hit hard. Danr's fist clenched. Insults to himself he had dealt with his entire life, but his mother was something else entirely. Before he could consider the idea further, he closed his right eye and peered at the dwarf with his true eye.

The dwarf flashed into full view, and Danr saw through

the red silk and velvet. He saw pieces of the dwarf's past and present. With everyone watching, Danr stumped over to the dwarf with a friendly little smile on his face and tapped his cheek under his eye with a thick fingernail, ignoring the staring crowd, who was having the best night ever.

"Go ahead," he murmured, "and ask me what I see."

"What. . . . what you saw?" the dwarf echoed, a little nervous now.

Danr decided to take it as a question. He kept his voice low. "You make golems, and no one knows if they're alive or not, if you're creating life or not. You don't know it, either. That bothers you, but you're afraid and you need money, so you sell your craft like a Rookery prostitute. And you're afraid of the Obsidia, so you sell yourself to them, even though someone else offered you more money." He leaned closer. "But you don't have to, friend Stane. All you need to do is walk away. You can go home to the cool darkness, to your old, comfortable workshop, where all the corners are worn smooth and where the forge is always hot. Just walk out that door and don't look over your shoulder. Leave the mermaid to us. I'll arrange for Queen Vesha herself to protect you from the Obsidia."

The dwarf hesitated, and for a moment Danr was sure he was going to turn and leave. Then he crossed his arms. "I don't need the protection of a half-blood." He looked at the auctioneer. "My bid is still twenty!"

Shit, Danr thought. Aisa only had thirty fingers of silver to bid with. Now Hector was smiling. In that instant, Danr saw that the entire auction had been a scam from the beginning. Even Hector's distress had been false. The Obsidia had never intended to sell the mermaid in the first place, and they had given their loyal dwarfish servant a pouch filled with gold to ensure that she would stay in their possession. The auction was an empty show, and Danr's plan had been a mere hiccup along the way. But what had it been for? The mermaid shifted weakly at the bottom of her tank as Danr cast about for something to do.

"The mermaid is sick, friend," he said, still having to try. "What if she dies before the week is out? My friend here wants to—"

"Twenty-five," the dwarf said, louder.

"You already hold the maximum bid," the harbormaster said. "Why bid more?"

"Thirty," Aisa called.

"One hand." The dwarf produced a gold coin and held it up. Aisa's face fell and Danr's heart went with it. He looked at the prince in mute appeal, but the prince set his mouth regretfully.

"One hand is the bid," said Hector, playing up a patently false relief for the entranced crowd. "Once? Twice? Three times?" He clapped his hands sharply. "Sold to the Stane in red."

In the pandemonium that followed, Danr slipped up to the mayor. "Do you know where the Obsidia live?"

The mayor looked up at him. "I do, I do."

The morning sky had grown heavy, and a salty wind was soughing in from the Iron Sea to the west. Bits of rain tapped the ground. In a grassy courtyard, water sloshed as two golems hauled the listless mermaid from the tank and dragged her, dripping, across a perfectly manicured lawn to a pool of salt water while the red-clad dwarf squinted at them from under a maple tree. The mermaid's tail left a trail across the grass. She was quite beautiful, even with, or perhaps because of, the mask of blue and black tattoos that covered her face. Marble rimmed the pool's edges, and the little brass fish that seem to be a requirement of every ornamental pond in the world spouted streams of water into it.

The golems gently dropped the mermaid in. She sank beneath the surface while the golems, who had been given no new orders, stayed at the edge. The dwarf was battling a fierce headache from even the weak sunlight, and he wanted nothing more than to disappear into the cool, welcoming depths of the basement and sleep.

The mermaid regained her energy quickly in the fresh, clean water. She shook her head, and then, before the dwarf could quite follow what was going on, she shot halfway out of the water, grabbed one of the golems, and dragged it into the pool. The golem! The precious, precious golem! It had taken him weeks to construct it! He knew every inch, every fingerprint he had left on the clay, every bit of magic and machinery that made up the interior, every rune on its surface, every drop of blood it had taken to grant it life. The dwarf skittered to the water's edge, then stopped himself, not wanting to get too close. The second golem didn't react.

"Connect to your brother golem and report what is happening," he barked at it.

The dwarf had used the same blood—his own—to bring the golem's to life, which allowed the two of them to share certain properties. From the golem's azure eyes projected a silent image, half-size, of the bottom of the pool from the first golem's perspective. The mermaid had broken the golem's arm off and was beating it over the head.

The dwarf put both his hands on top of his head in consternation. It felt as if the mermaid had torn off his own arm. "Tell it to leave the pool!"

From the bottom of the pool, the golem strode in slow motion for the side of the pool, but the mermaid darted in like a shark to whack it on the knee with its own arm, causing more damage and slowing it down. The dwarf howled. "Tell it to hurry!"

More rain was falling, but the sky was saving the big

show for later. "My brother golem is moving as fast as it can, master," the golem said. "Shall I tell it to fight back?"

"Yes!" The red-clad dwarf was hopping with agitation now. "Tell it!"

The golem projecting the image cocked its head. The golem in the pool shot out an arm and caught the mermaid around the throat. Her shriek was muffled by the water. She thrashed and fought, but the injured golem's grip was too strong. Her tattooed face bore an expression of terror. The dwarf smiled.

"Now," the dwarf said, "tell it—"

"Tell it," interrupted a new voice, "to let the mermaid go and leave the pool as best it can without injuring the mermaid in any way. Now."

"Yes, master," said the second golem, and in the pool the first golem obeyed—or tried to.

"And you, Hokk, should know better," continued Hector Obsidia mildly. He was still wearing his black evening clothes.

Hokk the dwarf spun and jerked into a bow. "My lord," he quavered. "I was just trying to preserve your property. I didn't mean—"

"The only reason I'm not sending *you* into that pool to help the golem out," Hector said thoughtfully, "is that I need you to make more golems."

"She *is* a beautiful specimen," Sharlee Obsidia observed, peering into the thrashing water from a safe distance. A stiff breeze rustled her night-black dress, and the leaves on the trees flipped to show their pale undersides. "Her ailment seems to have cleared completely. Really, I expected something better from Aisa than the old trick of making a slave look sick in order to bring the price down. I do wonder what she poured into the tank, though."

"Your eye for detail is a delight as always, my love," said Hector. "However, I have to say that you missed the troll boy's true eye. He turned it on me in the tavern, and I found it an extremely . . . uncomfortable experience."

"Darling!" Sharlee was instantly at his side. "What did he say? Did it hurt?"

Hector's face was a stone. "He said I was rich and that I carried insatiable darkness and hunger inside me."

"But none of that is news!" Sharlee cried. "That dark ambition is one of the things I love best about you. That and your perfect taste in a wife."

"I agree with you," Hector said peevishly. "But it wasn't his place to *say* it."

"Oh." Sharlee took his hand and stroked the back. "Then once we get what we need from him, we'll crush him. *I* will crush him. For you."

Hector gave her a fond smile and stroked her hair as the rain fell a little harder. "You always know what to say, my shining star. But now I have to deal with our dwarfish friend."

Here, Hokk stiffened.

"I think a onetime reduction in salary equal to twice the amount it will cost to fix this golem will be sufficient punishment." Hector paused, his arm still around Sharlee. "That, and ten lashes by the golem itself, once you've finished repairing it."

"I want to watch," Sharlee whispered in his ear. "And I want you to watch me watch."

Hokk the dwarf paled beneath his red swaddling. "But, my lord—"

"Twenty, then," Hector said amiably. "We'll watch for the bone to appear. Is there anything else you wish to add?"

"Please do," murmured Sharlee.

Hokk looked down at the grass. "No, my lord."

The golem hauled itself uncertainly out of the pool, using one arm and favoring its bad leg. It was followed by the sort of spitting sound a whale might make, and the golem's arm flew out of the pool to land at the dwarf's feet. Sharlee turned away from Hector and regarded it thoughtfully.

"Hokk," she added, "I believe my husband may be persuaded to curtail part of your punishment if you repair the golem by tomorrow morning."

The dwarf straightened. "Yes, my lady." He snatched up the arm and led the golem away.

"Now, why did you do that, my dear?" Hector asked. "You said you wanted to watch."

Sharlee kissed him on the cheek. "You never do learn about people, do you? You must punish with one hand, which makes them fear and loathe you, and with the other hand, you must lighten the punishment, which changes the loathing into love even when the lash falls. In the end, he'll beg you to beat him. We do need more dwarfs, eventually."

"Ah! Very good," Hector said with a clap of his hands. "I should know better than to doubt you, my Sharlee."

Sharlee patted back a yawn—it had been a long night—and wandered over to the pool. "How long before they come, do you think?"

"They'll come tomorrow night," Hector replied. "They've found our house by now, and are examining the place as we speak. They'll snatch a few hours of sleep next, make another trip to see the house in the afternoon, draw up their plan in the evening, and drop by after sunset."

"Are you sure they won't come tonight?" Sharlee said. "I could pop down to the Docks right now and wake Captain Greenstone."

"That can wait until tomorrow," Hector assured her. "If Danr were working alone, I might be worried, but we're talking about a group, and groups tend to be more cautious. It'll be tomorrow night."

"Then in the morning we'll have breakfast out here in the garden by the pool, despite the storm, so we can enjoy the mermaid before she leaves us, and then I'll go down to the docks. Captain Greenstone won't need much persuading when I remind her what she owes us."

The wind rose again. "Never give your enemies a choice," Hector agreed. "Never do."

Ranadar, minus the stupid robe, finished his circuit of the house. It was a *big* house, deep within Old City. Old City housed commoners who came from old money and nobility who couldn't afford the sumptuous Diamond District, which housed the Gold Keep. It was broad daylight, if cloudy, and the street was heavily trafficked—horses with laden carts, wealthy carriages, donkeys with pannier baskets, servants in livery, slaves with bands around their necks or wrists. The noise of clopping hooves and clattering wheels and shouting people swirled about him, mingling with the manure and urine in the streets—no sewers here as there were in Palana. Disgusting. Humans had no idea how to run a city. And was that a troll out in broad daylight? Even with a hat and heavy cloak to protect it from the sun, it thundered through the streets like a falling tree, and everyone ignored it except to get out of the way. Now that the mountains had opened up, Balsia was too welcoming for its own good. He snorted to himself. Humans tolerated full-blooded Stane in their cities but spat venom at half-bloods. Ranadar wondered if he would ever understand the Kin.

Ranadar pulled the hood of his cloak a little lower and concentrated on keeping the glamour up. This was difficult with all the iron about, but he managed. When people passed him by on the street, they went around him without truly noticing him, the way they might go around a tree in the forest without paying attention to it. This wasn't true invisibility, but it would do.

The house Ranadar was scouting had three stories and was built of carefully mortared stone, itself surrounded by a high stone wall that took up most of the block. Ranadar failed to understand the need to build with stone. Stone was dead and dull and you could not change it easily. Wood was a much better choice. It had a life and voice and if you listened to it, the wood told you how it wanted to be shaped. Iron was even worse than stone. The awful black metal poisoned everything it touched, and some things it didn't. Ranadar could feel it everywhere in this human city, dragging at him and sapping his strength. He wasn't a particularly powerful magician, but he was still used to using at least a bit of glamour here and there, and it was damn hard in this idiotic city the humans had built. Half the time he had a headache, and the other half his stomach felt ready to empty itself on any available surface. He refused to complain, however. Even in exile, he was an elf and a prince, far above petty problems.

Besides, he had Talfi.

Rain came and went, pattering the cobblestones with tiny ant feet before it retreated. Ranadar could feel the tension sliding in from the Iron Sea, taste the salt on the air, sense the water on his skin. When the full storm arrived, perhaps it would wash away the stink and the manure, at least temporarily. He drifted through the street traffic. In his home forests of Alfhame, he had learned to slip into a herd of deer and wander among them without their notice, a skill many of his own kind had forgotten, and it came in handy here.

Around the front of the house, the house of the Obsidia couple, he abruptly encountered an enormous iron gate. The soap bubble glamour popped, and his gorge tried to come up. A pair of human women gasped at the sudden realization that an elf clad in green and brown had been standing in front of them all the while, and Ranadar turned his head to hide his face as the women bustled away. He swallowed burning acid and crossed the stones to get some distance from the iron.

The gate was wide enough for a pair of carriages. Beside it, a smaller gate was set into the wall so individual people could come and go without having to open the main gate. Through the poison bars, Ranadar glimpsed groomed gardens and perfect lawns—nature beaten into submission. It might as well be dead. Guarding the gate was a pair of golems. That showed real wealth. Only the dwarfs could make golems—tireless, obedient, incorruptible workers who cost twenty times the most expensive slave. They were also highly alert and all but impossible to sneak past.

Ranadar chewed his lip thoughtfully. According to the mayor, this was the Obsidia house, and the mermaid lay beyond that imposing iron. Ranadar had no feelings about the mermaid one way or the other. But the mermaid was important to Aisa, and *that* made her important to Ranadar. Aisa and Danr had been instrumental in bringing Talfi back to life after the Battle of the Twist, so if they wanted to rescue the mermaid, Ranadar would help rescue the mermaid. If Danr and Aisa wanted Ranadar to swim to the South Pole to hunt diamonds in the ice, Ranadar would do it. That was more than a little frightening—he was used to giving orders rather than taking them—but the exhilaration of having Talfi was utterly worth it.

Ranadar kept the memory of the first time he had met Talfi close inside him like a wyrm guarding gold treasure. Talfi had been a new slave in the palace, one among several, and Ranadar had been given the task of touching each one and infecting them with glamour, the addiction that made humans adore their elven owners and give them their utmost loyalty. Talfi stood before Ranadar in bronze shackles, his eyes downcast, and Ranadar lifted his chin so he could better look into Talfi's eyes. He had expected to meet fear, resignation, or perhaps even defiance, but when this slave's sky-blue eyes met his, Ranadar found . . . intrigue. That, and an open interest that went through Ranadar like a hot poker. Ranadar inhaled sharply.

"What . . . what is your name, slave?" he stammered.

"Talfi," the slave said, and the word rolled over Ranadar like silken thunder.

"Talfi," Ranadar repeated. "You are . . . mine."

And instead of sighing or weeping or begging, as most slaves did, Talfi only grinned a grin that made the skies open wide. "As you wish, my lord."

Eventually, Ranadar took Talfi on as his personal body slave, and they were rarely apart. Talfi became Ranadar's *Talashka*, and Ranadar became Talfi's uppity elf, but only when no one could hear.

They still had to be circumspect. Elves could keep human playthings, but actual emotion toward one was considered filth. Unfortunately, as a prince who normally did as he pleased, Ranadar was unused to keeping secrets. His father even tried to warn him once. One spring while they were standing on the shore of Lake Nu, Father pointed to a swarm of insects and said, as if in idle conversation, "Look at the mayflies there. They hatch, mate, and die, all within a single day, while we remain behind. And some of them—" As if on cue, a trout rose from the depths and gulped down a number of flies at once. "—die prematurely. That is a pity indeed, especially for those left behind to watch."

Ranadar ignored the hint. He could not imagine a world without Talfi, and therefore such a world could not exist. One cool spring night, Talfi whispered that he could not imagine a world without Ranadar, either, and their hearts became forever one. They were young and they both knew with every fiber of their beings that love would find a way around even death.

Only a week later, the door to Ranadar's rooms banged open and both Father and Mother strode in like a pair of thunderheads. Behind them flitted a glowing sprite named RigTag Who Sings Over the Stormy Sky. Ranadar leaped out of bed, outraged and frightened, leaving Talfi tangled in the bedclothes behind him.

Father seized Talfi by the hair and yanked him naked out of the bed. Talfi, unable to resist the touch of an elf, dropped to the floor. "RigTag Who Sings Over the Stormy Sky overheard you talking, Ranadar," Father snapped. "This human called you *uppity*, and you used a term of endearment with him in return. Is that true?"

"True blue, who knew?" giggled RigTag Who Sings Over the Stormy Sky.

Ranadar opened his mouth to lie, then felt the truth glamour settle over him. Father was a powerful magician, and he had RigTag Who Sings Over the Stormy Sky to feed him power. Ranadar tried to fight the truth, but the power was too strong.

"It is true," his mouth said.

Mother's lips tightened and the tendons on her neck stood out. Father sighed. "Do you love him, *Ranashka*?"

The word caught Ranadar off guard, as did Father's expression. Father had shown Ranadar no real affection for more than forty years now. The unexpected gesture broke Ranadar's resistance, and words came out in a rush.

"I do, Father, and he loves me. It is the truth."

"Truth of youth, in sooth," said RigTag Who Sings Over the Stormy Sky.

"You know that in no time at all he will grow into a decrepit old creature," Mother said, "with rheumy eyes and

wrinkled skin and spotted hands and clawed fingers and
shriveled organs. And that he is not Fae, with no real thoughts
or feelings of his own."

"That is not the truth," Ranadar said. He looked down at
Talfi, his *Talashka*, who was kneeling uncertainly on the
wooden floor. "Talfi thinks and feels just as I do. And we
will deal with the problems of age when the time comes."

Father nodded once. "Perhaps it is best to deal with
it now."

In one quick move, he drew a bronze knife, pulled back
the unresisting Talfi's head, and slashed his throat. Before
Ranadar quite understood what was happening, Talfi was
falling to the floor, clutching at his neck in a growing puddle
of blood. He looked at Ranadar with sky-blue eyes, shuddered hard, and died.

Ranadar left the palace, unable for decades to even share
a room with his parents. He put aside the rich robes and
wealthy chambers of the court and instead roamed the forests of Alfhame, looking for he knew not what. His parents
showed no concern. In two or three hundred years, they were
sure, he would come to his senses and return to the duties of
a proper prince. Ranadar felt sure this would never happen.

But then, one hundred and forty-seven years later, on a rare
and chance visit to the palace at Palana, he had heard RigTag
Who Sings Over the Stormy Sky arguing with someone at the
trader's door. To his complete shock, he found an orc woman
with slaves for sale, including one who looked and sounded
exactly like his *Talashka*. Ranadar had, at first, refused to believe it. The slave must be a relative, or this was a wild coincidence. Even if Talfi had somehow survived in secret, he would
still have died of old age long ago.

But no, it had been Talfi, his *Talashka*, back from the dead,
able to return from the dead every time he died because of the
Iron Axe. And Ranadar had been worried that *he* would

outlive *Talfi*! Until Danr had been forced to kill Talfi a final time to free the Axe's power and Ranadar had, once again, been forced to watch him die with no hope of return.

It was no wonder that later, when he stood before Death herself, he had immediately offered up half his remaining days to Talfi so that he could come back. Even now, a year later, his head still spun with the implications, though when he woke up next to Talfi every morning, he found it worth every day. Perhaps, in some cases, love was indeed stronger than death itself, but only after Death had collected her sacrifice.

Lightning forked across darkening clouds, and thunder boomed against Ranadar's bones. People glanced uneasily upward. At the house, the smaller front gate opened and from it emerged that dwarf, still clad in red. Ranadar came quietly alert. Twice in one day this dwarf was out in sunlight, occluded though it was by storm clouds. What role did the dwarf have in all this? He had essentially bought the mermaid back for the Obsidia, that much was obvious, but why? Perhaps it was meant to be a fail-safe in case the bids weren't high enough, as had turned out to be the case. If it were, Hector and Sharlee Obsidia must be master chess players. Or perhaps the Obsidia hadn't wanted to let anyone buy the mermaid in the first place. But if that was true, why put her up for auction? To curry favor with someone? They were missing something, and Ranadar itched to know what it was.

He glanced over his shoulder at the golems, which were closing the little gate, and an idea began to form. Thinking quickly, he followed the dwarf at a slight distance. The golems recognized the dwarf. They let him come and go freely, either because he lived there or because he worked for the owners. That made the dwarf a way inside. If only—

"What are you doing?" hissed Kalessa in his ear, and Ranadar jumped. She had slipped up behind him in the crowd. "We are watching the house, not strolling toward the Merchant District."

"I am watching, he is strolling," Ranadar hissed back, more than a little miffed that Kalessa had managed to creep up on him. "That dwarf might get us into the house."

Kalessa fell into step beside him. She also wore a hooded cloak, though Ranadar wondered how well the disguise would work—he still caught glimpses of her green-tinted skin and golden eyes. Orcs were unnerving under the best of circumstances, and Kalessa showed a casual love of violence that alarmed Ranadar. One would think that a people as short-lived as the orcs would hoard what little life they were given, but orcs often seemed to welcome death, and Kalessa was no different.

"How can this dwarf get us into that house?" she demanded.

The dwarf was definitely heading toward the market. Hmm. "I can't spin a glamour that will hide all of us from everyone. But if I had a bit of that dwarf's blood, I could spin a glamour that would hide us from the golems. Unfortunately, I fail to see how we can get his blood."

"I see," Kalessa said.

Another peal of thunder. They were entering the merchants' and mongers' section now. No simple stalls and unsightly wagons allowed here. Shops and stores were the rule, each with a wooden sign that said in words and symbols what was sold inside. The dwarf was heading toward an ironmonger's shop, no doubt to buy something for a project.

"Wait around that corner," Kalessa added. "I will return."

"Wait!" Ranadar said. "Where are—"

But she had already trotted away. Swearing, Ranadar faded into a smelly alley and watched as Kalessa strode up behind the dwarf at the ironmonger's front door just as the dark skies opened and water poured down. Kalessa's knife, the enchanted one that could turn into any blade, leaped into her hand and with practiced speed, she slashed the back of the dwarf's upper arm, tearing his sleeve and cutting his skin. The dwarf squawked in pain and surprise. He spun around, but Kalessa was loping away, and the people on the street were mostly trying to escape the rain. In a few seconds, Kalessa rejoined Ranadar in the alley, which was already ankle-deep in mud. She brandished the bloody end of her blade under the shelter of her cloak.

"Will this do?" she asked.

"Er . . . yes." Ranadar wiped water from his face. "Why did you do that?"

"Sometimes," she sighed, "you Fae think overmuch."

Chapter Seven

Wind tore at the windows of the rooming house and rattled the shutters while water eked in around the edges. Aisa paced within the confines of her room. Danr watched her warily.

"It is nearly midnight," she raged. "We know where the mermaid is, but the storm traps us here."

"It will pass," Kalessa said philosophically. "We will find her."

"I failed her," Aisa said. "The tincture of foxglove and marigold made her ill, but the trick still failed. It is my fault she is still a slave."

Danr took her hand. It was small and callused in his. "Don't beat yourself up, Aisa," he said. "It's not the fault of the people who're trying to help her."

She looked at him. The moment stretched out, longer and longer, and he didn't want it to end. He smelled smoke from the fire, felt the heat from her hand, saw the deep brown of her eyes. Then she took her hand back and looked away. "I know that here," she murmured, tapping her head, "but not here." And she tapped her heart.

Kalessa, who was still drying herself out by the fire, gave a small cough. "We still do not know why the dwarf bought the mermaid back for the Obsidia."

"Do we know that's what he did?" asked Talfi from his perch at the edge of the bed. "Maybe he really did buy her for himself."

"No." Kalessa waved a hand. "No one with enough wealth to buy and keep a mermaid would be working as a servant for someone else, and he is very much a servant."

"It's really obvious Hector and Sharlee Obsidia never meant to sell her in the first place," Danr rumbled. He could still feel Aisa's hand in his. "So what are they up to?"

"It almost certainly has something to do with the way Sharlee drugged Aisa," put in Ranadar. "What did she learn from you, Aisa?"

"Nothing important," Aisa said quickly. "We must move, before Hector and Sharlee move the mermaid."

"Maybe we should go out despite the storm," Talfi said.

Ranadar shook his head. "It will wash the dwarf's blood away. We must simply wait until—"

The rain stopped as if a bucket had been emptied. The damp weight left the air, and the wind died down.

Aisa polished her nails on her blouse. "You were saying, O wise one?"

Danr, who had grown up much farther north, far from the volatile weather tossed in by the sea, checked the window in amazement. "Will it start up again?"

"Not until the next one, whenever that is." Ranadar held out his hand to Kalessa. "Your knife. Make it bronze, if you please."

"Are you asking to play with my blade, elf?" Kalessa asked archly.

"Only with your permission, my lady." Ranadar kissed the back of her hand.

"You are an orc woman flirting with a *regi* elf," Aisa observed.

"One who's attached," Talfi added.

"How far the mighty have fallen," Aisa finished.

"I do need to get out more." Kalessa sighed and handed Ranadar her knife, the one that had stabbed the dwarf. The blade, now bronze, still bore streaks of blood. Ranadar turned to Talfi.

"This will not hurt." He touched the flat of the blade to Talfi's forehead, leaving a bloody smear, and spoke some words. A blink of light, and Talfi was no longer there. Instead a dwarf stood in his place, and in Talfi's clothes. Now that his features were uncovered, Danr could see the dwarf had slightly bulging eyes and a long, thin nose matched by a long chin. A black beard spilled down his—Talfi's—tunic, and unkempt hair made a bushy mess on his head. His hands reminded Danr of trowels with fingers, and his back had a slight hunch. Danr whistled under his breath. The others moved closer to admire. The dwarf looked up at them. His face was the dwarf's, but his expression was definitely Talfi's. It was eerie.

"Very nice," Aisa said. "How did you make the clothing fit? I was half expecting him to be naked."

"That would be awkward," the dwarf said in Talfi's voice, and that made Danr's skin crawl.

"It's a glamour, not a change of shape," Ranadar replied. "I know what Talfi's clothing looks like, but I didn't understand the dwarf's appearance until I had the blood."

"Will this glamour fool a golem?" Kalessa asked.

Ranadar nodded. "That was the whole point. It was cast with blood, so it will."

On impulse, Danr closed his right eye and looked at Talfi with his true eye. The dwarf vanished, leaving Talfi in his place. When Danr opened his eye, the dwarf reappeared.

"My true eye sees right through it," Danr reported.

"Then it is fortunate the golems do not have true eyes," Ranadar observed. "Your turn, my orcish princess."

He smeared Kalessa's forehead with the blood, and in an instant, an exact copy of the dwarf took her place, except this one wore woven leather armor.

"How do I look?" the dwarf said in Kalessa's voice.

Aisa burst out laughing. "Oh my! Hearing a woman's voice come out of that body . . . Kalessa, you and I had better say as little as possible."

"Is that how you keep an orc quiet?" Talfi observed.

"It is a fine thing for you that your lover has my knife," Kalessa said, but it was hard for her to keep a straight face—she was arguing with her dwarfish twin.

Ranadar smudged Aisa's forehead next, creating a dwarf in the loose skirt and blouse Aisa preferred. Here, Danr laughed. "Er . . . maybe you should wear something else?"

Aisa the dwarf twirled, and her beard stood out. "Is this not what dwarfish women are wearing this season?"

"Just put on a cloak for the trip to the house," Ranadar said tightly. He was sweating a little now. "We only have to fool the golems, and they will not care what we are wearing."

He reached up to swipe Danr's forehead with the blade. Danr felt a slight tingle. All the other dwarfs in the room clapped their hands over their mouths in startlement or silent laughter.

"That was so strange!" Aisa said. "You are short now!" She reached out to touch the air above where the dwarf's head would be and touched Danr's chest. He automatically took her hand and pressed it to his heart. Even though it looked like a stumpy dwarf's hand, it felt like hers.

"I'm here," he said simply.

"Oh, that hurts." The Talfi dwarf rubbed his eyes. "Your hands are in the wrong place, but also in the right place. I can't make it work."

Ranadar smeared the last of the blood on his own forehead and became a dwarf in brown and green silk. He handed the knife back to the Kalessa dwarf, who sheathed it. "We need to move quickly," he said gruffly. "I can only hold this for a short time."

They hurried down the back stairs so the other inhabitants of the house wouldn't notice them. Outside, the sky had cleared, leaving crisp, bright stars. Danr, who could see perfectly well in the dark streets, took the lead. Fortunately, the house where the mermaid was being held wasn't that far away, and the streets were all but deserted at this time of night, allowing them to move with speed, though once they heard tromping feet. The entire group of them pressed against a house and stared wide-eyed at half a dozen trolls trudging down the street. Each troll topped Danr by a good three feet, and their arms were heavy as glacier ice. They were pulling great wagons loaded with what smelled like clay. The one in front, clearly the leader, caught sight of the group, and Danr's heart stopped.

"Heading for the Bosha Temple?" the lead troll called out without stopping.

"No," Danr replied truthfully.

"We'll be there later," Talfi jumped in, making his voice gruff. "Lots of clay, huh?"

"You would know," the lead troll said, continuing on his way with the others.

"What was that about?" Kalessa asked when they were out of earshot. "Why are they bringing clay to the temple of Bosha, and why would *we* know anything about it?"

"They think we're dwarfs," Danr reminded her.

"I still do not see any significance. Did you not tell us Prince Karsten allowed the trolls into Balsia to dig sewers? What do sewers have to do with cartloads of clay?"

"We must move along," Ranadar interrupted.

The elf was all but panting when they arrived at the high wall that surrounded the stone house.

"Will you be all right?" Talfi asked in a worried voice.

"Just keep moving," Ranadar replied tightly.

Inside the iron gate, a golem stood guard. Aisa walked straight up to it and waved her hands. The golem didn't respond. Kalessa drew her knife and it flicked into a full-length sword. She feinted at the golem through the bars. It still didn't react.

"A fine job with the glamour," Kalessa said with satisfaction. "But how will we get inside?"

Danr strode up to the small iron gate beside the large one, grasped the bars, and heaved. The muscles on his arms bulged and the bars dug into his fingers. The iron gave, then bent open with a quiet *screech*.

"All in," he said.

"I forget just how strong you are," Kalessa said, and slipped through the opening. Aisa followed with a smile of approval that made Danr's heart swell with pride, even if the smile came from a dwarf in a dress. Then Talfi went.

"I cannot go through." The Ranadar dwarf was still standing some distance from the gate. "If I touch the iron, it will disrupt my spell."

"They touched iron," Danr said.

"They are not holding the spell together."

"Right." Danr strode back to him. "Brace yourself."

Without further warning, he picked Ranadar up. The glamour flummoxed Danr a little until he hit on shutting his right eye so he could see the elf's true form. Then he tossed

Ranadar lightly over the wall. There was a soft yelp and a thump.

"Are you all right?" Danr whispered.

A number of curse words followed. Danr assumed they meant yes, and he ducked through the gate himself. The golem standing guard, meanwhile, didn't seem to notice. It didn't even move.

On the other side, Talfi was helping Ranadar to his feet. Aisa and Kalessa had spread out to scout. All of them were still in their dwarfish glamours.

Danr felt large and conspicuous, even in the darkness. His troll's eyes could see quite well in the starlight, and it was nice not to be speared with pain every time he glanced at the sky, but it was nervous work being here. The great house loomed like a stone dragon over a treasure of carefully sculpted bushes and well-laid flower beds. Crickets, emboldened now that the rain had ended, chirped softly all about. Danr heard faint splashing.

"This way," he whispered, and led the others around the side of the big house. The windows were dark, thank Rolk, and they came across only a single golem, which ignored them completely.

"We have to hurry," the Ranadar dwarf said through clenched teeth. "The glamour will fail soon."

"Hold on." The Talfi dwarf took his hand. "You can do it, Ran."

Aisa and Kalessa moved ahead without comment. Kalessa had her blade out. It was in the form of a curved sword— bronze so it wouldn't bother Ranadar.

In the rear garden, they found a large open space. A pavilion with a canvas roof had been erected there, and just past it lay both the mermaid's tank, now empty, and a pool filled with water that reflected the stars. Danr's heart gave a little jump. This had to be it, and no one seemed to be around. They could get out quickly, without trouble. Aisa would be happy, and then they could go off to find Grandfather Wyrm to regain the Kin's power of the shape. For the first time in his life, Danr would be fully human, fully accepted, and able to live a normal life.

Aisa hurried over to the stone-lined pool. Kalessa, however, caught up with her and yanked her back. "You do not know, sister, how the mermaid will react."

As if in response, a great splash erupted near Aisa's feet. Aisa gasped. A moment later, the mermaid's head and shoulders appeared amid a ring of ripples. The tattoos masking her face gave her an angry, savage look.

"Who are you, dwarf?" she hissed.

Aisa, still in her dwarfish disguise, knelt at the edge of the pool. "I am a human, not a dwarf. This is a spell that allows me and my friends to slip past the golem guards. My friends and I have come to bring you out of this place."

The mermaid considered this. "Any place is better than there. I will go with you."

Danr exhaled, and Aisa relaxed, too. He hadn't thought the mermaid might refuse.

"What is your name, not-dwarf?" The mermaid glided closer across the smooth water of the pool.

"I am Aisa," she said. "This is Ham—his name is Danr." Aisa pointed at the others and made quick introductions. "I have long wished to actually touch a mermaid."

"My name is Ynara." The mermaid put out a dripping hand. "Take my hand, cousin."

Aisa reached out. Danr discovered his heart was pounding. He understood how deeply important this was to her, and he felt proud and thrilled to stand next to her while she fulfilled one of her dreams. Her fingers stretched toward the mermaid's.

Ranadar screamed in pain. The dwarfish disguises vanished with a *pop*. Aisa, now human, snatched her hand back. Danr whipped around. Ranadar had gone down to the ground with the shaft of an arrow sticking out of his shoulder. Talfi shouted his name and knelt beside him.

"An iron arrowhead," Talfi cried. "They know we're here!"

"Intruders! Intruders!" A dozen rune-covered golems poured into the garden. Their molded faces and empty azure eyes were blank as stone, but they moved quickly, and they were stronger than even Danr. Kalessa managed three or four swings that carved pieces out of one golem before two others got her by the shoulders and disarmed her. Her blade thumped to the grass and changed back into a small knife. One golem grabbed Aisa, which sent Danr into a rage. He managed to pull the head off one golem, but four swarmed over him and forced him to his knees. Talfi hesitated, not sure if he should run or stay, and the moment cost him. A golem caught him in its stony grip. Ranadar proved no resistance whatsoever. The mermaid vanished to the bottom of the pool.

Hector and Sharlee Obsidia strolled into the garden. Sharlee was holding a bow. Behind them came the dwarf, still dressed in red.

"My golem!" the dwarf cried, and rushed over to the one Danr had pulled apart.

"So glad you made it!" Hector boomed.

"Darling! I wanted to say that," admonished Sharlee.

"You got to shoot the elf," the man reminded her, "so I get to make the entrance. Next time we'll do it the other way."

"Sharlee!" Aisa struggled in her golem's implacable grip. "Why are you doing these things? I thought we were friends."

"Never, honey," Sharlee purred. "I'm a little surprised

you didn't notice. Now you're going to do as you're told. Right down to the ship you take on your journey."

"What journey?" Danr demanded. The four golems held him with eight hands, all of them as hard and heavy as iron chains. Danr strained against them—he couldn't help himself—but they wouldn't move. "What do you want? Let Aisa go, and I'll give it to you."

"I know you will," said Hector. "And I'll be quick, because I know you appreciate that." He paused, giving lie to what he had just said. "We want you to bring us the power of the shape."

The words hung like poisoned water droplets in the air. No one spoke for a long moment. The friends traded confused looks.

"So I think you need to explain a little more," Talfi said from his own golem. "But let me get that arrow out of Ranadar first."

"And give him his glamour back? Hardly," Sharlee said.

Danr clenched his teeth. "Explain fast. You may think these golems are strong, but they're only clay, and clay breaks."

"No . . . ," moaned the dwarf. He was cradling the golem's head in his lap.

"This is the half-blood who looked at me with a true eye and told me how to behave." Hector strolled over to Danr and looked up at him. "You may have beheaded a city of elves, boy, but it's not a half-blood's place to give me advice."

Calmly, as if he were picking a flower, he sank a fist into Danr's groin. Pain burst through Danr and coiled in his lower abdomen like a cold snake. He tried to double over, but the golems held him upright.

"Shit," Talfi muttered.

"I'll give *you* some advice, troll boy," Hector said in the same soft, amiable voice. "For months, I've had you watched, and I know you've spoken with Death since the Battle of the Twist. My wife told me that once I planted thoughts about the power of the shape in your head, you would go crying to Death about it. She has a soft spot for you, so she must have told you where to find it. You and your slattern will fetch the secret of the shape magic and you will bring it here to us, and only us."

"That is quite a chain of logic," Aisa said. "You take a lot for granted."

"No," Sharlee said. "You common people are terribly transparent to anyone who bothers to look."

"If we are so transparent," Kalessa said in a too-even voice, "how did you miss the fact that we would never go on such a journey for a pile of wyrm shit like you?"

Hector said, "Hokk, if you please."

Grumbling, the Hokk the dwarf produced a set of iron wrist shackles. With surprising deftness, he clapped them on Ranadar's wrists and drew the arrow out of Ranadar's shoulder. Ranadar cried out again, and once again, Talfi tried to escape his golem, to no avail.

"Let me go to him!" Aisa demanded as blood ran down Ranadar's shoulder.

"Of course. We aren't barbarians here," Sharlee said. "You'll find what you need in that pavilion over there."

To Danr's surprise, the golem released Aisa, who shot Danr a look before she hurried into the pavilion and came out with bandages, dressings, and other supplies. Her golem followed, remaining a pace behind.

"Here's what'll happen," Hector said. "We're giving you the mermaid. With our blessing."

"Because . . . ?" Danr asked suspiciously.

"Because she will guide you to the shape magic," Sharlee said. "That's why we had her captured in the first place.

We've already sent a number of slaves and servants and hire-lings to find the secret, and none of them ever came back. But you, Danr—you and Aisa are heroes of the Twist. It'll be a small thing to fetch us the power of the shape."

Danr worked his jaw. "There's going to be a threat here somewhere, I know it."

Sharlee gestured to the golem holding Ranadar. It hoisted the elf over its shoulder and without ceremony, tossed Ranadar into the empty mermaid tank. Ranadar, bound by the iron shackles, was barely able to land without injuring himself. Talfi shouted Ranadar's name.

"Water," said Sharlee to the golem. It trudged over to a well and windlass several paces away.

"What are you doing?" Aisa demanded.

The golem cranked the windless, hauled up a dripping bucket from the depths, extracted a cup from the bucket, and trudged over to the tank. It climbed the ladder, emptied the cup into the tank, and headed back to the well for more. Ranadar watched, but was too weak from the iron to do any-thing about it. A quiet horror stole over Danr.

"At the rate the golem is working," Hector said, "it will take four days and nine hours, give or take an hour, to fill the tank to the point where your friend won't be able to breathe, though that will depend on how well he can swim with those shackles on."

"You're the boy who lives forever," Sharlee said to Talfi. "If he dies, you're going to live a long, long time without your true love."

Hector asked Danr, "Will you let your best friend mourn a loss that will pain him even after your bones are dust?"

It was a direct question. "No," Danr said. "We'll get you the power of the shape. If you promise to let Ranadar go when we bring it."

"Danr!" Aisa said. "We can't trust them!"

"We'll find the power of the shape and bring it here," Danr repeated dully. "You have my word. And you know I can't lie."

"Indeed!" Hector clapped his hands. "I knew I could count on you! Didn't I say they would do it, Sharlee?"

"You did, darling. I've never met a more intelligent man."

"Which is less a compliment than you might think," Aisa sniped.

Hector ignored her. "So. You'll sail immediately. We have arranged for a ship—"

"What about the storms?" Talfi said.

"Captain Greenstone owes us a great deal." Sharlee glanced at the golem, which was climbing the ladder to the tank again. It dumped a second cup of water and tirelessly headed back to the well. "She'll brave the storms. With the merfolk's help, you'll muddle through, honey, I'm sure."

"But if we just wait a month or so," Danr said, thinking fast for once, "we could—"

"Are you familiar with the work of Carolan of Dansk?" Sharlee interrupted.

"I'm . . . not," Danr had to reply.

"Garon the Venerated? The Books of Dust? The story of Old Lady Pearl?"

Danr blinked at her. "No."

"Then you'll have to take our word, our carefully researched, very expensive word, that the power of the shape is in the Key, and the Key is only open during the stormy season."

"The Key?" Talfi said. "What in Vik's name is that?"

"You'll understand when you get there. You had better go now. The tide goes out at sunrise."

"Except"—Hector held up a hand—"the orc woman will also remain as our guest."

Kalessa's head came around. "What?"

"If you don't return in time and the elf drowns," Hector said, "we will empty the tank and start over with the orc, just to ensure that you don't give up. That gives you nine days, more or less. Be grateful for the extra time."

"Sister," Aisa breathed.

"Danr, honey," Sharlee asked, "I know your first thought is that you should run to Prince Karsten and tell him about this. Isn't that so?"

Damn it. Another direct question, and he couldn't avoid it. "Sure. Karsten likes me, and he's just looking for an excuse to dump the debt the crown owes you. The guard will arrest you for kidnapping, no matter how many golems you have, and I'll watch and laugh while they burn your house."

"I can't blame you," Sharlee said. "There are other factors you don't know about, but just to keep you honest, one of the other golems will shadow you out there and will remain in contact with one of the golems back here. We will always know who you talk to and what you do. If you betray us, both your friends will die immediately. Do you understand, half-blood hero?"

"Yes," Danr was forced to say.

"So you set up a fake mermaid auction just to lure us here?" Talfi said.

"I do love a good party," Hector said.

"Ludicrous," Aisa spat.

"Effective," Sharlee countered. "We needed to ensure that you knew where the mermaid was and that you'd try to sneak in without telling anyone where you were going so we could conduct our business in privacy. Honestly, Hector, these are the people who found the Iron Axe?"

"The irony," Aisa said softly, "is that we were already planning to seek the power of the shape. We would have brought it to you if you had simply asked as a friend."

Hector shook his head. "Never give your enemies a choice."

"Never make an enemy where you could have a friend," Danr corrected.

"Wouldn't it be nice if the world really worked that way?" Hector said.

The golem emptied another cup of water into the tank.

Chapter Eight

Ynara the mermaid didn't speak during the awful walk through the city to Bosha's Bay. Instead she clung to Danr's neck with arms of iron. She smelled of seaweed and saltwater, and not at all of fish as Danr expected. Her muscular tail curled around his body, and that felt weird, indeed it did. He was careful not to stare at her bare breasts. Aisa and Talfi followed, also without speaking. Danr was sure they were all thinking the same thing—that Ranadar's tank was filling with a terrible steadiness.

The golem followed as well. Its footsteps were even and precise, and its azure eyes glowed a faint blue beneath the runes carved into its head. Danr had no idea whether it was craft or magic or both that made it move and see and hear. He didn't much care. All he cared about was getting Ynara down to the docks so they could go on to the next step. One step at a time was the key. If he looked at everything at once—needing to return with the power of the shape before Ranadar died—it overwhelmed him with impossibility. But steps he could handle: bring the mermaid to the bay; find the ship; talk to the captain; sail to the Key; find Grandfather Wyrm; use the squid ink to bribe the power of the shape from him; return in time to keep Ranadar from drowning.

Was this to be his life, lurching from one crisis to another? He was a farmer, for Rolk's sake. A farm was home, and all he wanted was the simplicity of plowing rich earth in the spring, planting small seeds, and coaxing them to grow while a small herd of cows lowed in the upper pasture. Even better if that farm was close to the ocean so Aisa could befriend the merfolk. A calm, predictable life without visits to Death, without unexpected journeys, without kidnappings and threats.

"I hope he'll be all right," Talfi said, not for the first time.

"He will be," Aisa said firmly. "And so will Kalessa. We saved the entire world once, you know. Saving an elf and an orc will be simplicity itself."

Danr nodded in agreement, but felt a tiny flicker of gladness that it was Ranadar instead of Aisa in the tank, and then he felt guilty over that gladness. He certainly didn't want Ranadar to drown or even be hurt—the elf had proven a good friend and ally, even if he was a bit snooty. But Danr was still glad it wasn't Aisa, and he prayed Talfi never asked him a direct question about it.

"Are we nearly there?" Ynara asked. Her tail's grip around his waist was weakening. "The air is becoming painful."

"The docks are just ahead," Danr said. "You can probably smell the water."

"I can. It hurts to scent it and not be in it."

"How long can you last outside the water?" Talfi asked.

"It hurts after several minutes," Ynara replied. Her voice was low and musical, like liquid silver. "After an hour, I will probably lose consciousness. Once that happens, death follows quickly."

"Do you need to be immersed, or can you be doused?" Aisa asked. "I know little of the merfolk, and . . . I am curious."

"Dousing will delay death, but it is difficult to breathe the air for a long time, cousin." Ynara exhaled shakily against Danr's chest. She felt light, like foam. "My people once walked on land, you know."

"Before the Sundering, yes," Aisa said.

"A tiny few of my people still can." Ynara exhaled hard again. "The power of the shape still runs among some merfolk."

Danr halted in surprise. The golem stopped, too, and its eyes never left him. "Then maybe we could talk to them! It would be less dangerous than seeing Grandfather Wyrm. Can you take us?"

"It will not help you," Ynara sighed. "The merfolk who can change their shape can only do it once, and they cannot change back, and it is not a secret they can share. Either you are born with the talent, or you are not." She closed her eyes. They were masked by her tattoos. "We must hurry now."

"Sorry." Danr hustled forward again. The golem followed.

The streets around the Docks never quite slept. Enormous beer wagons, too big for day traffic, lumbered over the cobbles. One was pulled by a troll, though it looked like a toy behind him. Bakers worked at night so their wares would be ready by morning, and the smells of new bread mingled with oven smoke. Danr caught sight of more than one group of thugs, but when they saw Danr was a head taller, with muscles like a sack of cantaloupes, they sank back into the damp, chilly shadows.

Ships creaked and loomed in the dark like twisted trees. Some were hung with yellow lanterns. Occasional shouts and laughter floated about, and once, a distant scream. Each dock had at its head a statue of one of the Nine, starting with Olar, the king of gods, and moving through Grick, his queen, to Belinna and Fell (the warrior twins, who counted as one

god), Urko, Rolk, Kalina, Halza, Vik, and Bosha. Tikk, the
tenth god, was the Stane interloper and trickster who had
changed himself into a fly and perched on Grick's vulva so
he could appear at the moment Fell was born and be wel-
comed among the gods as Fell's brother before anyone
noticed the deception. Still, he had a dock, because no one
wanted to offend him. When an eleventh dock was built, the
city had put two statues of Olar on it, and called it Two Olar.
A twelfth dock became Two Grick, and so on. They were
now up to Four Halza. It had become customary for the
captain to make a donation to the temple of whatever god's
dock his ship was docked at. This caused a certain amount
of friction among the temples over the naming of any new
dock, since each one became an instant and steady source of
revenue.

Hector Obsidia had said the *Slippery Fish*, the ship he and
his wife had coerced, was moored at Three Bosha, and that
was where Danr headed. The mermaid became restless as he
padded closer to the water, and twisted almost frantically
when he passed the trio of knee-high Bosha statues at the
front of the dock. One statue showed Bosha in her aspect as a
mermaid. Four ships were moored farther down the dock.

"The water," Ynara whispered.

"Wait." Talfi put a hand on Danr's arm, and his face was
hard. "First, you have to swear that you'll take us to the Key,
that you won't just swim away and leave us."

"Talfi—" Aisa said.

"The Key?" Ynara's voice was barely audible. "You seek
the Key?"

"Swear!" Talfi said again. "Or Danr won't put you in the
water."

Talfi had a point. Danr halted, the mermaid still in his
arms. Her hair was dry, her tail was limp, and he wondered
if he truly could stand here on the dock and let her die in his

arms. The golem continued its dead blue stare. Were the Obisidia couple watching and listening right now? Laughing at them? Vik! He wanted to reach into the golem's head, through it, and grab Hector and Sharlee by their throats.

"Swear!" Talfi said again.

"I . . . swear," Ynara whispered.

Danr knelt at the edge of the dock and let Ynara drop from his arms into the murky water with a soft splash. For a moment she floated there, limp as a dead flower, her hair splayed about her head. Aisa put her hands to her mouth, and Danr touched her shoulder. Then Ynara jerked to life. Water exploded in all directions, catching Danr in the face with salty spray, and she was gone. The water rippled and smoothed around the dock pylons. Danr, Aisa, and Talfi watched the surface with concern.

"She will return," Aisa said. "She swore."

But there was no sign of the mermaid.

After several moments, Danr said, "I think we're on our own."

"She betrayed us," Aisa whispered. "I did not think she would do such a thing. Not a mermaid."

"The merfolk aren't perfect," Danr said. His hand was still on her shoulder. She reached up for it, and he knew she was drawing comfort from him. It made his throat thick.

"What do we do now?" Talfi asked.

Danr straightened, and Aisa dropped her hand. "We go to the *Slippery Fish*. Captain Greenstone may know where to go. If she doesn't, we'll sail into the Iron Sea until we find the Key ourselves."

"And what about Ranadar?" Talfi said.

"We'll just have to hurry." Danr looked at the sky. Dawn was coming, and he realized he was missing his hat—and other things. "Talfi, you're the fastest. Run back to Mrs. Farley's and grab some extra clothes. Don't forget my extra hat. And—I can't tell you how important this is—bring the bottle of squid ink."

Talfi put his hands in his hair. "Vik! I forgot all about that!" He turned and sped away, faster than anyone Danr had ever seen.

"That'll give him something to keep his mind off Rana-dar," Danr said. The sky was lightening now, and the docks were coming to life. Bells rang on the ships, and shouts from the sailors and merchants who sold to them rose from the docks.

"You think like a leader," Aisa said with a nod. "I am impressed."

Danr shook his head. "I'm no leader."

"You sell yourself short, my Hamzu," she said. "You are more far-sighted and intelligent than you give yourself credit for. Where is that ship?"

The *Slippery Fish* was moored at the end of the dock. The sailor on duty at the gangplank didn't want to let them on board until Danr mentioned the name Obsidia, where-upon he vanished through some kind of door, though Danr doubted sailors called it that. He knew as much about ships as he did about mining molten lava. The deck rocked a little beneath Danr's feet, which felt decidedly odd, as if it might decide to tip him over.

From the door emerged a woman. A large woman. She was nearly as tall as Danr, and certainly as wide and mus-cular. Short black hair framed her face beneath a heavy, wide-brimmed hat, and her lower jaw jutted pugnaciously forward, showing heavy lower teeth beneath a small nose. Her skin was swarthy, just like Danr's. She wore a loose white shirt belted over bright red trousers, but she went barefoot. Danr stared in disbelief. It was like looking in a twisted mirror.

"You're half Stane," he blurted out.

"Takes one to know one, kid," she grunted.

"By the Nine," Aisa breathed.

Danr felt as if he'd been poked in the stomach with a feather. "I thought I was the only one!"

"Really?" She raised a thick eyebrow. "You must have grown up in the ass crack of nowhere."

"I . . . well . . . ," Danr stammered.

"And why is my first mate standing around starin', Harebones?" she bellowed to the first sailor, who had followed her onto the deck. "We sail when the ball-licking tide goes out, so get those Vik-shit sailors up here!"

"Yes, Captain!" Harebones rushed away.

"You gotta keep an eye on those men," the captain said with a wink to Aisa. "Lazy sods who can't keep their hands out of their trousers, every one of 'em."

"Indeed," said Aisa.

"Sharlee, the armpit of Halza, told me we had to take passengers into the Iron Sea or she'd cuts my tits off with a dull knife, but I gotta say, I had no idea one of them would give Fell himself a run for it." She swept her hat off and, to Danr's consternation, took his hand and kissed the back of it. "Captain Greenstone at yer service."

"Uh . . ." was all Danr could manage. His face felt as if it might catch fire. He couldn't call Captain Greenstone pretty, but she owned the salty air around her, and ropes that came down from the masts seemed to lean out of her way. Something about her made him feel privileged just to be standing near her.

"The stammering one is named Danr," Aisa put in. "Our friend Talfi will arrive presently. The golem here has no name that I'm aware of."

"Golems." Captain Greenstone spat at its feet. The golem didn't respond. "Dwarfish spies and bad luck on a ship."

"Aren't Stane bad luck on a ship?" Aisa asked.

"Sure. Bad luck is why I'm in the debt of the Obsidia bitch." Captain Greenstone hadn't released Danr's hand yet. Danr wasn't sure what to do about that.

"My name is Aisa," said Aisa, coming between them so Greenstone would have to drop Danr's hand. "We are together."

"Really?" The captain raised an eyebrow again. "That's disappointing. Half the half-bloods I meet are uglier than I am, and the other half are rotten in bed. You got a brother, handsome?"

Danr was starting to regain his composure. He was handsome? Kalessa had called him that once, but he hadn't quite believed it. "Yeah, but he's a full troll and I don't see him much."

By now, sailors were boiling up from belowdecks. They swarmed around the deck, hauling ropes and raising sails and doing other things with the rigging that Danr's farmer eyes couldn't follow. Danr was surprised to notice that several of the crew were female, though now that he thought about it, this made certain sense on a ship with a woman captain.

"So why're we heading into the Iron Sea during storm season? The Obsidia bitch"—she leaned toward the golem when she said this—"weren't too specific."

"We need to find a place called the Key," Aisa said. "In the middle of the Iron Sea."

"Yeah, good. Where's that on a chart?"

Danr spread his hands and thought of Ranadar in the tank. "We were hoping you would know."

"I don't sail the Iron Sea if I can avoid it, handsome. A thousand years since the Sundering, and it's still stormy, even when it ain't storm season. Only the merfolk know the place."

"We had a merfolk guide, but she . . . left," Aisa said. "Perhaps we can speak to the merfolk in the Iron Sea."

"There's a time limit," Danr put in. "We—"

"Attention! New information," said the golem.

Captain Greenstone stiff-armed the golem and it flew backward, fetching up on its back on the deck. The sailors paused briefly amid the creaking ropes, then went back to their work. "Oops," the captain said. "Startled me. I didn't know it talked."

The golem got to its feet, unperturbed, and walked stiffly back to Aisa and Danr. "New information," it repeated. Light flowed from its jewellike eyes and coalesced on the deck. A miniature version of the tank with Ranadar in it appeared on the deck. The whole thing reminded Danr of the table he had found in the elven throne room in Palana. Ranadar sat wretchedly in the bottom of tank, which now had perhaps an inch of water in it.

"Nice," Captain Greenstone observed. "Who's that?"

"He's mine." Talfi jumped aboard from the gangplank with a pair of sacks over his shoulders, out of breath and red-faced. "Is he all right?"

"Just wet," Danr replied shortly, and the image vanished.

"You're Talfi, I take it," Greenstone said.

Talfi noticed the captain for the first time. "Holy Vik! Are you Danr's sister or something?"

"I think Aisa here wishes I were. You're a delicious-looking one." She leered at Talfi with comic emphasis. "Too bad you're with that elf. Or are you hooked on him because of a glamour? We could have him killed."

"Not glamour," Talfi said, looking up at her with a mixture of wonder and awe on his face. "Are we leaving soon? I'm trying not to go out of my head with worry."

"We'll leave as soon as the harbor guide— Wait!" Greenstone turned like a catapult in a turret and pointed at Danr, Aisa, and Talfi in succession. "Half troll. Human woman.

Human man. Elven lover. No glamour. Vik's balls! You're the Hero of—"

Danr clapped a hand over her mouth. "Don't! Don't say it."

Greenstone's eyes were wide under the brim of her hat. But she fell silent, and Danr cautiously took his hand away. Greenstone drew them closer to the door of her quarters, or whatever they were called, and glanced about. "I've heard a lot of stories," she said more quietly. "I want to hear the whole thing. A half-blood who . . . did what you did? You could help a lot of people, you know."

"What do you mean?" Danr said.

"People don't like our kind," she said. "If a half-blood who saved the world and stopped the Fae from taking slaves spoke up in our favor, maybe people wouldn't spit on us so much. And maybe we wouldn't have to be so bitchy and nasty all the time to get anything done." She raised her voice. "Roker! That foresail is crooked. Raise it right, or I'll nail your balls to the helm!"

"How many of us are there? I thought my father was the only troll who could come out from under the mountain," Danr asked, feeling a strange excitement. His heart beat faster. All his life, he'd thought he was the only one. The idea that there were more like him made him want to run and shout and look for more.

"There are hundreds of doors under the mountain, and even Queen Vesha doesn't know all of 'em," Greenstone said. "Look, there aren't a lot of us half trolls, just like there aren't a lot of half elves and half dwarfs and such, but we exist all right."

"Half *elves*?" Aisa said. "The Fae glamours sterilize humans."

"That takes months. You ask your lover boy when we get back, Talfi. A few citizens of Alfhame walk around with short ears under their hats, if you get my meaning. You know what it's like to grow up half-blood, handsome. Sometimes you hate yourself and want to hide who you are. If you can."

Danr nodded. He knew, oh yes, he did. The sun had half risen now, and the bright sky was becoming painful. He fished about in the sack Talfi had given him for his own hat and sighed with relief when the brim was shading his forehead.

"Any road," the captain continued, "we'll get under way as soon as the temple's harbor guide gets here."

"Harbor guide?" Talfi asked.

"Bosha's Bay is filled with snags and sandbars, friend. And that channel in and out at the mouth is narrow as an eel's ass. The priests of Bosha are the only ones who know their way around, and they charge your left nipple to pilot for you."

"A fine way to put it," said a deep, rich voice behind them.

Coming up the gangplank in flowing robes of white and pale blue velvet was Harbormaster Willem. His silver-white hair blew across his forehead, and his blue staff, topped by a gold dolphin with amethyst eyes, thumped the wood. Behind him came an entire retinue of beefy-looking priests, all clad in blue trousers and spotless white shirts. Sea met sky. Strangely, the smell of wet earth and clay clung to the them, and most of them had dirty hands. The priests folded their arms and waited patiently behind the man, who stopped at the head of the gangplank. Punsle, the worried-looking bald man, stood just behind Willem.

Danr stepped in front of Aisa and watched cautiously. Was nothing in his life simple?

"Harbormaster Willem?" Captain Greenstone sounded more than a little shocked. She whipped off her hat, so Danr did likewise, and the sun speared his eyes. "I wasn't expecting you. Give me half a mo', and I'll call my sailors to give you a proper welcome aboard."

"No need." The harbormaster boarded the ship and pointedly held out a fist adorned with his gleaming amethyst ring. Danr was in no mood, but he leaned down.

"It's actually customary to kneel," the harbormaster said. "You did it wrong before and looked foolish in the attempt."

Danr stared at him. The harbormaster's bearing had changed. He had been at least a little friendly at the prince's gathering, but now hostility lurked behind his eyes, and he was deliberately putting Danr in a difficult position. If Danr knelt, the Hero of the Twist was showing subservience. If he didn't kneel, he was showing a lack of manners. What was going on? Slowly, Danr got to one knee. The harbormaster gave a narrow smile. Danr took the harbormaster's fist, and planted the wettest, sloppiest kiss he could manage on the man's ring and fist. The harbormaster snatched back his dripping hand in horror. Talfi coughed hard to hide a laugh.

"It's a surprise to see you again, my lord," Danr said to him with a toothy smile, unable to say it was a pleasure.

The captain jumped in. "Might I ask what brings the harbormaster himself aboard my poor ship?" Greenstone seemed more than a little nervous, and this made Danr uneasy.

Punsle whipped out a handkerchief, and Willem hastily wiped his hand on it. "I'm here to pilot you out, of course," he said with a false jovial grin that failed to match his deep, buttery voice. At least he didn't seem inclined to offer his ring to anyone else.

"The harbormaster himself?" Greenstone said again, echoing Danr's thoughts. "Is there a reason?"

"Are you asking me if I need one, Captain?" Willem replied levelly. "Perhaps you're hiding contraband on this ship. Perhaps we should search it—and your crew. Thoroughly. We may need to pull the pegs out just to be sure nothing is hidden beneath the planks."

"No need, no need, great lord," Greenstone said, running

her hands around her hat brim. "Whatever you say. I was just curious."

"Keep your curiosity between your legs where it belongs, half-blood," Willem said with a wide white smile. "Acolytes! Take the ship!"

The priests on the gangplank swarmed over the deck and into the rigging like locusts devouring a wheat field. They elbowed Greenstone's crew aside, adding curses and blows when they didn't get out of the way quickly enough. The ropes creaked in protest, and the sails shuddered. Greenstone looked about, trying to conceal her horror.

"Great lord," she said meekly, "my own crew knows the *Slippery Fish* backward and forward. Maybe they could handle her with your men's direct—"

Willem pulled a belaying pin from its socket and cracked her across the face. Greenstone's head snapped back. On the deck, her sailors tensed and Aisa and Talfi flinched. Danr noticed for the first time that the priests were all carrying swords. They continued working, but he saw several of them touch their weapon hilts.

Greenstone staggered, then righted herself. A moment hung in the air, tense and angry. Then Greenstone bowed. "Apologies, great lord. Everything'll be as you order."

"Go to your cabin, troll." Willem's gray eyes raked her with flint knives. "And order your sailors to go below. We'll handle the ship like real humans."

"You heard the lord!" Greenstone bellowed. "Get below until you hear otherwise! Harebones—my cabin!"

The sailors, male and female, slunk belowdecks. Greenstone gave Willem one last look before retreating to her cabin with Harebones, the first mate, close behind. Danr and the others cast about at a loss, unsure where to go. Greenstone's door clicked shut, and the priests rushed about the creaking, groaning ship.

"That's how you handle a half-blood," Willem said to no one in particular.

Danr's hands twitched. For a wild moment, he considered snatching up the man and simply breaking his back. It would be easy. It would also be easy for the acolytes to bring him down with their swords. He let out a breath and forced back his temper. Aisa and Talfi exchanged nonplussed glances.

Willem ignored them and strode off, shouting orders to the men. Aisa pulled Danr out of the way, and he put his hat back on. Talfi followed. So did the golem.

"A fine man," she murmured. "What is he doing here?"

"I was going to ask you the same thing," Danr rumbled back. "He was different at the Gold Keep."

"It has to be something with us," Talfi said. "It's too big a coincidence. But what do we do about it?"

"I do not know." Aisa chewed her lip. "Ynara broke her word, we do not know how to find the key, Ranadar is in danger of drowning, and now this."

Danr put his hat back on and cracked his knuckles. "I could've thrown him overboard. Simple."

"That kiss was sufficient," Aisa countered. "Rolk only knows what his men would have done if you had given him a full bath."

"So." Talfi lounged against the rail. "Another half-blood."

Some of Danr's enthusiasm returned. "I know! I want to hear everything about her. Which side is which half? How did she become a captain? Where did she grow up? I've never met anyone like her before."

"There will be time for that," Aisa said shortly.

Danr cast an eye at her. Was she jealous? Hmm. For a moment, he was tempted to check her with his true eye. But once, long ago, he had done that very thing and Aisa had been deeply hurt by the invasion of her privacy. It had nearly destroyed their relationship. Danr had sworn he would never do it to her again, and so far he had kept his word. He wouldn't break it now. He did want to ask her straight out if she was worried Captain Greenstone might steal his affection away, was readying the very words. Then he stopped. Not here. Not now. Not with the harbormaster tromping around and strangers everywhere and the golem within earshot. And, he had to admit to himself, it had become a habit over the last few months for the two of them not to ask such questions, and it was easier simply to stay quiet.

Aisa brushed nonexistent dirt from the front of her blouse. "I think all we can do now is wait."

"It's going to be a long wait," Talfi said morosely.

The priests were more efficient than Danr expected. In a short time, the *Slippery Fish* was gliding carefully through the harbor with Willem's long white fingers curling around the helm. A pair of longboats trailed the ship to bring the priests back to shore once they handed the ship back to her sailors. Ahead lay the long sword of land that sheltered the bay from the rest of the ocean. Seagulls flocked overhead, screeching high and free. Cool salt air washed over Danr's face and threatened to carry his hat away. The boards rocked gently beneath his feet, and he kept one hand clenched firmly around a guy rope while his stomach bobbed up and down. He prayed he wouldn't get seasick.

"The harbormaster wants to see you," called a sailor. "Now."

They climbed up to the helm, where Harbormaster Willem guided the ship across the harbor. The breeze tossed his silver hair about, and Punsle stood behind him, a worried shadow. Danr wondered, almost hopefully, if he was expected to kiss Willem's ring again, but Willem didn't offer it. Danr did remove his hat, and the sun speared his eyes with diamond knives.

"A great city, Balsia," Willem said. "It used to be the

crown jewel in an empire greater than any ever seen, back in the days of Alessander the Grand."

"The man who turned back at Irbsa because his lover died?" Danr said.

Willem glanced at him, clearly surprised. "You know of him?"

"Death used him to lecture me on petty desires. When she tells you something, you don't forget it."

"Ah. Yes." Willem's fingers tightened on the helm. "Petty desires overcome big thinking. Do you know how Alessander conquered? He brought order."

"Order," Danr repeated, unsure where this was going. Why did so many people enjoy talking nonsense at him?

"He required streets to be built in straight lines, buildings done around square courtyards, people in castes so everyone knew their places from birth onward. Very orderly. No chaos. It worked beautifully."

"Until his love died, and it all fell apart for him," Danr couldn't help saying.

"You understand perfectly!" Willem thumped his hand against the helm. "When chaos invades, order breaks down. Rules fall apart. No one knows what to do. A city can't run this way."

"It seems to move along," Aisa observed.

Willem made an annoyed sound. "The economy is a mess. The army is undisciplined. The guilds try to pry every bit of power they can out of the crown. I try to bring order by regulating the harbor, but it's a losing battle. That's why I'm here, young half-blood."

"I don't understand." Danr shook his head.

"I know about your quest to find the power of the shape. Sharlee and Hector Obsidia are friends of mine, and they've been obsessed with it for years."

"That's why you came out here personally?" Danr said. "To tell us this?"

"Hardly." The *Fish* creaked, and the sails flapped a little. Most of them were down so the ship would move more slowly and let the outgoing tide do most of the work. "The Obsidia will do anything for that power. They're both descended from families that used the shape before the Sundering. Sharlee wants it again because it's her birthright—or she thinks it is. Hector wants it—"

"Because he thinks it will fill the hole inside him," Danr finished.

"Don't interrupt your betters," Willem corrected, though the rebuke was idle. "You're perceptive for someone of your background. At any rate, you're right. Hector has squandered a trio of fortunes trying to find that secret, and Sharlee eggs him on. And they definitely shouldn't have it."

Aisa cast a glance down at Talfi, who was still staring out to sea with the golem behind him. "Not that I disagree with you, but why do you believe this?"

They were nearly to the gap between the spit of land and the shore. A temple sat at the tip of the spit, one made of gold and obsidian and dedicated to the warrior twins Fell and Belinna. Willem guided the ship with almost casual skill.

"They would misuse it," he said, watching the water ahead of them. "Badly. You've seen their wealth and power. They trade in slaves, alcohol, weapons—and politicians. They don't want to known in public, so they quietly buy aldermen and nobility and even priests. Half the Diamond Court at the Gold Keep owes them money or favors, including the prince. If these two had the power of the shape, they would use it to control Balsia the city and eventually Balsia the country. The chaos would be incalculable." He shuddered, and his gaze turned faraway, as if he were looking at a jewel only he could see. "This was a great city once, back before slums and smugglers and ships polluted Bosha's beautiful harbor and turned it into a cesspool. Balsia could be great again, noble and orderly, if it had a leader who didn't flinch from what needs doing."

"And that leader would be?" Aisa asked.

"My lord," said Punsle quietly behind them.

The harbormaster came to himself. "Perhaps it will be our good Prince Karsten. We can but hope."

"How would the power of the shape let Sharlee and Hector conquer Balsia?" Danr asked. "So they could change into rabbits or snakes or chickens. Big deal."

"You have to think big," the harbormaster warned. "I've read the scrolls, and the power of the shape is more insidious than you know. Someone who has changed his shape can more easily share his power with someone else. Imagine if Hector enslaved a dozen shape-shifters and stole their power. Imagine if Sharlee could change other people's shapes. Now imagine if they were the only people in Balsia with this power."

"We would happily abandon this quest and go home," Aisa said to Danr's consternation, "if you could arrange for the Obsidia to release our friends. You seem to have an army at your disposal, and you do not fear Sharlee and Hector Obsidia."

"I could do that," said Willem, "but then you wouldn't be able to bring the power of the shape to me."

A moment of silence fell over them, broken only by the wash of waves and the snap of sails. Danr blinked at Willem in the hard morning sunlight.

"You want us to bring the power to *you* instead of to Hector and Sharlee," he said slowly.

"Obviously."

"Why would we do that?" Aisa asked.

"For the greater good," Willem replied easily. "Think big! If you bring it to me—to the temple of Bosha—the power of the shape will be controlled properly. The priests are in the best position to train new magicians in its use. We have all the old books and scrolls that refer to the power of the shape and how it works, even if the actual practice has disappeared. We have the money and the resources to ensure that word of the power spreads in a properly controlled manner. It would restore more balance to the world. Everything would be proper and fine, completely unlike the chaos Sharlee and Hector would bring if you gave the power to them."

Danr closed his right eye, but it was hard to see on the harbor, with the bright daylight reflected off the surface of the water. Even so, he got a glimpse of Harbormaster Willem. The man stood firm at the helm, resolute and in control. Every stitch of his clothing ran in straight lines, every inch free of wrinkles. He stood with his head high, high up among his principles, which were more important to him than possessions, position, or people. He also wasn't lying at the moment, but he would lie to people to keep his principles, indeed he would.

"He's telling the truth, Aisa," Danr reported.

"Can we trust him?" Aisa asked, then clapped her hand over her mouth. She had forgotten Danr would have to answer.

"Nope," Danr replied. "He would throw us overboard in a moment to get what he wants, and he'll betray his so-called friends the Obsidia for the same thing. That's why he's asking us. He's betraying them for something higher."

"Order," Willem said, without rancor. "We must have order. You plan to introduce a new form of chaos into the world, but I will make it into a form of order."

"You could simply stop us from going on this trip in the first place," Aisa said acidly. "I cannot imagine that the death of an elf and an orc would mean much to someone like you."

"He wants to control the power himself," Danr said before Willem could answer. "He thinks he can leash it like a dog and use it to force everyone around him into obedience. He's just like the Obsidia, really. They all three want the same thing, just for different reasons."

Willem's face turned red. "I could have your head struck off, boy."

"You couldn't do that any more than a miser could throw gold coins into a river." Danr spat over the side. "You swim in the desire for this power like the merfolk swim in the ocean, and you don't see how deep it runs. But I see it. You need me and my friends to find this power for you, and that means you won't hurt me. Not yet." He put his hat back on, and sighed with relief.

"So you'll bring it to me, then?" Willem pressed. His fingers were pale around the spokes of the helm. "And not to the Obsidia? If you do, I'll see to it they release your friends unharmed. And I'll reward you. The temple's treasury is generous to her friends."

"It's nice to know we have options among traitors," Danr said with a mock bow. "Come on, Aisa. Let's go below."

"My lord can stop slavery," Punsle called after them.

Aisa halted, and Danr came up short. His stomach tightened into a drum and Aisa's entire body tensed. They both turned back.

"What do you mean?" Aisa asked, unable to keep a quaver from her voice.

Willem nodded. "Punsle is right. As the harbormaster and High Priest of Bosha, I have more power in Balsia than the mayor and the prince combined." A small smile danced on his lips. "Especially with the prince so young and dependent on his mother for advice. I can forbid our temple to keep slaves. The high priestess of Grick will ally with me in a heartbeat, and she'll bring the priests of Olar. Once that happens, *all* the temples will stop buying slaves and preach against slavery instead. With a stroke of my quill, I can raise tariffs and import duties on slaves so high that it drives the slavers out of business. I can press the mayor and the prince into raising taxes on existing slaves so that it becomes cheaper to free them and hire them as servants instead. It will take time, but within a few years, slavery in Balsia will disappear. I swear by Bosha's heart that if you bring me the power of the shape, I will do these things. Together, we can truly think big. Do we have a deal?"

Aisa was actually trembling. She murmured, "Is he telling the truth?"

"Yes," said Punsle.

Danr checked. "He is."

"Then we have a deal, Harbormaster," Aisa said.

CHAPTER NINE

D anr watched the longboats row swiftly back toward the harbor with Harbormaster Willem sitting stiffly at the head. The sea breeze was stiff and cool out here, and the ship rocked beneath Danr's knees and feet. The sea itself was gray and topped by small whitecapped waves.

"This makes me sick," Danr said to Aisa at the rail. "Everywhere we turn, things get worse. Ranadar and Kalessa are still in danger, and now we're working for that harbor rat."

"He will end slavery," Aisa pointed out. "That forgives a great many sins, in my mind."

Danr grunted. "He's not doing it because it's right. He's doing it so he can become more powerful. Didn't you hear him? The Obsidia trade in slaves. Wiping away what's left of the slave trade will hurt them and give him even more power than he already has. And he'll have total control of the magic. He's not a good man."

"Even a bad man can do good things," Aisa observed philosophically. "And sometimes . . . sometimes we must sacrifice something small to gain something large."

"Thinking big?" Danr said.

Talfi had gone below to scout out their quarters, and the golem had gone with him. Captain Greenstone was back at the helm several steps away from them on what Danr had learned was called the quarterdeck, and her crew swarmed over the rigging, checking for damage. The captain's hat shaded her eyes, and a leather thong tied under her chin kept the cool salt breeze from carrying the hat away. Danr, who was constantly snatching at his own hat, would have to ask for one himself.

Harebones hurried up to her. "It don't look like the Boshites did much to ropes or sails, Captain. We're hale and hearty and ready."

"Where are we going, handsome?" Greenstone asked Danr.

"The Iron Sea," Danr said. "The center, as close as you can figure it. And have your lookouts watch for merfolk."

"They hide during storm season," Greenstone said. "They don't even surface to collect tolls because no one is stupid enough to sail across the Iron Sea in the autumn. If you're figurin' on finding merfolk to guide us, we'll never—"

A great gout of cold water fountained over the gunwale and sprayed Danr in the face. He sputtered and slapped at his eyes. When his vision cleared, he gasped. Sitting on the gunwale was Ynara, her long brown hair in wet tangles across her breasts, and her facial tattoos looking fierce and blue. Aisa gave a low cry.

"Aisa and Danr," Ynara greeted them. "I apologize for abandoning you, but I needed time to recover and spread the word. Do you still want us to take you to the Key?"

"We do," said Danr, a little dazed.

"Then follow!"

With that, she leaped back over the side and vanished with a splash.

"Wow," Greenstone said. "Usually, they want silver. What did you do for her?"

Aisa ran breathlessly to the gunwale and peered over. "I *knew* she would keep her word. But what did she mean by *us*?"

In answer, a great gray shape rose from the depths beside the ship. Water spouted from its back, and a tail the size of a rowboat slapped the water.

"A whale!" Aisa clutched Danr's arm in excitement. "It is a whale! Look how big it is, Danr! I have never seen anything so beautiful!"

Danr leaned over the rail, grinning from ear to ear. Her excitement was contagious, and in that moment, he would have given his right leg to make sure she always felt this way.

Ynara was perched on the whale's back. She waved at them, and Aisa waved back. The whale swam past the ship and made a lazy circle in the waves before it.

"We are meant to follow them," Aisa called to Greenstone over her shoulder.

"So the lady said," Greenstone replied. "Harebones!" She barked orders to the first mate, who relayed them to the rest of the crew. With more creaking and snapping, the ship heaved about.

"The wind will be against us most of the way, so we'll be tacking," the captain said, whatever that meant. "If the Key is in the center of the Iron Sea, and if we don't run into no trouble, we should find it in two days, maybe three."

"And then the same time to get back," Danr said.

"Nope. Less time to get back because the wind'll be with us. Just hope we don't run into trouble."

Talfi climbed up to the quarterdeck with the golem behind him. Apparently, it had decided to follow him most of the time. "There's a mermaid on a whale at the front of the ship!"

"Bow," the captain said from the helm. "The front is the bow, the back is the stern. Left is port, right is starboard, and those big things stickin' up from the deck are called masts."

"I have to go watch," Aisa said. She skittered down the ladder to the main deck and rushed across it toward the aforementioned bow.

"One hand for yourself and one for the ship!" Greenstone boomed after her. "I don't need no one washed overboard!"

Talfi folded his arms unhappily. He had already learned the trick of bending his knees with the motion of the ship so his upper body remained still, though he was a thousand years old and Danr supposed he might be remembering an old skill more than learning a new one.

"Every time I look at the water," he said, "I think about Ranadar in that tank."

Danr put a hand on his shoulder. "I wish I could tell you not to worry, but we're hurrying, yeah?"

"I know." Talfi looked at the floor. *Deck,* Danr reminded himself. "It's just . . . I want him here."

"Kalessa might tear their hearts out."

"It's a good wind," Greenstone said. "We'll be there and back before you know it, especially with the merfolk on our side."

The sea stretched out ahead of them, and the sails boomed overhead. Danr edged up to her. It felt strange but nice to stand next to someone who shared his height. "Uh . . . where did . . . who was your . . ."

"You want to know about my family?" she asked archly.

He straightened his hat, a little embarrassed. "Yeah. I've never met another half troll."

"I'd say you're half human."

Danr barked a small laugh. "Depends on who I'm with. Humans see the troll, trolls see the human."

She glanced at him, then returned her eyes to the horizon. "You've talked to other trolls? I mean, visited with 'em instead of just fighting at the Battle of the Twist?"

"Sure. My father was Kech the troll, and he took me under the mountain when the humans exiled me. I met his wife and my half brother and my grandmother." His throat grew a little thick. "Her name was Bund. I liked her. But she died."

"I never knew my birth family." Greenstone turned the wheel hand over hand for reasons Danr didn't understand. The ship turned, and some of the sails went slack until the sailors adjusted them and they caught the wind again. "My parents—the people who raised me—were shepherds. They found me in the mountains. They raised me with their own kids, and I never saw a troll my entire life."

"Were you . . . did you feel alone?"

"Every damn day. When you're twice as big as the other girls, they don't want to play house with you, and the boys are scared to wrestle with you."

"They call you names," Danr nodded. "Freak and Stane filth and monster."

"Yeah. Until you knock a few heads together and they shut the Vik up about it."

"I never did that," Danr said. "I was a thrall, and my mother always said if I hurt someone, they'd come for me—for us. I thought I really *was* a monster."

"What changed?"

"Her." Danr nodded again, this time toward the bow, where Aisa was watching the mermaid with palpable excitement. "She showed me that I was a person, not a monster."

"Lucky," Greenstone said. "I never had a love. Lovers, yes. Love, no."

"For me it's the other way around." Danr ran his hand over his face. "How did you get to be captain of a ship?"

"That's a long story. Short version is, I got tired of being the strange one at home, so I set out to find a place where no one cares how strange you are. Lots of that kind of thing on a ship, it turns out. If you're big and strong and can hold your own in a fight, you can bully your way into work. I'm good at sailing. Maybe my dad was a sailor who caught himself a trollwife—I don't know. When the first mate washed overboard in a storm, I got his job. I had to break a few noses, but the crew finally accepted me, and the same happened when the captain retired. So here I am."

"Do you miss your family?"

"Yeah. I still see 'em sometimes, and write letters. My mum was big on making sure everyone could read at least a little." She peered under the sails across the multiple decks. The whale and the mermaid were holding course a good hundred yards ahead of the ship. "So you wielded the Iron Axe and stopped the war."

"Yeah. I had to. It was the only way. Aisa and Talfi were there."

"You'll have to tell me about that over a drink some-time, handsome." She paused. "You don't mind that I call you handsome, do you? I don't want to get you in trouble with your lady."

"Oh." He flushed a little again. "No, she's not mad. We're just going through . . . It's a little difficult."

"She's with a half troll. Other people probably don't like that."

He turned to look at her in surprise. "How did you know that?"

"It's happened to me a few times." Greenstone shrugged massive shoulders. "It's why most of my men left me. Their families and friends gave 'em hell for liking a half-blood. It's not easy for anyone."

"That's right!" A finger of relief ran down Danr's spine. Here was someone who understood, who knew how he felt. "It's hard. Everyone looks at you all the time, and you have to be the one who proves that half-bloods aren't bad. You never get time to be . . . yourself."

"On this ship, you can be yourself all you want, handsome. No need to hide like some of those elven halfbloods."

"Have you ever met a half-blood Fae?" Danr asked.

"Not that I know of," Greenstone said. "But I hear they can pass for either half, and they have some of that elven glamour, so it's easy for them to hide. Or maybe they don't exist at all. What the Vik do I know? Any road, we Stane halves gotta stick together." Greenstone clapped him on the shoulder. "That hat looks pretty thin. Sun must be killing your eyes."

"Yeah, the orcs gave me a thick felt one, but I lost it when I fought the . . . I lost it. These straw ones don't work very well."

"Got a couple spares in my cabin. Get one and then have a talk with your lady."

Talfi sat morosely on the deck of the tiny cabin. The ship tipped and dipped, but he barely noticed. Whether it was because he wasn't susceptible to seasickness or because he had gotten used to it in some former life, he didn't know or care right then. He only had one thought on his mind.

"Attention!" said the stupid golem in the corner. "Update."

It projected from its azure eyes twin beams of light that formed an image on the planks. A pint-size Ranadar huddled in the bottom of the tank. The paired golem was just pouring another cup of water into it. The water level now reached Ranadar's ankles. Talfi knew it was just an image the Obsidia were sending to torment him, but he couldn't help reaching out to touch the captive elf. His hand passed through the light. When it did, the image of Ranadar looked up and his eyes made contact with Talfi's. Then the image vanished.

Talfi swiped at his eyes, glad no one was here to see. "I'd say you're a shit son of a bitch," he told the golem, "but you don't even have a mother."

The golem remained in the corner, silent and motionless. Some of the runes carved across its body showed dried blood. Talfi should have wondered whose blood it was, but right now he couldn't get up the energy to care.

The ship dropped abruptly, and Talfi's stomach went with it. Obeying a reflex he didn't know he had, he looked out the tiny round porthole to check the weather, but what he could see of the sky was clear. That kind of thing went on a lot with Talfi—something happened to him, and he responded automatically with a skill he didn't know he had. Now that he knew he was a thousand years old, this made a lot more sense, but it didn't make it easier to cope with. The idea that he had been walking the earth longer than some cities had existed, that when he was born, some of the tallest trees hadn't even been saplings, that even some mountains had changed since he was a little boy, made him feel strange and quivery inside. It also made him kind of upset, as if someone had stolen something important from him. He didn't even remember his parents or if he had brothers and sisters. Though they were long dead by now. He had no memories of them at all.

And yet . . .

Sometimes at night, while Ranadar breathed evenly beside him, he clutched one or both amulets at his throat, and it seemed it all might come back to him, if he just thought carefully enough. The amulets helped. The first was a battered silver medallion. The other was the little pouch Danr used to wear around *his* neck. It contained the splinters from Danr's eyes and from the eyes of Danr's mother. The pouch was a piece of truth, and it had helped Talfi regain a piece of his memory after he'd been killed once. Talfi had offered to give it back to Danr, but Danr had told him to keep it, just in case it helped bring back memories. Talfi couldn't find a polite way to refuse, and like a tongue that sought an aching tooth, his hands often stole toward one or both amulets to see if the memories would return. Sometimes they nearly did, hovering in shadowy corners of his mind. All he had to do was turn and look.

Instead he pulled away.

The idea that memory might return always filled him with a nameless dread that tightened his skin and made his breath come in tiny gasps. His fist always opened, and the amulets fell away. The memories remained buried, and in the coffin darkness of night when no one else was around to know, he admitted to himself that he hoped the memories would *never* come back. Not even Ranadar knew.

Ranadar. Talfi sighed and clasped his hands around his knees. One of the problems on this ship was that there wasn't much to do, which let Talfi's thoughts come back around to Ranadar. His uppity elf. In his head, another cup went into that damn tank and the water level edged up a tiny bit more.

This was what bothered Talfi the most. Danr and Aisa hadn't noticed, but Talfi had done the math. He unfolded a piece of paper with numbers scrawled on it, numbers in his own handwriting. It had started off as idle scribbling, a way to keep his mind busy down here in the cabin, and then his hand took over by itself. Given a six-ounce cup, a tank that was seven feet high, seven feet wide, and four feet deep, and a slow-walking golem that took two minutes to make a

round trip between the well and the tank, it would take the
golem approximately two thousand nine hundred and thirty-
two minutes to fill the tank, less time to send the bucket
down and refill it. That was barely over two days, not the
four Hector Obsidia said it would take. Without a miracle,
Ranadar would be dead by the time they got back, and likely
Kalessa, too.

In the image, Ranadar's wrists were growing red and raw
from the iron shackles, while he, Talfi, sat in dry comfort
aboard this ship. He felt like a lion in a cage with a golem for
his guard.

Another cup of water went into the tank.

At the bow, Aisa stared and stared at Ynara the mermaid. The
whale she rode looked large and clumsy, but it glided through
the water, easily outpacing the *Slippery Fish.* Ynara perched
on its back like a queen on her throne, her powerful silver tail
folded beneath her and her long hair streaming in the wind.
Her skin was bared to the breeze, and that fascinated Aisa
as much as anything else. The idea of a woman showing herself this way, proud and unafraid, excited Aisa in a way she
couldn't name. She had no physical desire for the merfolk.
She wanted to embrace them, be like them, be a part of them.
It took all her willpower not to leap overboard and try to swim
to the whale, even though she knew she would drown.

It seemed a little unfair and . . . wrong. Aisa had been
longing to find the merfolk for years, and now that she had
finally done so—or found *one* of the merfolk—she could
not touch her, or even speak to her. It felt like taking two
steps back from a great banquet.

Danr padded up to her in his bare feet, and she gave him
a small smile. It was nice to have him near. He was wearing
a new hat, one of thick black felt. It must have come from
Captain Greenstone.

"Beautiful," he said.

Aisa arched an eyebrow. "The mermaid or our captain?"

"You," he said, "standing here at the bow with the wind whipping at your hair. You look like the . . . the carving at the front of the ship."

"The figurehead," she laughed. "All right, I forgive you, my Hamzu."

He scratched his head. "For what?"

"You were flirting with the captain." She meant to say it lightly, but it came out with more intensity than she intended.

"I don't know how to flirt," he replied seriously. "I never had a chance to learn." He paused. "Are you . . . jealous?"

The direct question caught her a little off guard. "Hmm! Perhaps I am. A little. She is a half-blood, like you, and that means you and she have more in common. Should I be worried?"

Only after the question escaped her did she realize how foolish the asking was, and she clapped a hand over her mouth. It was too late. She saw the struggle on Danr's face as he tried to keep the harsh truth to himself, but he lost as he always did.

"That's a stupid question," he blurted out. "I risked execution for you, accepted exile for you, fought an orc chieftain for you, and nearly cracked the continent in half to save your life. You don't need to worry about a ship's captain I've known for less than half a day. I'm sorry I had to say that. Please don't make me do that again. I'll always love you, Aisa."

The final words came out in a rush. Tears pricked the back of Aisa's eyes. How could she be so thoughtless to this kind man? She reached out to touch his arm. "I am—" she began.

The scream echoed inside her head. For a moment,

Danr—Hamzu—was a snarling monster wielding a bloody Iron Axe, and the ship was drenched in scarlet. The sailors were rent to bloody shreds. Amid them stood a woman in a cloak made of autumn leaves. In her hand she held a small sickle. With it, she sliced one of the sailors in half. Except it wasn't a sailor. It was one of the merfolk, a woman. The mermaid dropped to the deck in a puddle of blood and scales.

Sometimes one plant must die so the garden can live, said the autumn woman, and the face within the hood was sad and tired. *Can you let one plant die?*

Aisa pulled back in fear. Her heart pounded like a trapped bird inside her chest, and her knees shook. The vision vanished, along with the woman and her sickle. The sailors went about their business, unaware of what had just happened.

"Aisa?" Danr said fearfully.

"I . . ." She glanced out at the sea. Ynara was riding the whale, alive and free and unbothered by visions and screams and blood. "I am sorry. I . . . should not have asked you that question in that way. You are a truth-teller, and you cannot help your words sometimes. I am not truly worried about the captain."

"Really?" he asked.

Now she wished he would go away and let her gather her scattered thoughts, but she could not tell him that. "Really."

He moved to embrace her, and now she could not help but flinch away. With a hurt expression, he dropped his arms to his sides. Her heart ached for him, but she could not bring herself to speak just now. He leaned on the rail beside her instead. The ship plowed through the waves, away from the steadily rising sun.

"I know what's bothering you," he said.

Aisa turned, startled. "Oh?"

That wasn't a real question, so Danr was able to give a simple, grave nod beneath his hat. "There's another reason to find the secret of the shape besides rescuing Ranadar."

"Yes. The harbormaster said he will end slavery if we bring the magic back to him," Aisa reminded him. Her heart was beating fast again.

"That's not what I'm talking about." Danr cleared his throat. "I know why you pull away from me."

"I do not understand," Aisa said, though she was afraid she did. Somehow he had learned about her visions of blood. Had he looked at her with his true eye? He had promised never to do that again.

"You're nervous about the way people will treat you—us—because I'm a half-blood." Here he flexed his hands, perhaps unconsciously. "That's why I asked Death if there was a way I could become human. Then no one would recognize me, and the whole half-blood problem would just disappear."

"I . . . see." Aisa couldn't think how to respond. Thoughts rushed about her head like mice trapped in a grain bin. Danr's main reason for attempting this dangerous and difficult journey was flawed. She was indeed afraid, but not for the reasons he thought. And why was this cloaked woman now part of it? Everything was such a tangle.

Danr did not know about her visions of the past, after all, and that was a relief. Or was it? Perhaps if she told him, shared the burden . . .

But no. There was no way to say it without hurting him. Danr had had no choice but to wield the Axe, and if she could go back in time, she would not stop him. The visions came because of some fault in her, not him. Telling him about them would not change them or rid herself of them. Best to keep them to herself.

The trouble was, she didn't know if she could. The visions were growing stronger and stranger. Perhaps if she shared them with him, despite the short-term pain, he could help her.

"What do you think, Aisa?" Danr said. "If I become human, can we be together?"

She took his hand. "Danr, I—"

"Storm!" bellowed a sailor. "Storm ahead!"

Startled, Aisa whirled back to the bow. Where there had been clear sky only moments ago, black clouds now rushed down on them like an angry army. The wind turned cold. Ynara shot the ship a look; then with a splash both she and the whale vanished below the surface. Sudden waves slapped the ship, jerking it up and yanking it down so quickly Aisa felt she was standing on air. She grabbed a rope just in time to keep from losing her balance. Danr had managed the same. He looked green.

"Get those sails down!" bellowed Harebones. "Secure the rigging! Move, move, move! You passengers—get below!"

The sailors rushed about the ship, their faces tight and pale. Wood creaked and complained. Aisa staggered toward a hatch, trying to keep her footing on the heaving deck. Danr came with her. All around them, the sails were coming down like dying clouds. The storm stomped across the ocean with frightening speed and ferocity. The day's weather had begun so well Aisa had forgotten how fast autumn storms brewed in the Iron Sea. Heart thudding, she was reaching for the hatch cover when a great wave washed over the deck and crashed into her. Her mouth and eyes filled with salty water, and the wave swirled her around like a toy. She was rushing, sliding across the deck toward the gunwale. Terror gripped her heart. A strong hand grabbed her shoulder. Danr! Relief swept her—until the water wrenched her away again. Aisa spun across the deck.

She tried to scream, but salt water filled her mouth and eyes. The gunwale rushed toward her, and she flailed about, trying to catch hold of something, anything, but the water was too strong. It muffled her final cry as it swept her over the edge.

Chapter Ten

L iquid darkness stopped her mouth and nose. Aisa flailed about, trying not to panic but not knowing what else to do. Her own weight pulled her down. She was going to die. A thousand regrets peppered her thoughts—she would never see her homeland again, she would never see her potted garden again, she would never stand next to Kalessa at her mating ceremony.

She would never again be able to tell Danr she loved him. She prayed he knew.

Aisa sank further into darkness. A strange, high-pitched wailing, almost like a song, reached her. She could not imagine what it was, and what an odd thing to be worried about while she could not breathe, while her lungs begged for air. The world dimmed and she slid into a gray place.

Can you wield the sickle without flinching?

The grayness lightened. Around Aisa stretched the strangest garden she had ever seen. Row upon row of twisting vines and stems and rainbow flowers pushed to the horizon in all directions. Plants that had no business sharing a row twined with each other—marigolds mingled with mums, clematis clumped with catnip, asparagus intertwined with ivy. And yet there was a strange order to it, a pattern Aisa couldn't quite grasp.

The woman in the autumn cloak trudged down a row toward Aisa, the little sickle in her hand. *I've seen you cut a bloom so the flower can grow,* she said, and her voice was the sound of dying leaves falling to earth. *How much bigger can you think?*

Aisa felt she should be frightened. A moment ago, she had been drowning in the Iron Sea, and now she was facing an armed woman in an outlandish garden. But the orderly chaos of this garden was a calming sort of place, and her fears ebbed away.

"Who are you?" she asked, though she was already sure of the answer.

I've already spoken with your young man, the woman said. *You were supposed to be there, too, but he made a petty choice and changed the garden.*

"Pendra," Aisa said softly. "The third Gardener."

The woman Pendra drew nearer, and Aisa smelled cinnamon mingled with funeral flowers. Her autumn cloak fell open. Blood was running down long cuts on both her arms. Aisa drew back with a gasp.

The Tree tips. Blood pooled at Pendra's feet and ran into a crack in the ground. *Have you thought about why it tips?*

"I . . . no."

She sighed again. *We make a small sacrifice for the larger gain, child. Listen to the harbormaster and think big.*

Think big. Aisa looked around her. In the distance to her left and right, the garden eventually dropped over the horizon. But no, it was too close for it to be the horizon. The ground was curving downward, as if they were on a great hill. She turned her head. Far, far behind her, the garden climbed upward, as if scaling a wall.

No. Not a wall. The world *wrenched*, and Aisa saw it,

truly *saw* it. It was as if she had owned a drawing of a young woman all her life, and now had abruptly seen it as an old hag.

They were standing on the branch of an enormous tree, the biggest tree the universe had ever seen. It was ancient. It was rotting. And every inch, every leaf, every top and underside of every branch, was covered with the great garden.

"Ashkame," Aisa whispered.

Now you see it, Pendra said with approval. *But bigger still.*

Aisa's awareness spread further still, beyond her body, beyond herself. She saw that every branch had an identical root, or perhaps every root had an identical branch, and if Ashkame flipped over, the Tree would look much the same. And the Tree *was* tipping. Slowly and steadily, but it was tipping. Some of the garden would slide off into the void, and some of it would use the opportunity to grasp the bark more firmly, but in the end, the tipping would invigorate and heal the rotting Tree. The Tree would survive, and the garden along with it.

Yes, Pendra said. *And why?*

Aisa's awareness rushed back to herself. Pendra's blood tapped the ground in soft scarlet rain. Blood—her own blood—stained her sickle. The red pool at Pendra's feet drained into the crack. Into the ground. Into the Tree. Aisa put her hand over her mouth in shock as understanding crashed through her.

"The life of a Gardener is no small sacrifice," she whispered.

If you think big enough, anything becomes small, Pendra replied evenly. *And when I am done, my sisters will find themselves alone.*

Abandoned. A second woman in a rich cloak of green and brown rose from the garden like a sunflower. She carried a hoe.

Forlorn. A third woman in pale green floated down from the sky with a bag of seeds. They formed a triangle with Aisa in the center.

Aisa trembled. "What are you telling me?"

The Gardeners are not cruel, said Nu.

Not callous, said Tan.

Not unkind, sighed Pendra. *But we can forget what it is to be Kin.*

Stane, said Tan.

Fae, said Nu.

And so it has been that when one of us leaves, we turn to the Nine People to find another sister, said Pendra. *She must be someone who understands loss, so she knows compassion; one who understands hatred, so she feels love; one who understands petty details and thinks big.*

Aisa's mouth was dry and her heart rattled inside her chest. "Are you telling me you will die soon and you want *me* to—"

You are one among several we watch, interrupted Nu.

Observe, said Tan.

Inspect, said Pendra. *A Gardener must be able to make a sacrifice, even those that cause her pain.* Here, Pendra held out her own bleeding arms. *The Tree tips on blood, and more than just mine.*

You will be tested, said Nu.

Tried, said Tan.

Examined, said Pendra.

"How?" asked Aisa.

First, said Pendra, *you must live.*

The garden vanished. Salt water filled Aisa's mouth and clogged her lungs. She tried to gasp, but she had no air. Aisa struggled, but the ocean gave her nothing.

Two hands came under her arms. Aisa was propelled upward, up toward the light, up toward the air. Aisa had almost no time to understand what was happening before she burst above the surface. She coughed hard, and sweet, sweet air filled her lungs. Lightning cut the sky in two with a white blade. Thunder boomed in her ears, and a new wave towered above her, ready to smash her down.

"Take your breath!" order Ynara. It was she who had Aisa. Aisa had just enough time to inhale sharply before Ynara pulled her under again. They swam under the wave and surfaced on the other side. Aisa breathed like a breaching dolphin.

"Good!" Ynara said. "Do not fear. You will not drown. Take your breath!"

This time, Aisa was able to take two or three breaths to saturate her lungs before Ynara took her under. Her fear for herself had evaporated, and she was able to look about. The ship made a great shadow up and to her left, and it was clearly listing to one side. The strange, eerie song wailed through the water. Ynara's arms were strong and steady around her. It was peaceful under the sea, almost as peaceful as the garden. The cool water held her up, made her feel light and buoyant, almost as if she were flying. She could go anywhere, any direction, she chose. And it felt familiar somehow. It felt *right*, as if she had been reunited with a long-lost friend, or she were visiting a long-forgotten childhood home.

Then they broke the surface again, and wind howled in Aisa's ears. She breathed and shook the water from her eyes. The wave they had dodged crashed into the *Slippery Fish*, listing it hard again.

"The ship!" Aisa cried. "It will sink!"

"Take your breath," Ynara ordered as another wave came at them. They plunged underwater again.

If not for the danger to Danr and the others, Aisa would have enjoyed it. She was swimming with a mermaid! The incredibility of it made her light and buoyant. Ynara towed her along with casual strength. The ship, however, was now tipping with all the inevitability of a wounded elephant going to the ground. Aisa pointed desperately, heart pounding in her ears.

"It will be all right," Ynara said, and her voice carried perfectly well under the water.

How? Aisa mouthed.

"There." Now Ynara pointed, and Aisa clapped both her hands over her mouth to keep from gasping. Incredulous wonder swept over her, and she could do nothing but gape at the incredible sight. A pod of whales, more than fifty of them, swam up to the ship and pressed up against it, protecting it with their gray-blue bodies. Pale flukes waved like flat hands in the water, and their tails pumped in unison. Wise, ancient eyes reflected the ocean, and Aisa thought she caught her own self in some of them. The eerie song grew louder, and slowly, the ship creaked upright.

Ynara towed Aisa above the water, and air burst into her lungs. "That is amazing!" she gasped. "How do they know what to do?"

"We tell them," said Ynara. Another wave approached. "Take your breath."

"We?" But Ynara was already taking her under again. The whales continued to press the ship upright, but now from below came . . . merfolk. Dozens and dozens of merfolk. Women and men, children and babies. They streamed up from below, their long gleaming tails, covered in scales like jewels, propelling them in graceful arcs through the water and filling the water with delight. Their upper bodies were corded with muscle, and neither the men nor the women covered their chests. Blue and black and red and green tattoos covered their faces and necks in fierce designs. Several merfolk waved to Ynara—or was it Aisa?—as they passed, and Aisa felt she might burst with happiness. A tiny mermaid girl swam in joyful loops around her parents, her black hair floating behind her in a cloud. Aisa felt as if she had somehow come home.

The merfolk rushed around the ship and whales in a great circle. Like a great school of powerful fish, they swam faster and faster. Aisa felt the currents shift across her body. Ynara popped them above water so Aisa could breathe, then pulled her under again. The merfolk's tails glowed, gleaming as bright as gems caught in the sun as they whirled around the ship and the singing whales holding it up. The *Slippery Fish* creaked and started to spin.

What is happening? Aisa mouthed to Ynara.

"Watch!" Ynara said.

Another breath above the water, another dive. The merfolk had created a dizzying whirlpool, and it was pulling both Aisa and Ynara into the current. Worry returned to Aisa, but Ynara seemed unconcerned. The whales sang again.

The whirlpool current gained strength. It wrenched them both around. Aisa tumbled, and suddenly Ynara was no longer there. Panic seized Aisa again. The ocean blurred into a chaotic mess of sound and light, of fins and flukes. Aisa shouted, and water flooded her mouth.

And then she was standing on something solid. She looked down and realized she was on the back of a whale. Its great body stretched before and behind her, and its powerful flukes spread to either side. Before she could react, it pushed her above the surface and she could breathe again. Water exploded from the whale's blowhole and showered her with mist. Aisa sank to the whale's smooth back and clung to it as best she could. Where was the ship? Where was—

The storm was gone. Ended. Overhead, the sun shone in a clear sky. The sea lay flat and calm. The *Slippery Fish* floated a dozen serene yards away. Aisa blinked, trying to take in the enormousness of it.

"Aisa!" Danr was leaning over the gunwale, reaching for her, though she was patently too far away. His face was filled with a relief that both buoyed and pained her. "Aisa! I thought you were dead!"

She waved back to him. "I am well!"

Captain Greenstone appeared next to him. "What happened to you? What happened to *us*?"

"I will explain, but later! Do not worry!"

Merfolk surfaced all around her and the ship, like mystic flowers springing from the forest floor. They laughed and shouted, and several swarmed up the sides of the ship to perch on the gunwale. Greenstone and Danr backed away.

A pair of merfolk, a man and a woman, splashed out of the sea and slid onto the whale's back. Aisa drew back uncertainly. Their facial tattoos gave them fierce expressions, and they carried thin spears on their backs. Both had brown hair, long muscles, and smooth skin. In fact, they reminded Aisa of—

Ynara burst out of the sea and clung to the whale's back. There was no more room for her to sit. "Aisa! I wish for you to greet my parents, Imeld and Markis."

"You risked your life to return our daughter to us," Imeld said with a wide smile. "You and your friends. We thank you."

"And we salute you, kind one," Markis added. "You are now our daughter."

Before Aisa could react, he took her face in both hands, kissed her forehead, and released her. He smelled of salt water and spice. Aisa should have felt frightened or distressed, but instead she felt a small wave of . . . affection? It was like being greeted by a relative she had met long ago and only just now found again.

"You are indeed one of us," Imeld agreed. She touched

Aisa's cheek with a gentle hand, and for a moment, a tiny, heart-wrenching moment, Aisa's own mother was there. "You will be a sister to Ynara."

"I will?" Until Imeld said those words, Aisa hadn't even considered such a thing. She had a sudden vision of swimming bare-skinned under the waves like these women, and a joy suffused her every pore. It felt right, and it felt powerful, and for a moment it came as a surprise when she looked down and saw legs instead of a tail. The reality came crashing down on her. She was no mermaid. She was a human, a bystander who had done the merfolk a kindness, and they were saying simple words of gratitude.

But Ynara took Aisa's hand. "Sister," she said solemnly.

Aisa managed a smile. She seemed to be collecting sisters—first an orc, now a mermaid. And perhaps the Gardeners. But that thought was big, too big, and she pushed it aside to consider later. Too much was happening now.

"Sister," she said. "I was glad to help. Is that why you saved our ship?"

"Of course, my daughter." Imeld took her other hand while all around them, the merfolk swam rings about the *Fish*. "Ynara said you needed to find the Key, and we have brought you here."

A mental lightning bolt yanked Aisa upright. "The Key? We are at the Key? But that was at least two days away!"

"The merfolk are one with the sea and we have ways, especially for our friends." Markis grinned beneath his spiky tattoos, and Aisa wondered what it would be like to grow up with a father so fierce and proud instead of one who drank and gambled away his daughter's life. A twinge of envy for Ynara pinched her.

"Where is it, then?" Aisa asked. "The Key?"

"Perhaps four or five leagues that way." Markis gestured. "We will thread our way through the Nine Isles to find it.

But the Key is a dangerous place, daughter, filled with perils you cannot imagine. Why would you wish to go there?"

Aisa swallowed. "We are looking for Grandfather Wyrm."

At those words, all three merfolk gave her a sharp look. "Grandfather Wyrm?" Ynara repeated. "But he . . . he is unkind."

"To say the least," Imeld spat. "Thank Bosha he spends most of his time asleep. When he wakes, he hungers. He has devoured countless of our kind, created earthquakes and tidal waves and storms. What do you want with him?"

"He can give us the power of the shape," Aisa said, "so our friends do not die." And she briefly explained.

Markis ran his finger over his facial tattoos. "I see. We want to help you, my daughter"—there was that little wave of affection again—"but we must keep our distance. Grandfather Wyrm is too great a danger. And in any case, we cannot enter the Key."

Warm water sloshed over the whale's back, and it spouted cool mist again. Aisa asked, "What exactly is the Key?"

"It is a place between worlds," Imeld said. "Only the bravest go there. You will have to see for yourself."

"Who are your parents, Aisa?" Markis asked suddenly. "You look so . . . familiar."

This took Aisa aback. "My parents? Er . . . my family lives in Irbsa."

"The desert country." Imeld shuddered. "How did you bear it?"

"My father was Bahir, son of Muhar. I do not know if he is dead or alive these days. My mother was Durrah. I have two older brothers—"

"Durrah," Markis interrupted. "Durrah. I must think."

"In the meantime, daughter," Imeld said, "we must return you to your ship. You look exhausted. When did you last sleep?"

Aisa thought about it, and realized she couldn't remember. The expression on her face told Imeld everything she needed to know.

"That is what I thought," she said with a tart maternal tone. "It will be several hours before the ship arrives at the Key. We will be sure to wake you."

"Aisa!" Danr caught her up in an embrace that encompassed the entire world and squeezed half an ocean out of her. Aisa sighed, letting his scent come over her and feeling safe, if only for the moment.

They were on one of the upper decks. Talfi was running toward them along with the golem, Captain Greenstone, Harebones, and half the crew. The *Fish* remained rock-steady, and even after her short time in the water with the merfolk, it felt strange to be on a solid surface in dry air.

Everyone swarmed around her, asking questions all at once. The spiral of voices combined with her exhaustion into an overwhelming whirlpool, and she put up her hands.

"Enough!" Greenstone barked. "Full story later. For now—Aisa, did the merfolk bring us here?"

She nodded.

"Is this the Key?"

"It is a few leagues away. They will lead us."

"Update," said the golem. "Update." Its eyes projected an image of Ranadar sitting at the bottom of the tank. Nearby, Kalessa was chained by one leg to a tree. Water had reached Ranadar's shins.

Talfi sank to the deck with his face in his palms, as if all his strength had left him. Alarmed, Aisa knelt next to him in her sodden blouse and skirt. "What is it?"

"The tank," he said into his hands. "I was so afraid." And here he said something about numbers and volume that Aisa did not follow. "We can do it now. Ran doesn't have to die."

"Everyone back to work!" Greenstone bellowed. "Passengers below so you're out of the way."

Danr hauled both Aisa and Talfi upright, and they climbed down one of the hatchways belowdecks. Aisa's clothing sloshed and her shoes squished with every step, but she did not feel at all uncomfortable.

Talfi led the way with the golem through the hold, twisting around crates and barrels and ducking under beams. Aisa caught him swiping at his face, then noticed Danr doing the same. She touched his arm.

"I am fine, Hamzu," she murmured. "The merfolk saved me, as we saved Ynara. I was able to swim with them, after all this time!"

"You got your dream, Aisa." He took her damp hand. "I'm . . . so happy for you. And I'm relieved that you're alive. When that wave took you over the edge . . ." His voice caught. "You took my soul with you."

"I was terrified," Aisa said, skirting a tall coil of rope. "But only for a moment. Ynara caught me quickly. I was worried for all of *you*."

"I should have been there to save you," Danr maintained. "That's my job. I'm your—"

"There was nothing you could have done." Now she reached up to touch his face. How fine it was just to touch him. "I am glad you were worried for me."

"Update! Update!" said the golem.

"Shut up!" Danr roared at it. To everyone's surprise, the golem fell silent.

"Now, *that's* magic," Talfi said.

They arrived at the tiny cabins. Aisa had one to herself, while Danr and Talfi kept one together. So much privacy was no doubt a luxury to the sailors, who shared rooms by the dozen, but Aisa was too tired to give it much thought.

Talfi went into his and Danr's cabin, and the golem went with him. Danr paused at her door.

"Aisa," he said in that soft, husky voice, "I meant it when I said my soul went with you."

He touched her face with a warm, callused hand. His liquid brown eyes melted her heart and weakened her knees. Soft love spilled through her, filling her like a wineglass. She remembered her earlier regret at not telling him about her visions, and now there was so much to say. The words piled up inside her, but it was suddenly hard to speak again. Why was it easy to say these things inside her head but not with her voice?

"Danr," she managed, "Danr, I . . . I . . ."

"I'm going to bring you the power of the shape," he said stoutly. "I'll be human for both of us, and we can get married and even have children. Do you want children? Death said you can have children again, but we've never talked about it."

She fumbled. "Oh, Danr—this isn't the time to—"

"Yeah, sure." He ran a hand through coarse black hair. "Look, I'm ready to drop, and so are you. Let's get some sleep."

Suddenly, she wanted to hear the truth, absolute truth, and she blurted out the words. "Danr, will being human make you happy?"

"It will," he said without the usual harshness, "if it means we can be together. And there's more to it."

Before she could ask what he meant by that, he continued, propelled by his status as a truth-teller.

"I've always walked between worlds, half Stane, half Kin, and not belonging to either one. It's always made my life hard. Finding the power of the shape will be my chance to change that. I want to be more than half a man."

"You are always a man," Aisa told him. "You could be nothing less to me."

"Tell that to my troll side," he said with a wry twist to his mouth. "We should get some rest. We're both ready to pass out."

When he said this, it became more true. Fatigue pulled so heavily at Aisa's limbs she could barely keep herself upright. Calling up one last piece of courage from her mental merfolk mask, she stood on tiptoe and kissed his cheek.

"Thank you," she said, feeling at least a little better. Once they had the power of the shape, both their problems would end. "And good night. Or day."

She closed the door to her cabin, stripped off her sopping clothes, and dropped into a dreamless sleep.

"The Key is just past that island." Ynara pointed. Wind whipped at her long hair, trailing it behind her and making her facial tattoos stand out. Danr had to force his eyes upward. Even though all mermaids' breasts were bare, it felt strange and rude to stare at them, and he did his best not to. But it was difficult. Women were supposed to keep covered except when they were nursing a baby, and it was both strange and a little exciting to see something this exotic. He sent up a fervent prayer to Olar that Aisa never asked him about this, because he doubted she would like a truthful answer. He followed the line of Ynara's finger.

Ahead was one of the Nine Isles, one isle for each of the Nine. Each was the top of what used to be a mountain, but the Sundering had put them at the bottom of an ocean. The island ahead, peppered with twisted trees and towering rocks, was Urko's, and Greenstone was steering clear of it. None of the Nine Races lived in the Nine Isles—monsters twisted by the magic of the Sundering had eaten any brave enough to try.

Aisa and Talfi, newly wakened from their own sleep, came

up to see. The golem, as always, followed close behind, its dead azure eyes taking in everything. Danr was really beginning to hate the thing. Talfi's face was pinched with worry, despite the time they had gained from the merfolk.

The sea ahead of them was still calm. The merfolk had dispersed, though Ynara assured them that they were still nearby, watching. Everyone waited in silence. Even the sailors went about their work with hushed voices. A dark tension settled over the deck. Aisa stood uneasily next to Danr, the wind teasing her own hair. He wondered if she would let him touch it, touch her, then decided not. Instead he eyed the bottle of squid ink sticking out of Talfi's pocket. Very soon they would have the power of the shape, and everything would be all right. They would hand it over to Harbormaster Willem and he would both free their friends and end slavery. Danr would learn how to change into a human, and Aisa's last reservations would fall. All their problems would be solved.

Would they? murmured a treacherous inner voice. Harbormaster Willem might not be able to force the Obsidia to release Ranadar and Kalessa. Danr might not be able to become a human. Aisa might find she didn't want him after all.

He told himself to shut up.

Greenstone heaved the ship around Urko's Isle. Danr drew in a breath beneath his new heavy hat. Perhaps half a league ahead lay a great circle of water, a disk that stretched to the horizon. It was a pale gray instead of sea blue, and calm as ice. The little ocean waves came up to the edge and flattened like iron. The fluffy clouds coasting through the sky skirted the circle, unwilling or unable to cross the boundary. The very air grew thick and heavy, and a chill ran down Danr's back. Several of the crew stopped their work to stare.

"The Key," Ynara said unnecessarily. "Your captain knows it would be suicide to sail across it."

"Why?" Aisa asked.

"When the Key opens in autumn at the time of the Sundering, it becomes neither water nor air nor land," Ynara said. "Your ship would plunge straight to the bottom. Only those who walk between worlds can go there."

Danr straightened his hat. That was another problem with being a half-blood—you were somehow expected to do things no one else could. "Those like me."

"And me," Talfi said in a small voice. "I walk between life and death every day."

"That is the place where you first died," Aisa said.

Talfi just nodded.

"Do you remember anything about it?" Danr asked.

"Just some shadows." Talfi fingered the silver amulet around his neck, probably without realizing. "Screams. Pain. A blond woman. And fear like ice down my balls. I don't want to go down there."

"Then don't," Danr said. "You can stay up—"

Talfi held up a hand. "I need to. And I'm not letting you go alone, you big oafus maloafus."

"Oafus maloafus?" Danr repeated. "What the Vik is that?"

"I must have studied with priests at some point."

"And that's what they call each other?"

"And I will be there as well," Aisa said. "Someone has to make sure the two of you make no foolish mistakes."

Ynara, looking shocked, laid a hand on Aisa's arm. "My sister, you are not going to the Key."

"What?" Aisa was clearly taken aback. "Of course I am! I have gone under the mountain, I have argued with giants, and I have stood before Death herself. This Key cannot possibly compare."

Danr felt strangely stretched in two directions. The idea

that Aisa wouldn't go to the Key relieved him—he wouldn't have to worry that she might get hurt or killed. The idea also filled him with indignation. Aisa's deeds were greater than his own, and who was this mermaid to tell her where she could and couldn't go? In the end, indignation won.

"She can go if she wants," he said gruffly. "You may as well try to stop an elephant."

"Probably not the best metaphor," Talfi said out of the side of his mouth.

Ynara and Aisa didn't seem to notice the exchange. "We do not question your bravery or your deeds. We celebrate them like Rolk celebrates his monthly mating with Kalina. No, sister—the Key will not let you in. It is neither—"

"Earth nor air nor water," Aisa said impatiently. "I understand that, and I am—"

"You do not understand," Ynara interrupted. "In the Key, merfolk dry out. Stane drop to the center of the world. The Fae are shredded by bits of iron. And humans drown. The only ones who survive are those who walk between worlds."

"I *have* walked between worlds." Aisa planted her feet on the gently rocking deck. "I served in Grick's house. I stood at Death's door."

"Did you actually cross Death's threshold like Talfi has done?"

"I . . . did not," Aisa admitted.

"Then you will drown in the Key," Ynara said gravely. "Danr's half-blood heritage will protect him. Talfi has crossed Death's threshold more than once. But you . . . you are fully human, my sister, and the Key will be your death."

A hard line grew between Aisa's eyes, and her mouth became a gash in her face. "I love the way you bring good news," she said tartly. "I will bow to the inevitable."

Danr let himself have a tiny, purely internal sigh of relief.

He wanted Aisa with him, but at the same time he wanted her to stay safe. It was hot and cold in his stomach, and he was glad that the decision had been made by someone else, even if it made Aisa unhappy.

"You'll have to take a longboat out there," put in Captain Greenstone, who had come up behind them. "We've dropped anchor, and we're goin' no closer. That thing spawns storms and monsters and Vik knows what else."

"You could come with us," Talfi said suddenly. "You're a half-blood, too."

"Not me," said the captain. "The *Slippery Fish* is *my* true love, and I ain't leaving her, not even for the Obsidia. We'll row you out and give you a long piece of rope."

"Rope?" Danr asked.

"So you can climb back up." Ynara touched Aisa's cheek. "I beg you not to be angry with me, Aisa. My parents say you have earned your face. While your men are gone, we will give you one. Perhaps that will make up for it."

And she was gone with a splash.

"Earned your face?" Danr echoed, staring over the side. "What did she mean by that?"

Aisa's hand was on her cheek, her expression shocked, as if she had swallowed a live halibut. "How did she know? I never told anyone."

"Know what?" Danr demanded, more than a little peevish now.

She shook her head, and the dark tresses of her hair flowed like little waves. "A long time ago, when I was first sold into slavery, a school of merfolk stopped the ship that was transporting me to Palana. One of the mermaids told me that the slavers had stolen my strength away, so I had no face. When we stayed with the orcs, I worked in the house of Grick, Lady of Grain. I fought demons from my own head, and when I won, Grick said I had earned my face. Now the merfolk said I can have my face. Will they . . . truly give me one?"

She sounded so hopeful it gently tore Danr's heart in two. "They will! She said they would, right?"

"I hope so, Hamzu." The words came out in a whisper. "I want to swim with them again, bare my breast, and let my hair stream in the water behind me. I want to show my face, my good, strong face to everyone who will see it."

Danr, who was privately trying not to stagger under the image of a bare-breasted Aisa streaming through the water, put his arm around her shoulders. "We will make it happen. Together."

"A nice sentiment, but I cannot go with you on this part of the journey," she said, now more sad than angry. "Do not get hurt, do not die. If you allow yourself to get hurt, I will ensure that your recovery is quite painful. And if you die, I will have to go down into Halza's realm to haul you out by the ear."

He barked a laugh. "You would, too."

"Do I appear to be joking?"

"No." He looked into her eyes, her endless brown eyes, and suddenly he didn't want to leave, he wanted only to stay on that ship with her, and hang the rest of the world. *The world turns on petty desires,* whispered Death in his head, or maybe it was the memory of her words.

"I will at least accompany you to the edge of the Key," Aisa said with folded arms. "I did not come all this way to miss seeing it."

"Then come," Danr said heavily.

They boarded the longboat—Danr, Talfi, Aisa, and the golem, whom they still couldn't shake. Danr considered giving it a good shove, but the Obsidia, who were watching everything through this golem's mate, might decide to hurt

Ranadar or Kalessa if he did. Eight men and women came along to row. Years of working as a thrall made Danr feel he should help with the oars instead of sitting like a lump, but he knew nothing about boats and would just get in the way, so he crouched low and tried not to notice how much more than the ship the longboat rolled up and down. And his hands ached.

"Nervous?" Talfi asked him.

"Yes," he said truthfully. "Why?"

"You're crushing the gunwale." Talfi pointed, and Danr realized his fingers were white around the wooden rim. He forced himself to ease up, and the ache abated. Fortunately, the sailors knew their job and they reached the edge of the Key in short order.

The closer they got, the calmer the sea became, until it was like rowing across a pond. Danr stared down into the clear water and with that came the sickening idea that they were floating over thousands of feet of nothing. There was no bottom, nothing below but unforgiving ocean water. Before he could consider further, the sailor in charge of the rowing—Danr never did catch her name—called for a halt. The other sailors back-rowed furiously for a moment, and the boat stopped. Danr clapped his hand on his hat and raised his head.

They reached the edge. The water changed color here at a clear, sharp boundary. It was dark blue beneath their boat, and a blue-white a few yards past. The blue-white Key spread out before them, a great flatness that ate the horizon. Although the surface was flat, the Key seemed as bubbly as a child's bath. Danr caught his breath in amazement. The . . . liquid? . . . somehow swirled with sediment and bubbles and even light, all without creating a ripple on the surface. His hands now ached to touch it. It was only a yard from the front of the boat now, and he could just about do it.

The wonder of it quickened his heartbeat. Talfi and Aisa, meanwhile, moved to the prow for a better look. Even the golem came, probably so the Obsidia could see, and that made Danr grind his teeth. Danr and his friends had earned this incredible, amazing sight, and the Obsidia were getting it for nothing.

"It's hard to believe this is the Sundering," Talfi breathed.

"It's also the place all those storms come from," the sailor in charge reminded him. "So we need to hurry along before a great bloody tempest pops out of that thing. Sometimes you get waterspouts, you know."

"Where's the rope?" Danr asked. A great coil looped around the bottom of the boat. One end was tied to the prow. Danr picked up the free end.

"If it looks like we're being dragged in, I'm cutting it," the sailor said.

Danr nodded. "You have the ink, Talfi?" he asked for the fifteenth time.

Talfi, who was wearing a backpack, wordlessly pulled the bottle out, showed it for the fifteenth time, and replaced it.

"Then we're off," Danr said, and gave Aisa one last look. She nodded, and he tried to steel his heart, but suddenly he couldn't leave her. Not now, not ever. And a new thought was forming in his mind.

"What is it?" Talfi asked, seeing his expression.

"Look," he said slowly. "Maybe this isn't the best idea after all. How about we turn back?"

"Ranadar!" Talfi said insistently. "And Kalessa! The Obsidia—"

"It's kind of occurred to me that we're only doing what the Obsidia say because they're threatening to kill Ranadar and Kalessa. But if they actually *do* it, they lose their hold on us, which means we'd be completely free to hunt them down and destroy them. Not only that, Hector said he hated giving people a choice. No, they won't kill Ranadar and Kalessa because they'll lose their hold on us."

"An interesting idea," Aisa said, "if we are willing to bet our friends' lives."

Danr dropped the rope and turned to the golem, boring his gaze into the golem's glassy stare. "It's true, isn't it? You won't hurt Ranadar or Kalessa. Not really. You need us too much. Maybe we'll just turn this boat around and come back to—"

"Attention! Attention!" said the golem. "New orders received." With that, the golem picked Aisa up and flung her straight into the Key.

Chapter Eleven

Talfi watched in horror as Aisa vanished into the Key. Danr shouted and dove after her. Of course he would. The boat rocked, and the startled sailors flailed with their oars to steady it. Danr hit the Key and disappeared without even a splash. Talfi only hesitated half a moment himself and leaped after both of them with his heart in his mouth. Just before he hit the surface, he caught a glimpse of the golem staring after him with implacable eyes.

Warm water closed in around him, filled his ears and mouth. But it wasn't water. It felt greasy like melted lard, but billions of tiny bubbles bumbled against his skin with a faintly crisp sensation. He couldn't see for all the bubbles, in fact. His body also felt strangely buoyant, more buoyant than it did in water.

Talfi swam grimly downward. He had to find them, even if the task was hopeless. He couldn't see, and he was groping around, hoping against hope to find them by touch. And what would he do if he grabbed Danr? He couldn't pull someone that heavy to the surface. Aisa had probably already sunk to the bottom. She was drowning right this moment, in a panic, while Talfi was up here, flailing stupidly.

Don't think about that, he told himself. *Just search. Find one of them. Both of them.*

He dropped farther underwater, trying to see through the bubbles. His pack weighed him down and his lungs were beginning to complain. Still he swam, pushed on by fear over Aisa and Danr. They were his closest friends, and he wouldn't let them die. Or was Danr in danger? He was a half-blood and able to survive here—somehow. Aisa wasn't. She would drown. Come to that, how was Talfi himself supposed to survive? He couldn't die, not until he ran out of however many days Death had given him, but did that really mean he wouldn't die down here? If he did, what would happen to him?

The bubbles closed in, effectively blinding him. His lungs ached for air. He glanced up, but he couldn't tell how far away he was from the surface. Then an undertow caught him and yanked him downward. Talfi flung up a hand, reaching for the surface in terror, but the light was fading around him.

You can't die, he told himself. *You're the boy who can't die.*

And what would happen if he died and returned to life down here? Would he spend an eternity of days drowning and coming back and drowning and coming back? Death would be kinder. Ranadar would never learn what happened to him.

His chest hurt, and he wanted air more than anything while the water closed its gentle, relentless embrace around him. His heart was a sledgehammer in his ears. At last the need became too great and he couldn't stop himself. Air burst from his chest. For a tiny moment it felt as though he was breathing normally. Everything would be fine. Then he was forced to inhale. It was horrendous. Oily water flooded his mouth and nose. He tried to cough, but he had no air to cough with.

Good-bye, Ran, he thought, praying that somehow Ranadar could hear him. *Nine Gods, I never thought—*

He inhaled again and tried to cough again. This time it
was . . . different. Not as bad. It even seemed as though he
was breathing, just a little. Automatically, he exhaled and
inhaled again. The oily water bubbled through his chest. It
felt nothing like air. It was heavy, and he could feel it moving
in and around his lungs in a sensation that was both sickening and sweet. His need for air lessened. He breathed the
strange water again. His head cleared and his body seemed
almost . . . normal. Talfi hung there in the dark, not sure what
to think.

Neither air nor water nor earth, he thought, and relief
swirled through him. Danr was certainly discovering the
same thing even now. But what about Aisa?

Now that Talfi wasn't panicking about himself, he was able
to take better stock. He could breathe after a fashion, good.
The undertow was still pulling him downward. No—it wasn't
an undertow. He was falling. The water wasn't dense enough
to hold him up, and he was falling farther and farther down.
Every other time he had gone deep underwater, he felt the
pressure against his ears and his stomach, and he had heard
stories about people diving too deep and their eardrums bursting. There was no pain or pressure, though. Maybe inhaling
the water or whatever this was dealt with that problem. All
right, then—maybe he could get through this.

Beneath him, he saw a faint green glow. He fell a little
faster, though not nearly as fast as he would fall in open air.
The glow grew brighter. It was luminescent, like mushrooms. A gentle current pushed Talfi down toward it, and
he decided it would be better to go along with it instead of
fight it. The same current had probably taken Aisa and
Danr. He spread his arms in an attempt to control his fall,

both relishing the strangeness of breathing underwater and trying not to worry about both his friends.

No. One friend. Best not to worry about Aisa. She was certainly dead by now. The thought punched him cold in the stomach, and a lump of grief thickened his throat. Danr would be devastated. Talfi wouldn't be far behind. Aisa was one of the few people he remembered clearly. He had been there that wonderful day in Xaron when she emerged from the shadows with her face uncovered, and he had seen Danr's joy at the sight of her simple beauty. She had been there that awful day he came back to life among the orcs, and had explained who he was. That terrible day the elf king had murdered him for the second time, Aisa helped him regain part of his memory. She had accepted his status as *regi* and his love for Ranadar without batting an eye, and for that he would have trotted across hot lava for her. Sarcastic and witty and just a little nasty—Aisa was always there, and Talfi loved her for it. Not in the way Danr did, but he loved her nonetheless, and the thought of her drowning because of the Obsidia's golem jolted him with fury even as it crushed him with sadness.

The glow spread out, bigger and brighter now. It illuminated a regular pattern. It was like looking at a map drawn in green ink. With a start, Talfi realized he was dropping steadily toward a ruined city, one covered in luminous green plant life. Streets and wrecked stone buildings formed the spokes of the world's biggest broken wheel. Talfi was drifting toward the outer rim. In fact, he was rushing toward it now. Talfi backpedaled, trying to slow himself down, but the current swept him toward it. He was coming at the stone street at an angle, too fast. In desperation Talfi spread his arms and legs wide, trying to put up as much resistance as possible. It worked, at least a little. He slowed slightly, and hit. Talfi bounced and rolled, feeling every slippery stone pound along his body. He all but slammed into a wall so hard it knocked him breathless, or whatever that meant here underwater. At least he had stopped.

He leaned against the slick wall and tried not to pant. The water slid in and out of his lungs, making him uncomfortably aware of his breathing. It also occurred to him that he could see. The bubbles had disappeared.

"That's a luck," he said aloud without thinking. To his surprise, he heard his own voice, just as he might on land. He tried again. "Heigh-ho! Nice day! Danr!"

There was no echo, but the sound was otherwise clear. He shouted a bit longer, but got no response. The water was a constant presence, tugging at him, shoving him gently or insistently, forcing him to grab at the wall to stay in place. Luminescent slime covered his hand and made a trail in the water when he pulled away. Carefully, he edged around the wall and half walked, half swam into what he supposed was a street.

Rotten stone buildings covered in waving plant life stared at him with their empty windows. Many of them had fallen over or disintegrated into piles of rubble. Doors and shutters had long rotted away, but other objects remained. A cracked pot perched precariously on a stone bench. Empty circles of stone showed where trees had once shaded the streets. A doll's head stared emptily up from a blanket of glowing green slime. Sections of the building and block had been utterly destroyed, and other sections looked untouched, except for the glowing slime that grew everywhere. Often parts of the ground felt spongy, and Talfi remembered that Stane who came here were supposed to drop to the center of the world. Everything was desolate, abandoned, dead.

And something else was missing.

"Fish," he said aloud. The place was empty of marine life. Maybe they couldn't survive here. That made him think of Aisa again, and the grief hit him. He had to find Danr and look for Aisa's . . . body. Then they still had to look for Grandfather Wyrm. It all seemed overwhelming, especially now that Talfi was by himself.

The current pushed at Talfi, and he drifted down the street. He often felt that way, as if he was drifting through the world, with nothing to anchor him. He had no past, no family, no real memories of who he was. He didn't even know if Talfi was his real name. Talfi the drifter. But this place . . . this was the place where he had died the first time. Maybe he'd been born here.

The dread tightened his skin again. He didn't really want to know if this had been his home.

None of it looked familiar, at least. He touched the amulets at his throat, the leather pouch Danr had given him and the silver medallion with the Iron Axe on it. Death had shown him his first death in images, and watching it had been like letting someone grope inside his chest with a hand of ice, but it hadn't triggered any memories, thank Olar. The only thing he got was a vague sense of metal clashing on a battlefield, and screams, and blood. And then it was water, all kinds of water.

"Danr!" he called. "Danr, where are you?"

No answer. His voice sounded dead, and the buildings stared back at him. Talfi swam-walked farther down the street, leaving footprints in green slime. What now? Maybe he should find Grandfather Wyrm on his own. He could find the power of the shape and bring it back to rescue Ranadar before—

A cold hand grabbed his shoulder and yanked him sideways into a cracked house. Talfi's heart all but leaped out of his chest and he twisted in the grip, frantic. A toothy face came into view. Talfi tried to fight, but the water slowed his reactions.

"It's me, you oafus maloafus," Danr said. "Quit yelling!"

Talfi relaxed, though it took some time for his heart to slow. Now that his eyes were adjusting, he could see the outline of his friend, and a little cloud of happiness burst over him. "Vik! I thought you were . . . how did you . . . ?"

"I'm all right." Danr patted him roughly on the shoulder. "But keep it down, yeah?"

Talfi hated to ask, but he had to know. "Did you find . . . Aisa?"

"I did."

Another voice said, "He did." From behind Danr's massive form stepped Aisa herself. Even in the dim light, she looked perfectly well. Her dark hair floated in a cloud around her face.

Talfi gaped, then swept Aisa into a fast hug. It was a strange thing to do this underwater. "Aisa! You're . . ."

"Not feeding fish, yes," she said, gently freeing herself. "Not yet, anyway. Look!" She inhaled and exhaled pointedly. "Ynara was wrong. I did not need to cross Death's threshold to walk between worlds. Though I believe there must be less exciting ways to learn this."

"The Obsidia tried to kill you." Danr cracked his knuckles, a strangely crunchy sound underwater. "I won't forget that."

"Hector must have decided we were making a choice," Aisa said. "He had the golem throw me into the Key, knowing you would follow."

"I'll give him a choice," Talfi muttered. "Vik or Halza."

"Hmm. I am planning to make him choose between his left and right testicle." Aisa produced a knife and tapped it against her palm.

"We can do both," Talfi said.

"I look forward to it."

"Not so loud," Danr warned.

"Why?" Talfi asked. "What's wrong with—?"

In answer, Danr clamped a hand over his mouth and pointed at the door. A long, scaly form glided silently up the broken street. A toothy head big enough to bite a horse in half swayed above powerful-looking flippers. Talfi's eyes went wide and he tried to gasp around Danr's hand. The creature lashed past them with its powerful tail and was gone.

"Quiet, yes," Talfi gulped. "That's the way to go."

"When I first landed, I saw bigger ones," Danr said, eyeing the door. "And stranger. A four-headed turtle the size of a house. A thing that looked like an octopus fighting with a tree."

"I haven't seen any fish down here," Talfi said. "What do they eat?"

"Each other," Aisa said. "Did the bottle break, Talfi?"

Fear twinged through Talfi and he yanked his backpack off to check. To his relief, the bottle of ink was still in it, corked and undamaged. "That would've been difficult."

"You do enjoy your drama," Aisa said. "We should go. Carefully."

They crept out of the building like shy minnows and slipped down the street. Talfi twisted his head in every direction, watching for monsters. They could come from above, too, and that made it worse. He couldn't die, but he didn't relish the thought of being eaten alive and returned to life afterward.

"Stick to the walls." Danr picked his way over some rubble.

"Does any of this look familiar to you?" Aisa asked.

Talfi shook his head. "I'm not sure I want it to. All these people." He gestured at the ruined city. "Ripped to pieces. I still can't believe I was there. That I . . . caused it."

"You did not cause this," Aisa said stoutly. "The Stane did."

"The Stane thanks you," Danr put in.

"He makes a joke!" Aisa poked him. "He thinks he is funny."

"Her sarcasm returns," Danr shot back. "I don't—"

From around the corner rushed a terrible shape. All Talfi saw was a wide mouth and serrated teeth and dead black eyes. Then Danr was there. He caught the creature—it was a lean shark with a mane of suckered tentacles, and it was at least ten feet long. Danr had grabbed its snout in one hand and its lower jaw in the other. The shark thing twisted its head, wrestling with Danr. The tentacles lashed at him, and a cloud of slimy silt rose from the ocean floor.

Aisa didn't hesitate. She leaped in with her knife, slashing at the tentacles. Three of them wrapped around Danr's arms and body. Talfi had no knife, and he cast about for something to do. Danr gritted his teeth and strained. The shark thing shook its head again and tried to bite at him, but Danr's arms bulged and the shark couldn't close its mouth. Blood tanged the water. Talfi snatched up a sharp bit of rock from the ground and tried to move for the shark thing. His motions were slowed by water. It was like moving in a dream.

"The eye!" he shouted. "Aisa! Hit its eye!"

Aisa changed tactic and stabbed at the eye closest to her and missed. Talfi hit the thing with his rock and scored a hit on the dead black eye. The creature didn't seem to notice. Another tentacle wrapped around Danr, this time around a leg. He grunted, and the veins stood out on his tree trunk arms.

"Together!" Talfi yelled. "Now!"

At the same time, he and Aisa hit the creature in both eyes with their makeshift weapons. The creature shuddered once and let up on its attack for just a moment. That seemed to be all that Danr needed. He strained hard and with a primordial roar, gave a great heave. The creature's jaw and part of its head tore off. Blood gushed into the water in a black cloud. Convulsions racked the creature. Its tentacles released Danr, who stumbled backward, still holding the thing's lower jaw in his hand. The creature rolled over, thrashing and sweeping with its tail. It smashed into a wall, bringing down rubble. Danr dropped the bloody jaw.

"Run!" Talfi barked.

They ran—or tried to. The water made it slow going. They bounded and swam away from the dying creature until exhaustion forced them to halt. All three of them huddled in a ruined doorway, trying to catch their watery breaths. Talfi found it was hard to rest when even breathing was an effort.

"Are you injured?" Aisa asked Danr.

"Yes," Danr replied, always the truth-teller. He held out his hand. Blood rose from a series of slashes. His arms and legs were also covered with sucker marks.

"The golem did not allow me to bring my kit, so I have nothing to sew this with," Aisa said. "But a bandage will benefit you, even underwater. At least the wound is clean." She cut pieces from her skirt with her knife and set to work while Danr tried not to wince.

"Vik!" Talfi said in admiration. "Sometimes I forget how strong you really are."

"We should move as soon as we can," Danr said shortly. "The blood and that thing's corpse will attract other monsters."

As if in answer, a bellow boomed down the street from the creature's death throes. It was answered by a second bellow. The trio exchanged nervous glances and edged out into the street again, sticking close to walls and rubble.

"Where are we supposed to find Grandfather Wyrm?" Talfi asked. "We don't even know what he looks like."

"For all we know, he's back there having lunch," Danr

muttered. "I have no idea how to find him. To tell the truth, I thought he'd find us, or that the merfolk would show us."

"We cannot stay down here forever," Aisa agreed. "The boat will leave."

A dreadful thought stole over Talfi. "How are we going to get back *up*?"

"Up?" Danr echoed.

Talfi wet his lips, even though they were soaked. Force of habit. "You were supposed to bring the end of the rope down with you and tie it to something. How are we going to get back up without it?"

A horrified look crossed both their faces. In answer, Aisa tried to swim upward, but after clearing a couple of feet, she drifted back down again.

"This water is too . . . light," she concluded. "That is why we walk and do not swim."

"So we're trapped at the bottom of the Key with a bunch of monsters and no way to find Grandfather Wyrm," Talfi said. "Well, we've been in worse situations."

"When?" Danr demanded.

"Give me a minute and I'll remember one."

"While you are remembering, we should continue on," Aisa said, moving into the street again. "This city is built like a wheel. If Grandfather Wyrm is the most powerful being here, it seems likely he would be at—"

"The center!" Talfi said. "You're right! Let's try there. It's a place to start, anyway."

"I don't know." Danr paused doubtfully, the bandage on his hand waving faintly in the current. "I think he might—"

The ground beneath them moved. Startled, Talfi lost his footing and stumbled, thrashing in the water to regain his balance. Danr snatched both him and Aisa away, flinging them farther up the street. Talfi managed to regain his feet and land with at least some grace.

The stony street cracked and crumbled. From it rumbled an enormous thing, taller than four elephants, wider than the street itself, and long, long, long. Its back was so broad, the top was flat and had merged with the street itself. Danr tumbled away from the rising form. It shed sediment and slime in a glowing cloud as it rose.

"Hamzu!" Aisa screamed. She tried to run for him, but Talfi held her back. Danr managed to scramble free and half run, half swim toward them.

It was the biggest wyrm Talfi had ever seen. Its golden eyes were easily a yard across, and a platoon of men could have marched down its gullet. Boulders clung to its back like pebbles. But it was clearly ancient. Crevasses snaked through its scales. Its teeth and horns were yellow and blunted. Long hairs grew from its snout. Talfi backpedaled in chilly terror, but the ground was shaking and he kept losing his balance. So did Aisa and Danr. The wyrm opened its dreadful mouth wide and Talfi saw the end.

"You spoke my name three times, yes," the wyrm said in a voice like measured thunder. "You woke me, yes. Your lives will pay the forfeit, for when I wake, I am *hungry*."

Grandfather Wyrm. Talfi's first fear-addled thought was that he was bigger than the legends said. His second fear-addled thought was an attempt to remember how many times they had said that name aloud. Was it three? His third thought was how stupid it was to think these things when Grandfather Wyrm was ready to devour him.

Before Talfi or Danr could react further, Aisa prostrated herself on the ground in front of the wyrm. "Oh, great one!" she cried. "I beg mercy of you. We were foolish and did not know we disturbed your well-earned rest. You are truly a being of great power and wisdom, and even the Nine must live in fear of you. The stories do not do you justice."

Grandfather Wyrm hesitated. "Stories? What stories, yes?"

"The terrifying, world-trembling stories of Grandfather Wyrm." Aisa coughed pointedly in Talfi and Danr's direction. *Right!* Talfi thought, and dropped to the stones like Aisa. Danr hastened to imitate. "Every child has heard the stories of how Grandfather Wyrm called up storms to fight Fell and Belinna themselves, and how Grandfather Wyrm creates whirlpools that sink entire fleets, and how Grandfather Wyrm makes the earth tremble when he is angry. I never thought I would actually see such power in person, and I tremble before such awesome might."

Aisa was really laying it on. On the other hand, Grandfather Wyrm hadn't eaten them yet, so she must know what she was doing. Talfi lay still and tried to look unappetizing.

"They tell stories, yes," Grandfather Wyrm said. His slow voice thrummed against Talfi's bones. "How long have I been asleep?"

"It has been a thousand years since the Sundering, great one," Aisa said.

"A thousand, yes?" Even when Grandfather Wyrm sounded surprised, his presence filled the water until he became the entire world. Talfi felt as insignificant as a grain of sand. "Then it has been fifty years since I last woke, yes. There were storms and . . . merfolk. I did not know they told stories. It would be a fine thing to hear them, yes. It becomes tedious in the deep."

"Would you like me to tell you one?" Aisa offered quickly.

"I would, yes."

Aisa raised herself up a little and spoke. It was a story Talfi had heard more than once, about how Fell and Belinna, the twin gods, went fishing together in a boat with Tikk, their trickster brother. Tikk, however, put a secret spell on the ox's head they used for bait, and when Fell and Belinna pulled up the line, Grandfather Wyrm was on the hook. A great battle ensued, but instead of the usual ending, in which Grandfather Wyrm sank defeated back into the sea, Aisa spun a new ending, in which the gods fled back to Lumenhame with their tails between their legs.

"And so Grandfather Wyrm roared his triumph to the skies," Aisa finished. "Such is the story."

A moment of silence followed. Stones ground against Talfi's knees, but he didn't move. Water pushed unceasingly against him.

"A fine tale," Grandfather Wyrm boomed at last. "And well told, yes. But still you have wakened me, and I have not eaten for fifty years."

Aisa gulped. Talfi scrambled to his feet and came forward. It took all his nerve to walk toward a wyrm whose head was as big as a ship. "We brought a gift, Your Divine Wisdomness," he said. "We have it on good authority you'll enjoy it."

"A gift?" Grandfather Wyrm repeated. "It has been long since I have had a gift."

Talfi opened his pack. For a terrible moment, he was afraid the bottle was broken, but it was whole, with the cork in. "This, Your Muchness."

"What is it?"

"Ink. From a giant squid. Very fresh."

"Squid ink?" Grandfather Wyrm cocked his head, sending around new currents that nearly knocked Talfi off his feet. The bottle flew from his hand and tumbled toward rocky rubble. Gasping, he scrambled after it and caught the neck with his fingertips. "Squid ink is . . . a fine treat, yes. Bring it to me."

"I live to obey, Your Wondrousness."

"Don't overdo it," Danr hissed from his position on the ground.

Trembling more than a little, Talfi edged closer to Grandfather Wyrm's head, which now rested on the ocean floor.

Massive gills opened and closed behind his eyes, and his teeth were taller than tombstones. Talfi was all too aware that if Grandfather Wyrm opened his mouth quickly, the motion would suck him in like a minnow. When he was a yard away, he held up the bottle.

"Would you like me to open it, Your Wyrminess?"

Desire and even avarice glowed in Grandfather Wyrm's eyes. His voice became husky. "Do. Now, yes."

Talfi pulled the cork. Black ink puffed out in a dark cloud. Grandfather Wyrm inhaled gently, and the ink sucked into his nostrils like smoke. He slitted his eyes in pleasure, and Talfi quickly replaced the cork.

"Yes," the great wyrm murmured. "Yes. A delightful gift. Perhaps you are worth keeping, yes. And oh! I can see now. The Tree, yes."

"The Tree?" Talfi echoed.

"The Tree tips, yes." Grandfather Wyrm's golden eyes were heavy-lidded. "It tips indeed. What a shame. A thousand years ago, the Fae trounced the Stane. Now the Stane attempt to trounce the Fae, yes."

"They do?" Talfi asked, startled. "Excuse me, Your Wonderfulness, but the Fae tried to wipe out the Stane. We were there."

"You do not see everything, yes." Grandfather Wyrm blew contented bubbles. "The Kin always pay when the Fae and the Stane fight. I am living proof of that, yes."

"Both of us are," Talfi couldn't help muttering.

Danr cautiously got to his feet now and bowed before Grandfather Wyrm, who was currently looking much more mellow. "Er . . . we've come a long way for your wisdom, great one."

"A truth-teller," Grandfather Wyrm observed. "It is always a fascination to converse with your kind."

Danr looked taken aback. "How did you know?"

"I am old, yes, and I know much more than you." Grandfather Wyrm shifted, sending rumbles up and down the street. "What do you want?"

"The Kin have lost the power of the shape," Danr said.

"No," said Grandfather Wyrm. "They have not."

"I don't understand, great one," Danr replied. "The Kin can't change their shapes anymore. Not since the Sundering."

"When the Tree last tipped a thousand years ago, the trollwives took that power from the Kin, but they didn't take the talent," Grandfather Wyrm said. "I saw it happen."

"You were there, too?" Talfi couldn't help blurting out.

"Too?" Grandfather Wyrm echoed. He leaned in to stare more closely at Talfi, who forced himself to stand his ground, no small thing against the rush of water and cloud of sediment. "Ah! You were the young squire whose blood spilled on the altar, yes. Such a bright young lad you were. How are you alive to see the Tree tip twice?"

Talfi's mouth felt dry, despite the ocean. "When the Axe was sundered, its power went into me. It brought me back to life every time I died."

"Very good," Grandfather Wyrm murmured. "Delightful, yes. We are the same, you and I, yes, kept alive by a power that changed us." He chuckled.

Talfi swallowed. The idea that he had anything in common with this thunderous wyrm was more than a little overwhelming.

"How were you there, great one?" Aisa asked. "The legends of the Sundering don't mention Grandfather Wyrm."

"They would not, yes." Grandfather Wyrm's golden eyes took on a faraway look. "I was Kin back then, a human, a magician, yes. But very powerful. Perhaps the most powerful magician of the shape the world ever knew, yes. My wife was powerful in her own right, a general in the army. I was so proud of her. She wore a golden star on her shield, and her hair was the same color, but I have forgotten her name, yes. How could I have forgotten her name?"

"It was long ago," Danr said. "And you've been sleeping a long time."

"Yes," said Grandfather Wyrm sadly. "The king who commanded her allied with the Stane. I begged him not to, yes, asked him to throw in with the good Fae, but he refused to listen. The Stane had forged the Iron Axe, and the king was sure it would end the war with the Stane victorious. But the Fae stole the Axe away, yes, and the Stane decided the only recourse was to destroy it. My wife's army guarded the trollwives and their ritual. I wanted nothing to do with it, and I stood on a mountain far away, and when the trollwives stole the Kin's power to destroy the Axe, yes, I felt it coming and I was able to keep my power even as everyone else lost theirs. Then the earth cracked and the sea rushed in. My wife cried out and I changed into a wyrm to dive after her, but I could not find her, and when the earth settled down, I saw no reason to rejoin the Nine People, not with my wife dead and gone, yes. I wish I had her name to keep me warm in this place."

Talfi noticed Danr's hands curl, as if around the handle of a weapon.

"So you have your power of the shape," Aisa said. "You are the only one."

"I am not," said Grandfather Wyrm. "The talent for shape magic still runs strong in all three branches of the Kin, yes. They just lack the power to use it. I have seen a very few who still manage to change shape, merfolk who find a way to walk on land, or orcs who bond too strongly with their wyrms, or humans who become wolves during the full moon, yes, but only two or three in every generation."

"Where is the power now?" Talfi asked.

Grandfather Wyrm raised his head as if testing the breeze,

though they were underwater. "Interesting. It was bound up for centuries, but now the power has been restored to the world. It wanders about like a lost child. All it needs is focus, yes."

"Can . . . can we learn to focus it?" Talfi said hopefully.

"Not yet," Grandfather Wyrm said. "If you have the talent for shape magic, yes, then power needs an opening, a portal to reach inside you. To open that portal, we will need the same tools that closed it in the first place, yes."

"Tools?" Aisa said. "What tools?"

"I am hungry," said Grandfather Wyrm, raising his head again. "Perhaps I should eat before I tell you more, yes."

Danr and Aisa both backed up a step, fear written on their faces. The same fear bolted through Talfi, but he uncorked the ink bottle with shaking hands. More ink floated out of it, and Grandfather Wyrm inhaled appreciatively. He brought his head down slowly, with slitted eyes.

"Yes," he sighed. "Yes."

Talfi swallowed at the close call. "The tools," he prompted faintly. "The focus."

"You'll need the knife that first spilled your blood, yes." Grandfather Wyrm looked contemplative, even mellow. "It is still there, as is the altar, in the center of the city. Now that it has tasted power, only the one who died beneath its blade can touch it safely, yes, so it is fortunate you came, Talfi. Bring me the knife, and I will show you how to restore the power of the shape, yes."

Chapter Twelve

Talfi followed Danr and Aisa down the ruined city street. It was tiring, pushing against the water every step of the way and watching for the monsters created by the loose magic of the Sundering.

"Grandfather Wyrm knew me," he said quietly. "From before. Do you think he knows more?"

Danr drew him into an alcove, and Aisa piled in as well while a crablike creature with four claws skittered across the ruins past their hiding place. They emerged once it was gone.

"More?" Danr asked.

"About who I was," Talfi clarified. "Who my family was. Where I came from."

"I don't know," Danr said. "We can ask him when we get back."

"I don't think I want to know," Talfi said.

"The amnesia boy wishes not to remember," Aisa said. "What an odd choice."

Talfi didn't answer. They picked their way farther along. Aisa was right—it *was* an odd choice. Why shouldn't he want to remember? He was a thousand years old, but he didn't *feel* that old. He only remembered the last couple of years with any clarity, and had only snatches here and there before that, mostly memories of Ranadar. Maybe he was avoiding this because his family was long dead. If they had somehow survived the Sundering, they would have died of old age anyway. What good would it do to remember the pain of losing them? Better to let old memories remain buried.

But as they moved closer to the city center, faint memories now stirred. A building looked familiar. An open marketplace made him think of a hundred booted feet marching in rhythm with pennants snapping in the wind. For a moment a tall man with brown hair and blue eyes like his own stood next to him with a hand on his shoulder. Then he was back under the expansive ocean with Danr and Aisa.

"All you all right?" Danr asked.

"I'm remembering," he replied. "I don't like it. But we have to keep going—we need the power of the shape to get Ranadar out of that tank."

"Ironic, is it not?" Aisa said. "We are breathing at the bottom of the sea to save Ranadar from drowning in a tank."

"If that was a joke, it wasn't funny," Talfi retorted. "If it wasn't a joke, it was a shitty thing to say."

"Hey, now—careful how you talk to Aisa," Danr said. "It's not her fault we're here."

"Isn't it?" Talfi exploded. "If she hadn't wanted to see mermaids so much, we would never have come to Balsia, and if we hadn't come to Balsia, Ranadar wouldn't be chained in that tank."

"If you had not fallen in love with one of the Fae, you would not be worried," Aisa shot back.

"So you're saying that it's the fault of a *rasregi*?" Talfi snarled.

"Maybe it is," Danr growled. "And I can see the truth, so I know."

"See this, then." Talfi grabbed his own crotch.

"That will do!" Aisa stepped between them. "We have all been hurt by other people and do not need to hurt ourselves."

Talfi turned his head and ground some teeth. Dead, slimy buildings crumbled off into the distance, and the bubbly sea rose high overhead like a dome prison. "I'm just . . . I'm pissed off. On edge."

Danr put a hand on his shoulder, and right then the last thing Talfi wanted was kind words. Fortunately, Danr only said, "Let's keep going, then."

They swam-walked closer to the town center, and the city became familiar. More memories dripped into Talfi's mind like hot wax. He was a little boy with pride in his chest, watching his father teach soldiers to fight with swords in that courtyard. He was eight years old and arguing with his older sisters on those steps. He was ten years old and exploding with happiness while he received his position as a squire from the king in that square. He was thirteen and stealing an exciting kiss from a boy named Gavren in those stables, and the boy had red hair. The city flipped between fantastic and fractured.

"Move!" Danr's voice popped the memories like soap bubbles. He herded them both into an alcove in time to avoid a cross between a lizard and a manta ray that glided malevolently overhead. Once the creature had passed, they continued, and more memories wormed their way into his mind—learning to use a sword himself, falling off a roof and breaking his arm, receiving the news that General Bathilda herself wanted to see him.

His chest tightened and his hands trembled, but he kept

going. They could see the center of the city now. It was named Malennsa, he remembered that now. A dozen streets led into a great round space more than a hundred paces across, now filled with rubble. Not one building survived in this spot. But against all expectation, in the exact center of the space, a high platform with stairs on all four sides rose three stories above the floor. It was clear of rubble, but the remains of thick, pillars stood all around the top. Talfi remembered the place. It was a temple to the Nine, or what was left of it.

"Up there," he said hoarsely.

"I don't like it," Danr said. "No cover."

"You watch while we climb," Aisa said.

Cautiously, they clambered over the rubble. It was easier than Talfi thought—the light water let them scramble or bound over large pieces—and they reached the stairs, which were of cracked gray marble. Talfi was playing sword games with his best friend, Jak, he was flushed with anger when another squire called him *regi*, he was following General Bathilda up the steps to the temple. The general had a gold star painted on her armor, and she had told him his father had recommended him for an important mission. Mystified pride suffused him. What kind of mission started in the temple?

"Talfi, you look pale," Aisa broke in. "Are you well?"

"This was the spot where I died the first time." His heart beat a frantic rhythm and he wanted to pant, but the airy water wouldn't let him. "Grandfather Wyrm's wife brought me here."

"Should we turn back?" Danr asked.

Talfi almost said yes, but then he thought of Ranadar huddling cold and wet in the tank while the water inched toward his chest, his throat, his mouth. They had to hurry. For Ranadar.

"Let's go," he said.

They were halfway up the steps now. Talfi was leaping away from the redheaded stable boy Gavren in terror, realizing they had been seen. He was brushing Sir Devrit's horse, and when the nasty beast nipped his shoulder, Sir Devrit cuffed him on the ear for upsetting the horse. He was standing bewildered among the temple pillars in a strange circle of dwarfs, trolls, giants, humans, and orcs. General Bathilda was there, too.

They were close to the top now. The altar rose above Talfi, and the water rose above the altar. He could barely walk under the weight of the memories. Two strong men grabbed him from behind and clapped fetters to his wrists. He fought, but their arms were iron. A slow chant rose from some of the robed priests.

"What is this?" Talfi gasped. "You had a special mission for me."

"I do," said General Bathilda. The star on her armor seemed to glow. "You've been selected special, Squire Talfi. Your mission is to die so the rest of us can live."

The men dragged him to the altar and yanked his wrists over his head. "Papa!" Talfi shouted. "Papa! Stop them!"

The general leaned over him and clasped a medallion around his neck. The trollwives shuffled toward the altar. They were massive as trees, their arms thick as branches. Their swarthy skin gleamed like obsidian, and their jaws jutted forward, revealing yellow teeth. But their clothes— robes and well-cut dresses—were rich with embroidered velvet and heavy with silk. They chanted together in harsh voices like grating stones. One of them raised a long, jagged dagger. Desperate, Talfi looked into the crowd. Part of it was obscured, blurry. He couldn't see who was there. He didn't *want* to see who was there. It was pain, it was fear, it was betrayal.

Danr, Aisa, and Talfi were at the top now. The altar stood before them, and gleaming on the stone floor next to it, inexplicably untouched by time, the Sundering, or luminescent slime, lay a long, jagged dagger. Talfi was shaking now. Danr propped him up, and Talfi clung to him, terrified to take another step. The knife blade curved like a snake.

"Talfi," Aisa said, "you are not well. We should back away and try again when you've rested."

"We can't," Talfi said faintly. "Grandfather Wyrm said I'm the only one who can pick up the knife."

"Bull's balls." Danr left Talfi and strode to the knife. He bent down to snatch it up.

"Danr, no!" Talfi cried, but too late. Danr touched the knife. A great crack of thunder slammed Talfi's ears. A bolt of red lightning from the knife blasted Danr so hard he flew backward and slammed into one of the ruined pillars. The lightning held him against the stone like a red spear for a terrible moment, then vanished. Danr slid groaning several feet to the floor.

"Hamzu!" Aisa cried, and rushed to him as best she could through the water. He groaned faintly.

Talfi looked down at the cruel knife. Every nerve screamed at him not to touch it, to walk away and leave it, let the past die. But if he did, his future with Ranadar would perish. Slowly, in a watery dream, Talfi reached down and clasped the knife.

He was chained to the altar. The trollwife raised the jagged dagger over his chest. Desperate, Talfi looked into the crowd. Papa was there. Papa, with his own sword at his side. Papa, who knew the king!

"Help me!" he cried.

Papa put his hand on his sword, and for a split second everything was all right. He was going to step forward and parry the trollwife's knife with his sword. Then Papa's face hardened.

Regi, Papa mouthed, and turned his back.

Talfi was back in the stable, leaping away from Gavren. Papa was in the doorway. His face was a stone. He left without a word. The next day, Gavren was gone, no one seemed to know where or why.

Regi, Papa mouthed, and turned his back.

The general had a gold star painted on her armor, and she had told him his father had recommended him for an important mission. Mystified pride suffused him. What could she want him to do in the temple? "You've been selected special, Squire Talfi."

Regi, Papa mouthed, and turned his back.

The trollwife pressed the dagger into Talfi's chest. The point pierced his skin, then meat. Pain like nothing he'd ever known sliced through him, tore him in two, and he screamed. The knife met his heart. He felt it beat against the metal, and he begged the trollwife with his eyes to go no further. She thrust her lower jaw forward and leaned slowly on the blade. It burst into his heart with an agony that flooded every cell of his body.

Regi, Papa mouthed, and turned his back, and Talfi couldn't tell which pain was worse.

He was kneeling beside the altar under the airy water, breathing the strange liquid and gripping the dreadful knife hilt in his right hand. Tears formed in his eyes and drifted away.

"Now I know why I didn't want to remember," he whispered.

And then Aisa and Danr were there, with their arms around him. They shut out the dim light and blocked out the world, let him draw strength from them. He was glad for their presence.

"We are here, Talfi," Aisa said. "You need not worry."

"I'll try," he said.

"How much do you remember?" Danr rumbled.

"All of it," he said, wiping stupidly at his eyes. "It was . . . I'll tell you later. For now, we have the knife—and something else I think we can use. We should go."

Talfi stuck the knife in his belt and they headed for the steps. Then Talfi caught both his friends by the arm. "I didn't mean any of those shitty things I said before. I'm glad you both are here."

Aisa nodded wordlessly, and Danr's meaty hand squeezed his shoulder. Nothing more needed to be said.

Grandfather Wyrm was dozing in the spot where they'd left him. Danr threw a small boulder at his nose in a blow that would have killed a full-grown ox, but only served to rouse the great wyrm.

"Do you have the knife?" he asked.

Talfi held it up.

"Very nice. Still, I have not eaten, and I am beginning to think a meal is a better idea than giving you the secret of the shape, yes."

Gulping, Talfi sheathed the knife again and pulled the ink bottle from his pack. It would be dreadful to have gone through all that only to be devoured. He uncorked the bottle once more, and a few faint wisps of ink drifted from it. Grandfather Wyrm inhaled them anyway. The bottle was empty.

"Very well, yes," Grandfather Wyrm murmured like a sleepy mountain. "I may as well give you a little help. The power of the shape is passed on through the blood. You can inherit it from one or both parents, yes, or sometimes you can be granted the power, if you are strong enough. Let me look at you, young Talfi."

Talfi stood perfectly still while Grandfather Wyrm's

massive head looked him up and down. Abruptly, a tongue the size of a team of horses flickered out and licked him. Slime covered him. Talfi staggered back, horrified. At least the water quickly washed it away, but he could feel it in his ears and up his nose.

"You have no talent for the shape, yes," Grandfather Wyrm said. Then he turned and licked Danr, who shuddered. "You have a little talent, half-blood. You could change into one other shape if you are lucky, yes."

"One?" Danr said in his husky voice.

Grandfather Wyrm ignored the question and licked Aisa, who didn't respond at all. Talfi had to admire her fortitude. Grandfather Wyrm's eyes widened. "You, my dear, taste quite . . . tremendous, yes. Your talent outstrips most Kin, if you could only use it."

Now Aisa did stagger. "My talent?"

"I do not envy you," Grandfather Wyrm continued. "You will have to learn to use it on your own, for I cannot teach you. Or rather, I do not wish to. I have grown lazy, yes."

"How does the talent work?" Aisa asked.

"It is great fun, yes. You can change your shape, that's the first thing to learn. If you become good at it, you can learn to change the shape of other people or of other animals or even plants. Perhaps you will learn to crush two or more together into new shapes."

"The chimera," Aisa breathed. "The unicorn."

"The wyrms," Grandfather Wyrm added slyly. "Yes. But all this shaping takes power. You will find that you can borrow power from other people. It flows better if they let you, but the truly talented can even take it from the unwilling."

"Is that where the legends of vampires come from?" Aisa was clearly interested despite herself.

"You are intelligent, yes. It is much easier to take power

from someone who has changed his shape, which is why in my day, witches had familiars. Toads and frogs and cats that had once been Kin."

"How do we start?" Danr asked impatiently.

"Perhaps I shouldn't tell you." Grandfather Wyrm's eyes were clearing of the ink's influence now. It had been a small dose. "The Kin have helped ruin the world once already, yes. Why should I help them do it again? Especially when I am so *hungry*."

Talfi stepped in front of Aisa. Confidence flowed through him. "If you eat us, you'll never learn your wife's name."

Grandfather Wyrm reared back a little. "My wife's name? It would keep me warm, so warm to know it, yes."

"I was there," Talfi said firmly, "and I remember it now. Give us the secret to the power, and I'll tell you her name. I swear on the dagger that took my life." Here, he touched the hilt at his belt.

Grandfather Wyrm paused only a moment. "Very well, yes. I agree. But I cannot give it to you, Talfi. You have no talent. You never did, and that is why our continent lies in ruins, yes."

"I don't understand," Talfi said.

"Did you never wonder why this most careful spell wrought by the world's most powerful trollwives should go so badly wrong? Did you think it was *meant* to sunder both the Axe and the continent, yes?"

"I never thought about it," Talfi said, but he backed up a step.

"Yes." Grandfather Wyrm slitted his eyes. "The sacrifice was supposed to be a changeling boy, one filled to the brim with talent, yes. I believe his name was . . . Gavren. Strange that I remember that, but not my wife's name, yes."

Talfi felt the blood drain from his face. "Gavren? He was supposed to be the sacrifice?"

"But you ended up on the altar instead, yes, and why did that happen? I never did learn. But I do know that without the blood from a child of the shape, the spell took a bad turn, yes."

"My father." Talfi's lips were numb around the words. "He didn't know anything about magic. He sent Gavren away and put me on the table instead. Because we were . . . because *I* am . . . *regi*."

"Is that why?" Grandfather Wyrm blew bubbles from his nose. "Such a small reason to destroy the world."

"The world turns on petty desires," Danr muttered.

"Petty indeed, yes."

Talfi swallowed. He couldn't take it all in. The ruined city, the cracked continent, the sundered world. It was his fault so many people had died. His fault the Stane had gone underground for a thousand years. It was him.

Aisa touched his shoulder. "You are weaving poisonous vines about yourself. I can see it. Do not. You are not responsible for your father's choices. He did this, not you."

"If I had been more careful with Gavren—"

"It was your father's job to be a father," Danr said, "and a general to his people. Not a petty person. He betrayed you. You didn't betray him or anyone else. I know." And Danr tapped his eye.

Danr and Aisa were right. Talfi straightened his back and some of the guilt drained out of him. Not all of it, but enough.

Grandfather Wyrm said, "That was a long time ago, and right now I have a bargain to fulfill. The power, yes."

"I'll go first," Danr said quickly. "Show me."

"The secret is in the blood. Stand before me, little one. Talfi, bring the knife, yes."

The pair obeyed, more than a little nervous. It was hard to maintain their balance whenever Grandfather Wyrm inhaled.

"This requires a much smaller sacrifice, yes," he explained. "Talfi, you must cut my skin so I bleed into the air and water. Use that knife and no other, yes."

Talfi hesitantly cut at a bit of scaly hide near Grandfather Wyrm's snout with the dagger's point. It barely made a mark, and Grandfather Wyrm chuckled scornfully.

"Cut, boy," he said. "This is magic, not a baby's game."

Talfi tightened his mouth and drew back his arm. This time the cut slashed deeper, and a stream of dark blood gushed into the water.

"Very good, yes," said Grandfather Wyrm. "Ready, little one?"

Before Danr could respond, Grandfather Wyrm bit off Danr's right hand.

Chapter Thirteen

Pain flashed up Danr's arm. He didn't even have time to react. Almost instantly, a cloud of dark blood enveloped him, and he tasted copper. The white-hot pain went to his shoulder and rushed over his body, sending him to his knees. He realized he was screaming. His bones filled with hot lead, and he writhed on the slimy stones. The pain swallowed his entire world. It raked over every nerve with red coals and poured boiling poison into his gut. He screamed and screamed and if Death had asked to come for him, he would have begged her to take him. His strength drained into the airy water around him. His arms and legs shrank and pulled into themselves. A line of fire ants pulled his jaw inward and his forehead up. Danr felt his bones crack and reform themselves, and he screamed through it all.

And then it stopped. The pain ended as if it had never been. Weak and exhausted, he lay gasping airy water on the cold stones. He became aware of Aisa kneeling next to him with her cool arms around him. When had she gotten so large, her arms so thick? The back of her left hand had an open cut, and tiny streams of blood twisted upward from it.

"What did you do to him?" Aisa demanded.

"He has what he wanted, yes," came Grandfather Wyrm's voice somewhere above him. "You are naive to think it would come easily or painlessly."

"I'm all right," Danr said, and his voice sounded strange in his ears, higher and reedier. He pushed himself upright and for the first time he noticed his hands. He had two of them again, and they were different. Smaller. Thinner. The skin was pale, and the hair had disappeared. Tendons stood out like strings when he flexed them, and all his calluses were gone. Pale blue veins snaked down wiry wrists.

"What happened to me?" he demanded. His clothes were too large. They half hung, half floated about him. His hat drooped over his eyes, and he pulled it off.

"You're . . . human," Talfi said in awe. "Look at yourself!"

"Allow me, yes," said Grandfather Wyrm. A large rock lifted from the ocean floor beside him. Its shape went soft as taffy. It stretched and flattened itself with the sound of a finger running around the edge of a crystal goblet until it was an oval just as tall as Danr. The surface silvered over, and it rotated over until Danr could see his own reflection. Danr gasped through the bubbles around him as a dark-haired, brown-eyed young man came into view. His body was much thinner and leaner than before, and he couldn't have weighed more than a third what he did before. His clothes still enveloped him, and he had to catch at his trousers so they wouldn't fall. Danr was now perhaps an inch taller than Talfi, who was a little short anyway. Short. Danr had never in his life been so short. It was the strangest feeling. In awe, he put out an arm. The sleeve fell back, revealing wiry, nondescript muscles and none of the dark body hair he'd been growing since he was ten years old. His skin was so pale.

Thick dark hair floated about his head. That was the same. But his eyes looked so much bigger. And his nose was smaller. And his jaw had pulled so far back. He worked it back and forth. No teeth thrust upward, and he felt them with his tongue. He was Kin. He was *human*.

He turned to Aisa in wonder. She was so . . . tall. He was used to her head coming up to the middle of his chest. Now he could look her in the eye. It was disconcerting, and the world wobbled a little.

"Your face," she said softly. She put out a finger and ran the back of it down his cheek. He shivered a little at the touch. "You look your age—eighteen or maybe nineteen. You have a pug nose. I never thought I would see such a thing. But your hair has not changed, and I can reach it." She touched his hair, too, creating another shiver. "And your eyes. They are the same, too. Big and brown and . . . you. I am glad for that. I can see you are the same person inside."

"Do you like it?" he asked softly.

"Your voice is so different. You sound like a boy who is still becoming a man instead of a troll speaking from under the mountain."

"But do you like it?" he pressed, nervous now.

"You are handsome as a human, Hamzu," she said, "but I love you, not your shape."

She leaned in, her face turned up, but only a little. Danr's heart beat faster, and he leaned in as well. Desire for her flowed over him like silk and water, and he put his hand on her cheek. Their lips came closer.

"It is not just you," interrupted Grandfather Wyrm.

They both jumped and pulled apart. Danr had forgotten Grandfather Wyrm was there, indeed he had. Talfi, too, for that matter.

"She has the power like you, yes," Grandfather Wyrm continued. "The cut in her hand."

Startled, Aisa held it up. The cut was already fading.

"I jumped when he bit you and accidentally scratched her with the knife," Talfi explained.

A dreadful thought struck Danr. "How am I surviving here in the Key, if I'm Kin now?"

Grandfather Wyrm chuckled. "You can change your shape, yes, but you cannot change your nature. You are still half-blood, yes. You are still a truth-teller."

"Can I . . . change back?" Danr asked, not sure if he wanted to know the answer, and equally unsure what he wanted the answer to be.

"Perhaps you can, perhaps you cannot, yes," Grandfather Wyrm answered. "The power of the shape is chaotic. You will find yourself drawn to Tikk."

Danr automatically stamped his feet twice at the mention of the trickster god's name and he tried to spit, but met with mixed success underwater. "Or maybe I won't."

Grandfather Wyrm rumbled, "My blood now runs in both you and Aisa, yes. You can wake the power of the shape in any Kin. All you must do is share the blood, yes. If the recipient has the talent, he—or she—will be able to use the power. Whether they do or not, the power may pass to any children in their line, yes."

"So we have to run around bleeding on people?" Danr said incredulously.

"And they in turn must bleed on others, yes. Nothing comes without sacrifice, young one. Great Ashkame tips once every thousand years, moving between the Stane and the Fae with the Kin caught in the middle. But now that the Kin have their power back and they have their champion, perhaps the Tree could stop tipping, yes. The wars could end, if the Kin use their power wisely."

"A sacrifice," Aisa said softly, and Danr caught a strange note in her voice. "Is that why you gave us the power? Because we can stop war from breaking out between the Fae and the Stane every thousand years?"

"I think you *can*, yes," Grandfather Wyrm said, "but I do not know if you *will*. And now, Talfi—" Grandfather Wyrm turned his massive head toward the other young man, who reflexively backed up a step. "You will fulfill our bargain and give me the name of my wife."

"No." Talfi folded his arms.

A stab of fear went through Danr's chest. "Talfi—"

"I said no," Talfi said. "You broke the bargain, Grandfather Wyrm. You said you wouldn't eat us, and you ate Danr's hand."

Grandfather Wyrm managed to look miffed. "He has it back, yes."

"You still broke the bargain," Talfi replied stubbornly.

Grandfather Wyrm roared. Every tooth in his massive maw gleamed like a sword, and a wave of water shoved them all several yards backward. Grandfather Wyrm rose high above them. *"You challenge me, boy?"*

Heart pounding, Danr regained his feet. His mind raced. The creature was going to attack, and he needed to get its attention so Aisa and Talfi could find cover, get away. Automatically, he tried to pick up a nearby chunk of rubble, intending to throw it at Grandfather Wyrm's head. But the rock didn't budge. He strained, and his muscles popped. The rock, which wasn't even the size of a sheep, was too heavy. Then he remembered—his troll's strength was gone.

Talfi also got upright, looking unfazed. "You kill me, and you'll never learn your wife's name."

Grandfather Wyrm hesitated. Danr helped Aisa to her feet—she was so *heavy* now—and edged away with her as best he could.

"What do you want, then?" the great wyrm asked at last.

"Get us back to our friends unharmed," Talfi said, "and your debt will be repaid."

"That is all?" Grandfather Wyrm sounded surprised. "Very well, yes." He blew a bubble. It expanded until it encompassed all three of them. Danr found himself standing in open air on the ocean floor, his sopping clothes hanging off his lean body. Fluid gushed from his mouth and nose, and a series of wild coughs shook his body. The airy water cleared quickly from his lungs, and it was a fine thing to breathe thin air again.

"Tell me her name," Grandfather Wyrm said in a soft grumble, "that I may be warm again, yes."

"Bathilda." Talfi wiped fluid from his own mouth and chin. "Her name was Bathilda."

"Bathilda," Grandfather Wyrm sighed. His golden eyes closed and his massive head sank back to the ocean floor. "That was it. My Bathilda. Thank you, Talfi and Aisa and Danr. Perhaps we will speak again, yes."

The bubble moved, and Danr's stomach lurched. Aisa reached out to steady him, and he marveled that she was strong enough to do it, and then he remembered how much smaller he was. It was something he constantly tripped over. But he was *human*. No one would look at him and see a monster or a Stane or a troll. He was a human among humans, a key in a lock. He felt as light and free as the bubble that coasted slowly upward with them in it.

"You look so happy," Aisa said. "You smile so."

"Do I?" Danr put a hand, a human-sized hand, to his face and felt human-sized teeth in a human-sized grin. "I can't think of any other way to feel, Aisa!" He swept her into a hug, drenched clothes and all, that should have lifted her off the bottom of the bubble, but she was too heavy for him. He flushed a little and settled for dancing around a bit with her instead. "Look at me!"

"You're a good-looking man," Talfi said rakishly. "Take it from someone who knows."

Danr ran a hand through his hair. "Yeah?" He didn't know what to think of that, either. All his life, he'd been the ugly one out. In a stroke, that had changed.

"Why didn't you change shape, Aisa?" Danr asked. "Grandfather Wyrm said you have more power than I do, and you got his blood, but nothing happened to you."

Aisa held up her injured hand. The wound had healed completely. "I do not know. But you went through considerable pain, and I am not sure I wish such a thing for myself."

"We still don't know why Aisa was able to survive the Key, either." Talfi poked the side of the bubble with a finger, and Danr caught at his wrist. His fingers barely wrapped around it.

"What the Vik are you doing?" Danr demanded. "If you pop this thing, we're dead."

"Sorry." Talfi grinned. "I can't seem to help poking."

"Hmm," said Aisa.

"Maybe we could find out why she survived and why she didn't change shape," Talfi said brightly.

"How?" Danr was examining the rubbery sides of the bubble and discovering his own urge to poke at it. Damn Talfi.

"You could *look* at her." And Talfi tapped his own left eye meaningfully.

Aisa inhaled sharply. Danr turned, his stomach tight. The air in the bubble was getting hot and stuffy. Unbidden, his thoughts fled back to the last time he had looked at Aisa with his true eye, when he had learned of the depth of her hunger for the Fae and of the private pain she had lived with. He had seen her longing for the ocean and seen a strange, fluid strength that he hadn't understood. Aisa, however, had felt violated beyond measure, and it had nearly cost their love, their friendship, everything. It had been the worst month of Danr's life since his mother's death, and since it had happened, he did his best not to think about what he had seen. Now he did think about it. What was that fluid strength he had seen? The power of the shape, hidden inside her?

"I promised I would never do that to her again," he said shortly.

"Unless Aisa gives permission," Talfi replied. Poke, poke. "Don't you want to know?"

Talfi had, perhaps deliberately, directed the question so it could go either to Aisa or Danr. Aisa said nothing, but Danr was forced to respond.

"Of course I want to know," he retorted. "Only a fool wouldn't. She might have power we can't dream of, power we need, and this is one way to find out, and while I'm at it, I'm going to add that you're licking Vik's balls by asking me that and making me answer."

"Keeps my mind off Ranadar," Talfi said with more than a little heat. "The love of *your* life is standing right next to you, and you're a human now. You have what you want. Does either of you care if Ranadar lives? Or Kalessa?"

Danr's words flew like darts. "Of course we care. You're so wrapped up in whether or not the world accepts you, *regi* or not *regi*, that you can't see true friends when they're standing in front of you. All you care about is the elf that's behind you."

Talfi's face went white and he made a fist. "You're not so big now, and I can bloody your damn nose. I can—"

"No," Aisa said quietly.

Both young men turned. "What?" Talfi said.

"I do not grant permission for anyone to gaze at me with a true eye," Aisa said.

"But—" Talfi said.

"Just like a man," Aisa sniped. "He can't hear *no* from a woman."

"Hey!" Talfi said. "I didn't—"

Danr crossed his arms, and noticed how much thinner they were. "If she says no, it means no."

"Fine." Talfi turned his back, but Danr didn't miss the glimmer in the corner of his eye. Hesitantly, he put a hand—how long would it take before he stopped noticing how small his body was?—on Talfi's shoulder.

"We'll get him out, Talfi," Danr said in his new tenor voice. "Both of them. I . . . I . . ."

"You can't say that you promise," Talfi said with his back to them both. "It's not the truth."

"We are near the surface," Aisa said suddenly.

It was true. Sunlight was penetrating the bubble and the water around it. Danr automatically threw up a hand to shield his eyes—he had lost his hat somewhere back with Grandfather Wyrm—but found to his surprise that the light didn't hurt. Before he could consider this astonishing development further, the bubble breached the surface like a strange whale and sailed across the border of the Key into normal water. Danr had time to glimpse the wide blue ocean stretching in all directions before the bubble popped and all three of them dropped into the sea with a splash.

Danr flailed about, expecting to sink promptly and becoming surprised when he didn't. His oversize trousers fell away and he struggled within his oversize tunic. A hand grabbed the back of his collar and hauled him none too gently into a boat. It was the one they had left at the edge of the Key, with all the sailors in it. Talfi and Aisa were dumped beside him.

"Never seen anything like that in all my life on the sea," remarked the head sailor. "Glad to see the girl didn't drown after all. So who the Vik is this, and what happened to the big guy?"

Danr lay on his back, only vaguely aware that he wasn't wearing pants and blinking up at a bright blue sky that didn't hurt at all. The sun was a friend to the Kin.

"You!" Aisa scrambled to her feet and lunged for the azure-eyed golem, which was still on the boat. The boat rocked. "You tried to kill me!"

"Whoa! Careful!" The head sailor and a pair of others caught and held her back. "No fighting on the boat. You want to capsize us?"

"Attention! Attention!" said the golem. "Message from the Obsidia masters." Its voice changed into Sharlee's silken tone. "That was unexpected, honey! I was sure you would be a casualty of forcing Danr and Talfi to explore the Key. But I can see Danr has found the power of the shape, unless you kidnapped a handsome mermaid. Hurry back! The water is up to the elf's chest, poor chick. Message ends."

Talfi scrambled to his feet. "We have to move!"

"Later," Aisa growled at the golem. It didn't respond.

They rowed back to the *Slippery Fish*, still at anchor. Captain Greenstone waved at them over the railing. "Where's Danr?" she called. "He all right?"

"I'm fine!" Danr called up. "We're—"

The water around them erupted in merfolk. The sailors shied away while the golem sat impassively in the bottom of the boat.

"Aisa!" Ynara reached across the gunwale to embrace her while the male sailors gawped. "You have returned unharmed! We were so worried!"

Ynara's parents, Imeld and Markis, were there as well,

and they insisted on similar embraces. Danr watched, wondering what it would be like to have a family, even a new one, that showed so much enthusiastic affection. There were also two other merfolk he didn't recognize, a man and a woman. About then, Danr also became aware that he had lost his trousers in the ocean. He flushed and did a quick check. His tunic, which was five sizes too large for him, covered everything that needed covering, though it was like wearing a giant wet sack.

The boat sloshed and rocked as Captain Greenstone slid down a rope into its center, her heavy hat clapped firmly on her head. "I couldn't wait to find out what in the Nine's name is going on down here," she declared. "Let's hear it! Starting with who in Vik's house this is." Greenstone jabbed a thick finger at Danr.

"It's me, Danr," he said with a grin. "Grandfather Wyrm gave us the power of the shape and I'm all Kin now."

"Are you?" Greenstone sounded more than a little disappointed. "Well, start from the beginning, then."

Talfi and Aisa quickly told the story while Danr watched the new merfolk. Why were they here? These two were older than the other merfolk Danr had seen, with wrinkles on their faces and white streaks in their hair. They listened intently to the story, especially to Aisa. Danr was getting used to the nudity, though the tattoos still looked fierce.

"And now you possess the power of the shape, sister," Ynara said.

Aisa replied, "So Grandfather Wyrm said, but I do not yet know how to use it."

"You will learn quickly," the older merwoman broke in. "It is your birthright."

"Yes?" Aisa said politely. "And who are you?"

The old woman reached across the gunwale and took

Aisa's hand. "Very occasionally, the power of the shape appears in our family. My daughter learned she had the power to change shape, but only once. She fell in love with a human man, and she used her power to walk on land and live with him, even though it meant she could never return to the sea. We never saw her again. Her name was Durrah."

Aisa paled. "That was my mother's name."

The old woman nodded. "The name of her human love was Jibran."

"But . . . my father's name is Bahir," Aisa whispered. "Jibran was his brother. My uncle. He died just before I was born."

"So we heard," the older man said. "The laws of your country require a widow to marry her dead husband's brother. Durrah could not change back into her true form, so we could do nothing to stop him."

"Then you are my . . . grandparents?" Aisa said.

The older man took Aisa's other hand. "We are. Markis told us you had come. We did not even know you existed, and then we arrived too late. You had already entered the Key."

"So this is why you love the merfolk so much," Danr said in awe. "You're one of them."

"Join us, sister!" Ynara held out her arms. "Take your true shape and your face!"

Aisa released her grandparents' hands and stood tall in the center of the boat. Then, with a low cry, she leaped for the water. Danr gave a shout of his own. With a slim splash, she vanished beneath the waves. The sea bubbled and boiled.

"Aisa!" Danr lunged for the gunwale, making the boat rock sickeningly. "Aisa!"

A gout of water erupted before him. In a shining arc, Aisa leaped over the boat, trailing sparkling ocean behind her. Her breasts were bare, her body was long and sleek, and her silver tail gleamed in the noonday sun. Her eyes met Danr's as she passed over his head, and he could do nothing but stare with his mouth open. The merfolk shouted and pounded the sides of the boat. Aisa cut into the water and vanished.

Chapter Fourteen

Water flowed around Aisa like a silken friend, holding her up and letting her fly. She was *free*. Her tail—her *tail*—swept in easy arcs, propelling her through the sea at breathless speeds. Breathless. She was breathing water like air. It rushed through her mouth and nose and through gills in her neck. It was both strange and comforting, something she had been waiting to do all her life. Her clothes were gone, and she had not realized until now how confining they had been. She grinned and dove, reveling in the freedom and not minding the change in temperature or pressure in the slightest. The change of shape had not pained her, either. A rainbow school of fish darted out of her way, and at the bottom, a rich forest of flat-leaved algae waved gently in the soft current. A great garden stretched out in all directions, including above and below, and it was hers to explore.

A garden. Was this why the Gardeners were considering her to . . . She could not complete the thought. The idea was simply too impossibly big to consider. She was a mortal woman. How could an ordinary woman plant the seeds of fate?

Water, gentle and free, coursed over her body. What would it be like to garden with the Three? Or, she supposed, the Other Two? How would she know what to do? If it was anything like regular gardening, you planted the seeds where you wanted them, kept out the weeds, and pruned what needed—

Pruning. Aisa swallowed. Cutting something in the garden of the Gardeners meant ending a life. Could she do that? *Should* she do that? The Gardeners oversaw the lives of not just Kin, but of Stane and Fae. It seemed to Aisa that the Gardeners needed to be impartial, but it was impossible to be fair when the Fae were involved. Just thinking of them made her remember the elven king and the way he had laid hands on her and addicted her to his touch. And the elf queen had tried to exterminate every Stane on the planet.

No. Being a Gardener was too much responsibility for a mortal woman like her. It was not her place, and never would be.

Aisa shook her head. Here she was, a new-made mermaid, swimming in the bright clear water, and she was thinking about fate and gardens. She should be reveling in her new-found shape, her newfound home, not thinking about Pendra and high-flown offers of fairy-tale power.

"Aisa!" Ynara swam up, her face alight with joy. "You have come home!"

Home! The word brought raw emotion crashing over Aisa. So much was happening so fast, and she was having a hard time keeping up. She wished the world would slow down for a moment and let her catch her breath, or whatever it was that mermaids caught. Mermaid! Rolk! She was a mermaid! Tears formed in her eyes and floated away.

"This is . . . I cannot describe!" she stammered.

"Then do not." Ynara took her hand. "Come now! You must see."

They swam together in silence for some time. Aisa found her body moving in new ways, responding to new cues. She could sense changes in the water. This area felt lighter, that one heavier. And her hearing had become sharp as cut glass. Aisa could hear the shape of the algae below her, sense the shape of a pod of dolphins, hear their squeaks and chatters, even though they were more than a mile away. She felt her heart would swell and burst, and she wished she could share this with Danr.

Danr. Who had himself changed his shape. Her tail spread and she swam harder as she remembered. The shock and startlement rocked her through, and although she was not glad to see the pain of his transformation, she had been glad of the distraction. Even without his true eye, he saw a great deal. She had to admit his new form was boyishly handsome. Those soulful eyes and his tousled hair and his fine, careful features would now make any woman glance twice at him.

And Aisa hadn't cared.

He thought that public approbation mattered to her, that she was afraid of what the world would do to her if she married a half-blood. But she did not care about that. She never had cared. It was the bloody visions of him and the attacks of panic that made her unhappy.

The longer she went without telling him, the harder it became to speak. The lie had grown between them like poison ivy, becoming harder and harder to remove with every passing day. Now he had changed his shape for her, and he would expect their problems to disappear. They had sought out the power of the shape for many other reasons, but Danr's reason was deeply personal—and based on a lie. What would she do now?

Ynara's parents and Aisa's grandparents joined them now, and Aisa learned her grandfather's name was Bellog

and her grandmother's name was Grell, but she should call
them Grandmother and Grandfather. Aisa, who had never
known her grandparents on land, felt like a princess come
home to her castle.

"We are nearly there," Grandmother said.

At her words, Aisa halted, hovering in the water. It
would be easy to go with the merfolk, leave Danr and the
others behind forever. He had the power of the shape now
and could rescue Ranadar from the Obsidia on his own.
What did he need with her? But no. The thought of leaving
him made her chest tighten, and she owed him more than
cold desertion. "We have come so far," she said. "I cannot
abandon my friends."

"You will not," Grandfather said. "Imeld, would you swim
back to the human ship? Tell them to set sail, and Aisa will
catch up with them soon."

Imeld sped away. Aisa watched her go. "Will I truly be
able to catch up with them?" she asked.

Grandfather laughed, and his gills flared. "Human ships
sail slower than coral grows. You must trust yourself, granddaughter."

Ynara took Aisa's hand. "Come! You will see!"

The ocean floor dropped into a canyon. They skimmed
down into it, passing a pod of whales that drifted along like
great ships, and their eerie songs echoed through the sea.

At the bottom of the canyon, Aisa paused and caught her
breath, if she could catch breath underwater. Ahead of her,
stretching like a rainbow coral reef, spread a city. It covered
the canyon bottom and climbed up its walls. The houses
and buildings were constructed of everything imaginable—
cut stones and giant shells and pieces of coral and colored glass and polished bone—like a rainbow that had
shattered across the sea floor. And there were hundreds of
merfolk, in all ages and shapes, all of them bare-skinned

and tattooed. Laughing children chased each other like dolphins in midair—or midwater, Aisa supposed—while adults and elders watched or attended to tasks Aisa did not understand.

The city was also alive with fish. Aisa did not know one fish from another, not yet, but they swam past in bursts of gold and scarlet and azure. Anemones waved in reefs, and octopi darted about. Dolphins giggled, and one boy even rode a killer whale.

But what stole Aisa's breath was the city. The entire city was laid out like a great tree. It was something she could only notice approaching from a distance as she was. Bright coral formed its trunk. Algae gardens made leaves that waved in an invisible breeze. Busy streets and houses ran along the branches. The merfolk swam about like seeds fluttering from a maple. The tree lived and breathed with a power made up of everything and everyone in it, and Aisa longed to join it.

"Incredible!" she said. "Why is it a tree underwater?"

"It is Ashkame," Grandfather said.

"How did you form the city this way?" Aisa swam toward it delicately, as if the city might burst like a bubble.

"Form?" Markis raised his eyebrows. "We do not form the Tree. The Tree forms us."

Ynara and the others guided her into—over—the city. Once Aisa got closer, she lost the ability to see the city as a tree, but she found the symbol of Ashkame everywhere—carved on doors, etched on stones, even tattooed on faces.

They swam about what passed for streets, though they seemed to be more avenues of convenience or etiquette than actual streets, since the merfolk and the creatures that lived among them were not bound to the land and could swim in any direction they chose. Aisa found the concept both confusing and intoxicating. Merfolk and fish and other creatures parted for them as they passed, though more than one stared.

"Why do they look at me so?" Aisa asked, and felt suddenly self-conscious about being bare-breasted, even though no other woman here covered herself. Ever since she had seen the merfolk, Aisa had dreamed of freedom from modesty, and now that she had it, she could not bring herself to enjoy it.

Ynara said, "You look strange to them without a face."

And then it happened again. Blood covered the faces and hands of Ynara and her parents and Aisa's grandparents, and the water could not wash it away. Terrible axe wounds gaped in their chests, and Aisa heard the whistle of the Iron Axe spinning through the air. But it was not the Axe. It was a sickle, and Aisa was wielding it. Cold fear twisted her insides. The algae about her twisted in a thousand directions, but also converged on this spot. Everything met here. Aisa made a small choked sound.

The blood vanished. The wounds disappeared. Everyone was fine. Aisa's heart pounded and her gills flared. The others noticed she had stopped, and they pulled up short. A small shark coasted by.

"What is it?" asked Markis.

"I . . . it was . . . ," Aisa stammered. *It was just a memory, nothing more,* she told herself. But she realized a small part of her had been hoping from the moment she changed her shape that these visions would disappear, and the disappointment put a heavy stone in her heart. Another reminder that Danr's change had changed nothing. But why was she seeing the sickle and the Garden? What did Pendra have to do with any of this? Anxiety twisted her bones. She was not a Gardener, and never would be, but she felt like a leaf in a current, rushing toward a waterfall.

"Aisa?" said Markis.

"I am just a little overwhelmed by all this," she said lamely.

"Easily understood," Grandmother said. "Look—we have nearly arrived."

They came to a house built of a ramshackle collection of shells, bones, and living coral. It occurred to Aisa that a house among the merfolk would be built more for privacy than shelter. Small fish wandered among the cracks, feeding on the waving plants that grew there, and Aisa's spirits rose at the simple beauty.

They swam down to a set of stones that formed seats in a kind of courtyard outside the house. Grandfather and Grandmother took up the stones on either side of her. Grandmother touched Aisa's face with a long-fingered hand.

"You look so like your mother," she said. "How can this be you?"

"It is hard for me to understand that I am here," Aisa said. "The first time I saw merfolk, I wanted . . . I did not know what I wanted. It hurt so much."

"Of course it did," Grandfather said. "It is painful in all ways for our kind to leave the sea, even when we are in human form."

A flash of insight came over Aisa. "Is that why my mother took ill? Is that why she . . . died?"

"I suspect so," Grandmother's gills pressed tightly against her neck in sorrow. "She gave up her shape for love, and it turned to sand. Her new husband—your father— would not even allow her to visit the sea, and she became weaker and weaker."

Aisa twisted her hands in her scaly lap. Sadness made the water around her heavy. "So my father did more than gamble my life away. I thought I had let that go, but still it makes me sad. And angry."

"Of course it does," Grandfather said. His own gills were

tight. "Feelings come and go like the tide. Just when we think something has washed away, it returns. The Nine have made us so."

"The Nine are cruel to make us remember so much fear and sorrow!" Aisa burst out.

Grandmother touched her cheek again, and for a moment, Aisa's mother was alive again. "Young one, you have been through so much. Fear holds you back. I can see it in your bare face. But rejoice in your power and it will overcome the memory of fear."

"I do rejoice in my power," she protested.

"You do not," Grandmother said. "Not yet. But you have only recently come into it. First you need your face."

Now the women gathered around her. Imeld returned and clapped her hands, ready to help. Grandmother reached beneath a rock and produced a startled octopus while Ynara came up with a box of tools that included a set of bone needles.

Aisa felt a strange mixture of anticipation and fear, and water rushed hard through her gills. "Will this hurt?"

Ynara looked confused. "Of course. But you have earned your face already, and the pain will be nothing to one such as you. Besides, after a while, the pain will become pleasure."

Aisa swallowed and made herself sit still, though her tail trembled while Grandmother, Ynara, and the recently returned Imeld set to work with the needles, octopus ink, and other objects. Aisa sat rigid while the burning sensation of pokes and prods crawled over her face. Her gills flared and tightened under the pain, and she kept her eyes shut. But Ynara had been right—after a while, the pain felt *good*, like the pain of pulling an old scab away from a sore or the relief that followed the lancing of a boil. She wanted this. She had *earned* this. She inhaled more water and gave herself up to the women.

And then they were done. Ynara came up with a hand mirror clearly of human manufacture—perhaps from a shipwreck—and gave it to her. Aisa inhaled and put a hand to her face. Her fingertips found little bumps and ridges over her eyebrows.

"Those are seed pearls," Grandmother said, "as befits a family of our status. The octopus"—she released the animal, which drifted away, looking stunned—"is bred just for our clan. We are known for our ink."

"It is . . . beautiful," Aisa whispered. It truly was. The tattoo that masked her face was a simple design of blue and purple points that curled around her eyes and nose. Two fang-like spikes ran down her cheeks, and the line of seed pearls marched across her forehead. Back when she was a slave, she had worn scarves to mask her face from her owner. Then she had gained the courage to walk about in public with a naked face. Now she had both a mask and a face at the same time, and it was a wonder.

Aisa looked at the trio of women, and at the two men who hovered a few feet away. "Thank you," she said.

"You are our daughter come home again," Markis said. "There is nothing else we could do."

"And now," Grandfather said, "we should discuss this power of the shape."

"Oh!" Aisa came upright. "Yes! I got it from Grandfather Wyrm."

"Your friend can only change to one other shape," Grandmother observed. "Can you change to more than one?"

"I do not know," Aisa admitted. "I do not know if I can even change back into a human."

"We will not have you attempt it down here," Grandmother said quickly. "Humans are weak, and the pressure would kill you before you had a chance to drown. I think you were able to change into a mermaid because it is in your blood—your half-blood, if you like. So perhaps you need an example to get started."

She plucked a bright yellow fish from a passing school of them and handed it, squirming, to Aisa. "Here."

Aisa accepted it with hesitation. It wriggled in her grasp. "What should I do with it?"

"Eat it. Take its form into yours."

She paused, then crammed the fish into her mouth before she could lose her nerve. It wriggled all the way down. Aisa shuddered.

"Good," said Grandmother with a nod. "Now think of the fish's shape. Its color, its fins, its gills. Imagine your shape changing. Take that shape for yourself."

Aisa imagined the fish. It seemed she could feel its form, but it was more than that. She *knew* it, too. Understood it down to the tiny parts that made up its muscles and skin and scales. Her body slid and shuddered, and suddenly she was floating in the water, able to see in all directions at once. Her mouth was enormous, and she hung sideways, ready to bolt forward at a thrust of her tail. She had become the yellow fish, but Aisa-sized, and there had been no pain.

Her new family scattered, then recovered themselves with murmurs of amazement. Imeld hung back. Ynara clapped her hands in glee. "That was a wonder, Aisa!"

Aisa slowly rotated in the water, enjoying herself hugely. The fish shape wasn't hard to understand, though she felt the loss of hands and she had no voice. Her mouth opened and closed ceaselessly while life-giving water rushed through her gills. She wondered what Farek, her previous owner, would have thought of this, and gave an inner smile at the thought of him running for the mountains in a panic.

"Now change back," Grandmother said. "Imagine your mermaid shape. Let it call to you."

Aisa tried to close her eyes and discovered she had no

eyelids. Well, that was all right. She would simply stare into the distance while she thought. It was easier than she imagined. One moment, she was a fish, the next she slithered back into her mermaid shape. The moment she did, however, exhaustion pressed her to the sandy sea floor.

"That . . . was tiring," she gasped.

"The old stories said magic takes power," Grandmother said, helping her float to a table. "You should eat."

At the mention of food, Aisa realized she was ravenous. Grandmother brought her cut fish and roe and algae salad and something spiky that had a soft center. Aisa gobbled it all down, not caring that it was raw and finding it all delicious. She felt better but still tired. Through it all, Imeld still hung back, but Aisa was too tired to take much notice.

"Can you . . . show us how to do it?" Ynara asked.

Aisa pushed herself upright and nearly floated away before she righted herself. "Yes, of course! That is why I have come. If you have a talent for the shape, my blood will let you use it. Once you have changed shape at least once, your blood will let others use their talent. If you have no talent for the shape, you will still pass the power on to your children. But I warn you—the first change may be painful. It was for Danr."

"What do we do?" Ynara asked.

Aisa thought a moment. "Give me a knife." They did, one made of a pink shell, and Aisa held it above her arm.

"Wait!" Now Imeld shot forward and put her hand under Aisa's arm. "Should we do this? Do we have the right?"

"What do you mean?" Aisa asked. Was this why Imeld had pulled back?

"Look." Imeld gestured at the underwater city. The merfolk were going about their lives on the sea floor and up along the canyon walls. "This single action will change everything we know. The very word *power* will have a different meaning. Wars will be fought, red blood will spill. The children swimming over there will grow up in a world completely different from the one we had. This moment will change history. This moment will change *everything*. And those people there do not know it. Do we have the right?"

Aisa considered this. A little girl chased her brother up the canyon wall in a game only they understood. Imeld was right. How would her actions change their lives, and how much right did she have to change them?

"The Stane took the power from us a thousand years ago," Grandfather said. "They changed everything for everyone, without the right. We cannot change it back, but we can set it right. The Kin need the power of the shape so we can be on equal footing with the other six people."

"And Grandfather Wyrm said that the Kin may be able to stop the Tree from tipping every thousand years," Aisa added. "It will be a change, but for the better, I hope."

Aisa started to bring the knife down, but before she could move, the knife transformed into a sickle and Aisa was wearing a cloak of autumn leaves. Her arm swept around and the sickle sliced through a faceless merfolk's neck. The head dropped to the sea floor like a cut flower as the water gushed with blood. But it was more than one merfolk. Other people—Kin, Stane, and Fae—died under her sickle as well. And the city around her changed. The algae took on new colors. Schools of fish and pods of whales changed direction. The tree that made up the merfolk city shifted so that the branches looked like roots, the roots looked like branches.

Can you wield the sickle without flinching?

And then it all disappeared. Aisa dropped the knife.

"No!" she moaned. "Not again!"

Ynara was there. "Sister? What is it?"

"It is the worst of my life," she said.

"Tell us," she said. "We are your family."

Aisa looked at them, strangers who had become her new family. Perhaps it was because they were family, or perhaps it was because they were strangers, but she found herself telling everything. She told about the Iron Axe and the Battle of the Twist and the bloody visions that followed. And she told how Danr had come to change his shape, both because he wanted to escape fame and his half-blood status and because he thought she feared the consequences of marriage to a half-blood, when it was actually her fear of what he had done. And she told of Pendra bringing her to the garden of Ashkame. And she told of holding a sickle that caused bloody death. From behind her new face, she told it all, and when it was done, she drooped to the sea floor, weakened by the telling.

After a moment, she became aware of arms around her, of strong tails sliding beneath her, lifting her up. She felt more buoyant now that the words had left her. Her family drifted back and let her go.

"So much for one young person to bear," Grandmother murmured. "You have seen more in two years than many see in ten lifetimes."

"What do I do?" Aisa half choked. "I have learned that I am a half-blood, I have the power of the shape, and the Gardeners believe I could walk their rows one day."

"Perhaps it is because you have done all these things that the Gardeners are looking at you," Ynara pointed out. "You are a powerful woman and you have seen much of the world. You have faced down Death and Grandfather Wyrm. You have been to the world of the Stane and of the Fae and of the Kin. You have walked among all races of the Nine People. You have been the lowest slave and now you are becoming the highest sorceress. You know the world, Aisa. Who better to become a Gardener?"

"Hmm." Aisa straightened at such words. "I had not

thought of it that way. But all this responsibility. I am not strong enough to make such decisions."

"You are one of the merfolk," Grandfather said. "The strength is in your blood. You only have to believe it."

"But you must also talk of these visions with your young man," Imeld said. "It will hurt you both if you keep the truth from him."

"It will hurt him if I tell him," Aisa said. "And so the words never come. I am too weak."

"You are merfolk. The strength is in your blood," Grandfather repeated. He handed her the knife. "Let us begin with the power of the shape. It runs in our family, so share your blood with us."

"It will change history," Imeld whispered.

"As it must," Grandfather said.

Aisa pressed the cool blade against her skin, and the world flickered. The garden stretched around her, and she stood in the center with the sickle. A number of plants were poised to die beneath it, but a number of others stood ready to burst into blossom once the first plants were removed.

Can you wield the sickle without flinching?

Then she was back with her new family under the sea. Her fingers tightened ice-cold around the knife. With a single, petty stroke, the Kin would regain their power, but some would die in the process. How many people now alive had no idea that their death was imminent? How many orphans would Aisa's knife create? Her hand refused to move.

Can you wield the sickle without flinching?

She handed the knife to Grandfather. "You do it."

An autumn cloak fluttered at the corner of her eye, and she thought she heard a disappointed sigh, but she ignored both. Grandfather took the knife with a gentle nod. Aisa looked away, and he made a quick cut on the back of her arm. She flinched. A red line of pain flowed up her arm, and dark blood floated into the water. Aisa avoided looking at it, but memories of the Axe still crackled faintly in her head. For a moment, she thought she saw Pendra turn her head away in sadness.

"Inhale!" Grandfather ordered.

Everyone leaned in and drew in Aisa's blood. Even Imeld did so, though her face was set hard. For a moment, nothing happened. Then Imeld squirmed and shifted and changed. She cried out under the pain as Danr had. With a bloop she became a small walrus.

"Halza's tits!" Grandfather swore, and Grandmother slapped his shoulder.

"Imeld!" Markis said. "After everything you said, you have become a shape magician!"

"Well," Aisa said as Imeld flapped her flippers in consternation, "that would seem to be—"

Ynara choked. Her face turned blue and she went into convulsions. Her tail split into a dozen writhing tentacles, then mashed back together. Her face contorted and blurred into hideous, malformed shapes—a crushed seal, a shark's snout, a dolphin's beak. Her arms became fins and flippers and arms again. Markis cried out in alarm and swam to her, but it was over in seconds. Ynara's mangled corpse drifted to the garden floor.

"No!" Markis grabbed his daughter by the shoulders. He was already weeping. "No!"

Imeld rushed back into her own shape and joined Markis, fruitlessly shaking Ynara, as if she might just be sleeping. "Ynara!" Imeld begged, her face white with exhaustion. "Daughter, please!"

Aisa had both hands over her mouth in icy shock. But before she could react further, Grandmother stiffened. She gave a low cry and writhed in the water. Her skin turned a pebbly yellow. Horns spiraled out of her head. A dozen eyes popped open all over her body. In moments, she sank dead to the ocean floor beside Ynara.

Grandfather dropped beside her. He held her deformed head in his lap and made a low wailing sound that burst into the full keening of a whale. Markis and Imeld joined in, and the sounds of their sorrow made the sea heavy for all who heard. Aisa backed away in horror. Ynara could not be dead. Grandmother could not be dead. It was impossible. These mangled . . . things could not be them, could not be the beautiful, free mermaids Aisa had only just met and swum with and received her face from. They could not. But they were. And her blood had brought it about. Shame and remorse suffused her, weighed her down with black stones. She didn't deserve to live when they were dead.

You flinched.

Bitter tears gathered in her eyes and were washed instantly away by the sea. Hesitantly, she reached down to touch Imeld's shoulder.

"Imeld—" she whispered.

The woman rounded on her. "You killed my daughter!"

The words punched Aisa in the stomach with an almost physical force. She backed away into a school of fish, which scattered. Their slippery bodies rushed over her skin and away. Markis and Imeld keened like orcas over Ynara's corpse while Grandfather sobbed over Grandmother's, and other merfolk swam hurriedly toward them from other houses to find out what was wrong. Aisa turned and fled.

"There is your ship, Aisa." Grandfather, his eyes red from weeping, pointed at the bulk above them, but Aisa had already heard it crashing loudly over the waves on the surface. It was indeed loud and slow, just as Grandfather had observed.

"I am so sorry," she said for the hundredth time. The

grief over what she had done threatened to drag her down to the bottom and she could barely swim. "If I had known—"

"It was not your fault," Grandfather interrupted firmly. "I spilled your blood, and your Grandmother . . ." His voice tightened in a way that broke Aisa's heart in half. ". . . your Grandmother wanted it to happen. We knew the risks. Still, I do not know if Imeld will forgive it."

"Grandfather, I am so sorry." Aisa's eyes were red, too, and her nose would have been running if she had not been underwater. "I do not know what to do. I wish—"

"Listen to me, granddaughter." Grandfather took both her shoulders. His eyes were serious within his blue tattoos, and Aisa could see the wrinkles around his eyes and at the corners of his mouth. "Change always brings death. It also brings new life. If you had shared your blood elsewhere first, the power of the shape would still have reached Ynara and Grell eventually, and their fate would have been the same."

"I killed Ynara," Aisa said.

"You rescued her," Grandfather said. "If not for you, she would be a slave on land, a life worse than any death. Imeld and Markis will eventually come to see that. But for now, perhaps it is best that you stay away. Let me spread the power of the shape among our people."

Aisa stared at him in disbelief. "After all this, you still think we should—"

"Of course."

"But others will die!" Aisa cried.

"And if we do not regain the power, yet more will die." He sighed, and bubbles floated about his head. "Nothing comes without sacrifice. The Nine and the Gardeners know that."

"What is the point of being a Gardener if I have to sacrifice the ones I love?" she demanded. "Why should I do it?"

"Only you can answer that," Grandfather said.

Aisa wiped at her eyes out of habit. "I need to catch the ship."

"If you ever need the merfolk, take your mermaid shape and cry for us like the orca," Grandfather told her. "We will hear you, and we will come."

"How . . . how do I cry like an orca?"

"Every mer knows how. Shout your name as loud and high as you can. Shout it three times."

Aisa did. To her surprise, she produced a high-pitched wail that spread in all directions. Grandfather nodded.

"We will see you again, granddaughter." He embraced her, and her forehead pushed into his shoulder so she felt the new pearls press her forehead. "We are proud of you, the mermaid who changed the world."

Catching the ship was simple enough. Aisa found she could swim more than twice as fast as it sailed. Remembering how Ynara had done it—the fresh sorrow renewed itself at the thought—she propelled herself straight up with great sweeps of her tail and leaped gracefully into the air. But she had never done this before, and found she had pushed too hard. Instead of leaping up to the rail, she catapulted right over it and flopped gracelessly onto something hard that collapsed under her.

"Aisa!" Danr, still human and small, was there. He pulled her upright, or tried to. She couldn't stand, and he wasn't strong enough to hold her upright.

Something squirmed beneath her. It took a moment to work out that she had landed square on the golem. It rocked about, confused. Several sailors and Captain Greenstone came running across the rocking deck. Sails snapped and creaked overhead in a now-familiar song, and a fat orange sun was dipping into the ocean behind them.

"I was so worried!" Danr pulled her into a breathless embrace. "You have tattoos! Are you all right?"

"Yes and no," she said. The golem tried to wriggle out from under her. She let go of Danr and flopped back onto it, causing it to crash back to the deck again. Words tumbled out of her and tears threatened again. "Oh, my Hamzu. Ynara and my grandmother are dead, and it is my doing."

Danr's large eyes went even wider and the blood drained from his face. "Dead? How?"

This time Greenstone picked her up as easily as a doll, and the golem jerked itself upright, managing to look annoyed even without facial features. "All right, all right," Greenstone said. "Let's put you somewhere more comfortable, and we'll get this sorted out."

"Give me a moment, and I can walk," Aisa said to her.

She concentrated, remembering her true shape, her birth shape. The power moved, and she felt herself start to change, but she was suddenly too tired. After three changes, a great deal of swimming, and all the awful things that had happened, the energy just wasn't there.

Then Danr took her hand. A spark jolted her, and power rushed through every cell. She was drinking sunlight and feasting on stars. Her very bones tingled, and she felt strong enough to uproot trees and lift mountains. Danr inhaled sharply, but she barely noticed. She drank in more and more power. Her tail painlessly split and formed into legs. Her gills merged with her skin. Her body shortened. Awed, Greenstone set her down, and Aisa stood on the deck in her birth shape. The sailors all backed up.

"The Nine," Danr panted. His face shone with sweat and he sank to one knee before her. For a moment, Aisa thought he was going to knock his head on the deck. Then she understood he was exhausted. She, meanwhile, felt ready to fly twice around the world.

"What happened?" Danr gasped.

"Grandfather Wyrm," Aisa said. "He told us it would be

easier to take power from someone who had changed shape. He was right. Are you hurt?"

"No." He struggled to his feet, and this time Aisa helped him. He felt light as foam. "Just tired. And . . . Aisa, you're naked."

Aisa glanced down. Indeed she was. The fact should have sent her fleeing for cover in horrified embarrassment, but now . . . now that Ynara had died, it barely seemed worth noticing. One of the larger male sailors stripped off his shirt, and Aisa pulled it on as an impromptu tunic.

"Where are your tattoos?" Danr added. "They've disappeared."

Aisa put a hand to her face. It was perfectly smooth again. Even the seed pearls had disappeared. A pang went through her. Would they come back when—if—she became a mermaid again?

"Where's Talfi?" she asked suddenly.

"Sleeping below," Greenstone said. "Between worry and wyrms, he's damn exhausted. You should probably sleep, too. You see that?" She pointed behind them. Dark, heavy clouds gathered in judgment on the horizon. "Gonna be a real titty-twister. We can stay just ahead of it if we hurry, but if you want sleep, get it quick. You hungry?"

"Starving," Danr said.

Chapter Fifteen

So you're human now." Captain Greenstone stared over the helm out to sea. "How's it working?"

Danr self-consciously looked down at strange arms. He had rough trousers and a patched tunic from the ship's stores that fit him decently enough, and even a pair of shoes that he felt every moment against his feet.

"I feel short," he said, and his voice sounded too high in his own head. "And the sun doesn't hurt, and I can't see in the dark for much."

"Hmm." Greenstone adjusted the course. The *Slippery Fish* was dashing northeast along the Balsian coast, which put forested land on the ship's left—port side, Danr corrected himself. The storm had been chasing them for the last day, but it pushed a wind ahead that sent the *Fish* scurrying along like a toy boat. Part of the storm stumbled on the continent behind them, which luckily slowed it down.

"We'll be in the city before nightfall," Greenstone predicted.

Another relief. They would fulfill Aisa's deal with the harbormaster and he would get Ranadar out of that tank.

The harbormaster would start the end of slavery, which would thrill Aisa, and they could . . .

Danr swallowed. He still had to propose to Aisa!

"My debt to the Obsidia will be paid off," Greenstone continued, "and I can get the Vik out of this city, storms or not."

"Where are you going?" Danr asked, surprised at how much he was disappointed she was planning to leave. "Otrania?"

"Otrania's a Fae city, and they don't like Stane mongrels, so we'll head down to the Flor Isles, or maybe Briat. When the storm season ends, maybe we'll risk a spice run from Nik in Irbsa."

Mongrel. Half-blood. Those words didn't apply to him anymore. He looked down at his human hands again. They were so long and thin. He liked them.

As if reading his mind, Greenstone said, "You're glad, are you?"

Danr had to answer, "Yeah. Who wouldn't be?"

"Well, me, really." She heaved the helm over, then hauled it back. The *Fish* responded with a creak.

"You?"

She avoided looking at him from under her heavy hat. "I was kind of hoping you'd find your way clear to help out. You're a hero, with a big name. Half-bloods need other half-bloods to look up to."

"I didn't even know there *were* other half-bloods in the world until I met you," Danr protested.

"Yeah, I know. I used to think I was the only one, too. That makes it easier for everyone to say there's somethin' wrong with us—and it makes it easy for us to believe it. Then we hate ourselves, and want to hide who we really are."

Monster, echoed a memory in Danr's head.

"But if we have someone big, someone who does great

things, like wield the Iron Axe, and that someone stands tall and says he's proud to be a half-blood, other half-blood kids will believe they can be proud, too. They might come out of hiding and do more great things. And regular folk might start thinkin' that half-bloods ain't so bad."

"I'm not that kind of man," Danr replied. Her words stung more than a little. "That's not me."

"It *is* you," she said in a strangely gentle voice. "Or it used to be. You wasn't happy with your troll side, so you went on a quest to dump it. I get it. Still hurts the rest of us."

"That's not what I—" Danr started to say, but the words died in his throat. He couldn't finish a lie.

He blinked. How could that be a lie? He had gone after the power of the shape to save Ranadar and to spare Aisa public condemnation, not because he wanted to reject— because he wanted to reject—

He wanted to reject.

Huh.

"I don't like being famous," he said too quickly. "I didn't want to wield the Axe, either. I only did that to save my friends."

"I know," she sighed. "Kinda moot now anyway. I mean, can you change back?"

Not for the first time, he tried it, reaching inside himself to find his birth shape the way Aisa said she had done. Nothing. "Nope. I must be one of those people who can only change once. Grandfather Wyrm did say I only have one other shape."

Really, it came as a relief. No more half-blood. No more fame. No more pointed fingers, no more people stamping after him, no more royal receptions. Just him. An anvil lifted off his back, and the wind threatened to carry him away.

"Then there's no point in talking about it, handsome."

Greenstone pointed. "Well, we're at Balsia, so you can rescue your elven friend. Good thing, too, with the storm behind us and company up ahead."

Danr followed her pointing finger. Coming toward them was a pair of ships. Both flew the flag of the city of Balsia.

"That's the *Golden Wyrm*," Greenstone said. "Prince's ship. The other one belongs to the harbormaster." She hawked and spat.

Harebones, the first mate, rushed up. "What now, Captain? They're approaching fast."

"They flying a battle flag?" she asked.

"Just Balsian colors, ma'am."

"Then drop sail and see what they want. Keep everyone alert, but I don't want a fight. We're way outnumbered."

"I've met Prince Karsten," Danr told her. "He's not a bad guy."

"In my experience, nobility's nice only when they need to be."

Aisa came up on deck. "What is wrong?"

"Guests," Captain Greenstone said. "I told Harebones to get out the good china."

"But hide the silver," Aisa murmured.

Danr shook his head. "How you can joke at—"

"Listen." She took his arm and drew him aside. "It looks that everything is about to move very fast. I should speak with you first."

He eyed the approaching ships. A longboat dropped from each. "Looks like we have a few minutes. Where's Talfi?"

"Sleeping below. The golem is watching him again." The two of them were standing at the gunwale, with Greenstone still at the helm some distance behind them. Aisa looked out over the strip of sea toward the land, her expression hard. Danr tensed.

"What is it?" he asked.

"When I was with the merfolk," she said, "I . . . learned many things. Things I need to discuss. With you."

The boats rowed closer. Danr shifted uneasily in his new, smaller body. It was still strange to look straight into her face instead of down into it. "All right. What did you want to talk about?"

She paused for a long moment. "I am so weak. I do not know where to begin."

"Anywhere you want," he said. "But you'd better hurry."

"I . . ." A strange look crossed her face. It seemed to Danr that she started to find her nerve, then abruptly lost it. "Danr, will you marry me?"

And he had to answer the truth. "Of course I will. I love you. And—hey! I was supposed to ask you!"

She smiled. "We half-bloods were never ones for rules."

The words slapped him. Half-blood. Aisa was a half-blood, too, even if she didn't look like one. It hadn't really hit him until that moment. Could two half-bloods come together and make a whole?

"My turn," he said. "Will *you* marry *me*?"

"Yes, my love. One time or a hundred. As many times as you ask."

It was exactly right. He kissed her now, his long fingers entwining her hair. She sighed and kissed him back. They shared this quiet moment, with the boats rowing toward them and the storm building behind them.

"Is that what you wanted to talk about?" he asked when they parted.

Again, she hesitated. Something else was in her eyes, something powerful, but he had no idea what it was. Then she looked away, and whatever it was disappeared. She said, "That is all, yes. I was . . . so nervous and I wanted to know. Before everything happens."

He paused. Was she telling the entire truth? He had the

feeling she wasn't, but he didn't want to ruin this soft, quiet moment with an accusation. So he only said, "Hmm. Then it's a good thing you proposed now."

"And a good thing you said yes," she said with a flash of her usual sarcasm, and Danr couldn't help but smile.

Already the pair of longboats had reached the *Slippery Fish*. In short order, two groups of men swarmed aboard. Some wore the pale blue and white outfits of acolytes of Bosha, and others wore dark blue military uniforms with a gold wyrm insignia. This time, however, they didn't take over the ship. Instead a man who Danr assumed had a high rank demanded, "Where's the golem?"

"Guest quarters, with the boy who can't die," Greenstone said. "Pleased to meet you, too."

The high-ranker nodded toward two men, who hurried below.

"What are they doing?" Danr demanded, tense now.

"Guarding his door so the golem won't come up and let the Obsidia know what's going on," said Prince Karsten, climbing onto the deck. Everyone bowed. The harbormaster, in his crisp blue robes, clambered up behind him, fumbling with his blue dolphin-topped staff.

"You believe physically trapping the golem in that cabin will lead the Obsidia to believe nothing is wrong?" Aisa said. "I can see why your mother is reluctant to let you out to play."

"Aisa!" said Danr, shocked.

"And where's Danr?" Harbormaster Willem asked in his deep voice.

"That's me," Danr said, and wondered if Willem would extend his ring again. "I've changed a little."

Willem glanced at him dismissively, then turned and stared. His fingers went white around the dolphin staff, and a look of awe stole over his face. "No," he whispered. "You couldn't have."

"Why not?" Aisa asked. "Did you think we would die in the attempt like all the others?"

"Frankly, I did." Still looking shocked, Willem reached out to touch Danr's hair. Danr pulled away.

"Grandfather Wyrm made fascinating conversation," said Aisa. "We would love to introduce you someday."

"Look, we really need to get to shore," Danr said.

"I know," Karsten said. "The Obsidia have the elf and the orc you befriended."

Danr's heart jumped. "Did you rescue them?"

"We tried," the prince said. "But the Obsidia reminded us that elves are slavers and orcs are barbarians, and neither of them are citizens of Balsia, so what happens to them is no concern of the crown's."

"You are saying it is not a crime in Balsia to kidnap an elf or an orc?" Aisa said in disbelief.

"That's exactly right. And we still owe the Obsidia all that money."

Danr ground his teeth. Hector had chosen his hostages well.

"At any rate," Karsten continued, "you came back with this power, and we need to decide what to do with it."

Danr shot a nervous glance up the coast to the city. Rana-dar was in there at the Obsidia house, and the water was rising. The storm continued to build on the horizon behind them. Anvil-topped clouds turned gray.

"Do with it?" Aisa echoed. "We'll complete our deal with the harbormaster, of course. He said if we gave him the power of the shape, he would . . ." She trailed off and looked at the prince. Danr tried not to bite his lip. Prince Karsten might know about their journey to find the power of the shape, but he might not know—or approve of—their deal with the harbormaster. An end to slavery in Balsia would create a major upheaval in Balsia, and Danr didn't think the prince would enjoy this idea.

"The harbormaster said he would help us," Aisa finished lamely.

Willem straightened his blue and white robes, pretending to take no notice of Aisa's words.

It suddenly occurred to Danr that the harbormaster was friends with the Obsidia, and the Obsidia were slave dealers. If the harbormaster abolished slavery, his friends would be ruined. Abolition would also dry up countless millions in taxes and tariffs for the temple of Bosha. Harbormaster Willem had said he was worried the Obsidia would misuse the power of the shape, and that was why he wanted Aisa and Danr to bring it to him and only him, but the more Danr thought of it, the weaker that argument seemed. Unless . . .

Danr followed this line of thought. The Obsidia were sitting on a small army of golems and at least one dwarf who could make them. If slavery was abolished in Balsia, golem servants would gain enormous value. A golem factory would become nearly priceless, especially if someone, someone like a wealthy high priest, knew ahead of time that he should build a stock of golems. A priest with the space and the money for a new golem factory.

Golems were made of clay, by dwarfs. And a line of trolls had been hauling cartloads of clay toward the temple of Bosha. Those very trolls made it clear they expected to see a great many dwarfs at the temple as well.

When Harbormaster Willem promised to end slavery, just who was he hoping to help?

Danr closed his right eye and looked at the harbormaster. He appeared just as he did the last time Danr had examined him, all lines and edges. "Are you working with the Obsidia to end slavery," he asked bluntly, "so you can replace it with a golem market that you alone control?"

Aisa gasped. Prince Karsten folded his arms hard, his expression unreadable. The harbormaster turned hard gray eyes on Danr. "Impertinent and rude! Just what I'd expect from . . . from . . ."

"A filthy half-blood?" Danr fixed him harder with his single eye. "You gave a pretty speech before the prince about love and acceptance, but you hate half-bloods. You hate all Stane."

"Nonsense! All creatures are Bosha's—"

"Another lie," Danr spat. "I see it. You and the Obsidia are good friends, and you cooked up a plan. You pushed the prince into letting the Stane enter the city with big talk about troll tolerance and sanitary sewers, but what you really wanted was dwarfs. Dwarfs make golems. They make golems in your own factory. They're making golems for you as we speak. Your men stink of clay! You meant to end slavery long before you made a deal with Aisa, and you wanted to replace it with an army of golems that only you and your temple could produce."

"Neat, orderly golems," Aisa put in. "Tidy. No chaos."

"Drivel from a simpleton!" the harbormaster cried. "Your Highness, are you going to let him—"

"Speak?" Karsten said. "Yes. We'll definitely let him speak."

"But your friends the Obsidia objected, didn't they?" Danr drilled relentlessly ahead. "They were already hurting because the elves stopped buying slaves, and *they* wanted to produce the golems themselves. You found yourself in a difficult place. You had the space for a golem factory, an army of workers who will keep a secret, and the power to end slavery, but all the dwarfs worked for the Obsidia. What to do? Except the Obsidia wanted something else: the power of the shape. They want it more than gold or golems. So you made a deal—they could have the power of the shape in exchange for the dwarfs."

"You were going after the power of the shape long before I got involved," the harbormaster pointed out.

"Another lie. We only truly decided to find the power of shape after Aisa learned about Ynara." Danr closed both his eyes for a moment in sorrow, and Aisa's own eyes were downcast. "Before then, we might have gone or might not. We never did ask how the Obsidia captured a mermaid. They didn't— You did, Harbormaster. Once Sharlee found out that Aisa was drawn to the merfolk, you gave them Ynara and helped them set up the auction that lured us to their house."

"I don't need to listen to the mouthings of a half-blood piece of—"

"I'm human now," Danr said. The moment the words left his mouth, the captain's face turned to stone, and the anvil settled onto his back again. "The only thing I don't see is why you would offer *us* the end of slavery in exchange for the power of the—oh. Oh!"

"What is it now?" the harbormaster scoffed. "A surprise twist to the end of your story?"

"You *were* telling the truth," Danr said. "You really are afraid of how much power it'll give the Obisida. You really do want to stop them from abusing the power."

"Doing the right thing for the wrong reasons," Aisa said quietly.

"How is this wrong?" the harbormaster suddenly burst out. "What is wrong with anything I have done? Bring my plan to fruition and everyone wins! You"—he pointed at Aisa—"despise slavery as inhuman. Go along with this, and slavery will indeed end, and we will instead have an army of workers who don't think or feel pain or get tired. Our economy will change with almost no damage. And you"—he pointed to Danr—"hate being the center of attention. You brought back the power of the shape, and your fame will soon evaporate. Do you *want* the Obsidia to have this power?"

"Vik, no," said Danr truthfully.

"Everyone has won!" the harbormaster said. "I should be praised, not pilloried!"

"Except," Aisa said, stepping forward, "that this plan makes you the single most powerful person in the world. You are already the most powerful priest in Balsia. The golem monopoly will make you the wealthiest man alive. And the power of the shape will put the might of a hundred armies at your disposal."

"So I gain a little something for my trouble," the harbormaster said. "Is that wrong?"

"Did you intend to share this power with the crown?" Karsten asked. "The power of the shape?"

"Don't lie." Danr tapped his left eye. "I can see it."

The harbormaster started to answer, then glanced at Danr and folded his lips.

"I see." Karsten glanced at Danr as well. "That's an interesting power you have, Danr, your ability to see truth. None of the stories mention it."

"I've kept it quiet," Danr muttered.

"Maybe you should be a judge," Karsten said. "Anyway, I don't think we'll allow your plan to come about, Harbormaster."

The harbormaster looked genuinely shocked. "Why in Ashkame's name not?"

"It's treason, or did you forget what happens when you plot against the crown?" Karsten said grimly. "Men, take the harbormaster—"

The harbormaster moved so fast Danr didn't quite understand what was happening. A knife leaped into the man's hand

and he slashed at Danr. Danr automatically grabbed the harbormaster's wrist to yank the weapon away. Not long ago, the
harbormaster would have had no chance, but Danr's new
shape was far weaker. The harbormaster's knife fell, and red-
hot pain sliced Danr's chest. Blood spattered the deck. Aisa
shouted.

The deck bristled with sudden weapons. The prince's
guards, the blue-clad acolytes, and Greenstone's sailors all
produced swords, knives, and truncheons, but none of them
seemed to know who they should fight. Captain Greenstone
jumped in and grabbed the harbormaster easily enough.
The knife spun away. Danr went to his knees, clutching his
bleeding chest. He was so weak! The harbormaster was grinning in Captain Greenstone's bear hug while warm blood
ran down Danr's arm. More of his blood dripped down Willem's face.

"The poor half-blood. It'll make me rich." The harbormaster laughed and licked a scarlet drop from his cheek.
His body glowed with golden light. Startled, Greenstone
released him, and the men on the deck took a step back. The
harbormaster's shape lengthened. He grew taller, thinner.
His features, already handsome, sharpened into preternat-
ural beauty. His hair changed from white to silver, and the
tips of his ears poked through.

"Half-blood!" Danr said. His chest hurt like hell, and he
felt stupid for letting the harbormaster get the better of him.
"You're a half-blood. Human and elf."

"You would have seen it if you had thought big enough,"
the harbormaster said. "My father would be pleased. And . . ."
He stretched out his arms. His sleeves fell back, now too
short. "Now I can feel it. I always had a little of the glamour
and none of the Twist, but now I can feel both. Thank Bosha!"

"You hated half-bloods, including yourself," Danr spat.
"So you hid."

"I'm not half-blood now, you Stane moron," the harbormaster spat back. "I am Fae!"

"Men!" Karsten barked. "Take him!"

The soldiers, none too happy to see a hostile elf in their midst, turned their iron swords toward the harbormaster, who blanched.

"You don't have me yet," he said, and with a flicker Danr recognized from countless Twists with Ranadar, the harbormaster vanished.

A moment of silence followed. Then Greenstone said, "Hidden in plain sight."

"That was . . . frightening," Karsten breathed. "And incredible! Will your blood let anyone do that?"

"It only works for a few people, my lord," said Danr. "Some feel horrible pain from it before they change. Some die."

"You looked at him with that true eye," Karsten said. "Why didn't you see he was a half-blood?"

"I . . . don't know," Danr said, surprised. His chest still hurt. Droplets of blood spattered the deck. "I didn't see Aisa was a half-blood, either, so maybe a true eye doesn't tell you that."

"The bigger question," Aisa said, "is what delightful plan will the harbormaster drop on us next?"

"We need to find him," the prince said. He raised his voice. "Men! I want the harbormaster arrested! Occupy the temple of Bosha. Find out if they're making golems. Meanwhile, detain these men for questioning in the Gold Keep!"

The guards on deck turned their swords toward the acolytes, who were just now recovering from the surprise of seeing their high priest transform into an elf and Twist away. The acolytes, who matched the soldiers man for man, snapped their own weapons to readiness. Danr realized he was staring at the sharp, shiny beginning of a civil war. Karsten, meanwhile, at last seemed to notice that while his ship was only a few dozen yards away, a number of priestly blades were pointed at his heart. The sailors on the deck backed up several steps and folded their arms. Karsten shot them a glance, then looked at Captain Greenstone. She shrugged massive shoulders.

"Five gold hands," Karsten said to her.

"Up the prince!" Greenstone boomed.

Knives and cutlasses leaped into the sailors' hands. The priests' blades wavered. Danr tensed. He'd seen more than enough fighting in his life, and every swing of a sword put Aisa in danger. Before the sailors and soldiers could react further, however, the acolytes all leaped overboard and, lithe as porpoises, swam toward the harbormaster's ship. Karsten watched them go, mouth set.

"Will the harbormaster's ship try to smack us around?" Greenstone asked.

"Not without the harbormaster himself to give the order," Karsten said grimly, and turned to one of his men. "But they're getting away, and they know what's going on. Lieutenant, I want you and the men to row to shore and take my commands to the Gold Keep. I want the harbormaster found and arrested."

"My lord," Aisa said, "if a former slave could offer some advice?"

The prince looked at her and seemed to see her and her beauty for the first time. He straightened his tunic. Danr suppressed a growl. Karsten said, "Advice?"

"It will take time for your orders to reach the Gold Keep, and then it will take more time for the guard to assemble men and carry out your orders. But I would guess that the harbormaster is already at the temple, giving thrilling commands to his loyal acolytes. If he now has the full elven glamour, his people will be breathtakingly eager to obey him."

Karsten folded his arms. "What are you saying?"

"Prepare for a long fight. That temple is a fortress, and they are readying for war even as we speak. The harbormaster has stolen our magic to commit treason, and such men do not seek mere money."

"You think he wants the crown," Karsten said flatly.

"Along with the head that holds it up," Aisa returned. "Can you stop him from taking both?"

"We'll take his filthy life," the lieutenant said, heading for the longboat. "You can't trust a shape-shifter."

He said the word exactly the way other people said *half-blood*. A chill crawled across Danr's skin.

Karsten didn't seem to notice. "Lieutenant, I'm going with you." He climbed down the side of the ship, and the men followed, including the two who were guarding Talfi's room. Danr heard measured footsteps thudding up from below. The golem!

"Aisa," he urged, "very soon the Obsidia are going to find out that something went wrong. We have to get to their house soon or they'll kill Ranadar and Kalessa. Can you change into a mermaid again?"

"Easily."

"Then we'll need another longboat and a small favor from you, Captain."

"Oh, a *small* favor," Greenstone groused. "Just as long as it's *small*. The prince didn't even pay me the hands he promised."

"You'll like this favor, and that's the truth."

He spoke quickly as Talfi scrambled out of a hatchway with hair disheveled and eyes wild. He rushed over as the golem thumped up the ladder behind him. "What's—"

Danr clapped a small hand over his mouth. "Don't ask. Not yet. Captain, the boat."

When they climbed down the rope ladder into the craft, the golem started to follow.

"How about a stroll across the bottom?" Greenstone asked. With that, she heaved once, and the heavy golem splashed into the water. It sank in a blizzard of bubbles as thunder rumbled in the distance.

"What did you do that for?" Talfi gasped.

"So we could hurry," said Danr.

With a flick, Willem appeared atop one of the tall, domed towers within the temple of Bosha. There was a bad moment when his boots skittered on the smooth stone of the dome and he nearly slid over the edge, but at the last moment and with Bosha's grace, he managed to grab the spire at the top. He stood for a moment, catching his breath and slowing his heart, while the chill, wet breeze pushed at his hair. The storm was coming.

And he was an elf.

Since no one was around to see, Willem allowed himself a moment of giddy elation. He shouted and he thumped his feet against the dome. How *grand* it felt to be freed of the human pollution, to no longer be a half-blood. The childish inner part of him wanted to see the look on Father's face as he, Willem, strode into the house—through the *front* door— and claimed a place at the table as a son. Maybe he would Twist to Otrania right now and—

His face hardened. No. He had sworn he would never again set foot in Otrania, or any part of Alfhame. He smiled. Not unless he was bringing order to the place. No more family fights. No more children crying in corners. No fathers who refused half-blood offspring because there would *be* no half-blood offspring. Everyone would know his and her proper place.

The temple of Bosha, azure beneath the gathering clouds, spread beneath Willem's boots in sharp, tidy perfection. Tiny people moved about like blue and white shards while the gardens, laid out by Willem himself, kept to their rigid rows. Beyond the temple walls sprawled the city of Balsia, a fat and lazy wyrm wrapped around a gleaming jewel. There wasn't a part of it that Willem didn't know. The counting houses in the Diamond District, the weavers at the Tenner River, and the dyers at the Niner, the whorehouses near the Docks and in the Rookery, the desperate souls in the Sludge near the Shallows, the cooks ringing Old City—everything in its place. From up here, it looked unspoiled, perfect. Exhilaration made his elven chest thrum. This was to be a god!

Blasphemy. His grip on the spire wobbled. For a sickening moment, the world bobbled beneath him. Then he caught his balance again, and a few moments' scrambling got him under control. Control. That was the key. Keep it controlled.

The trouble was, control came harder and harder to maintain. The new prince made rash, hotheaded decisions. Hector and Sharlee Obsidia, fond as he was of them, let their obsession with power run them into the mouth of a wyrm. They didn't understand that Willem had a harbor to run, a city to oversee. Until now it had been relatively easy. Willem had used what little glamour he had to keep the old prince under a heavy thumb, and the mayor was barely worth bothering about, but now . . . now everything was getting away from him. The new prince resisted his weak, half-blood power. He allowed the Stane into the city so they could quite literally undermine it. He had brought the so-called Hero of the Twist into the very heart of the palace and listened to his demands. Despite all Willem's subtle attempts to interfere, Sharlee and Hector were inches away from getting their hands on the power of the shape.

Initially, Willem had been positive the power of the shape would involve an object, most likely the legendary knife used in the sacrifice. All the books pointed toward it. But the books had been wrong. The knife only spilled the blood, the true source of the power. He had planned to take the power for himself, rid himself of his half-blood status, destroy the prince's army, and then parcel out the power to selected humans who had fallen under his newly powerful elven glamour. Unfortunately, that didn't seem possible now, or even feasible. Danr and Aisa were already escaping into the city, and Bosha only knew how many people they had already infected with their half-blood magic. His plan was a chaotic wreck.

His eye fell on the long, L-shaped building that had received all the clay. Where the dwarfs lived and worked. Willem laughed, overjoyed again.

Destroy the prince's army. He had always planned to do that. He only had to think *bigger*.

Below, Willem caught a glimpse of a familiar pudgy shape crossing a courtyard. Punsle. Now that Willem could Twist, he was amazed that he couldn't see how to do it before. Willem reached through space, feeling for the route he wanted. It was like bending the branch of a tree toward himself, stepping onto it, and letting the branch snap back into place, sweeping him along with it. Willem Twisted and popped into the air two feet above the courtyard a little behind Punsle. A little breathless, he dropped to the ground, scattering a startled flock of acolytes and possibly scarring them for life. Quickly, he drew his hood over his new ears. The time would come to reveal his true self, but not yet. At least his voice hadn't changed.

"Summon the Whitecaps!" he barked at an acolyte who hadn't fled quickly enough. "Tell them to meet outside the manufactory at once!"

The acolyte scurried away.

Punsle whirled. "Excellency?" His blue and white robes

were even more impeccably maintained than Willem's. You could shave with the creases in his sleeves. "When did you return? And you're . . . you've . . ."

"Not now, Punsle." Willem tried to straighten his own robes, short as they were. He drew himself up. "Bar the gates and seal the entrances. We're going to war."

Punsle recovered himself. "Yes, Excellency," he said as if Willem had just ordered a plate of chips for dinner. "Against whom, Excellency?"

"The prince. I've committed treason, and it's time to make our move."

Punsle's expression didn't change, which was one thing Willem liked about him. "I thought we were moving next month, Excellency, when the golem army was fully completed."

"Plans have changed."

"As have you, Excellency," Punsle apparently couldn't help saying.

"The Tree tips, Punsle." Willem wrapped his cloak about him like a suit of armor. "We can drop with it, or control the fall."

"As you've said, Excellency. Do you need anything else?"

Willem was already striding toward the L-shaped building. Behind his back, Punsle snapped out orders to acolytes and priests, principals and primatures. Word spread quickly, and activity burst over the complex like water from a broken dam. The followers of Bosha lit fires, set pitch to boil, opened weapon stores, checked traps and barbicans at the entryways. In the distance the main gates grumbled shut, adding to the tension and urgency that already rode the air. Swords came out, and troops of armed Whitecaps in their pale leather armor scrambled toward the manufactory. Willem drew the hood on his cloak farther forward to hide his face as they joined the stream of men. None of them seemed to recognize Willem, or wonder why a priest of Bosha was wearing robes that were blatantly too short for him.

"The sea washes everything toward us, Punsle." Willem turned aside and entered the building through a side door with Punsle in tow while the Whitecaps hustled to the courtyard in front.

The moment Willem entered the building, a sick nausea nearly brought him to his knees. Clangs and thuds echoed through the great hall and bounced off the ceiling three stories above them. Smells of wet clay and wood smoke tanged the air, and through it all mixed the horrid, acid smell of hot iron. Iron had never bothered Willem in the slightest before this, and he had forgotten how difficult it made life for the elves. A headache ground at the back of his eyes.

He straightened. This was nothing. He would move forward, iron or no iron.

All the windows were bricked up, and the only light fell from a few torches and a pair of glowing forges—more iron—that also heated the room to sweat-inducing levels. A small mountain of clay sat in one corner. On the wide floor, a dozen golems stood motionless as chess pieces, their azure eyes staring eerily at nothing. Four dwarfs—two for each forge—moved among them, their sensitive eyes protected from the sun by the manufactory's thick walls. Parts for more golems were stacked on worktables amid tools Willem still didn't recognize. Some of the tools were sharp and, of course, made of iron. Willem forced himself not to step away. He was stronger than this.

Behind them all, against the far wall, a much taller shape crouched beneath the high ceiling. Scaffolding made a spidery lattice all about it. Truly, Willem mused, the troll boy thought he could see the truth, but even the truth could be wrong.

One of the dwarfs recognized Willem and scuttled over.

His twisted spine bent him so far sideways he had to look up to hold a conversation. "Excellency?" he mumbled.

"When will the golems be ready?"

The dwarf coughed. "Hikk is only now carving runes on their thoraxes, and then we'll need blood to bring them to life."

"They aren't alive," Willem spat. "Nothing men create can live."

"As you say, Excellency," the dwarf said in a tone that made it clear Willem was wrong in every way possible but who nevertheless decided how far the purse might open.

"How long?" Willem repeated.

"Hard to say, Excellency. Weeks still, I'm sure."

Willem ground his teeth through the awful iron headache. This was a problem. The Fae had trapped the Stane underground for centuries, something that had driven them to poverty, hunger, and desperation. They had become so desperate that they had chained up Death in an attempt to harness her power and escape. Control of Death herself. Willem couldn't help admiring it, even if it had failed. But thanks to that greasy half troll, the Stane had been released, and Willem had spotted an opportunity. Impoverished people were always willing to work, even for scandalously low wages. If you did the math right, you could even find ways to make *them* pay *you*. You just paid them in scrip they could only spend at the stores you owned, then pushed the price of food so high they had to borrow against future wages just to stay alive. A number of trolls had found themselves in the temple's debt this way. In some ways, it was better than slavery.

Dwarfs, however, were different from trolls. They kept their eye on the gold, and they knew how much their labor was worth. It also wasn't worth it to threaten torture or beatings. Dwarfs, Willem had learned, would go through a great deal of discomfort if it meant holding on to gold. Or silver. Or even copper. But in some ways, that made them easier to handle.

Willem gestured at Punsle, who produced a purse from under his immaculate robes. He opened it to show the soft, gleaming gold within. The dwarf sucked at his teeth.

"How long?" Willem asked pleasantly.

"We can have the dozen running about in a few days," he said.

"And the other project?" Willem said.

The dwarf looked longingly at the purse. Punsle obliged by jingling it. But the dwarf shook his head. "You can offer me a roomful of gold, and it won't change a thing. We can't do what we can't do. The problem is the blood."

"The blood," Willem repeated slowly.

"Golems need Stane blood to get started," the dwarf said. "Giant or troll or dwarf. A smear is enough for them"—he waved a hand at the dozen golems— "but for this, we need a lot more, and that takes time."

It was always about the blood, Willem thought. Blood for the troll boy, blood for the golems, blood for the shape magic. Everything came down to the blood.

"How do you usually get the blood?" Willem pulled the cloak off and handed it to Punsle, who accepted it without comment. Then Willem pulled off his robe.

The dwarf didn't seem to notice, either. "Cut my palm."

"I see." Dressed only in an undershirt, Willem hooked a large washtub with his foot, dragged it over, and pointed over the dwarf's shoulder. "Does that water pump work?"

The dwarf turned his head. "Sure, Excellency. Why d'you—"

Willem snatched a knife from the table. The hilt was wrapped in leather, but still the iron burned his hand like acid and his knees wobbled, though he ignored both sensations. One slash opened the dwarf's throat from side to side. Willem flung the dreadful knife aside even as the dwarf gurgled and collapsed. Gleaming scarlet, Willem held the corpse so the dwarf's blood gushed into the washtub.

"Will that be enough, do you think?" Willem asked.

"I'm sure of it, Excellency," Punsle replied.

Chapter Sixteen

The heavy sewage in the bay caked Aisa's gills with filth. No wonder the merfolk avoided Balsia. Disgusted and worried both, Aisa flashed through the water with the long-boat in tow so fast they left a wake. Danr and Talfi clutched the gunwales hard enough to leave permanent finger marks. People on ships and fishing boats and rafts turned to stare at the sight, but Aisa was beyond caring.

They reached the docks in moments. Danr and Talfi climbed onto the dock, round-eyed and white-knuckled, while Aisa pulled herself onto the wood and wrung the awful water from her hair.

"Your facial tattoos came back when you changed," Danr said. "They make you look so . . . fierce."

She touched her face. The ridges and the seed pearls had indeed returned. Relief swept her. She had forgotten to check when she first changed back into her . . . was the mermaid her true form? Or was her human shape her true form? Perhaps it did not matter. In any case, she had kept her face.

"Can we talk about that later? We have to reach the Obsidia house," said Talfi. "Ranadar and Kalessa are—"

Aisa reached into her memory. Her power was growing. She no longer needed the blood of an animal to change into it. The shape of any animal she had seen or touched seemed to form in her mind, and flowing into that shape seemed ridiculously easy, if somewhat tiring. Her shape melted and reformed. Tears pricked the back of her eyes even as her eyes changed their shape. Ynara had sacrificed everything so Aisa could have this power. Aisa had shared it, and Ynara and her grandmother had died.

No, whispered a voice in her head, and she couldn't tell if it was her own voice or Pendra's now. *Your grandfather shared the power, not you, and more people died than were fated to. Can you wield the sickle without flinching?*

Why must we give up blood for gain? she cried out. *Why must we lose before we can win?*

But there was no answer. Her shape finished changing, and she stood on the stones as a roan horse.

"Fantastic!" Danr said. "Aisa, I could kiss you."

"I'd pay a dozen silver fingers to watch that, but we're in a hurry." Talfi leaped onto her back, and Danr followed. Aisa snorted at how ridiculously light they were. She bolted forward. Talfi clung to her mane and Danr clung to Talfi as she cantered up the docks, gathering speed. It felt strange running with four legs, but she quickly got the hang of it. Air rushed past her nose and ears. Exhilarating!

"Make way!" Talfi shouted at startled pedestrians. "Move aside!"

They passed out of the docks and into the slave market. Rows of slaves were still chained within the pens. An auction was going on. The stench of the pens and the shouts of the auctioneer slammed into Aisa, and it became impossible for her to run another step. She skidded to a stop. Danr and Talfi nearly went over her neck. Unbalanced, they slid off.

"Hey, what—?" Talfi asked.

Before she could think more, she took back her human form in a small explosion of light. The noise of the market stopped, and everyone, slave, slaver, and customer alike, stared for a moment. Then pandemonium broke out. Most of the customers stampeded away. The slaves shouted in their chains. Naked and uncaring, Aisa snatched a knife from the belt of a slaver who was too stunned to react and ran into the closest slave pen. She held the blade above her forearm.

"What's happening, Aisa?" Danr asked behind her.

Aisa turned to him—

—and he was wielding the Iron Axe. Blood dripped from it. It spread across the slave pens—no, it was the elven city of Palana—no, it was the Garden. Aisa forced the tip of the knife against her skin, but she flinched and her knees weakened. She relived the violence, tasted the fear, felt the warm blood. The tip of the knife refused to move.

"I cannot," she said hoarsely. "I cannot do it."

Can you wield—

"Shut up!" she barked.

The slaves stared at her from their chains. Talfi ran up. He had pulled his tunic off, and he flung it around Aisa's shoulders, though it only partially covered her. "What's going on? What can't you do?"

"I . . . I want to share the blood and the power. But I cannot."

To her relief, Danr didn't question it. "I'll do it."

"No!" Talfi's face was red now. "We have to reach the Obsidia house. Now!"

"This'll only take a second," Danr said. He snatched Aisa's knife and scored his own arm with a fresh wound, even though his chest was still oozing. Blood trickled toward his fingers. Without heeding the filthy straw or the hard cobblestones, he dashed into the first pen and, by chance, knelt face-to-face with the women Aisa had treated that one day. The women cowered. Danr spoke to the woman who had flung water on Aisa after Aisa had refused to help her escape.

"You . . . you . . . ," the woman stammered. "How . . . ?"

"Do you wish to see if you are a shape-shifter?" Aisa asked over Danr's shoulder.

"Yes," the woman said.

Danr dabbed a bloody finger on the woman's mouth, then turned to the next woman to ask the same question. The first woman, meanwhile, howled and twisted in her chains. In a moment, she became a wolfhound, which easily slipped the fetters. The hound gave Danr a grateful look and sprinted away.

"My blood and the blood of anyone who tastes my blood might let you change shape, or it might kill you," Danr called in a voice that rang through the pens. "Share it! Share it all and you'll be free!"

But now the slavers recovered their surprise, and they objected to the idea of someone freeing their prize stock. Several of them closed in on Danr and Aisa. One of them grabbed Aisa by the shoulders. Once again she was back in Palana. Blood gushed over the ground, and the Iron Axe crackled in her ears. All the strength drained from her body and her muscles went limp as wax while the slaver glared steel down at her.

No! she told herself. *You are strong!*

Aisa reached into herself and found more power. Her shape shifted, and she exploded into a one-ton walrus. The slaver flew backward and skidded into a wall. The others fled. Aisa roared. More shouts of fear arose from the slave pens, but others cried out in admiration. So this was how

Danr felt all the time. Why would he want to give it up? This was strength!

The slaves in front of her cowered in their fetters, unable to run. Aisa pulled herself together. She had no time. Rana-dar was close to drowning, and the slavers would find their courage soon. She reimagined her true shape and changed back. The effort made her a little dizzy.

"She's a sorceress!" one of the slaves gasped to Danr.

"You might have the same power." Danr held out a bloody hand to her.

The woman took his blood, but nothing happened. Danr moved on to the next, and the next. Some people accepted the blood, others refused it. Three others changed shape. One died, and Aisa averted her eyes. Four others tried to change shape and glowed faintly, but failed. Talfi was grow-ing more and more agitated, so Danr handed the knife to a slave.

"Whoever's shared blood with me can share it with others," he said. "We have to go."

"Now," said Talfi.

Aisa tried to change into a horse again, but the power wasn't there. She tried again, and failed. The magic would not come. Oh, what a weak fool she had been. The slave market had drawn her, and now she had—

A wisp of power threaded through her. Eagerly, she fol-lowed it back to its source. Danr! He turned and gave her a white, handsome smile that thrilled right through her. Even though he was not touching her, his strength was there. She drank, and power came easily from him. Magic gushed into Aisa, stiffening her spine and firming her bare feet on the cobbles. Danr staggered a little, then righted himself with a nod. With a laugh, Aisa spread her arms wide and flowed back into her horse shape. She galloped away with Danr and

Talfi on her back while the slaves passed the knife around behind them.

Moments later, she halted at the gate to the Obsidia house. The gate still gaped where Danr had bent it open a few days ago. Had it only been days? Danr and Talfi dismounted, and Aisa squeezed through the opening. The golem standing guard shouted an alert, but Aisa planted a double-hooved kick with her back legs square in its chest, and it flew backward.

"Come on!" Talfi, who had regained his tunic, leaped back aboard and hauled Danr up. As more golems rattled toward them, Aisa cantered around the house, weaving and dodging and nearly throwing her passengers off her back. They arrived in the garden where Ranadar now stood in the tank with water up to his chin. He had to raise his head to keep his mouth and nose above the waterline. A human would have died of exposure long ago, but elves were not bothered by such things. Thank Olar. Kalessa was chained by one ankle to a tree not far away. She bolted to her feet.

"Who—?" she said.

The golem climbed up the ladder with another cupful of water. Golems, crying alerts, poured around the corner of the house. Aisa whirled, dumping Danr and Talfi unceremoniously off her back, and gave the glass a full kick with both rear feet just as she had done to the first golem. The glass cracked. Aisa kicked twice more, and the glass shattered. Struts broke. Water cascaded across the grass, drenching Aisa from the hocks down. Talfi ran into the tank and helped Ranadar sink gratefully to the floor. His wrists were raw and bleeding from the iron shackles. The golem reached the top of the ladder and emptied its cup into the puddle.

Thin applause drifted across the garden. "You did it!" Hector called from a safe distance. "And two of you have managed to change shape. I'm impressed. Let's have the power of the shape. Please."

Aisa reared up on her hind legs and screamed a neigh at them.

"Defiance?" Sharlee put in next to him. "We had a deal. What makes you think you can back out now?"

"Willem," Hector spat. "He must have betrayed us."

Aisa stamped. She didn't want to move away from Ranadar, but she couldn't speak, either. Not in this form. Many golems, at least a dozen of them, were now scattered about the yard. Where was Danr? She couldn't see him.

"Aisa, is that you?" Kalessa called from beneath her tree. She was wrestling in vain with her fetters.

"You will still give us the power of the shape." Hector's voice was hungry. "I will have it."

Aisa pulled herself back into her human shape, and Kalessa gave a shout of glee. "You have it! My sister!"

"I will give you nothing," Aisa said. "You have sacrificed nothing, and you deserve nothing."

"We sent dozens of other servants and hirelings off to find the power," Sharlee objected. "We sacrificed every one of them."

"And yet here you stand," Aisa said. "You have given nothing of yourselves, overcome no hardships, acquired no scars. The power of the shape will suck the life from your body and spit out your bones. It will leave nothing but an evil shadow. I will not give it to you."

"I didn't give you a choice," Hector said. "I never do." He snapped his fingers, and a golem dragged Danr into view with his arms wrenched behind him. One golem was more than strong enough. His chest and arm still oozed blood.

"Aisa," Danr gasped. His face was white with pain. Aisa froze.

"Don't move," Sharlee said pleasantly. "And don't change shape. Tell us how to share this power, or your half-blood lover will pay the price. And to show we aren't joking . . ."

The golem twisted Danr's arm. The wet snap stopped Aisa's heart. Danr cried out and went to his knees.

"We don't give second warnings," Hector said. "Its next move will be to tear his arm completely off."

"Don't give it to them, Aisa!" Danr said. "Don't tell them how it works!"

"Oh, but she will," Sharlee said. "She loves you, and can't bear to watch you suffer. It's been enough that she had to watch her sister mermaid die."

"How did you know about that?" Aisa demanded.

Scorn invaded Sharlee's tone. "Pay attention, dear—you were still sitting on the golem when you told Danr all about it. We're swimming in irony. You worked hard to free the fish girl, only to watch her perish. Did her people forgive you, Aisa? What was it like to hear a mermaid scream?"

The words pierced Aisa with a cold knife. Sorrow and exhaustion shook her like a wolf shaking a broken rabbit. Ynara was dead because of her, because of her blood.

But Sharlee wasn't done. "Tell us, Aisa. Or should I tell your Danr the truth first?"

"Truth?" Aisa said. There was a clanking behind her as Talfi struggled with Ranadar's shackles.

"So you haven't told him! Danr, darling, would you like to know what Aisa has been keeping from you?"

"No!" Aisa begged, not sure if she was speaking to Sharlee or to Danr. "Be silent!"

But Danr had to answer. "That's a truly stupid question for someone who's supposed to be smart. I have no idea if I want to know because I don't know what you're offering. You're— ow!" He groaned as the golem twisted his broken arm.

"Be polite to my wife, half-blood," Hector said with calm menace.

And Aisa saw Danr close his right eye. He looked straight

at Hector and then at Sharlee. He looked for a long, long moment.

What do you see? she wanted to ask, but she kept back the words.

Sharlee took a step forward, her dark eyes drilling into Danr's handsome face. She was enjoying herself, drinking in his physical and emotional pain.

"Let me give *you* some truth, Danr," Sharlee said, and Aisa's knees weakened. "Aisa never cared that you're a half-blood. She adores you for who you are, and would marry you no matter how many people stormed the castle to come get you."

"Thanks," he gasped. "So nice of you to say."

Sharlee's face was twisted into a cruel rictus, and her breath was coming in short bursts. Every moment of pain gave her a thrill of pleasure, and that fact frightened Aisa more than even Grandfather Wyrm.

"Sharlee, don't," Aisa said, and hated herself for the pleading tone that crept into her voice.

Sharlee was relentless. "But Aisa also remembers how you slaughtered the Fae with the Iron Axe. She remembers every drop of blood you spilled because she still sees it on your hands. She relives every scream, and smells the delightful scent of Fae flesh cooking in the fires you set. And you, half troll, were too stupid to notice."

The world crashed to a stop. A look of terrible pain, worse than any broken bone, washed over Danr's face as Aisa's exposed secret mocked her with its nakedness. A black lump choked her throat, and her heart slowly tore in half.

Sharlee continued gleefully. "Your quest was a lie. Your love is a lie. Your marriage will be a lie. While *my* love . . ." She took Hector's hand and received a fond smile from him. ". . . is as true as the rising sun."

Danr turned within the golem's grip and looked at her with both eyes open. Aisa couldn't meet them. Her entire body was cold and shivering. "Aisa," he said softly. "Is . . . is it true?"

"You know it's true. Hamzu," Sharlee said.

The hurt on Danr's face grew, and the awful black guilt pulled Aisa into the ground. He hated her, and he should. A person as weak as she was deserved no love. The blood from the wound on his arm and chest trickled down and spread across the grass in a scarlet sheet. He was hurt. Fires crackled in the trees and Fae screamed in her head. Behind it all stood Pendra with her sickle, ready to hand it to Aisa.

"You don't deserve this power, Aisa. You're afraid of it," Sharlee said, echoing Aisa's thoughts. "Tell us how to take it from you, and you won't have to worry about it ever again."

"I . . . ," Aisa said. He didn't love her anymore. It was all a great lie, had been from the beginning. She should have known from the beginning. How would she go on now?

"If you don't tell us, dear, we'll tear his arm off," Hector said pleasantly.

A lie. They said her love was a lie. But Danr was a truth-teller. She could ask—but if she did, he would answer. He would give tell the absolute truth. Did she want to know if Sharlee's words had stopped his love?

"Besides," Sharlee added, "what do you care if we have it? What has the world done for you but give you pain?"

"Why are you listening to them, sister?" Kalessa wrenched uselessly at her fetters.

"Leave her alone." Talfi got to his feet behind her, leaving the semiconscious Ranadar for the moment. "I'll—"

"Do nothing, Talfi," Sharlee said in a voice smooth as melted sugar. "If you move, our golems will rend your Fae lover to pieces while you watch." And Talfi froze.

"Give us the secret, Aisa," Hector said, "and we'll reward you. How does ten thousand gold hands sound? You'll be a wealthy woman, beyond the petty worries of a world that's kicked you in the face. What do you owe the world?"

They were right. What *did* she owe the world? She had been kidnapped and enslaved and raped and be-glamoured. The Obsidia were offering a real reward in cold, hard coins. Death herself sent Aisa on pointless quests with no real reward except the loss of her Hamzu. The Nine could take the world and—

Then she knew. Hamzu. Danr. He would tell the truth. Sharlee and Hector were aware that Danr was a truth-teller. Why did they not ask *him* for the secret? Sharlee and Hector were manipulating her. Why?

Because they needed to neutralize her, get her on their side.

Aisa drew herself up. "You fear me," she said. "You have always feared me. You know how strong I have become, and you need me on your side."

"We'd be fools not to want you on our side, honey," Sharlee said with a nod. "We'll give you whatever you want— money, mansions, slaves—"

Aisa's spine stiffened. Sharlee cut herself off, but too late. The reminder of the source of Sharlee's wealth hung there, tainting the very air with poison. Aisa would never accept a reward from a slaver.

"Thank you, Sharlee," she said.

This caught Sharlee off guard. "Thank you?" she repeated.

"For bringing out the truth. You tried to destroy my love for Danr and his love for me with a truth that became a lie because I hid it. You brought my truth into the open when I could not, and now I need no longer lie. For that I thank you." Aisa took a deep breath and forced herself to face the truth. "Danr, do you still love me, despite what you have learned?"

There came only a tiny pause. "Of course I do," Danr said from the golem's arms. "Every day and always."

Her heart swelled and she felt it join with his, swirl through the stars and stream together like paired comets. "And I love you. I will never join with the Obsidia."

"Ah well," Sharlee said. "It was worth a try. Danr, honey, how do we get the power of the shape?"

"You need to sip a bit of blood from someone else who has it," he said promptly, "but it'll only work if you have the talent."

"Aw, no," Talfi muttered.

"Is that all?" Hector rubbed his hands together. "That makes it easy enough." He snapped his fingers at a golem. "Slice his throat and drain the blood into a barrel."

"You do not need all of it!" Aisa protested. "A drop is enough, and he is already bleeding!"

"You got a lot of power from a bit of blood, honey," Sharlee said. "I want to see what happens when I *bathe* in it."

The golem strode toward Danr with a knife. Aisa recognized it as Kalessa's. Another golem rolled an empty barrel toward him. Danr tried to fight again, but his arm was still broken and a patina of sweat coated his skin. He looked desperately at Aisa, and mouthed a single word:

Ynara.

And then he closed his *left* eye.

For a horrible moment, Aisa thought he was looking at her through his true eye. But that was his left eye, the closed one. He was giving her a message. *Ynara.* Aisa swallowed grief yet again. Ynara had died under the power of the shape, and now—

She had died. And Danr was calling attention to his true eye, the one that had only just now seen the Obsidia.

"Wait!" Aisa took a step forward. "I have changed my mind. I will join you."

Hector held up a hand, and the golem with Kalessa's knife halted. "Why would we care? We know the secret now."

"But you do not know how to use it," Aisa countered. "I do. I can teach you. I can show you how to use it properly."

"Aisa, no," Danr moaned. And she noticed it was a statement that could be taken any number of ways. It was not a lie.

"Why should we believe you?" Sharlee said.

"I have stood before Death and Grandfather Wyrm and lived to tell about both," Aisa said. "You can trust me when I swear. If you take only a drop of Danr's blood and then let him go, I will teach you how to use the power. I swear by Rolk and Kalina, the sun and the moon."

Sharlee and Hector exchanged glances. "Wonderful!" Hector said.

He gave instructions to a golem, who plodded over, swiped its hand over Danr's wound—his face went paler than Aisa thought possible—and plodded back to the Obsidia.

"What are you doing?" Talfi hissed.

"Saving us all, I think," she hissed back.

Hector stared at the blood on the golem's hand with ravenous greed. "We've been waiting so long for this," he said in a voice that raised the hairs on Aisa's arms. "You first, my love."

"No, you, my darling," Sharlee replied.

"Together, then," Hector said. Together they lifted the golem's hand to their lips and licked.

"Damn you!" Kalessa continued to tug at her fetters. "Vik and Halza devour your souls!"

"We'll kill the orcish pig first," Hector said. "Her safety wasn't part of the bargain. Then the elf, and then Talfi."

"Do you feel anything?" Sharlee said. "I don't."

Aisa held her breath and shot Danr a look. His pinched face gave her nothing.

"No change," Hector said. "In every sense of the word."

"I told you that very few have the talent," Aisa said. "You may not."

Hector's face grew red. "Grick's tits, do you take us for idiots? The talent ran strong in both our families before the Sundering! I have the talent! I can feel it in . . . in . . ."

He dropped to the ground. A dreadful yellow glow started in his midsection and spread to all his limbs. Hector squirmed in obvious and horrid pain on the grass.

"Darling!" Sharlee dropped beside him, her face a mask of terror. "What's wrong?"

Hector made only a choked gargling sound. His right arm changed into a wing and then a chicken leg. His eyes bulged out of their sockets and turned into butterfly eye stalks, then sucked themselves back into his skull and migrated to the sides of his head. They widened and darkened, like those of a horse. His skin sprouted fur, then pulled it back and changed into leather scales. His legs went boneless, then turned into a glistening mass of jellyfish protoplasm that exploded, covering Sharlee with steaming ooze and leaving Hector without lower limbs. Hector shuddered hard and went still.

"No," Sharlee whispered. "Hector? Darling, speak to me!"

"Ynara," Danr said. "She died the same way."

"You saw it!" Sharlee rounded on him. Tears streaked her face. "You knew the power would kill him and you said nothing!"

"You didn't ask," Danr said.

"I'll kill you!" Sharlee screamed. "The golems will—"

A set of wrist shackles shot across the courtyard and caught her full in the forehead. Sharlee dropped sound-lessly to the grass with a splat into her husband's protoplasm. Talfi stepped carefully around Aisa with a pale Ranadar beside him.

"That shut her up," he said. "Sorry it took so long, but I had to get Ranadar out of those shackles."

"He has a fine arm on him," Ranadar observed.

"And we are grateful," Aisa said.

The golems, bereft of orders, went motionless except for the one still trudging back and forth between the well and the broken tank. Aisa ran to Danr, who remained in the grip of the golem that had broken his arm. Pain twisted his face.

"Are you all right?" she asked.

"No," he said truthfully. "It's like someone dipped my arm in lava and I think I'm going to faint. Thank you for making me say that."

"I am so sorry," she said, working at the golem's impassive hands. "I should have told you the truth before."

"Do you really see blood from the Battle of the Twist?"

The golem's fingers were stubborn, and it was difficult to force them open without hurting Danr further. Aisa finally picked up Ranadar's wrist shackles and smashed at the golem's forearm. Talfi and Ranadar, who was recovering steadily, were gingerly searching Sharlee's clothes and Hector's body for the key to Kalessa's chain while she fumed under the tree.

"You killed all those people. No—" She put a finger on his lips to hush him. "I know it had to be done, and if we could go back in time, I would have you do it over again. Know that I still love you, my Hamzu."

Smash, smash, smash. The clay cracked. Danr grunted but didn't speak. The silence stretched between them, pulling unexpected tears from Aisa.

"I am not strong enough to do what needs doing," she

said. "This is why the visions come to me. I had no strength when you were swinging the Iron Axe, and I had no strength when the world converged on you afterward. I had no strength to sacrifice Ynara so the merfolk could have the power of the shape."

"You're plenty strong," Danr gasped. "I lean on you. And now you have the power of the shape."

"A power I can barely use without exhausting myself," she said. "I have no real strength."

The arm finally broke off. When it did, the golem's fingers released Danr's arm. With that accomplished, he was able to wriggle painfully out of the golem's other hand and sit panting on the ground. When Aisa came over to examine him, he took her hand.

"Tell me now what you meant by a sacrifice," he said.

She looked into his eyes, the deep brown ones that had taken her through more than a world, and at last she told him the rest. She told him of Pendra, and the garden, and the sickle, and Ashkame. And when she was done, she realized Talfi and Kalessa and Ranadar were there as well.

"And you say you have no strength," Kalessa said in awe. "The Gardeners themselves want you to—"

"I do not want that," Aisa retorted. Lightning forked in the distance and dark, wet clouds piled high. "I have watched Ynara die because of me. I will not watch others die."

"I love you no matter what you decide," Danr said stoutly. "*We* love you."

Aisa's eyes filled like the rain clouds. She dashed at them. "A fine thing to be surrounded by so much love after so much hate. But now I need to check your arm, Danr, and—"

Danr kissed her as thunder crackled through the sky.

Sweat streamed down Willem's skin, and he ached from the iron in the manufactory, but he forced himself to stand upright, the high priest and harbormaster of Balsia. Everyone would know someone was in charge, everyone would know the world was properly ordered.

He stood on the steps before the crowd of Whitecaps, exactly ninety-nine men carefully chosen for their fighting prowess and command presence, all wearing the resplendent blue-and-white lacquer Willem had chosen exactly for this moment. No iron. Willem himself wore his increasingly tattered, short robes and cloak as if they were a suit of bloodied armor and kept the hood drawn like a helmet. More than half the battle was acting as if you'd already won. The other half was simple planning, and Willem had been planning for a long, long time.

From inside the manufactory came heavy clunks and thuds. The Whitecaps, encased in their lacquered armor, were too disciplined to react, and Willem swelled with a pride that momentarily overtook his aches and pains. These were *his* men, and in a few moments, this would be *his* city, and then *his* world. Under his hand, the world would become as regular and even as the tide through the simple expedient of destroying anyone or anything that wasn't.

"I'm not here to give a pretty speech," Willem said. "I'm here to tell you the prince is coming. He intends to dismantle this temple stone by stone, bring it down around our ears. He wants to throw us into prison while our Lady of the Oceans weeps salt tears and the twin war gods exult in our loss. He wants to put my head on a pike at the city gates."

Outrage rippled through the men, and several put their hands on their new bronze swords.

Willem said, "But I'm also here to tell you that we won't let that happen. *I* won't let it happen."

"Father Nikol!" barked Punsle at the first man in line. "Prepare your own hand to receive the blessing! The rest form a line behind."

Father Nikol stepped smartly forward, unable to keep a shadow of pride off his face at being called first. With his bare hand, Willem made the sign of the Sea Goddess over Nikol's head, then laid his palm on the man's cheek. Nikol stiffened in surprise at the unexpected gesture, then relaxed and stepped backward with a look of wonder and adoration on his face. The elven glamour had him full in its grip.

"Excellency?" Nikol whispered.

"Will you obey me and only me, now and forever?" Willem intoned.

"I will die to defend you." Nikol clasped Willem's hand in both of his own, weeping tears of joy. "If only you will let me."

"The Sea Goddess is pleased, my son," said Willem. Nikol staggered away, overjoyed and not knowing how to express himself.

"Father Fenrid!" Punsle called, and Father Fenrid came forward to receive the same blessing.

When it was all done, all ninety-nine men gazed up the stairs at Willem in adulation. He faced them, took a deep breath, and cast back his hood, revealing himself as a full-blooded elf.

There was a moment of motionless silence. Willem's heartbeat pounded in his ears. For a moment, he was sure the glamour had failed. Then, to a man, the throng knelt, and every man put his hand on his heart. Exulting in this new power, Willem spread his arms over them in benediction.

By now, word had gotten out about Willem's location, and messenger acolytes were piling up at the bottom of the stairs, all of them from Principals who commanded the walls and were sending updates or asking for orders.

From the front gates of the temple came a thunderous *boom*. One of the messenger acolytes, bolder than the others, dashed up the stairs. She hesitated when she saw Willem's new shape until Willem touched her face and her expression cleared.

"Excellency," she said, "I must report. The prince's army has surrounded the temple. They have armored battering rams at the gates and they are bringing siege engines. We are pouring pitch and loosing arrows. What are your orders?"

Another *boom*.

"Excellency," said another acolyte, and Willem touched him as well. "We have word that the prince is in negotiation with the trolls. In exchange for weapons and armor, they will fight on his side against us. When the sun comes down, they join his army. What are your orders?"

"Excellency," Punsle said, "it would seem the odds are very much against us. Should I prepare the emergency exit plan?"

In answer, Willem raised a fist. Behind him, the roof of the manufactory crashed upward. People fled in terror, and Willem pursed his lips at the chaos, temporary though it was. Wood and slate cracked and splintered, and a great form more than five stories tall heaved itself upright from its kneeling position, shedding bits of scaffolding as it went. The great golem rose high over the city, its three-foot azure eyes glowing ocean blue. Scarlet streams dripped down its head in a bloody baptism. The golem cracked its knuckles with the sound of snapping oak branches. Punsle and the few remaining onlookers gaped in a mixture of awe and terror. Willem couldn't help the thrill that went through him at the sight.

"The half-blood was half right," he said to Punsle. "I wasn't building an army of golems. I was building an army of golem."

"Yes, Excellency," Punsle whispered, still staring up and up. And up. "What do you intend?"

"First we—I—destroy the prince's army," Willem said. "Then the entire city of Balsia."

Now Punsle did jump. "The city, Excellency?"

"So it can be rebuilt, Punsle, in a fine and orderly fashion. Always think bigger, Punsle. Always."

"YOUR . . . ORDERS . . . EXCELLENCY?" asked the golem in a voice like an avalanche.

Thunder boomed. With a laugh, Willem twisted himself up to the golem's shoulder.

Chapter Seventeen

We must kill her," Kalessa said.

Sharlee lay unconscious beneath the tree. Hector's grotesque corpse bubbled next to her. With no one to command them, the golems stood scattered about the grassy courtyard, motionless as the clay statues they were.

Danr closed his eyes—both of them—for a tired moment. His arm had been dipped in melted iron and it was starting to swell. "Must we?" he said. "I've had enough of death, and I have a bad kind of feeling we're in for more without adding to it here."

"She tried to kill me," Ranadar said. "She tried to kill Kalessa. That is reason enough."

"For once the orc agrees with the elf," Kalessa spat. "We do not allow enemies to live."

"She kidnapped you," Danr the truth-teller pointed out. "She threatened you. She didn't actually kill anyone."

"She bought and sold thousands of slaves," Talfi said.

"So did thousands of elves and orcs." Still tired, Danr heaved himself to his feet, wincing as more pain flared across his broken arm. With his good arm, his slender human arm, he picked up a strut that had broken away from the tank.

"But do what you like. Just leave me out of it." With that, he trudged away from the tree. Aisa hurried to follow.

"You must let me see to your arm, my love," she said.

Talfi called after them, "So you're saying after all that, we should just let her go? That she shouldn't be punished?"

"I never said that." The truth popped out, as it had to. That and the pain and the incredulous looks on his friends' faces made him angry, and rather than respond further, he swung the strut as hard as he could and struck the nearest golem with it. The jolt snapped all the way up Danr's shoulder and jarred his teeth. Only a small crack marred the golem's chest. Damn it, this body was so weak! His birth form would have smashed the golem to rubble. Danr smacked the golem again, and this time it cracked more visibly. A third hit put a hole in the golem's chest, and a fourth finally smashed it in half. Panting, broken arm throbbing, Danr leaned on the strut.

"How's that for punishment?" he asked.

Kalessa and Talfi looked puzzled, but Aisa and Ranadar caught on quickly.

"The Obsidia have sunk their fortune into these golems," Aisa said. "A pity if someone destroyed them all. With no slave market to sustain her, and no golems to sell, Sharlee will soon find herself without a single copper finger."

"And without her beloved high-status husband," Kalessa agreed, "it would be almost worse to leave her alive."

Sharlee gave a quiet groan on the grass. Kalessa retrieved her magic blade from the ground and flicked it into a heavy two-handed sword.

"This," she said, "should be fun."

She smashed a golem. It hit the grass in shards after three more hits. Ranadar and Talfi grabbed pieces of their own. With an angry howl that pulled Danr's hair upright, Ranadar laid about, shattering clay and bringing down golems as fast as he could. Talfi did the same beside him while Kalessa worked on her own.

"Please let me see to your arm," she said again. "I cannot bear to see you in pain like this, and anyway, it is foolish of you to go without."

He nodded and sat down again, inhaling sharply as the motion brought sharp pain to his arm. The others continued to smash golems. Aisa examined his arm carefully, tenderly. Danr closed his eyes. It was nice to let Aisa take care of him, even for just a few minutes. But the truth-teller in him couldn't leave a question open.

"You relive the Battle of the Twist," he said.

"This seems to be a clean break. I can set it easily enough, though it will hurt."

He wanted to ask the next question, but at the same time, he didn't want to know the answer. He asked anyway. "Why didn't you tell me?"

"I can use some of those pieces from the tank for splints, and shreds of Hector's clothes will make a fine wrapping," she replied, then looked at his face and sighed heavily. "I did not wish for you to feel bad or guilty over something that could not be changed."

"I wouldn't—" The words halted in Danr's throat. He was unable to say he wouldn't have felt bad. He was unable to lie.

Aisa noted this and nodded. "You see? But you must listen to me. I do not fully understand these visions. My hatred for the Fae—except for Ranadar—runs deep. Yet watching you destroy them . . . the sight haunts me like an evil spirit." She paused. "The visions are not your fault. You did what needed to be done. As I said, I believe it is because I had no strength, no power. Not then and not now."

Smash. Thud. Crash. Clay shards continued to fly. Only the golem trudging between the well and the remains of the tank was left. Sharlee stirred on the grass and slowly pushed herself upright.

"You're a powerful woman," Danr said. "You've visited Death and the house of Grick. You killed the king of elves. And now you have the power of the shape and the Gardeners want you for one of their own. How much more powerful can you get?"

She smiled wanly. "So. Now that you have given me a sharp talking-to, I will believe it, and the visions will disappear. Hold still—this will hurt."

It did. Danr sucked at his teeth while Aisa swiftly bound the splint around his forearm. When he had been a half troll, his bones weren't nearly so breakable, and the one time he had broken his arm as a child, the pain wasn't half what this was.

"My golems!" Sharlee coughed. "What have you done?"

The golem with the cup spun just as Ranadar was drawing back the strut. With startling speed, it rushed over to Sharlee and pulled her upright. Ranadar missed.

"What have you done?" Sharlee screeched again. Tears streamed down her face. "Your blood killed my Hector!"

"And once the guards arrest you for collaborating in treason with the harbormaster, the prince's executioner will let you join him," Aisa said. "Honey."

For a moment, Sharlee pulled herself upright into her old haughty self. Then her gaze flicked over the wreckage of the courtyard and her husband's dreadful corpse. Her face crumpled into itself and she sagged like a dying tree.

"You won't know when the knife falls," she whispered hoarsely. "You'll only feel the blade."

She spat a few words at the golem. It lifted her up and sprinted away faster than any of them could run.

"You got your wish, my beloved," Aisa mused to Danr.

"I did?"

"We did not have to kill her. We only have to wonder what she might do next."

"It won't be much," Talfi said. "She has no money now, and Danr's blood didn't change her shape. She can live in the gutter for the rest of her days."

"Hmm," said Aisa.

Danr swung his broken arm and winced at the twinge of pain. "So now what do we—"

"YOUR . . . ORDERS . . . EXCELLENCY?"

The voice echoed around the city. Danr spun wildly, looking for the source.

"There!" Ranadar pointed with a pale finger. "Up!"

Rising above the skyline was the biggest golem any of them had ever seen. It was taller than the tallest giant. Its azure eyes glowed, and the great runes on its head ran with blood.

"Halza's tits!" Talfi whispered.

"It is at the temple of Bosha," Aisa said. "Or near to."

"The harbormaster." Danr was staring up at the golem, his broken arm forgotten. "We have to stop him."

"How do we stop *that*?" Ranadar asked.

"We can't do a thing from here," Danr said. "Come on!"

Not even a shape-shifted Aisa could carry them all, but they found horses in the Obsidia stable. While they were dragging them out, the dwarf Hokk met them at the door. He was swathed all in red against even the weak sunlight, and he moved stiffly, as if his back pained him, and he held a cracked golem head in his hands.

"You destroyed my golems," Hokk whimpered. "They were perfect. My masterworks! And you destroyed every one of them."

"You are free of the Obsidia," Aisa said. "You can make more, and make them for yourself."

Hokk shook his head under the heavy hat and within the

thick scarves. "That's not how it works, not how at all. You can't make a golem for yourself. You can only make it for someone else. To serve someone else. I need a master."

"Not us," Ranadar said.

Danr furrowed his forehead. "If you only make golems for someone else, friend, how does the other person control them?"

"It's a secret," Hokk said.

"Not much of one," Talfi said. "Not if golems were going to come up for sale."

"The world is changing," Hokk said to the golem head. "Dwarfs walk with the humans. Trolls burrow under the cities. Golem secrets are coming out."

"The Tree tips," Aisa said. "And we can't stop it. We can only try to control it. Tell us how it's done, Hokk. We need help, and only you can give it."

Hokk looked at her for a long moment, then nodded. "The blood. When the golem is done—perfection!—you have the owner, not the maker, smear Stane blood into the runes. To control a golem that big, the harbormaster used a lot of blood. Stane blood."

"Stane blood," Danr repeated. "So if I smear my blood on it—"

"Stane," the dwarf said. "Not human. And to control a golem that large, you'd need to do more than slash your palm."

"So what?" Kalessa said. "It does not help to know how the harbormaster controlled the golem. We need to know how to destroy it."

"Why would you?" Hokk said, genuinely shocked. "It's beautiful. I only wish I had helped create it. I should have gone with my brother dwarfs to the temple of Bosha."

"How can we stop it, Hokk?" Aisa said.

He shrugged, utterly defeated. "You can't. My little golems

are thin and elegant, but that one is big and heavy. Nothing can bring it down. You'd have to stop the harbormaster himself."

"Oh!" Danr said. "Remember what happened when we knocked out Hector and Sharlee?"

"The golems stopped," Aisa breathed. "Thank you, Hokk. As a reward, you can have anything you like from the Obsidia house. Hector is dead and Sharlee has fled, so feel free to plunder whatever you like to buy a new forge."

Hokk's eyes lit up. "I didn't like Hector much." And he shuffled out the door.

"You were awfully free with Hector and Sharlee's possessions," Ranadar observed.

"Why should *we* make all the sacrifices?" Aisa said tartly. "Grab the horses. We have to tell the prince what we know."

The golem didn't go unnoticed. People filled the streets, staring and pointing and speculating. Danr and the others had to shout for people to move aside so the horses could get through. Danr's splinted arm jolted with pain at every step. From the slave market in the distance, two ravens and an eagle rose and flapped heavily away. Danr felt a small twinge at that, as if a thread or thin web bound him with the people who had changed shape. He had felt it before when he shared blood in the slave market, but everything had happened so quickly he hadn't thought about it. Grandfather Wyrm had said that those who shared the blood could also take power from the ones they shared with, especially once they changed their shape. Aisa had certainly taken power from him so she could change shape several times in a row, and he had gladly given it to her. But he hadn't thought about taking power from other people himself. He supposed it didn't matter—he could only change shape once, and he had done it already.

The golem, for its part, still hadn't moved. Its implacable blue eyes and bloodred runes seemed to stare at nothing. The great storm swirled behind it, ready to break over the city. Tiny orange streaks rushed at the golem like darts of sunlight, and Danr realized that someone—a group of someones—was loosing fire arrows at the golem. They bounced off without any visible effect.

"Is it waiting for something?" Talfi clung to the back of a gray gelding.

"Probably," Aisa said. "And we also probably do not want to know what it is waiting for."

When they reached the temple, they found a chaos of guards and soldiers ringed by crowds of people. Surprisingly few seemed interested in running away. Great fires burned on the cobblestones, and men cranked catapults down to be loaded. The golem watched from behind the gleaming walls of the temple compound.

At the border of the civilian and military crowds, perhaps a hundred yards from the temple wall, Danr leaned down from his horse to grab a passing soldier. "Where's the prince? We have a message for him."

The soldier said, "The prince? He's—"

The golem moved. Its head came around and its leg came up. As cold raindrops spattered the cobblestones, the golem's massive foot came down over the temple wall. It smashed a great wagon to flinders. Horses screamed, as did the crowds of onlookers, who tried to stampede away.

"WE WILL RAZE . . . BALSIA," the golem boomed. "WE WILL BUILD . . . BALSIA ANEW."

"Fire!" someone shouted. The catapults shot their boulders, but they bounced off the golem's baked clay skin like stones from a boy's sling. Hundreds of arrows darkened the sky in a deadly rain of their own, but they pinged away from the golem and spiraled to the ground while the soldiers below ducked and tried to avoid their own ammunition coming back at them. Danr and the others stared from the backs of their horses. The golem was perhaps a hundred yards away, but a few steps forward and it would be right on top of them. People stampeded past them up the street in a panic now. Some of them stumbled, and the others rushed right over them. Kalessa leaped from her horse and pulled an older woman to safety, and Talfi dove into the crowd after a boy who had tripped.

Danr slid off his horse, which cantered away the moment he let the reins go. The golem stomped forward again. Its second step destroyed a house, and Danr prayed there was no one inside. Some of the fire arrows that had fallen back to earth landed among buildings and started fires. Danr wondered if the foolish commander who had given the order to use them would be removed from command, and then he wondered if any of them would survive to find out.

"There!" Aisa had abandoned her own horse near a low wall, and she pointed over Danr's shoulder. "Do you see?"

Sitting high on the golem's shoulder, well out of archery range, was the harbormaster. Danr could just make him out. He leaned into the golem's ear.

"BALSIA . . . WILL RISE AGAIN!" the golem shouted, and it smashed its way through a block of houses. Danr saw rag doll human figures fly through the air. "WE WILL RAZE HER DOWN . . . AND RAISE HER UP . . . IN PERFECTION!"

"He will destroy the entire city," Aisa said above the noise.

"I can't stop that!" Danr asked. "None of us can."

Kalessa pushed her way through the panicked crowd. "We need something big," she said. "My blade can grow to enormous size"—she held it out and once again it leaped into a two-handed sword taller than she was—"but what could grow big enough to fight that?"

The golem stomped through more and more houses,

destroyed shops and other buildings, ignoring the catapults and arrows of the army, while the harbormaster watched from on high. A river of people fled up the street, and the golem turned to look at them.

"No!" Danr shouted. "Don't!"

The golem's foot came down. Screams of fear and pain mingled with the blood under the golem's sole. Another step crushed more people. Danr's stomach twisted and his knees went weak. The horrible sounds echoed through his head, and his vomit spattered the cobbles. The harbormaster laughed like a boy stomping an anthill.

"WEAK!" the golem boomed. "THOSE WHO CANNOT STOP ME . . . ARE WEAK!"

More screams of fear and pain burst up just as the storm broke over the city, pouring water and lightning over it in equal amounts. Thunder smashed Danr's bones, and chilly water sopped his clothing and dripped down his face. The army rallied and rushed toward the golem, swords and bows aloft, but the soldiers only met the people fleeing in the opposite direction. The harbormaster laughed and made the golem tear an entire house off its foundations. It threw the building straight into the middle of the frightened mob. It wasn't possible for so much blood to exist.

"It is the Battle of the Twist all over again." Aisa's voice was hoarse.

"This is what the harbormaster wants," Kalessa said. "Sacrifice one thing—the city—to gain something else—a new kingdom. Think bigger."

"You are full of aphorisms today, sister," Aisa observed tightly. "What do we do? We cannot fight it like this. We are not strong enough."

Danr forced himself to ignore the screams, ignore the carnage, ignore the blood. He looked at Kalessa's sword, the sword that changed size and shape, and then he looked at

Aisa. A cold feeling came over him. There was a possibility, if they were willing to take it. He touched her arm. "Kalessa and I aren't strong enough. But we know someone who is."

"Me?" Aisa stared in disbelief. The rain soaked her hair, plastering it to her neck. "If you are not strong enough, I certainly am not."

"But you are, Aisa," he said. "The harbormaster was right. You have to think big. Really big." And he pointed at the golem.

"Think—" It took her a moment to understand. "Oh! Big! But . . . Hamzu! I cannot reach such heights. I have not the strength."

"You aren't alone, Aisa," Danr said quietly. "I can help."

The golem swept through another neighborhood. It was growing a little smaller in the distance. Houses and shops, halls and warehouses, fell beneath its tireless hands and feet. The army, caught completely off guard, seemed to have no idea what to do.

"I cannot," Aisa said. "I am not—"

"Don't let Ynara's sacrifice go in vain," Danr said.

Rain poured ceaselessly down over them, and the wind picked up, driving the water harder over the companions huddled in the small shelter of a street wall. Aisa watched the golem go.

"Kalessa," she said at last, "may I borrow your sword?"

Aisa stood in the center of the street with Kalessa's sword in both hands. Wind and rain swirled around her, and lightning crackled over her head, but she barely noticed. The golem's footsteps shook the earth and made her bones tremble, but she barely noticed. Instead she reached into herself, into the place where she found the power of the shape.

And then she paused. What if this failed her? What if she was too weak? What if Danr was not strong enough?

The harbormaster's golem destroyed another house. Blood had spattered it to the shins. Aisa straightened her back. That was what the harbormaster wanted her to think, what Sharlee and Hector wanted her to think, what the Fae wanted her to think. Before, she'd had the time and luxury to wallow in her weakness, but now there was no time to think about such things. There was only time to act. She would be strong because she had to be, and wasn't that always the way of strength?

Aisa inhaled, expanding her chest. She pushed outward and upward. And she *GREW*.

It was easier than taking on the shape of an animal. This was her own shape, but bigger. Bones lengthened and thickened. Muscles flowed like soft clay and grew. Her head came up to the rooftops, and it seemed to her that the city was growing smaller. Aisa expanded, up and up and up. Her clothes shredded and fell away. Kalessa's shape-shifting sword expanded with her. When Aisa's eyes reached the rooftops, her strength faltered, and she felt dry inside, like a glass suddenly gone empty. This was different from changing into an animal or a mermaid. Those shapes required a single change, and no magic to maintain. But this shape was more impossible. Her bones were too heavy to stand upright, her muscles too thick to move. She needed to draw on magic to keep the giant shape together, but already she was running out.

Then she felt the soft touch of her connection with Danr again. She looked down at him, so lithe and slender, and he waved at her. He closed his eyes, and she felt power flow from him. It knocked on her skin, and she accepted it, drinking as greedily as a baby from a bottle. He went down on one knee as she grew a little taller, and then the new power stopped. Danr panted in the street. Talfi and Ranadar rushed over to help him, but there was nothing for them to do. The power flagged. It was not enough. Aisa felt herself begin to collapse back down toward her original size.

The golem's head came around as it and the harbormaster caught sight of her.

"AISA," it boomed. "YOU WILL NOT . . . STOP ME. HALZA . . . WILL GRIND YOUR BONES."

Aisa shrank farther as the golem stomped toward them.

Chapter Eighteen

Danr tried to come upright, but even with Talfi's help, he couldn't gain his feet. He was simply too weak. Power rushed out of him and into Aisa, but he had already given her so much today already, and he was tired, so tired. The rain pushed him down, streaming over his head and down his arms. His heart slowed in his chest.

"I won't," he whispered to the cobblestones. "I won't give in."

But he had nothing more to give.

The stones shook under the golem's heavy steps, and the dreadful voice laughed. "HALF-BLOODS. ALL THE . . . TRASH. HALF . . . THE POWER."

"Vik!" Talfi muttered. "That thing is even bigger close up. Ran—what can you do?"

"I have no blood from its maker," Ranadar said. "It will not notice my glamours."

"Retreat!" Kalessa barked.

Aisa, still naked, stepped between them with slow, heavy steps of her own, but she was half the size of the golem, and she had no more chance than Danr did. Danr looked up and up and saw the harbormaster in his own shape clinging to the golem's shoulder at its ear. The harbormaster said something, and the golem drew back its hand to swat Aisa aside. Danr's heart twisted in his chest.

And then from nowhere, a soaked wolfhound dashed over to press its ribs against his shins. Two wet ravens flapped in a heavy circle around his head. Remembering the slave market, he closed his right eye. Instantly, his true eye saw the freed slaves in their true shapes. The wolfhound was the woman, and both ravens were men, and it was strange, indeed it was, to see the men fly in circles. The wolfhound woman looked into his eyes. He saw gratitude there while the raven men croaked around his head, and he felt all three of them, their blood, their energy, their lives, shared with his.

The wolfhound nodded once, and with a soft sound like a cloud tearing in two, their power rushed into him, filling him with sunlight and thunder. Danr came upright and raised a fist. The power of the shape, the power of the *blood*, cascaded into him, through him, in an invisible river that rushed straight into Aisa. Her arm snapped up, and the flat of Kalessa's sword caught the golem's arm. Aisa grew. She was nearly to the golem's chest. The golem hesitated, unsure how to react. Rainwater ran through its giant runes like rivers, but somehow failed to wash away the blood that stained its forehead. Aisa, still growing, pushed hard, and the golem was forced back a step. Rubble crunched under its foot.

"Vik!" Kalessa said. "She has become Belinna herself!"

More lightning forked across the sky, followed by thunder like the shout of an angry volcano. Wind tore down the streets, lifting loose rubble and sending terrified people in several panicked directions. In the meager shelter of the low wall, the wolfhound flopped at Danr's feet and the bedraggled ravens perched on his shoulders. Their power streamed through him into Aisa, but he felt more than that—he felt others beyond them, others they had shared blood with, and still others *they* had shared with. With his true eye, he could *see* it, see the silver threads of power that connected them all. In all, he felt more than a hundred people, two or even three steps removed. Some were easy to touch, others were stubborn and distant. What would happen if he touched that much power?

Aisa's growth had slowed. Her dark skin glistened with rainwater, and her muscles stood out as she inexpertly wielded the enormous sword, trying to push the golem back. The harbormaster seemed to have recovered from his surprise, however, and the golem was now pressing forward again. It still had a full head on Aisa, and it was as tireless as stone, while Danr felt the tremendous amount of power it took for Aisa to hold such a great shape together.

"YOU WILL . . . DIE, NAKED SLUT," proclaimed the golem, "AND HALZA WILL . . . DEVOUR YOUR . . . SOUL."

"I am friends with Death," Aisa said in a voice grown rich and deep. "We will open her door wide for your fat ass, Harbormaster."

The golem drew back a great fist and struck. It caught Aisa on the chin. Her jaw slammed shut, and Danr felt the pain as his own. The wind screamed with her voice as she reeled back and fell. The earth rumbled when she went down and took several houses with her. One of her outflung hands thudded onto the cobblestones only a few yards ahead of him on the street. Rubble scattered everywhere. Talfi and Kalessa leaped back, pulling Ranadar with them.

"Aisa!" Danr felt he should hope everyone in the houses had escaped, but he could only worry about her. Anger at the harbormaster colored his vision red. The harbormaster said he wanted to help Balsia, but he was like every other ruler Danr had met, hiding a desire for power under kind words. He abandoned the shape-shifted animals and ran toward Aisa's giant hand.

Aisa needed more power. Already, she was shrinking again, and Danr could feel the trio of shape-shifted animals growing tired as well. The power he had felt just beyond them beckoned with a silver song. The storm swirled and howled and pelted him with rain. Recklessly, Danr reached *out* as he ran. He reached through the trio whose blood he shared and toward the other shape-shifters he had felt. He reached into the web of blood and the power it contained, and just as he reached Aisa's outstretched hand, he touched it at once.

Magic thundered into him, and he cried out in pain. Every nerve raked raw. His skin split open. Lava poured over the open places. He screamed and screamed. Raindrops sizzled when they touched him. He was dimly aware of Talfi and Ranadar and Kalessa all at his side, but they could do nothing. The ravens and the wolfhound slumped to the sodden stones, unable to move, and still the pain tore through him. The power was more than his body could hold. He was clutching the sun, and it roasted him alive because he wasn't strong enough.

Aisa's head turned. He could have stepped straight into her kind, pain-filled eyes. They filled his universe, and some of his agony lessened. "My Hamzu," she whispered. "What are you doing?"

You're not strong enough now, he told himself through the pain. *But you could be.*

He knew. Even filled with the terrible pain, he knew. A half troll was much stronger than this small human form. All he had to do was take back the shape.

But no—he was trapped forever in human form. Grand-

father Wyrm had said he could only change shape . . .
change shape . . .

White-hot pain ripped every nerve, dripped poison and
acid into each individual muscle fiber. It wasn't true. Grandfather Wyrm had said he would only have one *other* shape,
and Danr had assumed he would be able to change shape
only once. He could go back to being a half troll.

Danr became aware that he was screaming. After everything he had gone through, everything he had worked for,
he should give up this new shape? It wasn't right. He had
fought for this shape, fought to become *human* at last, for
them. For Aisa. How could he give it up?

I love you, not your shape.

The memory of those words drilled through him now.
Who had he really taken a human shape for? What was the
real reason he didn't want to give it up? Tears that mixed
many kinds of pain ran down his newly human face.

But of course there was no choice. Aisa needed him in
his birth shape, and he would do it for her.

The burning pain devoured him from the inside. Somehow
he pulled a tiny bit of the power and called to his birth shape.
His body answered to it easily. His muscles thickened, his
head expanded, his chest barreled, dark hair sprouted. The
splint and his clothes tore off him in rags, and in less than a
second, he took his original half-troll shape. Even his broken
arm was healed.

Aisa was struggling to her feet amid the rubble of the
houses. The golem drew back a foot and kicked her in the
side. The crunch sounded like a river of breaking bones.
Part of her rib cage stove in. Another kick broke Aisa's arm
and sent Kalessa's sword spinning away down the street,
tearing apart more buildings until it shrank and vanished.
Aisa's scream of pain raked up a howling rage in Danr. He

threw back his head and roared a troll's roar to the skies. Blood power thundered through him, but his body was strong again. He roared a second time and sprinted across Aisa's hand, up her arm, and onto her shoulder. Golden energy flowed out of his hands and feet and into Aisa's skin.

The golem leaned over, its crushing fist ready to fall. But Aisa grew again. Danr felt her expand beneath his feet. Broken bones reformed and muscles knit together. She caught the golem's fist and sat up, forcing the golem back. Danr barely grabbed hold of her ear in time to keep his place on Aisa's shoulder. Sheets of rain crashed over all of them. The ground swooped into the dizzying distance. From this vantage point, Danr could see that big chunks of the city had been razed. Ships huddled like frightened dolphins in the harbor, and people surged through the crowded streets in a desperate attempt to flee the fighting giants. Even the army was fleeing, leaving toy-sized catapults behind. Was this how the Nine saw the world?

Danr sent an endless stream of power into Aisa, and she surged to her feet, now as tall as the golem itself. Danr stared across the distance between them at the harbormaster, the power continuing to flow through him. They were mirror images—the small man on the shoulder of a great golem, the half troll on the shoulder of the huge human.

"YOU . . . CAN HELP ME . . . DESTROY THE CITY," said the harbormaster through the golem. "YOU . . . CAN HELP ME REBUILD IT. YOU . . . CAN BE MY QUEEN."

"Men always say that when they are losing," Aisa boomed in her new voice. And she stiff-armed the golem. The golem staggered backward, and the earth shuddered. Danr surged with pride. All around the city, he felt the other people, the slaves who had shared his blood. Some of them had managed to change their shapes, and it was easy to take their power. Most had not been able to change their shapes, and taking their power was harder, but he did it anyway. Many of them were growing tired.

The harbormaster and golem rallied and came at Aisa. The two titans slugged at each other like thunderheads in battle while over them crashed near-continuous lightning and thunder and Danr desperately clung to her, feeding her power. Aisa tried to knock the harbormaster off the golem's shoulder. Each time the golem parried her fists with its forearms and dealt Aisa a harsh blow in return. The golem shattered her nose and broke ribs, and each time Danr cried out while the harbormaster cheered. But after each punch, Aisa changed her shape just a little and healed the damage. Aisa struck back, smashing at the golem with fists and feet. Once she sent the golem to its knees, but it scrambled upright. Bruises darkened her knuckles, and blood ran from her fingers, but she kept fighting.

"YOU . . . WILL LOSE," the golem said. "IT IS IN . . . YOUR BLOOD."

It—he—was right. Danr was panting now. The people he was drawing power from were drained nearly dry now, and the golem showed no signs of slowing. Aisa hadn't even cracked it. The moment Danr stopped feeding her power, she wouldn't be able to hold the giant shape together any longer and the golem would crush her to pulp.

As if in answer to this thought, the power stuttered and dimmed. Aisa staggered. The golem took advantage of weakness to deliver a gut punch that drove the air from Aisa's lungs. The world tilted and Danr nearly lost his grip on her ear. He was so close to the harbormaster that he could see the ice in the other man's eyes. Danr closed his right eye.

"You're losing, half-bloods," the elven harbormaster shouted. "Your race is weak, your kind is weak, your blood is weak. You don't deserve to walk the earth!"

Lightning flashed so close that Danr smelled ozone. It

illuminated the fresh, glistening blood on the golem's head just as the thunder smashed the sky. In Danr's true eye, the blood glowed with the same power as the blood that flowed through the harbormaster's delicate veins, connecting them. And Danr knew what he had to do.

Aisa recovered from the stagger and came upright. Pain and release washed through her enormous body in waves. One moment, she felt the pain from a ham-fisted blow. In the next, the wound was healed. She was sweating, for all that she was naked in a rainstorm, and fatigue was beginning to pull at her. This stupid man, the harbormaster, and his indefatigable golem, kept coming. She ducked under a punch and rammed into the golem with her shoulder, still trying to dislodge the harbormaster. The harbormaster clung to his perch even as the golem fell back a step, crushing more of the very city she was trying to save. She couldn't even think about the people. It made her sick. But she had to fight him, bring him down, or he would crush all of Balsia into dust and turn himself into the world's worst despot.

The power coursed through her, and she reveled in her strength. Unlike the Battle of the Twist, where she had been forced to watch, Aisa herself was fighting. Hamzu poured power into her, and she sizzled with it, felt the lightning in her fists and feet. All the anger and fear she had felt, all the rage and terror, came out of her now, and she directed it at the golem. She kicked its thigh with her hard heel, and this time the clay actually cracked with a satisfying *crunch*.

And then, a few paces away, she saw Kalessa's sword, lying in the abandoned street as small as a pin. Where Kalessa, Talfi, and Ranadar had gone, she didn't know, and she prayed they were all right. While the golem was off balance, she leaned down to scoop the sword up, and felt Danr cling harder to her ear.

"Are you all right, my Hamzu?" she asked, her voice as quiet as an avalanche.

"I'm . . . fine," he said in her ear. "But we can't kill it, Aisa."

She plucked the sword from the ground with her thumb and forefinger. It exploded to giant size in her grip. She swung it once, twice. Oh, this was delightful.

"We can, my Hamzu." Aisa aimed a blow at the harbormaster, but she missed and struck the golem on its upper arm instead. It chipped, and she felt the impact shock in her arm and shoulder. Rain lashed at her, but she ignored it.

"I'm running out of magic, Aisa," Danr said. "We won't last long."

And with his words, the magic fell away, just as it had done a moment ago. She staggered again, and the sword grew heavy in her hands. As if in answer to her need, the blade changed into a small knife. Her strength began to fade. She cast about for a way to bring the golem down quickly, but nothing came to her.

"Aisa," Danr panted, "it's the blood. You can stop the golem with blood. My blood."

Blood?

Aisa's eye went irresistibly to the bloody runes atop the golem's head. What could he possibly mean? How could his blood—

A chill slid over Aisa's skin. She glanced sideways at Danr, clinging to her naked shoulder, so small but at the same time so strong. When had he taken his original shape? She hadn't noticed. His trollish form was a comfortable shape, one she liked more and more as time went on, and she was glad to see him in it, half-blood or not.

Half-blood.

Aisa snapped her head around to look at the golem again. It was four or five paces away and advancing. Hokk said when a golem was completed, the owner smeared Stane blood into the head runes. Did that mean anyone who smeared more Stane blood into the runes would gain control of a golem?

The moment the thought entered her head, she knew it was true.

Can you wield the sickle without flinching?

The voice in her head was soft, insistent. The golem stomped across wet, slippery rubble toward her, and the magic that kept her shape together was fading again. She could feel her big, powerful shape shrinking, her new strength draining out of her. Danr, her quiet Hamzu, tugged her ear insistently.

"He'll destroy the city and kill thousands more," he said softly. "It's the only way. A small sacrifice."

Can you wield—

No! Anger thundered over her. "Leave me alone! Why must *we* always make the sacrifice? Why must *we* be the ones that bear the pain?"

The golem advanced another step. The harbormaster laughed his chalkboard laugh. "YOU ARE . . . SMALLER, HALF-BLOOD. HALF THE SIZE . . . ALL THE FILTH."

"Aisa, we don't have time to talk about it," Danr said. "We have to do it now."

"I could use my own blood," Aisa said desperately. "I have plenty right now."

Danr's voice was hoarse. "Golems need Stane blood. Small golems need a little. A golem that size needs—"

"No!" Tears heavier than lead spilled from her eyes and her throat choked with despair. "How can the Nine ask me to make this kind of sacrifice?"

Another step. Two more and the golem would be in striking range. The elven harbormaster whooped with laughter now, but Aisa didn't hate him anymore. She hated the Nine and the Gardeners and their damn Tree. Danr, her Hamzu. There was so much she wanted to say to him, so much she wanted to show him. They were to spend the rest of their lives together, and now their entire remaining time could be expressed in seconds.

Another step, and she shrank even more. Danr was larger on her shoulder now. She looked down at Kalessa's blade. It had become a small sickle.

Can you wield it without flinching?

"I love you, Aisa," Danr was saying in her ear. "I loved you from the day I first saw you in the village, and I loved you at the Battle of the Twist, and I love you now. Never forget me."

"I can't, Hamzu," she whispered through the rain.

"You have to, Aisa. Please."

"YOU AREN'T . . . STRONG ENOUGH," the golem barked. "YOU NEVER WERE."

And suddenly, Aisa was in the gray-lit garden again. The rain and thunder vanished. Chaotic rows of plants stretched in all directions around her, and the soft twilight settled around her like an autumn cloak. At Aisa's feet grew a trio of vines: a squash, a pumpkin, and a trumpet flower.

Pendra appeared before her, though she didn't quite step out of thin air. It was as if she had always been there and Aisa had only now noticed her. Blood gushed down Pendra's arms, flowing in a scarlet storm from her skin into the dry, cracked ground.

Look into the future, she said.

Aisa looked. The trumpet was choking the other two vines, and it had sent tendrils out to choke other plants as well. Ninety-nine blue and white flowers had just fallen victim to its snare, and the trumpet was running toward an even larger patch of the garden. Except the trumpet was bent on destruction. If it was not cut back immediately, its roots would sink too deeply into the garden, and it would never be fully removed. It had already strangled a great many plants. The trouble was, the trumpet vine had grown in such a way that the only way to kill the main vine was to cut out the squash vine first.

"No!" Aisa said. "I cannot do such a thing!"

Look into the present, Pendra said.

Aisa looked. The roots of the squash and the pumpkin started at separate places, but less than halfway up, they had twined together. The pumpkin was reaching outward, trying to grow in an entirely new direction, but part of the vine was wound around the squash, holding it back. The only way to let the squash grow forward was to—

"I cannot," Aisa said. "I am not strong enough."

Look into the past.

Once more, Aisa looked. She followed the rows backward and saw her own vine intersecting a row of algae and seaweed—the plants of her merfolk family. Ynara's plant, dry from its time on land, had withered and died. Grandmother's misshapen stalk lay shriveled and black beside it. A lump formed in Aisa's throat and she wanted to look away. Before she did, she saw how her own vine skirted the row a little and pushed Ynara's into a different path, one that carried the bit of algae to its death.

"I really killed her?" Aisa whispered.

Only your grandmother was fated to die. When you flinched away and asked your grandfather to take your responsibility, the garden had to make changes. Ynara died, too. Pendra sighed. *If you flinch away from this new sacrifice, the garden will suffer. Millions will perish. The Tree will tip again and again and again.*

Her throat choked with guilt and fear. "Why are you doing this to me?" she demanded. "Why *me*? I never asked for this."

The best Gardener, Pendra said, *is usually the one who least wants the position. Can you wield the sickle without flinching?*

Aisa noticed she was still holding the sickle. Millions of lives against one. She could not conceive of so many people.

But she could. In this garden, she could see all of them, twisting and twining together in an orderly chaos. Husbands and wives, free people and slaves, parents and children, lovers and beloved. Every plant here pivoted around these three vines. How would she feel if someone else had this decision to make and refused to make it?

"Damn you," she said in a hoarse voice to Pendra.

"You may be doing exactly that," Pendra said.

Tears filled Aisa's eyes. She touched the pumpkin vine and she could hear his fine voice, feel his strong warmth, see his kind eyes. Memories poured through her, of seeing Danr for the first time and recoiling in fear, then gazing in curiosity; of applying a poultice to his leg where a wyrm had bitten him; of finding his fire on the mountainside after she had run away from her owner; of facing Death and her knitting needles by his side; of their clumsy, tender marriage proposal. That last flower would never bloom now. "I love you forever, my Hamzu," she whispered, and leaned down with the cold sickle. Pendra sighed and closed her eyes.

We will speak again. Sister.

And then Aisa was back in the storm. The golem loomed ahead of her. Stinging rain pelted her bare skin. The harbormaster laughed. Danr sat on her shoulder, begging her to take his blood.

Weakness threatened, but Aisa thrust it aside. She was strong, she was powerful, and she would wield the sickle. With a scream from the bottom of her soul, Aisa plucked Danr from her shoulder and, without flinching, she sliced his chest open with the sickle. A flick of lightning split the sky. The stroke laid Danr's ribs bare to the stormy sky and his blood gushed warm over her hand. He howled his agony, and the sound tore her heart to shreds. His life ebbed away in her hands. Danr's wide brown eyes met Aisa's, and for a tiny moment, she thought he might have a last word for her. Then his eyes glazed over and he went limp. Her soul turned to lead and she wanted to lay down and die.

"YOU ARE . . . NOTHING!" The golem raised its mountain fist, but Aisa, tears streaming from her eyes, ducked under it and with a swift motion, pressed Danr's limp body against the golem's forehead and forced herself to squeeze. Aisa bellowed her pain and sorrow as Danr's bones ground together, and Stane blood rushed over the golem's runes, filling them with scarlet rivers.

"What—?" the harbormaster said. "What are you doing?"

The golem instantly froze. It stood still beneath the lash of the rain. Its azure eyes flickered, and then its head turned toward Aisa.

"MISTRESS," it said.

"No!" the harbormaster shouted. "Kill her!"

The last of the power Danr had given her was fading away, and Aisa was shrinking again. Danr grew larger and heavier in her bloody hand. Righteous anger thundered over Aisa. With her last bit of breath, she boomed to the golem, "Walk to the Flor Isles with the harbormaster in your hand."

"You half-blood bitch!" Willem screamed. "I'm harbormaster! You will obey me! You will obey—"

The golem plucked the harbormaster from its shoulder,

turned, and walked inexorably toward the bay, with Harbor-master Willem in its firm, gentle fist. The harbormaster struggled. The harbormaster shouted. But the golem walked forward. It crushed two docks and sank a ship as it waded into the bay. Ripples and white waves rushed outward from it. When the water reached the golem's waist, the harbor-master's shouts turned to screams. When the water reached the golem's chest, his screams turned to blubbering cries. And when the water reached the golem's head, his cries faded into nothing.

Aisa barely noticed any of it. She shrank to her normal size on the rubble-strewn ground with Danr's naked bloody corpse in her arms. Kalessa's blade, still a sickle, clattered to the stones beside her as the rain slowed to a mere drizzle, and the thunder grumbled to itself in the distance. A numb-ness overcame Aisa. He was dead. Her Hamzu. She should be screaming, howling, crying, but his death was simply too big to encompass. She had taken the life of this strong man to save the city, to save herself. Her own blade had spilled his blood. How could she ever live past this horrible time? In that moment, she wished the ground would crack open and swallow her whole.

"I will never become a Gardener," she whispered, and stroked Danr's bloody hair "They can fuck themselves with their own tools. Oh, my Hamzu."

Feet scuffled toward her, and she became aware of Kalessa, Talfi, and Ranadar. With them came the wolfhound, which had two ravens perched on its back. Talfi dropped be-side Danr, his young face twisted with pain. "How could this happen?" he cried in a broken voice. "What did you do?"

Black guilt rushed over Aisa, and her heart became a stone in her chest. "It was the only way. He begged me."

"Begged you to cut him open?" Talfi's frantic voice raked across wounds still fresh. "I thought you loved him!"

"Talashka," Ranadar said.

"He called it a small sacrifice," she murmured. "But his was the biggest."

"I have no words," Kalessa said. "My sister, you are brave and strong, and I cannot imagine my life without Danr."

And then Danr's eyes flickered open and he made a tiny groaning noise. Aisa gasped. He was still alive, but only a tiny bit. He couldn't speak, not with his chest laid open. He looked at Aisa, and she could see the last of his life draining away. She gripped his hand and summoned up enough strength to steady her voice. For him.

"I am here, Hamzu," she said. "You saved us."

"Why isn't his arm broken?" Talfi said suddenly. "The golem in the garden broke his arm, but his splint is gone now, and his arm looks fine."

Aisa glanced quickly downward. Talfi was right. She hadn't noticed before—his arm was completely healed. It must have happened when he changed shape from human to half troll. And then she remembered how her own wounds had healed when she changed from human to mermaid, how the hand bitten off by Grandfather Wyrm had regrown after Danr changed into human form. Changing shape . . . healed. A spark of hope flared inside her.

"Hamzu!" she said excitedly. "You have to change shape. You have to become human again!"

"Wait, what?" Talfi said.

Danr only made a small gasping noise. His eyes dropped shut.

"No, Hamzu!" she said. "Do not leave us! Change shape!" She rounded on the others. "He needs power. Magic energy!"

"I cannot share mine," Ranadar said. "The Fae—"

Aisa snatched up the sickle and slashed her arm. A blood sacrifice poured over Hamzu's gaping chest. Instantly, she felt the connection between them change. Instead of receiv-

ing power from him, she was able to give it to him. Recklessly, she fed him power, pushing harder and harder. Her
hands glowed gold and black spots danced under her eyes.
But the spark of life within him was too far gone. It was not
enough.

"Not now!" she cried. "Hamzu! Please! You can do it!"

But he faded away. Aisa's throat closed, and she wept
hard. How could she bear losing him twice in one day?

The soft padding of paws and the flutter of feathers
brought her head back up. The wolfhound was there, and the
ravens with it. Talfi drew back, startled. The hound licked
Danr's scarlet-spattered face, and the ravens nuzzled his
hands. Aisa thought she saw another golden glow. The animals! They were the shape-shifted slaves from the market!
They must have a small bit of magic left. Silently begging
the Nine for aid, Aisa fed Danr her own power again, draining herself to nothing.

"Please change!" she choked. "You are my life. My world
will not turn without you."

"You are the bravest and most honorable of men," Kalessa
begged, and went to one knee. "I have never knelt before a
man, but I kneel before you. Please do not leave us."

"We love you," Ranadar pleaded. "We need you. Stay
with us."

"You're my best friend," Talfi cried. "Don't die now."

"Hamzu," Aisa whispered.

A dot of light appeared in the center of Danr's ruined
chest. Aisa gasped. The light, golden as the morning sun,
grew and spread over Danr's chest. It enveloped his body.
Aisa wavered, drained of energy, and she felt a change begin
under her hands. She held her breath, and Danr's awful
wounds pulled together. His bones rearranged themselves
with cracks and pops. His muscles knit themselves whole.
His body, arms, and legs shortened, and his body hair fell

away. In a few breaths, Danr lay on the wet cobblestones, human again and utterly whole. His body shuddered once and his eyes popped open.

"Hamzu!" Tears of utter joy stained Aisa's cheeks. She snatched him into her arms and held him close, smelling his skin, feeling his hair. He was alive! The awful weight of guilt and grief vanished, feeling, the power of her sheer delight. Oh, he was alive!

Talfi and Ranadar and even Kalessa joined in the embrace before the animals could scramble aside, and for several moments, they made an awkward, laughing pile of people, fur, and feathers. Talfi shouted incoherently in everyone's ears, and Kalessa actually smiled. At last they disentangled. Exhaustion swept Aisa, and the ground swayed dizzily.

"I need sleep," she said. "Do you think Mrs. Farley will still take us in after all this?"

Danr, who looked as exhausted as Aisa felt, thrust out his human arms and made a face. "Death said that in the end, only I can decide to change," he sighed. "Looks like she was right."

"I love you, no matter what shape you take," Aisa said.

"I know," Danr said softly.

"What do you remember?" Talfi asked, probably because it was what everyone asked him whenever he came back from the dead.

"Death opened her door for me," Danr said, and put his arm around Aisa. "And I was ready to walk through it. But you, all of you, pulled me back." Then he knelt down and touched the head of the wolfhound while the ravens croaked from the cobbles. "Thank you."

The wolfhound whuffed once and trotted away. The ravens hopped into the sky and vanished.

"Can they change back?" Ranadar asked, looking after them.

"The better question is, will they?" Aisa said.

"An even better question," Talfi put in, "is why two people who have never shared a bed spend so much time naked."

Chapter Nineteen

It didn't end there, of course. Sections of the city lay in ruins and the docks were badly damaged, and countless people lay trapped under rubble. Prince Karsten rose to the occasion. He proved tireless, rushing about the city, mobilizing the army and his private guard into cleanup and rescue. The ninety-nine warrior priests, released from their glamour by the harbormaster's death, ordered all priests and acolytes to help as penance.

And when the sun set, the trolls came. They tromped up from the new sewer tunnels and out of stone cellars where they had been quietly living. The dwarfs burrowed out of the ruined temple of Bosha to join them, and they set about digging. The humans who had been desperately laboring for hours accepted the help gratefully. For the first time in a thousand years, Stane and Kin worked side by side.

Aisa and Danr and the others tried to help at first, but fatigue dragged them down.

"I will want to hear everything that happened later," Prince Karsten told an exhausted Danr. "For now, go home before you make a mistake and hurt someone."

Mrs. Farley's rooming house was untouched by the golem's

rampage. They crept in by the back door and slipped upstairs. Without even thinking, Danr went into Aisa's room with her. Kalessa merely nodded and took Danr's room. They dropped into bed and into dreamless sleep.

Aisa woke slowly and painlessly, like a sparrow gliding in to land. The blankets made a warm cocoon and the bed was deliciously soft and comfortable. Warm sunlight spilled across the green plants on the balcony and into the room. It was so nice to lie there, drowsy and content.

The bedclothes rustled. Danr, still human, rolled over and put his arms around her with a little sigh. Her heart felt so powerfully content, so delighted and happy, she couldn't imagine life any other way. How had she lived before this moment? Hamzu was still asleep. She examined his face, his human face. Dark eyebrows framed large eyes. His raven hair was tousled with sleep. Stubble dusted his cheeks. His chest and stomach, the muscles flat and well defined, rose and fell with his breathing. She could watch him, in either shape, for hours, and need no other meat or drink.

They had fallen into her bed last night and dropped into instant sleep, too tired to do more than share a good night kiss. But this morning . . . this morning, Aisa decided, it was time for more than a kiss. And was there any better way to wake a man?

But first, she needed to know something. Steeling herself, she deliberately thought of the Battle of the Twist. She thought of Danr wielding the Iron Axe. She thought of fire and blood and slaughter. She deliberately courted the visions, called them to her.

Nothing happened. The little room remained unchanged. Danr slumbered on next to her. The terrible visions were gone.

Her burden lifted, and she felt almost giddy, as light as a

soap bubble. The relief was almost as great as the relief she had felt when Danr changed his shape last night and came back to her. She leaned closer, and felt his warm breath on her cheek. He stirred then and opened his eyes. They were as warm and brown as she remembered.

"Good morning," she said.

"It is, isn't it?" he replied with a long, slow smile, and he gathered her into his arms. "The first one of many."

She sighed and pressed against him, feeling his heartbeat. And she felt something else press against her as well. Danr flushed a little, but didn't let her go.

"I like waking up this way," she whispered into his neck. Her hand slid downward. "And I think now is the time to explore so many new—"

His body stiffened. He jerked away from her and sat up. For a confused moment, she thought she had hurt him or done something wrong. Then she noticed it, too—a difference in the air, a change in the light, a soft, inexplicable sound. She sat up with him.

The plants on the balcony were spilling into the room. Before their eyes, they expanded and grew, crawling over walls, across the floor, and even into the tiny fireplace. Flowers bloomed, and a riot of color spilled over the vines and branches. In seconds, the room became a humid green jungle.

"What—?" Danr gasped. "How is this—?"

But Aisa put a calming hand on his arm. "It is fine, my Hamzu. We are having visitors."

Even as she spoke, a great bud grew at the end of one vine. It expanded to the size of a horse. A bloodred iris split open, and from the blossom stepped two women, one in a pale green cloak with a bag of seeds, and one in a green-brown cloak with a hoe. They looked sad.

"Nu and Tan," Danr breathed.

"But not Pendra," Aisa finished. Her heart beat quickly. What did this mean? Were they already here to bring her away?

"You wielded the sickle without flinching," said Nu.

"You made the sacrifice," said Tan.

There was a pause, and then both Gardeners seemed to realize there would be no third response. Tan pressed her lips together and Nu wiped at her eye with the corner of her cloak.

"What is this about?" Danr asked, then added hastily, "Great Ones."

"I never had a chance to tell you," Aisa said.

"He should have known from the beginning," said Nu.

"From the start," agreed Tan, and there was another pause.

"Should have known what?" Danr was clutching the blankets around his naked waist. "I don't understand, Great Ones."

"You did not bring Aisa to your last meeting with Death, so we had to make accommodations," said Nu.

"Changes," said Tan.

"To what?" asked Danr before they could pause.

"It would be easier to share with you directly," said Nu. She reached into her bag and blew a handful of pollen into Danr's face. He coughed, and then Aisa saw the knowledge come across his face.

"So you chose Aisa to replace one of you," he said slowly. "Has it . . . is it time for her to go? Is that why Pendra isn't here?"

Aisa realized she was clutching the blankets so hard her knuckles hurt. She had just found her happiness with Danr. How could she leave him now? Maybe they could continue their love anyway. But wouldn't she become . . . immortal? Could an immortal Gardener love a mortal? There was so much she didn't know.

"It has become complicated," said Nu.

"Difficult," said Tan.

"In what way?" Aisa asked tensely.

"You wielded the sickle without flinching," Nu repeated. "You showed that you could do what needed to be done."

"You have walked among the Stane, the Fae, and the Kin," said Tan. "You have been powerful and powerless. You know slavery and freedom. You have seen strength and weakness. We settled on you as our new sister and set the others aside."

Aisa put a hand to her mouth. "I'm not ready! I'm not—"

"It cannot happen now," said Nu.

"Not yet," said Tan.

Danr looked at the Gardeners, then at Aisa. "What do you mean? Why not?"

"Pendra," said Nu and Tan together, "has disappeared."

ABOUT THE AUTHOR

Steven Harper Piziks was born with a name no one can reliably pronounce, so he usually writes under the pen name Steven Harper. He sold a short story on his first try way back in 1990. Since then, he's written twenty-odd novels, including the Clockwork Empire steampunk series.

When not writing, Steven teaches English in southeast Michigan. He also plays the folk harp, wrestles with his kids, and embarrasses his youngest son in public.

CONNECT ONLINE
stevenpiziks.com
twitter.com/stevenpiziks

ALSO AVAILABLE FROM

Steven Harper

IRON AXE

The Books of Blood and Iron

In this brand new series, a hopeless outcast must answer Death's call and embark on an epic adventure....

Although Danr's mother was human, his father was one of the hated Stane, a troll from the mountains. Now Danr has nothing to look forward to but a life of disapproval and mistrust, answering to "Trollboy" and condemned to hard labor on a farm.

Until, without warning, strange creatures come down from the mountains to attack the village. And Death herself calls upon Danr to set things right...

Available wherever books are sold or at
penguin.com

R0211